W9-ABS-819

G. P.

G. P.

BY WILLIAM A. BLOCK

PRENTICE-HALL, INC., ENGLEWOOD CLIFFS, N.J.

G.P. by William A. Block
Copyright © 1971 by William A. Block

All rights reserved. No part of this book may be
reproduced in any form or by any means, except
for the inclusion of brief quotations in a review,
without permission in writing from the publisher.

ISBN 0-13-362111-1
Library of Congress Catalog Card Number: 76-127644

Printed in the United States of America *T*

Prentice-Hall International, Inc., London
Prentice-Hall of Australia, Pty. Ltd., Sydney
Prentice-Hall of Canada, Ltd., Toronto
Prentice-Hall of India Private Ltd., New Delhi
Prentice-Hall of Japan, Inc., Tokyo

Second printing. . . . . February, 1971

To my wife, Judy, without whom there would be no G.P.

48495

All characters in this book are a product of the author's imagination, and any resemblance to any persons living or dead is purely coincidental

G. P.

. . . .

"... Hold up the bus, here comes Dr. Shoemaker. Come on, Doc, look out for that mudhole—jump...."

Taxes in this town twenty-two percent higher—Johnny Shoemaker winced, stamping the heavier mud from his boots—and they can't put an old surplus Quonset hut out there for us? Mud up to my ankles, rain soaked through my cap, never took my flu shot this year. Stupid, chugging back in a bus to the locker room every half time. Freezing cold. Hope they keep Willie warm—"Gotta play, gotta play"—don't any of them know I *know* they gotta play? What am I here for, my health? After this rain Big Doctor will be home a week with the flu, I'll lay odds. This is my last year. Damn bus, shakes the kids' brains loose, whatever's left after that clobbering.

For twelve years Dr. Shoemaker could have ridden back to the high school locker room in the coaches' limousine— comfortable, warm, dirty jokes—but he continued to ride in the back of the bus. He sat in the last seat over the wheel. "The exercise is good for me," he would assure those who offered him a front seat. "Like jogging sitting down."

His earmuffs continued to hug his orange ears. His compact football emergency bag upended on his lap served as a support for his padded elbows, in turn a support for his chins which he warmed in the cradle of Mrs. McGibbon's hand-knit mittens. The school nurse had presented them to him ceremonially several years ago, and he wore them to every game. "Damn gloves, freeze through every game," Johnny mumbled. No room for his left thumb, but they never came off. Through thirteen straight winning games. How could the team doctor make himself responsible for a losing football game? The gloves stayed on—wet, cold, misfit, ugly.

From his vantage point in the bus, the doctor watched the boys. He saw past their lampblacked eyes; he smelled more than their boy sweat; and he searched beneath their mud bruises and their bloodstains and their hand tremors.

Joe Rizzo threw up. He was going in for Willie. Dr. Shoemaker wiped his forehead. Joe would be all right, Johnny convinced himself. Look at him, a giant of a boy, face like a bulldog, hands like chain links, legs like pistons. Scared shitless.

"You'll be OK, Joe," Johnny assured him.

"Thanks, Doc," Joe said. "No chance Willie gettin' back in today?"

"No chance."

Willie had played one of his regular miracle games today: two interceptions, three touchdowns (one a 97-yard punt return), two pats. Nothing unusual for Willie, the first freshman kid to ever play varsity. Dr. Shoemaker had worked with him for four years. Probably make all-state and go on to be big time pro someday. Dr. Shoemaker felt good he knew Willie, and he knew how it was with Willie. He kept him in vitamin samples and protein bars, got him a job driving Marvin's prescription truck, wrote a strong letter of reference to State College. Scouts were coming down next week. Things looked good for Willie.

Dr. Shoemaker felt a wave of nausea. He swallowed his dried-out sour saliva hard and shoved a Tums into his mouth. His stomach he knew would never be right from Labor Day until Thanksgiving. This, after all, was only a minor plaint to pay for the privilege of getting slobbering wet every Saturday and riding the back of the stinking bus. If only for self-preservation, Johnny Shoemaker, was not prone to self-pity—a belch or two, a Tums lemon wafer, it went away. What the hell, he shrugged. He *would* allow a certain humorous sympathy for himself. He shrugged and opened his palms as if feeling for rain.

In the locker room Dr. Shoemaker kept himself busy ferreting out injuries. Damn kids, unless it's gushing blood and a shower towel won't hold it they won't tell you. Surprisingly, in the rain, injuries were nil. A few smashed fingers, one smashed eye, one smashed knee, nothing sensational. The kids seemed to relish the rain and the mud. What a day for revolt! "Don't get your clothes dirty, sonny." "Stay out of the rain now, buddy." "Did you wear your rubbers?" "You're not to leave this house without your yellow rain hat." Only Willie lay quietly on a blanket in the corner. Three other black boys hovered nearby. There were four on the squad.

"You really gonna keep me out, Doc?" he pleaded with Dr.

Shoemaker, looking for that jelly spot that Doc had become known for. (You gotta work on Doc. Keep tryin'. You gotta try. It's a little spot back there someplace. Every so often it just squished apart, and suddenly you were in there playing ball.) Willie reached for the spot. "What if I just get up and play?"

"What if you just try?"

"Hurts like hell."

"Then cool it, man."

The kids dug Doc. They covered up their cuts and faked their sprains and turned their backs on Doc when he paraded the benches during the game. But weekdays—Doc's place is the place to go to get it fixed. Doc was In. He could say "Cool it, man," and they dug Doc. They smiled a little at his kooky gloves and his square earmuffs, but this was his thing—Doc they dug. So, when Johnny said "Cool it, man," Willie settled back cool.

Coach Bocca had three set operational half-time shows, right out of Pat O'Brien. Today, with the half-time score 20-21 against them, the rain, and Willie laid out—today was the day for the Academy Award.

Coach Anthony Bocca, Italian-made, all-city, all-state, fourth draft choice for the West Orange Aides, father of nine, two hundred and eighty-seven pounds, cried. Real, honest to glory cry tears.

"Our soul brother, Willie, lays over in the corner on a stretcher. Doc says he may never play again." (He *did*?) "Some sonofabitch clipped Willie from the rear, and two other sonsabitches stomped on his head after the whistle blew. We're four and nothing up until today. We're down by one point. We make today and we're over the hump for the state title. Now how the hell are we going to do it with Willie laying there stretched out almost killed by those sonsabitches? How are we gonna do it? I'll tell you how we're gonna do it, we're gonna play tough. We're gonna kill. Kill. *Kill*! Every last one of them sonsabitches has to pay for what they did to poor Willie laying here half dead. *Doc*—Doc—tell us—don't spare us, Doc.". . .And the tears flowed like Italian wine. "Tell us, Doc, tell us Willie's gonna make it."

All on cue, the coach and the coach's assistants bent over

Willie's stretcher and mumbled a silent prayer. The glassy-eyed colored boy turned practically gray with fear, screamed "Glory be!" and the entire squad fell to their knees and crossed themselves (except Sidney Goldstein, who covered his head), and they prayed to almighty Jesus for Willie's life and *they* cried. And the boys of Greenville High, as one, raised their voices in agony: "Kill, kill, *kill*!"

When the last cleat had clumped from the old locker room floor, and the last tear had flowed from Coach Bocca's eyes, he stopped alongside bawling Johnny Shoemaker and whispered desperately, "Jesus, Doc, let the damn kid play. What the hell's it to you? . . ."

. . . .

THURSDAY

1970	OCTOBER				1970	
S	M	T	W	T	F	S
				1	2	3
4	5	6	7	8	9	10
11	12	13	14	15	16	17
18	19	20	21	22	23	24
25	26	27	28	29	30	31

15

OCT. 1970

Morning

7:45—Hey, Pop, you gotta get me out of gym.

—Me too.

—You know what we're doing now? Square dancing.

—Say anything, Pop. Tell them I got a concussion.

—C'mon, Pop, you pull Willie out of a big game, you can pull your son out of square dancing.

—So long, folks. It's late, I'm going. . . .

—It's pouring rain, look at you. . . .

—C'mon, Mom, it's not even a drizzle.

—It's *pouring*. John, look at him in a short-sleeve shirt—I just *ironed* that shirt. . . .

—So long. . . .

—Put on your raincoat. . . .

—I don't *have* a raincoat. . . .

—Put it on. . . .

—How about my rubbers?

—All right, catch pneumonia, your father's a doctor.

—Pop, is that what you are? Man, we're rich.

—Jennie, take an umbrella. You'll get your earache again.

—I took three vitamins.

—Three pep pills, huh, Skin. Hey, Pop, Skin's gonna sell them for Bennies to her sixth-grade midgets. Hey, Skin, how about a pot party in the cafeteria? Mix it in their graham crackers. . . .

—Monkey see, monkey do, Pimples. . .

—Shut up, Skin.

—It's *pouring*. John, you see what they went out into, it's *pouring*

Only Mary saw it pour. She saw her wet children and her sick children. She saw all the wet and sick children and all the sick people and heard all the coughs and all the sneezes and saw all the people drenched in disease. She saw her husband drenched in sick people, and she prayed the rain would stop.

"If *Redbook* says wet feet can't possibly make you sick," Mary told her doctor husband, "then how come our kids get sick every time they go near a damp rag?"

Johnny squashed his toast into his mouth, avoiding an answer to Mary's aging charade.

"They *eat* pills. They swallow enough red, white, and blue pills in one day it's a wonder they don't rattle the Star-Spangled Banner."

Johnny smiled woefully through his egg.

"*Reader's Digest* had a thing about kids and pills—from the first day they open a mouth and say *ahhh* you drop a pill in it like it's a slot machine. No wonder they grow up expecting life to deliver them a jackpot."

Johnny pushed down his soggy Wheaties.

"The *News* says I'm going to get a hemorrhage into my brain from *my* pill. Lucky me, maybe it'll hit me before I find out why I've had no period for two months. It's ten days into the third, John, and no signs, I mean none. N-o-n-e."

Johnny dropped two saccharin tablets into his black coffee and tested it to his dried lips.

"Doctor, you sip your brew silently. Pray thee, my seer, give me a word of comfort—one word, a syllable, an *mmm*. Something in Latin?. . .How about one of Pop's old favorites from your magic black bag. like fried roots of thorn apple mixed briskly with dried skunk cabbage and smoked through a pipe? And if this doesn't work, maybe I'll try calling Tom in the morning. Send a wire to Southern Illinois Medical College, Brownsville House, Chicago, Illinois: Dear Tom. Father is clammy, and mother is rammy, and kids is calamity—help, help, help. . .

. . . .

SOUTHERN ILLINOIS MEDICAL COLLEGE
-BROWNSVILLE HOUSE-
CHICAGO, ILLINOIS

Friday

Hi, Pop,
Send M-O-N-E-Y

Tom

Naw, I'm only kidding. You've done right by me, don't I know it? And I know what it takes to keep me out here. But only five thousand more patients to see and you've got me made—Tom Shoemaker, M.D. Can't wait.

Guess you've got the new sign made. Knowing you, it's
probably up in the storeroom now ready for hanging.
. . .Well, it's been two months . . . learned more . . . you
seem to have gimmicks . . . science here . . . learned more in
two months . . . miss you . . . time away to think . . . medicine
is different here, you know, everything's up-to-date in Kansas
City—teaching hospital . . . new views . . . feelings change . . .
dreams . . . woke me up . . . thoughts worked out . . .

First of all, Pop, you always said, don't hedge, say it,
defend it. Well, right off, I've got to say it—I'm not going into
general practice with you . . . I'm not going into general
practice . . . I'm not going—with you . . . I'm not . . .

Johnny began skimming ahead, finding words he had read a
dozen times over. The process of folding the letter and
placing it in his pocket, then unfolding it and taking quick
glances had not worked out as he had hoped. The words had
not changed.

Johnny Shoemaker crumbled his son's letter back into his
pocket. Later this morning he would try reading it again. He
tore second gear out of the old Buick and headed her into
town, wondering wistfully whether he should trade up for an
automatic. Naw, Johnny was convinced it would never give
the performance of the old reliable stick. Three hundred and
fifty bucks of trouble. When you have country-style penicillin,
why go looking for Madison Avenue mycin?

"*. . .Dr. Shoemaker, there is only one car for a doctor.
How can you go on denying yourself? Only this past month I
sold Dr. Goldstein a Coupe de Ville, Dr. Fishman and Dr.
Klein an El Dorado, and Dr. Levy a Brougham Fleet-
wood. . . .*"

Senseless, medical prostitution. Johnny shook his head, his
gaze bouncing boastfully about the old Buick. Get another
three years out of this baby. The last thing I need is a new
car. Maybe my son, Tom, will come driving home in one after
his first year in medical school. Why "maybe"?

Johnny Shoemaker, the father, held the letter squashed
into the torn pocket of his beaver car coat—Mary never has
time to sew my things. I should get her a full-time girl. If her
estrogen level drops any lower, *I'll* end up doing the sewing.

Wonder what will be with me when *I* hit the change? Just gotta be sure I put away three thousand dollars. Arnie Frankel read in some underground medical journal that for three g's you can go to this place in Austria or Hungary— some damn place over there, they change names so much—and you get these glands of fresh-killed virgin sheep shot into your butt and you get locked into age thirty-nine and no lies.

It was a long, cold red light at Fourteenth Street, and Johnny took the chance of shutting his eyes. He wondered why he had been so tired in the past week. He recalled a time in the early years of practice when he had felt this way—a sense of eternal exhaustion—but then there had been reasons, like being poor and hungry. Then he had been working round the clock seven days a week covering for eight of the more successful and aging practitioners (thirty-three to thirty-nine), now heavy with the burdens of old, established practices, leaden with the gold of very smoothly running enterprises.

They were good days, Johnny thought. Those were the days when money alone was not all that was garnered; above all, it was the time to learn the unwritten lessons of General Practice.

In expanding Greenville the first thing young, bright, Dr. Shoemaker on call learned was—when called, never call right back. If you do, then it is assumed that you are not such a bright young doctor, or else you would be too busy to call right back.

The second thing he learned was never enter a sickroom without washing your hands, never exit (if there were more than two members of the family present) without loosening your tie, never speak without muttering. Announce the diagnosis gravely; the cure, lightly.

You never treat a cold, you treat an acute Upper Respiratory Infection.

Never take a check.

If Grandma was babysitting, Dr. Shoemaker prescribed a mustard plaster, senna tea, and an enema. If the new mother and father stood by shaking, he injected deep into the diminutive rump a double shot of penicillin, gave a bottle of sample cough medicine from his bag, and wrote an Rx for an antibiotic that would cost eight dollars.

And under no circumstances, never ever, did you leave a

call without giving a shot—of *anything*. If you did, the doctor
you had covered for would get a call in the morning and be
told angrily that the wet kid he sent out "didn't do a damn
thing for me—I still got the itch and he didn't give me no
shot."

And, Johnny smiled plaintively to himself, if you were very
very good at this and you ran your little ass off for a year or
two, before you knew it you yourself would soon be able to
shut off the phone on Wednesday, Saturday, Sunday, and
holidays, and take Peurto Rican jaunts, and again allow the
power of medicine to go full circle. "What's your name, son?
You new in town? How'd you like to cover me? Don't worry,
you'll learn fast. Go ye without fear, haven't seen an
emergency in seventeen years."

The light had changed and horns were blasting at that
sonofabitch doctor's old car. Johnny had stalled out. The
Buick had a history of chronic stall-out. He pulled open the
choke and pumped gas. Flooded. Damn car. (*"There is only
one car for a doctor."*) He turned the ignition and accelerated
halfway to the floor, then rammed it home, a trick his late
brother Lem had taught him. It started. "Thanks, Lem," he
said out loud.

"Don't mention it," he heard in return. "Just don't be so
inconsistent, and dammit, stay awake. What has been wrong
with you this past week?"

Johnny's hand wrapped around the crumbled letter as if to
squeeze some hidden warmth into his day. For October it was
cold, wet and cold, and for Johnny it got no warmer. The
heater in the '63 Buick still was blowing musty air-con-
ditioned dust into the car. Old protein energy-bar wrappers
circled Johnny's chilled feet. He flicked on his medical tapes
and was drowned in realistic stereophonic re-creations of Dr.
Stanislaus Bauminder, Dr. Geoffrey Langleman, and Dr. Ivan
Petrofsky, advising him of the cautions of Conception Control
including an Addenda on the Nymphomaniac and Satyrisiac by
Dr. Phyllis Smith.

Johnny Shoemaker settled down now, and in his traveling
auditorium he imagined himself back in seat number thirteen,
Southern Illinois Medical College. On the remaining seven-

minute ride into Greenville Center he hummed something
relating to a Mrs. Robinson.

8:55

HOURS: BY APPOINTMENT
9-12 A.M. DAILY EXCEPT WED.
7-9 P.M. MON. TUES. FRI.

JONATHAN J. SHOEMAKER, M.D.
GENERAL PRACTICE

1555 CENTRE STREET   TELEPHONE
GREENVILLE, N.J.   663-8225

RING BELL AND WALK IN

DOCTOR IS IN–PLEASE BE SEATED

NO SMOKING

NURSE ON DUTY: MRS. FRANCES COOPER

The day nurse was pushing thirty-five generously. After
Mary Shoemaker had had her fill as office wife, Frances
Podalsky, fresh farmed from Uncle Sam's nurse corps (Pacific
theater of duty) became Dr. Shoemaker's first real nurse. With
her shapely young behind, straight blond hair, and face of a
choir girl, she was just great to have around, great to look at.
And unbelievably great to work with. She organized the office
like only a four-striped top sergeant could, and Dr. Shoemaker knew never to come within five feet of her command
station.

Fourteen years, however, had sadly accented the loneliness
of a four-striper. A run-away marriage, a sixth-month baby, a
hit-and-run husband, a puritanical separation, a breakdown, a
Thorazine cure. Frances Podalsky Cooper didn't look too
great any longer. Her shapely backside overran her thighs, her
fun-colored hair blacked out at the seams, the face of the
choir girl was now that of the master. She wasn't too great to
work with, either. Sunrise, sunset, and Dr. Shoemaker came

often now to the command station. The rancid bitterness of
spoiled years curdled her voice; she saw in everyone a
reflection of her own hopelessness, and all patients were fair
game. . . .

. . . .

—I have Willie's skull films hanging on the dryers. He has no
more a concussion than I do. They're all fakers. His Uncle
Hooker canceled again, says he's too sick to come out and
wants a house call. I wouldn't go into that neighborhood
without the militia. They're all alike, seventeen or seventy-six.
Mildred Katz is here. I told her we could see her tonight as a
fill-in. She won't come out to the Lake office any more, she
said, wants in now. I told her she would wait an hour. She
loves you, but she uses the same energy to hate me. The
coroner called, wants a cause of death on Baby Lee. You
were out there three this morning? I'll bet right in the middle
of poor Billy Lee's sixth orgasm. Stupid kids, they'll never
learn, will they? . . . Nick Golopas is first, then Mrs.
Brownlee. She brought the weirdo son, no appointment, like
we have nothing to do but play truant officer this morning.
Then Klopp is here from Medical Supplies. I'll have to get
Katz in first, she sees his briefcase, she knows. What could I
do, she was *sitting* there when I came in? Pushers, that kind.
All pushers. I told Klopp uh-uh today, it's too jammed. All
we need is a thousand 23-gauge syringes and a box of 10 X
12 films, but he says what he's got is so hot he'll wait. So,
he'll wait. And there are two call-backs on your desk. And
please Dr. Shoemaker, please, keep it moving—no hearts and
flowers this morning, please. Here's your list. . . .

Thursday A.M. OCT. 15, 1970—Schedule—Centre St. Office

9:00	Nick Golopas	GP		
9:15	Clara Brownlee	GP	(and son)	
9:30	~~Silas Hooker~~	GP	Mildred Katz	W
9:45	Alvin Dekker	S		
10:00	Jeanette Dusharme	OB	Genevieve Lowrey	GP
10:15	Grace Miller	W	Rose Selena	GP
10:30	Willie Washington	GP (S)	Essie Howard	GP

10:45	Baby Denise Calvert	(Ped)	
11:00	Mattie O'Brien	GP	Jean Pilaggi	I
11:15	Chris Thatcher	TP	Pitkowsky	TP
11:30	Nelson Kids (3)	I	Robt. Loeffel	I
11:45	Frank Carlson	EKG	Mary O'Leary	I
12:00	Joe Jacardi	TP	Karl Appel	I
12:15	Herb Salem	I	Cyndy Lewis	W
12:30	Jenny May	W	Anne Kline	W
1:00	Elsie Schnauzer	W	Sol Roth	I
1:15	E. M. Spencer Brown	GP		
1:30	Fran Cooper			

9:00 GOLOPAS, NICK #7

> 1217 Park St., Greenville, N.J.
> Age 29
> Police Officer—Married—Ins.—Pol. Benefits (BC & BS)
> 7-12-54—This 29-year-old cop has a recurrent ++++ Wasserman. His wife doesn't know and he says he'll billy-club me and charge me with resisting an officer if I ever squeal. He's generally well—too much beer in his young fat belly. Penicillin. . . .

—Hello, Moneybags. Middle of October and you still got a goddam suntan. Been out pushing the little white ball around on Wednesday? "Sorry, sir, the doctor is not in today, sir. My *goodness* sir, you know it *is* Wednesday." Holy Chris', you guys got a strong union. What the hell would you do in my place putting in an eight-hour day pounding cement? Goddam, when I was your seventh patient, you sure as hell come runnin' on Wednesday—*and* Sunday—*and* Saturday night. It's a good goddam thing alls I got is syphilis and not some goddam emergency that could kill me on a Wednesday . . . ouch! Goddam, that's a hornier needle than I got. How many more of these I need? Still ten? Don't you guys make no progress? With all your damn money you'd think they'd figure out a better way to cure a guy. Hey, listen, what if I get another dose before I finish this ten, do I hafta start all over? . . .

.   .   .   .

—Good morning, Centre Pharmacy. Can I help you?...
Marvin, the licensed pharmacist speaking, available also for
wakes, whistlestops, PTA orgies, and Bar Mitzvahs for thirteen-year-old potheads. Dr. John? Glad you found time to
call. You certainly find time to write pretty little scripts for
Essie Howard—like fourteen in the past two months. I'm
warming up the soup which my little wife will deliver
barefooted daily to the local jailhouse, and when they move
us to the state penitentiary, she will mail it in plain Saran
wrapping. You know the Feds are in the neighborhood.
Picked up young Cardone, twenty-three unsigned scripts. You
got twenty-nine on Essie alone. So you know, Dr. John, like
the man says, c'mon down....

.   .   .   .

—I tried calling you all day yesterday. It's Jimmy. You know
how I worry about my Jimmy. He had this sore, you know,
the one on his finger? Well, I read in the papers yesterday
morning that a sore what doesn't heal might be—*cancer*—and I
tried calling you all day yesterday. Your service wanted to
send me this Dr. Peters, but he don't know my Jimmy. And
Jimmy would kick anyone else but you. You remember my
Jimmy, the nine-year-old? The one with the size-eight shoe,
you always laughed when those clodhoppers of Jimmy's got
your shins. He had this sore on his finger, you know, since he
was four years old, and you know he's nine now, and this
article in the paper got me all upset, and when I told Jimmy
there was this Dr. Peters, he said no he only wants Dr.
Shoemaker. I wish you had your son with you already, he is
such a nice boy. He would want your son if your son was a
doctor, he told me....

*...I'm not going into general practice with you. This is the
way it is. In the light of what I know now about general
practice, any other decision would be dark ages. In the past
month I've learned more about medicine than you have in the
past fifteen years, but don't take it personally, Pop. I won't
put you out to pasture. You still have a few old Establishment gimmicks they don't teach out here. Those I won't
forget. (Won't I miss the summer afternoons with you in the
office and rounds in the hospital.) But the gimmicks of your*

medical practice are fading into sad disrepute. Fact is, the way you practice now, Pop, be damned sure your malpractice insurance has you well covered. Since arriving here in September, I have had much time to evaluate a medical world I had been blinded to. I see it like it is and myself as I must be. Your office to the teaching hospital is like a dry, dry desert to the rip-roaring wet ocean. I've kept these feelings out of my letters to the family (miss all that noise around the table). What I'm saying, Pop, is you've got to ready yourself for a change in dream plans for me. . . .

. . . And the article says to call your doctor at once. Can you make Jimmy your first call today? I don't want to take a chance bringing him out. . . .

.   .   .   .

—Doctor, we can't get moving, Coroner Watson is on the phone, take it on line two. He sounds sweet today. . . .

—Dr. Shoemaker, hello there. I have the Lee baby here at the store, and we need your John Shoemaker on a little bit of paper that says it's OK for me to look over your hospital reports on the child. Crib death, eh? Crib death is so uncertain. Makes an honest coroner's job difficult. Oh, well, you know election is coming up in a few weeks. I certainly would appreciate serving you another two years, Doctor. Hmm, crib death. Seems to be a lot of it going around eh, Doctor? . . .

Laurie Lee's mother had had twelve pregnancies and fourteen children. When Laurie was sixteen, she knew if she were ever to shape up, she had better get her little pot a-boiling. So along came Billy Lee, as good a stud as was around for this ninety-two pound, half-toothless, diaper spartan.

At twenty-one Laurie had moved ahead of Momma in relativity and now scored five pregnancies, four births, one death: crib death.

Johnny had been unprepared for this, a forgivable state. After having dropped off to sleep around one-thirty, he expected Peters to cover the night. But Peters, too, was unprepared for this, for a scream of death speeds the unwritten law of coverage into rapid action. Don't call me, call *him*. The call came in at 3 A.M. ("Doctor? Shoemaker?! Come quick. My baby ... my baby is *dead*....") Johnny grabbed first his wife's blouse in the dark, his daughter's slippers (how in hell did *they* get in my closet?), a wet jock (he had been swimming at the gym). And he was there at three-fifteen. Dr. Shoemaker's Buick circled into Laurie's house like a homing pigeon. The wheels sunk into the overgrown mud driveway. The drizzle, that was to be *pouring* by breakfast time, already had softened the ground enough to slop up his quick-grabbed bedroom slippers.

Useless. He pounded and he sucked and blew and pounded. He shot medicine into cold veins, into cold arms, into cold butts. He sped in the ambulance with the infant, breathing and pounding, breathing and pounding, breathing and ... useless. Cold, dry, dead. He had delivered her just six weeks before to the hour—warm, wet, alive.

Johnny Shoemaker rocked himself in Laurie's nursing chair—it was soothing—and he listened. Laurie had a lot of talk in her at 5:30 in the morning. Laurie, eighty-two pounds, edentulous, always (which nobody can deny) a conscientious mother. Now Laurie Lee spoke (ignorantly, but reducing her guilt at least) with the sudden illumination of the condemned. . . .

"Dr. Shoemaker, it is three hours since my baby died. Why? What made her die?"

Johnny could only shrug heavily and explain the unknown.

Laurie Lee was unimpressed. She wiped her sweaty palms across her pocked face, a thing she did constantly, as if spider webs had suddenly enveloped her. "I just give her up and say, so she died?"

The doctor promised her an investigation.

She wiped a web from her lips and made munching sounds from her toothless mouth. "This baby just came out of your hospital yesterday after a week of tests and they found nothing wrong. Now all I got to show for it is a seven-hundred-dollar bill."

The doctor said he was sorry.

"You said I had a fine baby. Do you tell all your mothers a fine baby?"

The doctor *tried* to tell all the mothers that. Johnny thought about all the fine babies he had delivered. Maybe three or four hundred. I wonder where they are now? he thought.

"It's not fair. You don't expect a fine baby to die in her crib six weeks later." Laurie cried, her face a mass of red blotches, her hands massaging her skin in desperate attempts to free the encroaching webs.

He again attempted to explain to Laurie the elements of the unknown.

"Then I'm a rotten mother," she said brutally. "I killed her. I heard her cough last night, I should have stayed with her. She wouldn't be dead if I stayed with her, would she, Doctor? Would she be dead if I stayed alongside her bed all night?"

The doctor shrugged helplessly.

"Would she be dead if I brought her to another doctor?—or to another hospital?"

Now the doctor stopped, then rocked somberly.

"You're my doctor, why didn't you tell me to bring her someplace else? A specialist in Philadelphia? Will I have this to think about all my life? Dr. Shoemaker, you've got to give me something to hold on to."

Laurie Lee slapped at her face as if the spider had bitten her. Blood rose to the skin and bubbled from a pustular sore.

"Dr. Shoemaker, it is only three hours, and in the bedroom now Cathy is coughing, and Billy Jr.'s nose is full of yellow guk, and Clarence's bowels are running water. Are they all going to die?"

The doctor had assumed the total responsibility of the Lee family many years earlier, first with Laurie's mother, then with each kid in turn as she married and then had children. He chilled at the nurse's announcement that one of them was on the phone. No one ever was well, no one ever got better. The days were numbers on a calendar, the countdown to destruction.

"Are they all going to die?" The doctor said "No." And Laurie said "How do you know?" And the doctor said "I don't know...."

At River Drive Johnny had pulled into an empty lot

alongside an old boarded-up burger stand where he could stare
into the rotted wood. He bit away two fingernails from the
thumb and third finger and ripped open a hangnail on the
second, watching it bleed into his hand. He sucked at the
warm blood and tried to feel, but did not feel. He waited for
Lem, who did not come. Tom's letter helped less, but the
words offered themselves up as a surrogate. . . .

   . . . What am I going to do? You're my best Pop, but I've
got to give you up. I cannot go on as you in general practice
haphazardly detecting disease. And with your limited
background and at your age [*my age?*], you cannot even
hope to expand into the newer, more sophisticated medical
procedures now being churned out as rapidly as peanut
butter. Your overconfident, blindly misguided patients are
getting a poor quality of medicine and paying a high price for
it—their lives.
   This is hard stuff, Pop, but this is the way it is. And if I,
as your son, cannot present these truths to you in deep
honesty, and if at this early stage do not recognize the road
ahead is not the road back, as it were (quoth Karl Kleinert),
then I have destroyed your faith in me.
   Now then, Pop, I want you to do me a favor. During
the next week of practice, begin a very honest and
sincere soul-searching evaluation of each case you see.
Think about their complaints, their illnesses, their
potential diseases and eventual deaths. Think past your
natural, homey handling of them—think of them the
way *I* would now. Then, sit down and write to me
about them, and tell me in direct honesty as a physician/
healer/father/human being, whether some portion or *all*
of their cure would not be bettered if they were in the
hands of a specialist trained in their own specific problem.
   You are still in my book a fabulous father, and as for being
a doctor, unbelievably great. Would I ever let even the President's private surgeon remove a *splinter* before consulting
you? But the writing on the wall is loud and clear, and thanks
only to you, I am tuned in. Forgive me, Pop, but this is the
way the new medicine ball is going to bounce.
   Within the next ten years—maybe it won't count to you at
your age but it sure does to me—in ten years the GP as you

know him will be as obsolete as his ancient horse-and-buggy
brother. The backwoods, slipshod, shotgun, come-as-you-are
methods of yours will soon melt away. The pressure of
modern technological advances in the sciences will squeeze
you into uselessness.

Pop, did you ever sit back, like an observer, I mean, and
look at the way you run those sheep through your nickel-
odeon movie? Some of the weird ways you make your medicine
work give me goose pimples. How do you get away with it?

As a kid, it was a run-away adventure, great romanticism,
to visualize your father as a combination magician and
minister and medical man. But you run this scene over and
over again, year after year, and it gets cornier and campier
each time it's played.

And it will only get worse for you. *My* patient will never
know this hodgepodge, this hocus-pocus. My patient will
be plugged in and within seconds the computer will discharge his diagnostic card and the cure that would have
taken you days, weeks, years, or never will be as simple as
flipping a switch.

World Electronics Corporation just around the corner
from you is already working on these things. They have a
WEC MED. CALC. installed in one of our labs right now.
There has got to be a better way, Pop, can't you buy it?
You'll be a museum piece in less than ten years if you don't

Even Arturo Artuoro couldn't change my mind. Poor
old Arturo, they wheel him in, he sputters on about the good
old days, and they wheel him out. A symbol of something,
Pop? A message? How could I, knowing what I do, ever
return to old Greenville and hang out a ditto shingle alongside my Dad's and practice in his dying medicine? It certainly would be sad to spend eight or ten years of my life and
25 thou of your loot and come away with square wheels
when the world is riding around on compressed air.

Gotta go now, Pop, they're getting the old bodies un-
wrapped in the lab and the formaldehyde has already blurred
my lacrimal ducts. I'll cut off an ear and send it to you—how's
the art coming?

Love and Regards to All,

Tom

9:15 ⌐ BROWNLEE, CLARA #3423 ⌐

4 Centre St., Greenville—Age 58
Domestic—Widow—Ins. None—Tele. None
10-18-66 Fat. Sloppy. Menopausal. Good-hearted. Cries,
laughs in one breath. One track—her son. She has nothing
else. Probably estrogen. . . .

—I don't know, Doctor, I was hoping these hormones you
give me would help settle my son's problems. I don't see
them getting any better. Him and me, we just don't see eye
to eye. Even just to get him to talk to me is like pulling teeth
from someone with lockjaw. Kids don't listen to their old
ladies anymore. He goes his own way, never hears what I say,
never eats what I cook. It must be that girl he's got, kids get
awful bad when they get a girl. I think he must have it bad
for this girl. Why else does a kid eighteen have stains on his
underwear? Won't even come out in Lysol. He don't care.
Just drops them on the floor where he pulls them off. I pick
them up like I always do. Did it for his father, too. He knows
I keep a spotless house. Never lifts a finger. Says he's tired if
I ask him. Never talks to me. Never says nuthin' about this
girl. His father never talked neither. When he drank he'd get
talkative and sometimes I even liked it when he drank so'd I'd
have somebody to talk to. Once I tried to get the boy
drinking so'd I have someone to talk to. He just fell off to
sleep and dreamed of his girl. I was sure when you said these
hormones would help me with my sex problems that I would
be able to fix up Albert. But it hasn't meant one thing. Could
you see him? I know he don't have an appointment and
you're so busy, but I kept him out of school and it was hard
enough getting him here. If you could just use some of your
hormones on him, I thought, whatever his problems, you
being a father. . . .

9:25 ⌐ BROWNLEE, ALBERT #3491 ⌐

4 Centre St., Greenville—Age 18
Student—High School—Ins. No—Tel. No
10-15-70—

—I got no problem. . . .

· ·

MEMO: From Frances Cooper—

I can't buzz you because she is hovering over my desk like a vulture. If I don't let her in next, she will attack. Can you blame the Arabs? I'll give you seven minutes. Have you heard that *phone?*

· ·

9:30

KATZ, MILDRED #3280

1210 Erie Ave., Greenville Lakes
Age 38
Married—Housewife—Ins. B.C.B.S. N.J.
9-8-65—New neighbor. Sexy, chesty, high-style, had to tell her to quit lighting up in the office. Problem is eternal dieting. I'm the 8th doctor in past ten years. Pill—fast. Nothing works . . .

—Now look, Johnny, this weight has got to go. Year after year, up, down, up, down. I don't even know who I am most of the time. I have two separate closets of clothes. Most of the time I can fit into *one* of the closets, but this year is my worst. Danny comes home after a week on the road, he calls me a slob. You know he comes home after ten days, maybe two weeks, out in Stickville, Indiana, and he never touches me, *touches* me. Am I so *bad*, Johnny? Look, *you* know. Where could it be better? Here, here, look at me. So, I'm a little heavy this year, but I carry it, I *carry* it. I still have a damned gorgeous leg. You never would feel my leg, would you, Johnny? Like it's medical, feel, *feel.* It's so bad for Danny, a guy who's been in a hotel room with wet underwear for two weeks? I tell you, Johnny, honest to God, a few more nights and I will ex*plode*—all right, *Doctor* weigh me. . . .

. . . All right, I just got over my period, what the hell do you expect? You got to give me four pounds. Anyway, it's a heavier skirt. A hundred and fifty-three less the four, and one and a half for the skirt, so there you are, practically in the forties. Hell, I can *carry* it, I'm nearly five feet six with heels. And I had four martinis last night. Well, don't look at

me like you're a big temperance leader, I have seen *you* at a
few parties. What am I supposed to do when he turns his
behind to me, snoring away like he had already had me, and
I'm just getting into bed? I mean it, Johnny, a few more
nights and I will explode, I mean ex*plode*. Well, dammit,
don't look so—so like a goddam country doctor who just
found out his maiden aunt Matilda has gonorrhea. I'm
thirty-five years old and I have still got it. Johnny, look for
God's sake, this is a beautiful breast. Thirty-five years old and
two kids, and look at the firmness. I don't even wear a
bra. . . .

*". . . Be careful, Johnny, they get pretty tender this time of
the month. Careful. That's good. Good. You are good,
Johnny Shoemaker, I'm so lucky, so damned lucky."*

*The eleven-to-seven shift of nurses at Greenville Mercy
would grudgingly agree; Jonesy, the Night Supervisor, got
herself a damned lucky deal, the bitch. "After all, she's no
kid, she's had her share of those jackrabbit interns. It's not
like he's out for a quick lick and then you don't see him
again until his next night shift. Not Johnny Shoemaker. He is
a stable one, he is. He takes up with a Jonesy, you can
depend on him full time. After all, he's no kid either. He's
married, got a couple of kids of his own, has a great future
going for him over his father's drugstore. This has got to be
the real stuff. You just don't find the younger interns with
his hope-chest-type permanency."*

*Yes, after many losers Jonesy had a winner in Johnny
Shoemaker. She knew, too, that a bird like Johnny seldom
strayed from the nest, seldom allowed himself the unpredict-
able privilege of adulterous flight. But somehow in Jonesy he
had not only found a compassionate companion but a
collaborator in medicine, at a time in his life when Mary—at
home with the kids—could no longer fill this intense need.*

*After Lem, his brother, died, he had run scared and empty
until Mary. She filled the void with understanding and kids,
and he pushed on through school and graduation. It was a
good time. Johnny was able to forget. The tragedy of Lem
faded through the love of Mary and it was a good time, the
years of school. And now the internship at Mercy was good.*

And how it was that a Jonesy could turn-on a Johnny Shoemaker is easy to understand.

You take a nineteen-year-old boy, set in life, and you tell him one tragic day, "Go on, kid, your big brother's shoes have to be filled, go on and get walking," and you put him through a pressure chamber for ten years and keep him drugged with the compulsion of success, and then you suddenly open the escape valve and say, "The end is out there, go walk to light." Well, unless he is Saint Luke, he may come out with the bends.

So, Johnny Shoemaker, now depressurizing for three months at Mercy Hospital, found Nellie Jones, and Jonesy unbended Johnny.

Jonesy, surely thirtyish, with a bloody green smock hung like a potato sack over a formless body, and a washed out wrinkled rag tied over her sweating head, and a spit-stained mask clamped over her shapeless mouth, did for Johnny what Mary—young, graceful, nubile, genteel, soft, silken Mary—had not been able to do of recent times, fully gowned for a ball, or fully naked.

The third floor linen closet worked well for Johnny and Jonesy. The others downstairs, reconciled to their loss, covered for them. The housekeepers never used the storeroom at three in the morning. Only one night, later in the year, did the door open on the blanketed lovers. But old Manuel, the new man, frightened for his job, just tippy-toed over them, said a quiet, " 'Scuse me, folks," pulled some sheets and some pillowcases down from the rack, and tippy-toed backward over them, never to return again.

It didn't seem to work as well up there for the rest of the year (not as smooth as Johnny felt it worked before Manuel) but he was able to go on with it. Johnny had an unappetizing thing about getting caught at sex, and Jonesy could thereafter tell the difference. They never talked about it, but the meetings upstairs grew wider apart, and the time grew shorter, and the day Johnny Shoemaker hung out his doctor's shingle was the last day he ever touched Jonesy—or for that matter, any other. He just somehow never got around to it again. . . .

. . . And Johnny, I will not go out to that Lake office. I'm

coming back *here* from now on. You're here Tuesday night?
I'll be your last patient, I'll take a cab, you'll drive me home.
You *will* drive me home Tuesday, won't you, Johnny? Please,
please . . . ?

9:40

DUSHARME, JEANETTE #3288

> 190 Hideaway Ave., Greenville
> Age 26
>
> Married—Housewife—Ins. WEC (husband)
> 5-12-68—Scared innocent. First pregnancy. Ugly beauty.
> She knows and can't decide which. History of urinary
> complications. To refer her to Lenihan for consultation.

—I'm sorry to just disappear from you and then show up with
a big belly like this. But Dr. Lenihan is so busy, and he has
this partner I can't stand, and he turned me over to him
completely this past month. I might as well come to someone
I know. I always liked you, Dr. Shoemaker, but you did send
me to him. . . . Your examining gowns are nice, Dr. Shoemaker. You know, Dr. Lenihan doesn't use examining gowns.
Nothing at all. He says it's the only way to examine in truth.
At first it is total shock, let me tell you, but you go back.
Especially when you're twenty-six and married to the same
young kid for seven years and he is still copywriting technical
papers at World Electronics and going to school three nights a
week, and here this suave, graying, silver-tongued *doctor* is
paying close attention to your body.
 . . . Even the preparation at home getting ready for The
Visit, bathing, powdering, perfuming, this is great, like
dressing for a coming-out party. In the first few months
following the examination, Dr. Lenihan would pat me as I
tiptoed off to dress. I would flinch and pucker a little and
wonder—maybe hope. Then, as the months went by, he would
improvise on the examination, like showing me how to
prepare my breasts for good nipple health. He's a firm
believer in nursing, and I agree with him. Often he would kiss
my cheek, once even a little lingering breast kiss, and then

paddy-whack me off to my dressing room and home to Fred. . . .

Dr. Shoemaker remembered Fred, a third-string linebacker at Greenville High who never quite got to play more than once or twice because he was always in the office for sinus trouble and stomach trouble and ingrown nails and rashes. After he married Jeanette, his main complaint—early in life, but not for Fred—was prostatitis. . . .

—I had often heard whispers in his office of the "chosen" ones, who got to come back for appointments after hours, and soon I found my only purpose in life was to become one of Dr. Lenihan's after-hours. But the damn baby came on time. He delivered me, kissed me goodbye, and wished me back soon. Four months later I was pregnant. I remember you thought the pill was a flop. You even stopped three of my girl friends, but I couldn't say a word. It wasn't the pill, it was *me*, I just never took them! And in his stupid, helpless way, Fred had sent me back to Dr. Lenihan.

He was thrilled to see me, he said, and I died between visits. I began calling him more often for stupid questions and emergency visits, and soon I was all gone. Mercilessly gone. His paddy-whacks became delicious squeezes, and his playful kisses held us together until I thought I would bust if he didn't have me. He made my next appointment after hours. This was just three months ago. It was to be the Great Scene. He would fall madly in love with my body and we would be married. I came ready for the *Grande Passion*—explosion under my love, euphoria, utopia, ecstasy. Minutes after it was over I was turned out of his office as he readied for the next patient. I wanted him to love me. I came back, I told him so, I was in *love* with him. I wanted to marry him. He hurriedly and sickeningly buttoned me and told me that this was childishly foolish, and if I wanted to keep up our affair, he would be delighted. He thought I was very lovely—but he told me he was happily married and to go home to Fred.

I went back for more visits ... the same quick nothing, ending in goodbye and thank you. And now this, on my last visit, he was *not in*. I called, and I begged, and I made a stupid ass of myself. I told his nurse I *loved* him, and she said "The line forms to the right."

I can't go back there. I can't let that man *touch* me. Please, Dr. Shoemaker, help me. I know you said I needed an obstetrician, but you delivered my friend Jeannie and there was no trouble. I love you, Dr. Shoemaker, please take me on. Please, I need someone. . . . Before you examine me, do you want me to remove my gown? I seem to react better that way. . . .

. . .Now be honest with yourself, Pop, just think about it. . .and then tell me that all of your patients would not be better off in the hands of a specialist trained in their specific problem. . . .

. . . .

—You know, two people walked *out*. This girl had you there for twenty minutes. I'm sending in Klopp, he says he just wants a minute. Now don't forget what happens out *here,* doctor. The phone is already ringing for Friday, there's only two seats left in the waiting room. You have two calls before you see the big, black football hero. He's here, rippling muscles, rancid pants, and all. Klopp is coming in—*one* minute. . .

10:00 —J. J., you look great,—tired, but *great*. How come I don't see you on the course? I played with your buddy Lenihan yesterday. Broke 80—gin and tonics, that is. Ha! Hey, don't get up and leave me, I've been sitting in that damned waiting room an hour. When the hell are you buying new furniture? I got a spring up my ass in two chairs.

Maybe that's what those women come in for. Never saw so many pregnant and waiting women. Which is just what I came to talk to you about.

Now J. J., needless to say, The Pill is a problem, but like a lot of other problems, you're stuck with it until something better comes along.

So, quick, thirty seconds and I am on my way. J. J., I got for you the latest baby-stopper. But, ah-ha, the one where *you* make the brick, and the publicity is beyond reproach. It's the old Intra-uterine-Device trick. The women since the pill

scare are plugging away for this like mad. Up until now only the
OB-GYN men could do it safely—getting up to a hundred a
throw. Along comes this guy with this smart gadget—weighs less
than an ounce—blindfolded, you're in. We're the only outfit
that's got them, my boss picked them up at a Japanese
convention. Most of the G.P.'s are gobbling them up as fast as I
can deliver. Figure it out, J. J. Costs you two-thirty apiece.
Most boys are satisfied with fifty a throw. I'll leave you two
dozen for a start—that's a quick trip to Puerto Rico. . . .Now
what kind of remark is that, my minute is up? J. J. you're the
god-damndest fool. I'm your friend, the whole town is doing it,
you got to grab on to the new stuff, J. J.

   . . .All right, I'm going, I'm going. J. J., you surprise me.
You haven't bought anything new in years. Dammit. I'll leave
you a sample—try it on your best girl friend. . . .

.   .   .   .

—There are two calls hanging on. One is Laurie Lee, and she
sounds petrified. Wants you to come by this afternoon, all the
kids are sick. The second, well, use your own judgment—it's
Clara Dumbleton, third time in an hour. Don't women have
anything else to do mornings? . . .

.   .   .   .

—This is Clara, Doctor. Fran wouldn't put me through and I'm
near out of my mind. She knows when I call it's only an
emergency. . . .

   "*. . .and the sore on Jimmy's finger looks worse than it did
yesterday.*"

   . . .Can you imagine, I waited a full day? I wouldn't call you
yesterday on your day off. I know how you need a day away
from us pests, but I couldn't go on another mealtime with
this happening. This kid has got me crazy. You told me Lisa
should start on strained fruits. Well, I started her on apricots
because on our last visit you mumbled something about her
color and you know how apricots have three percent more
iron than applesauce. You said, and I wrote it down, in *red,*
you said she should progress a teaspoon a day until she is
eating a half a jar. Well, Dr. Shoemaker, get this, I tell you,
I'm scared, this baby has got me scared. . .

"...I'm scared, Dr. Shoemaker. Kathy is in there coughing like the baby, and Billy Jr.'s nose is full of yellow guk..."

...She had a teaspoon on Sunday, then two teaspoons on Monday. All right, then, three on Tuesday. Now, listen to this—she had *three* again on Wednesday. And this morning—the fifth day—my God! *Three* again. Dr. Shoemaker, I know you are busy this morning, but if I bundle her up and bring her right in....

. . . .

10:10 | WASHINGTON, WILLIE #SF

6½ Willow St., Greenville—Age 15
Student—Greenville High—Special Football Ins.
9-3-67—This is the young, wild, black boy Tom said to look for. He's going to make all-state. Arturo would jump cartwheels. Snotty, but good sense of humor. Enviable body....

—Now, look, Doc, I gotta play Saturday. I tell you my head don't hurt no more. We been together three years, would I lie to you? Look, test me, put that light in my eye, it don't make a move. I'm strong, man, let me tell you, I'm strong. See these pectorals?—man, you are going to make a big mouth of me—see these shoulder muscles, like cables of steel. See these... gastrocnemuisii? When these leg muscles start pumpin' Saturday, we are gonna run wild over that zero team. This is *the* game. Coach Bocca says there is gonna be scouts from State College. You know what that means to me? Sure you know—great day last summer when you drove me out into them hills, country like I never saw before, country air like I never smelled before.

State College! You told me it could be mine if I worked. Well, man, this is it. No one ever worked for anything like I worked. Free sleepin' and free eatin', new bedsheets every week. Man, I'd get my head clobbered every day for that deal.

You know they can't play without me, now you know that. We're four and zero, and when we take this one, we're on our sure way to state champions. Hell, Doc, you know how many cracks in the head my old man gave me in the last year alone? Each time he changes jobs, and that's like every ten days. He uses it like a scoreboard. And the crack I got last Saturday was like a love potion next to my old man's. You pulled me out of that game and we only won by shit luck cause it was rainin'. They gotta have me this week. Doc, I swear, I'm *solid*. Here, make me walk a line, lift a thousand pounds. See here, I can lift *you*,...

...and you are beautiful too, man, Johnny Shoemaker marveled from four feet up where Willie Washington held him suspended, parked against the ceiling tiles. Man, you are beautiful.

It was a game they played. Johnny was a game player. When the pressures moved in to make him feel like he might be happiest back in Cannes smearing up a borrowed canvas with neo-impressionistic abstractions of wrestling nudes, Johnny unconsciously resorted to game-playing. He had one for each trouble area. There was one with the kids at home—Skin, Pimples—in which he gathered them together and while he shut his eyes and counted to ten, they would disappear and he would never find them. Another he had with long-winded patients, where he would buzz Fran Cooper three shorts and a long and she would race in with a bloody towel and scream "It's awful, it's awful," and he would disappear, never to be found again until the causal patient had been removed from his consult room and sent on home with a new appointment well into the next month.

And there was his favorite, reserved for Mary, when she turned cold for no reason other than that he had arrived three or four hours late for dinner. As she pummeled him with wifely tirades relating to the inconsiderations of the male doctor and her absolute refusal to go on living this way any longer and how his mother should have brought him up with more manly qualities and how her father would never treat her mother so absent-mindedly and how sex was not all that makes a marriage, but that she had had it and he might as well stay out the rest of the night—as she ranted, Johnny would begin a slow, insistent count—five (your mother never liked me), ten, fifteen, twenty, (my father called my mother six times a day...), twenty-five, thirty (*erahna, erahna, erahna, erahna*) ... up to ninety, ninety-five—at which time he had advanced upon her unrelentingly so that she was unable to pace her battle strength, and finally, total capitulation—*one hundred*!

The game with Willie started a few years back following a freak bobbled interception. Willie had pulled a loose-flying ball out of the air behind his own goal post, and in ten-point-three he had touched the ball down over enemy lines to win a crucial game leading to Greenville's first state trophy. Willie, then only sixteen years old but already smoldering with strength, rushed to the sidelines and with one whoosh! had erected Dr. Shoemaker ten feet straight into the October sun (from *only* which—Johnny swears—the tears came). The school band, led by Mr. Rosy-Cheeked Purty, struck up his hand-written school victory march; the bare-legged cheerleaders bounced their new adolescence up and down the gravel track; the boys on the bench in their clean, green uniforms made a circle around the shiny black pole holding triumphantly aloft the pale white father; and the stands arose as one and screamed *Olé*.

As Willie held Johnny immovably against the cork tiles, Johnny could think only of the unbelievable miracle of strength this boy had become. There was no fear, no paling out like the first experience, no tears from the sun, just a feeling of absolute power one would feel if he were a shipping carton of steel bumpers now raised into the air by a massive electronic forklift. Wrapped mightily around his paunching waist (*Must get back to jogging*), the anatomical masterpiece of Willie's hand flashed through to the doctor. The most exacting machine ever created, the human hand, now here was embodied in a Willie Washington, and was folded around a Jonathan Shoemaker. He would never, without trembling in exultation, be able to comprehend the precision of this structure, the fascination of its function. His doodle pad by the phone was a mass of trapezoids and capitates, and hamates and lunates with styloids and facets and capsules and palmar metacarpal ligaments and digital muscles and cruciate and annular fibres and vinaculum longums and lots and lots of phalanges—long ones, short ones, up and down ones, sideways ones. Bloomquist, the headshrinker friend, once dialing from Dr. Shoemaker's telephone, glanced at his pad and said, "This doctor is a sex maniac."

"...*Gentlemen, my name is Professor Arturo Artuoro. I have six hundred and forty-seven muscles in my body, each of them with a name, each of them with an exact position, each of them with an exact origin, each of them with an exact insertion, each of them with an exact action. Before any of you graduate, you will know better than you know your own name the origin, insertion, and action of each of these six hundred and forty-seven muscles. I will call now for the first assignment on seat number thirteen. Tell me, seat number thirteen, the origin, insertion, and action of the Palmaris Longis. No hesitation, snap, snap, snap—like your name, number thirteen.*

Number thirteen flubbed the Palmaris Longis. He muttered that it originated where, in actuality, it inserted, and Arturo screamed to the shrinking thirteen that if this were the case, he would have to masturbate with his elbow. So, for such a stupid error, he was to write five hundred times in longhand the origin, insertion, and action of the Palmaris Longis and be prepared to give orally in class the complete hand group—of which the total is eighty-four.

"Remember," the shrill little man (where his four-foot-eight curved body housed the six hundred and forty-seven muscles none of his students were destined to know) sternly reminded number thirteen, "not only do you not graduate if you do not pass my course, but you are also a lousy doctor...."

...Johnny Shoemaker was now laughing uncontrollably into acoustic tiles so that the muffled sounds came back to him distant and hollow, not like they were the laughter of joy, but of fear. He had never felt fear in Willie's hand since the first tear-stained experience. It had always been a game of sheer exhilaration, the long shadow of little Arturo claiming another victim to its corps of medical forget-me-nots. But the laughter now bounced flatly into the little black cork holes, and they muffled a cry which sounded to Johnny like, "I won't let *you* down; now don't you let *me* down, Willie Washington."

"...*You will meet up,*" *Arturo had said glumly to him the day they parted, "you will meet up in the next years as a General Practitioner with the scum and the saints, with the dirt and the polish, with the sad and the lonely and the sick shells of what will come and go past your eyes as humankind. But they will only be shells, empty of substance, empty of livers and hearts and brains and muscle, but full of puke, snot, slobber, pus, debris, rot, and decay. And they will plead for life and health, and you will patch them like ripped inner tubes worn with age, frayed with misuse, set for instant blowout. Death will come welcome, health will be a dream. You will be a carpenter, a tailor, a plumber, a ditchdigger. You will hammer them apart and sew them together. You will cover them over and you will bury them, and prosper from them, and you will live in the country from them in a big estate with horses and pigs and boats and limousines. And you may very well live an entire life maddened and benumbed by them, and will die by them. But, one day, if you are saintly inscribed, one day along will come the gladiator, the lion, the perfect messiah of a patient. He will have six hundred and forty-seven muscles in exacting origin, with exacting insertions, and exacting actions. And he will be your gift, your only chance at being a real doctor. He will sicken only if you allow him to sicken, for his structure will regulate his function. And he will die only if you allow him to die, for his death must be a tragic blunder. So when and if he comes, save him, ploy him, cherish him. He only comes to the practitioner of General Medicine truly by accident. He is the total antithesis of what your General Practice will be. He is the absolute truth of what your practice could be. Good luck, Dr. Shoemaker, good luck. I hope you find one in the next thirty-five years alloted you. But remember—please to re-member—a retributive word from me who has known: The letting go may be more difficult than the finding. . . ."*

Who can tell of such joy, Johnny thought, looking up foolishly from the floor where his toothy, smiling, messianic clown with the ominous crack in his head had dropped him in a hysterical heap. Soon he will be gone, he thought sadly. Soon this tough, beautiful bastard will be gone and there won't be anything left but the shells. . . .

—Hey, now, Doc, I still gotta wear this stupid collar? My old man laughs like hell. I gotta take it off at home, he just keeps laughin'. Listen, will ya? Please, Doc, just listen. Screw the head, I gotta get away to State, and the only way I go is I gotta play Saturday. We talked about this a hundred times. I might as well be dead if I don't play Saturday. You're my buddy, Doc, you know what I mean? Just shut your eyes and don't worry so damn much, Doc. I'll be there when you open them. . . .

. . . .

At ten thirty Dr. Shoemaker was already fifty-five minutes behind. He remembered classically the president of the medical school's largest fraternity greeting the puerile freshman in assembly that first night. And he heard him say in conclusion to a ten-minute welcome to Chicago's bloodshot-eye-land, ". . .Doctors [other than number thirteen, that seemed to be all anyone called you], doctors, look at your watches. Check the hour. It is inevitably written—you are already two days behind."

At ten thirty-five Genevieve Lowrey, sickly thin, tobacco stains on her lips, smelling from butts and peppermint, coughed out that she wouldn't sit another minute without a smoke, and lit up. Dr. Shoemaker opened the window.

"Converts are the worst kind," Jenny puffed. "You doctors talk out of two heads. If you don't smoke, you turn your collars around and preach abstinence like it's the Saviour returned. If you do smoke, you join the air-pollution squad and serve notice on the local gas works. Heads got to roll, as long as it's not yours. Three months ago I gave up the darling weed. Big deal, I still can't stop the cough. It's getting worse. Words disappear right in the middle of a sentence. Suddenly I realize I lost three little words and you know, Doctor, what's that sentence without those three little words? It feels like I'm a tape recording and somebody scissored out an inch." Jenny coughed, and black phlegm lined her lips.

Dr. Shoemaker whipped out Dr. Irvin's letter and read to her the specialist's findings.

"So," she shrugged, "brother Albert had the same thing last May. You think old seventy-five-a-visit Irvin will crack open my case when I go in the hospital tomorrow? If I've really got it, why quit? Brother Albert puffed right into his coffin. I saw clouds coming up from the ground past the first dozen shovels of dirt. Unless, of course, you're going to give me the old soft-shoe speech, and you wouldn't do that to an old dying grandma, now would you, sonny?"

She pulled out a fresh, clean, crisp pack and pulled away the foil, "Got a light?" . . .

At ten forty Rose Selena shuffled her feet in, her body seemingly pulling up in the rear, separation in all areas of life her foil. This way, Dr. Shoemaker had observed, she needn't ever react as a norm and in so doing she needn't feel, or be. Rose Selena had prematurely returned from a Caribbean cruise and had been slipped in as an emergency. Frances did this at times for Rose, because Rose was a teacher to her kids at Mary the Blessed High.

Rose was over twenty-one, closer to thirty-six. And she was a virgin, Rose was. At this moment, not very blessed. "I had to come home, Doctor. I left three days early, I couldn't wait. I was going to call you from Jamaica." She was already crying, only not with tears but with sobs and starts and stops, also a mechanism adopted for fragmentation of voice from fact, from being. If you are careful to adjust your speech to broken segments, your chances of being understood are slim and you can continue not to exist.

"I did something awful—awful—just—oh yes I did, Doctor." She sighed and wiped a dry eye. "Doctor, you are going to hate me—me—yes—hate—you are. But, my God, help—yes—me, you must, help. I came right to you. I told them dysentery— yes—dysentery—me—they knew—it hurts. But the lump in my belly—uh—no dysentery—the hurt, the lump, like an anchor, the ship is sinking. You're going to think bad of me, but I—no—me—never—you know—my God. I was far away from home—home is far—and I was far—and he was clean and beautiful and kind and we laughed and we sang and he said beautiful things to me and suddenly that night he touched me with his—oh mother of God—he wet me all over. Doctor, you've got to help me, I'm pregnant."

Her voice trailed off into a chord of redundant organ sounds, and she, not realizing the clarity of speech she had found, but enjoying it, played it over and over and over. "I'm pregnant, I'm pregnant, I'm pregnant." But try as she might, she could not disassociate. "What will I do about school when the Sisters find out? And Sister Marie! What I told you—you told—oh no—me and Sister Marie. Oh, my God, awful—oh awful—yes—sweet Sister Marie, when she finds out what I did with a *man....*"

At ten fifty Baby Denise Calvert was brought in by mother Phyllis, who was still in glorious shock. The baby had come out looking like Frank. "It looks like *Frank.* I don't believe it. The eyes, and that same hook in the nose. God Bless you, Dr. Shoemaker, you made me hold on when I wanted to shove anything in there to get it out. Hold on, you said, you will bless the day. Well, bless *you,* you old sonofabitch, we did it this time. Even Frank's old lady says a spittin' image of her baby boy, Frankie. I have been laughing since five minutes after she was born. The intern wanted to give me a needle, he thought I was hysterical. And Frank with his stupid giggle—can't you give him anything to stop that giggle? He pokes at the kid and grins asinine grins and he struts around. Stupid ass. I came out of this smelling like a rose. A great feeling, a *great* feeling. He'll never know, the sonofabitch will never know. Doctor—will he? You think—you think I should ever tell him?. . .."

Johnny Shoemaker saw Mary Shoemaker kissing Santa Claus. He blinked hard, ran cold water over his eyes, and made a note to check the pill count when he got home.

An emergency call from Coach Bocca, blasting him for even *suggesting* Willie wouldn't play Saturday. "Chris', Doc, I got a job, too. . . ."

At eleven o'clock Mr. Arthur Green, local haberdasher, style-pacer of all Greenville city, *bon vivant* of Centre Street, and girl-winker, arrived with Mrs. Arthur Green, local beauty, memories of high school pageantry and queen of football homecoming, circa 1941. Each had a singular request: "She needs her hormone shot." "He needs his hormone shot."

At eleven ten Essie Howard was slipped in for a quick shot

of distilled water. She had just about reached her breaking
point, the shot without which she would never have made it
to nightfall. Dr. Shoemaker wrote out her regular Rx for
twelve pills, and Essie screamed and cried she'd never make it
sleeping next to *him* all weekend. "For God's sake, after
fifteen years, Dr. Shoemaker, twelve pills will never hold me.
What do I have to do, *beg*?..."

At eleven fifteen Mattie O'Brien kissed Dr. Shoemaker and
thanked him and complained about the other doctors who
never helped her, and left blessing Medicare.

At eleven twenty-five, after waylaying a dozen calls of
desperation, six pharmacy callbacks for Rx OK's, four
appointment verifications and two cancellations, one for last
Thursday, Fran allowed through a call to Dr. Shoemaker from
Mrs. Podalsky, her mother. Poppa couldn't get out of bed.
—Mrs. Podalsky, Doctor, Franny's ma? Hello, Doctor. I'm
sorry to bother you about Poppa, but he's got this terrible
pain in his back and you know he's got to get off to work by
twelve....Hello, hello, Fran—you on the line?...
Of recent date, Fran was apt to be. There was a time Dr.
Shoemaker never considered this more than her professional
curiosity, and often there was an advantage to a three-way
hookup. But recently, Dr. Shoemaker found himself automatically switching to his private line. He never thought of
why, it just seemed more desirable. Frances Cooper's commentary on the patients' problems was as much help to him
today as a leech on a leg.
...Dr. Shoemaker, Franny is off the line and quick I want to
talk to you about *her*. Poppa, that old Polack, I put a
mustard plaster on, he'll live to bury us all. Now, listen
careful about Franny. I don't know what she is telling you
lately, but that no good Irisher husband is back in town and
he has been playing with her like a cat pawing a dead mouse.
He calls her and hangs up. She gets in her car and he's in her
seat. She turns a corner and he is in her skirt. He wants her in
bed. That's all he wants, the dirty thing, nothing else. Not the
kids, no responsibilities, just her body, the poor girl. So listen,
Doctor, this is what you got to know—she is taking all kinds
of pills. I'm scared crazy. I don't know how she acts in the

office, but at home she sits in a dark corner sometimes for hours and never moves. All right, all right, I know this is not the worst thing to bother you about on a busy morning, but *somebody's* got to share with me what I found just now. That old Polack, I tell him and he'll bust a gut. I can't just keep this inside me. Who else but you, you're a doctor, ain't you? This morning I am fixing her clothes—she left so late—and I put away her nightgown into her bottom drawer, and sweet saints preserve us, she has got a gun. . . .

Aging hadn't dulled Fran's perception of her doctor's flushed face. "You lie like a wet towel," she didn't hesitate telling him. "It wasn't about Pop's back. The old bitch can't learn to butt out. Maybe if they had butted out at the beginning——" She drew herself back—no personal references during office hours, she had set up an appointment later—and as quickly the sergeant returned. "I put away Washington's skull films. They looked all right to me. Faker. Make him play. Don't be a wet nurse, they'll suck you dry. These kids need to get smashed up. They *want* to play, let them get smashed. What else they going to do with their lives? They all end up hero-bums. Don't I know, I got one.

"All right, so, up-to-date—cross off Thatcher, he got his diathermy. Sore knee, ha. Pitkowsky's still under traction. Maybe I'll push it up to forty pounds. You want to go in that room—do they *ever* change their underwear? The Nelson kids I gave their allergy shots, they both cried, the mother gives such a dirty look. I told her she wants to wait for you, she's got an hour more to go. Loeffel had his B_{12}, Carlson's EKG is ready, Jean Pilaggi got a reaction to the water shot, so I said maybe it's an allergy. And I'm getting O'Leary's B_{12} now. . . ."

There was a time this would have turned Dr. Shoemaker into a Dr. Jekyll. To allow hired help the sanctified privilege of attending to the sacred patient without even as much as a wave or a smile or a touch—hell's bells, Johnny would say, a guy's got to really prostitute his medicine. I don't know how the other guys get away with it, they run through seventy, eighty a day, maybe they see twenty, and the hired help practice the medicine. In the meantime, what the hell does *he* do?

"Whatever he does," Jerry Albert, his accountant had said, "you better do, too." Over a stack of blue-lined, red-penciled pages, Jerry had said this to Johnny, as he had said many things to him in the past years. Regardless, Johnny Shoemaker continued to practice medicine in his own abstract way. Apparently the obtuse patterns and bland colorings of the doctor's canvases left his accountant's mind devoid of cheer.

"Unheard of," Jerry Albert had said. "All I can tell you is you better find a way to increase your load or else you got yourself a medical phenomenon, a rotten year. With one kid in college and five more years to go, and whatever other *mishagos* he has planned for your bankroll, and the other three coming up fast, and the crazy market this year, and that stupid washing machine business you got hung up on— Johnny, keep up the medical load. . . ."

"*. . .You either reduce your medical load or find another way to make a dollar, doctor.*" So spoke Alvin J. Kronewitter, M.D., F.A.C.I. (Fellow, College of American Internists), following a recent examination of Dr. Shoemaker. "Your diastolic has stabilized at 110, your left ventricle is practically doubled in size. Statistics say fifteen years. Cut your load, doctor, see less people, take on a partner, no night work. Pardon me, but I must get on to my next patient. . . ."

"*. . .When I grow up, Pop, I wanna be a doctor like you, only I'm not going to work at night 'cause I'd miss Uncle Miltie, and the Merry Mailman, and Howdy Doody, and . . . .*"

. . . .

11:00 JACARDI, JOSEPH #3420

274 Kingston Terrace, Greenville—
Age 48
Married—Car Sales—Ins. (Litigation Att'y)
9-12-69—Accident. Rear-ender. Nonspecific injuries. Apparent whiplash. To be further studied and treated accordingly. . . .

—Look, Doc, you keep markin' me down, it's money in the bank. Hell, I can't leave the place to them dumb *schvartzes,* they'll steal every tool in the shop. And I got a Jew at the register, I trust him like a brother. His name I already turned over to the Mafia. And those bum football star salesmen, they sell a car and pocket under the table like they're still big heroes. How the hell can you stand workin' at that political school job with them kids? They figure the world owes 'em a livin' for runnin' a dirty ball all over the grass. Up their ass. While they were stealin' all the glory out there, I was scrounging for a dime selling hot dogs my old man picked up at the slaughter house. A little green, but we'd soak 'em overnight and with all that goddam noise out there, who knew what they were eatin'? It's a crooked world from the day go. You gotta screw before you get screwed, and the world laughs with you. That's my motto, Doc. What's yours? Make it out for cash? Don't give me no crap, you want to knock off the Buick for a Caddy. So feel the neck, it still hurts like hell. See? I can't turn it this far. You get the picture. Doc, nothin' drives like a Caddy. Mark me down, you hear, three times a week. The '71's are creampuffs, you can knock one off on my case alone. Sock it to 'em, Doc. Mark me down—you *hear?* Gotta get back—screw the heat treatment, can't leave that crook at the register alone a minute. . . .

. . . .

11:50 SALEM, HERBERT #2337

634 Garden Ave., Greenville Lakes—
Age 51
Engineer WEC—Married—Ins. WEC
1-6-62—Harmless little guy. Looks like a fly could swat him.
Engineer through and through. Precision medicine is. . .

—Well, Doc, it's just about here, we're off for Japan by Christmas. Maybe for a year, maybe two. You can't ever tell what's going on at the WEC Exec. Center, but when you're Company, away you go. You better deep freeze about a dozen vials of the stuff for me and have it ready-packed in dry ice. I hate to remember what I was before these shots. I could have tied the thing in a loose bow, but *now,* damn, like Washington's Monument. I worked my wife's ass down three sizes. Never says a word any more. How could she? What the hell can a guy have left, she figures. My secretary fondly shares the illusion. Doc, you guys have got it made. Stick your hand in that little black bag and you can fly to the moon, and none the wiser.

You got it straight now, Doc, a shot a week, figure two years, OK? Pack up a dozen vials. Hey, hold on, make it a baker's dozen—there's a Japanese housegirl I met last April. . . .

. . . .

Noon —Jenny May says screw the appointment. She has to get the hell back to work. Just give her a bottle of pills and take the rest of the day off. You want to touch her? . . .

. . . .

—Hello, Dr. Shoemaker, you certainly look well rested today. Weather was ideal yesterday for fall golf, now wasn't it? We at J. C. Campbell know that relaxation is the key to a successful and efficient doctor. Because of this, our in-depth research has come up with this fine new book written expressly for J. C. Campbell, expressly for you by the country's top ten golf pros. They have spared no expense to make this your constant Wednesday companion. Through in-depth analysis our research department knows that above all, your dream in life is to arrive at that stage where all you need do forever is swing down the lane below eighty, not a care in the world, not a telephone in sight. They know this through in-depth analysis of four hundred and twenty-seven outstanding doctors just like yourself. Now just look at this four-color abstract cover done for us by the world-renowned artist, Cassandra. They tell me he—or she?—pocketed $25,000 just for this cover which J. C. Campbell presents to you through me. Oh, yes—and just between us, please, Doctor—this was an unusually expensive undertaking, and I only have a few for my territory, and I know you always have been good to us, and my *kiddies,* too, so just between us, eh, Dr. Shoemaker? . . .Now, I am sure you have been receiving our sample mailings on the new one milligram *Vagex.* This is our product, you know, and it finally answers the problem of The Pill. It is a result of four hundred thousand case-months of study conducted by the world-renowned Louis Urbanshire of the Brazilian Medical Institute conducted under a nonprofit grant from J. C. Campbell Foundation for World Health and Population Control. If you will look at this four-color chart, you will see that compared to the old problem products, in the five main categories of side effects, *Vagex* one milligram shows the lowest possible index which is depicted as the heavy magenta line. *Vagex* shows a 63 out of a possible 100. The closest, whose name product you well know, only scored a 68. So, you see, for accurate and safe birth control—and isn't that what we're all after?—the *only* product you can feel totally safe with is Vagex one milligram. May I leave you some sample starters? And will you promise to start four new patients this week? Thank you, Doctor, I won't take up any more of your valuable time. You are a gentleman. Enjoy your Wednesdays and the book and the comfort of *Vagex* One. . .

. . . .

—Coach Bocca on the phone. Says it sure as hell is an emergency. . . .

—Doc, what the hell is *this?* Don't you know what's going on down here with the NAACP? First I get old man Washington down here this morning telling me Willie's gotta play ball, and I tell him I won't know until you give me the word tomorrow. Next thing I know, Dr. Leader calls me down the office, there's a big meeting this afternoon with some Reverend and this here character from the NAACP. Hey, Doc, what the hell, who needs this? Let the kid play, his head's like a billiard ball. Doc, hey, *Doc,* you want my kids to walk the streets bare-assed? . . .

. . . .

No, Johnny didn't want Bocca's kids to walk the streets bare-assed, nor did he want Willie Washington to play the game with a cracked head. Nor did he want to start four new patients on *Vagex* one milligram. Nor did he want to swing down the lane below eighty. Nor did he ever stick his hand in his little black bag and fly to the moon—but he thought about it.

By one ten he had seen five more shells. Fran buzzed him and said, "Four minutes to E. M. Spencer time. You're going to make it today. And so that the four minutes won't be totally lost, look who I'm sending in. . . .

. . . .

—R. J. Sanford & Company here, Doctor. Your girl sent me in, I promised her I'd only be four minutes. See that pretty little bellied girl who just left here—if you had had the new *Ovex* one milligram a few months back, she wouldn't have her pretty little self all blown up with baby fat. New *Ovex* one milligram offers you a background of trial with twenty million cyclic hours and only one pregnancy. And we hear this was in some Zulu tribe—one woman who couldn't read the instructions—gave a pill to each boyfriend. And *there's* an idea R. J. Sanford is on top of, too. However, I'm sure you have been receiving our sample mailings of the new *Ovex* 1. This is our product which finally answers the problem of The Pill. If you will look at the four-color chart prepared by Dr. Charles Santorino of the Mexican Institute of Birth Control, it demonstrates with finality our superior achievment. *Ovex* 1 offers you absolute conception control, and the incidence of side effects at a new low of 63 out of a possible 100.

The closest second product, whose name you very well know, is 68. I won't burden you with details, but if it's pregnancy control it's *Ovex* 1. If it's safety—and isn't that what we're all after?—it's *Ovex* 1. I'll leave you a dozen samples and I know you will start four new patients this week.

That's a picture of your four kids, isn't it, doctor? Hah—I'll leave you a *lifetime's* supply there, Doc. And a book for your Missus by the world-famous beauty expert, Madame Maria, with hints on how to remain young forever on *Ovex* 1. Damn well could have been welcome about ten years ago, huh, Doctor? Oh, well—don't tell the boss, but you're like me, I got seven, like to keep my wife the old-fashioned way—barefoot and pregnant. Whoever invented these damn pills had no guts. Some homosexual, wouldn't you say, Doc? . . .

. . . .

1:15 SPENCER BROWN, E. M. #3092

900 Westgate Drive, Newtown—
Age 63
Exec. V.P. WEC—Bachelor—Ins. WEC
10-2-64—Emptiest shell of all. Who is to figure, never sick a day in his life. Scary, our world revolves about his. . .

—Your punctuality is improving, lad, only thirty-three seconds off today. Soon you'll be ready to compute. Had to drop two of my top aides today—couldn't compute them. Punctual errors varying from thirty-three milliseconds to one-point-three minutes. One millisecond, lad, and the satellite fails to orbit. One millisecond and the terminal fibril in the cerebrum fails to discharge. One millisecond and a chain reaction destroys the universe. A few more years and unless you compute, you will be sand on the beach. World Electronics Corporation will make you compute soon, Doctor. No medical errors ever again. Tolerance less than plus or minus zero-zero-zero-zero-fourteen. Buy all the stocks you can, lad. WEC. Compute. . .It's 1:17.4, time for my B.P. What? 147.3 over what? 83.6? Fine. My pulse—76.3. Fine. My cardiac rate—regular. My lungs—clear to auscultation. My eye-grounds—negative for sclerotic changes. Fine. If you will give me my monthly shot of vitamins, one-point-three cc's this time, in the outer upper third of my gluteus maximus—*now,* it is 1:20.7 and time. . .all right, thank you, Doctor. You will have your secretary bill me in triplicate on the twelfth, afternoon mail. You are a fine doctor, as soon as you learn to compute you will go far. . . .Just one thing—wish you wouldn't be driving that Buick. Can't you afford a *Lincoln,* lad? . . . .

"...Hello, yes, this is the Shoemaker Neoluminous Electro-scientological Medical Center. No, doctor is never in. No, appointments are unnecessary. Your wife needn't come in and lose valuable time in a stuffy, overheated, overcrowded, germ-filled reception room. No, just send us a recent full photograph of her and Dr. Shoemaker will run it through his Neoluminous Electroscientological Data Processing Unit built specifically for him by E. M. Spencer Brown of World Electronics Corporation at a cost of four hundred and ninety-seven thousand dollars and twenty-seven cents and it includes a new Lincoln Continental. Twelve-point-three milli-scconds following the feeding in of your wife's photo, her prescription will be space-transferred via Neolumining Control to the City Water Commission where it will be piped directly into your house....If she is not feeling better in twenty-four hours? Why, have her take two aspirin and call us in the morning...."

. . . .

Moisture pouring from his hairy arms, his bushy gray eyebrows curled with sweat, Sam Sacks, the deli-man, quietly walked out of his store three days a week directly in the middle of the gluttony of his businessman's lunch hour. His wife, Myra, clutching at her pained breasts, swore after him in avenging Yiddish, and he, his round graying body looking like a ball of soft wool, bounced gaily across the street to his friend, the doctor. Three times a week he brought him his corn beef on white bread at one fifteen.

"Why not?" His finger raised in defiance at his place of business. "Why not," he repeated, as if to convince himself more than Fran Cooper. "Wouldn't he do it for me? Wouldn't he, in the middle of his busiest hour, in the middle of even a vaginal examination, wouldn't he come running over to me if even I coughed? This is how I prepare myself for the guilt I will have when the day comes he should have to do this.

"I worry so about such a man. He has a piece of paper says he is a doctor, so he acts like he is a doctor. Stubborn ox. His father was the same way. Somebody gave him a piece of paper says he was a pharmacist, he stopped making tuna fish sandwiches.

"When Myra and me came over from West Philadelphia—the *schvartzes* were beating me up once a month—his father sent over all his tuna fish lunch customers. Couldn't wait until the whole town was eating bagels, he said, so he could close down the lunch counter. He said a pharmacist running a lunch counter was like a doctor running a funeral parlor. He's the same thing, your boss, he takes care of these *mashugena* people like he's the last doctor who will ever live. Take it easy, Shoemaker, I tell him. Walk out in the middle of businessman's lunch and get a big surprise—they'll live. He thinks he's practicing medicine? He's practicing *tuches* wiping.

"Who's in there now, Spencer Brown? A *fagele.* You ever see his chauffeur? See-through pants. Mrs. Cooper, you are not eating again."

"I'm meeting someone for lunch," Fran moved the chicken salad aside, for the sixth straight day.

Sam knew. The other morning he had seen her husband slap her across the mouth for no reason when she got out of his car.

"You should call the police, that's what you should do," he said to Fran, his sunken gray eyes running little balls of gray water in each corner. He knew he should shut up—Myra told him every day he should shut up—but he never did.

"Tell *him,* him inside, our big doctor. Who else can help you? He'll tell you himself. If he can't help you, where you going to go?"

Sam coughed and cleared his throat. He still wasn't completely over his bout with pneumonia.

"I hate to admit it, but we all need him. There were three times in fifteen years I needed him, and look at me, I'm still alive. You know, last month, or was it last year, time flies, but anyway—*pisha, paysha*—I had a bad day and I got a few sneezes, just awful sneezing and running of the nose into the cole slaw. You just can't stick your head in the sand, you got to call a doctor, or else the whole neighborhood has got a cold. So, out comes Shoemaker. On the phone he says *get in bed,* like God he talks, and *out comes* Shoemaker, *to the house.* He gives me a real stubborn-ox checkup, a real examination to show me he is a real doctor. I told him give me something to stop the dripping into the cole slaw, the hell with all your fancy footwork, save it for the football field (another of his *mishagas*). But he goes on *after* the tap-tap, squeeze-squeeze, he goes on to the push-push, and pull-pull, and a look deep inside, and say *ahhh* from your *kishkes,* and breathe—deeper, *deeper*—jump up and down, take off your pants. Oh, Got! I yell at him, it doesn't drip down *there!* Eleven days the stubborn ox puts me to bed with goose grease on my chest, and Vicks up my nose, and a flaxseed enema up one end and apple juice down the other, and four bottles of stuff that made Marvin, the pharmacist, eighteen dollars closer to retirement.

"A good treatment for a cold, Mrs. Cooper? Virus pneumonia. Shoemaker, the big doctor, called it Virus pneumonia —he talks from his shoes when he is so professional, and don't you settle for less. It was a cold. But when you're a stubborn-ox doctor, it's a virus. So, Mrs. Cooper, here I am, right? Seven days a week? Working, right? Musselman from the shoe store had the same cold at the same time—I wouldn't tell you which *specialist* he goes to—he's still dripping into the shoes, and with pimples on his nose. For *me,* Shoemaker, this is a doctor. . . ."

.   .   .   .

1:30 PODALSKY, FRANCES #1307

COOPER

                   1619 S. Wilson Rd., Eastville—
Married   Age 23
Single   (separated) R.N. Ins. (B.C. B.S.)
5-3-57—Army nurse. Looks like she'll make a great office aide. If she can make herself ugly, Mary might consider leaving. Nerves (?). . . .

—Ready? It's my turn, Doctor. If you don't want to rupture your eardrum, you better tune out. . . .I'm so sick I could die. Your pills stink, my kids stink, my husband stinks, your patients stink. *You*—I don't know—don't you ever want to belt one of them in the mouth? I swear, if a green cow

walked into the waiting room and defecated purple manure
you would tell the animal to please sit down and you will get
to her problem shortly. . . .There's no end to it. Years ago
you told me it was seasonal. There's no more seasons, it's all
hell frozen over. You're going to cure the whole world from
this office. And you know how many telephone catastrophes
you *don't* hear about? Out there in my office I have in one
day enough galling idiocy to fill one medium-size nut
house. . . .And now I have to go home to *him.* He started
again on me. I am so sick of crying myself to sleep every
night. I have got to get away from him, he's killing me. I have
taken all your pills, nothing. I failed chemistry in high school,
you know, so maybe that's why my body doesn't know what
it's supposed to do. The barbiturates keep me awake, the
analeptics depress me, the amphetamines make me hungry. I
was a high-school beauty you know, homecoming queen and
all that idiocy. Now look at me, a side-show freak.

I am getting so sloppy fat, I have to cover up the mirrors. I
don't eat a thing and I'm gaining four, five pounds a week.
Crap—I sound like the rest of them, why don't you make it
easy and fire me? I'm no good any more—I send out bills
added sloppy, I get calls every day. I'm behind in the charts,
behind in X ray filing. I slapped a kid for coming over and
saying hello. I have a feeling like I'm not living. It's a weird,
awful feeling, like I'm dead and just moving around in
somebody else's body, but maybe that's the way I want it.
You know Leo, my seventeen-year-old, asked me the other
day if I wanted to smoke some marijuana with him. God
Almighty! He was dead serious. Said it might make me feel
good, poor kid. . . .Some boys beat up Eddie, he's the one
with the crippled arm. There's going to be a fight to the
finish, Susie told me, and he is really scared. I watch him
crying in his sleep, flaying that loose arm around. It's two
kids and they're both bigger than he is. I know he'll get
slaughtered, but he's got to do it. Susie tells me the same
boys want to lay her. Great, huh? Thirteen years old today.
She wants to know what it feels like, and what to do when
they do. . . .I've lost all control over them, and wouldn't you
know, their long-lost father shows up two weeks ago. I'm
desperate for money, you know, and he hasn't sent us a

penny in eight months. He asked me to take him back—for a
few nights. Some compliment! He waits for me by the bus
and tries to maul me. I'm going to kill him, I swear. I told
him I needed money, I do. Honest to God, I don't think I am
going to make it, even if I take the supermarket job on
Sundays. I keep hoping I'll win something. Dr. Shoemaker—
help me—I spent the petty cash for Susie's birthday. . . .

. . . .

AFTERNOON
    MAIL

GREENVILLE MERCY HOSPITAL
GREENVILLE, NEW JERSEY

MEMORANDUM
TO: Drs. Brown   Millikin
        Dempsey   Peters
        Goldman   Shoemaker √
FROM: Karl Kleinert, Executive Director
DATE: October 14, 1970
SUBJECT: Suspension of Staff Privileges

Dear Doctor:
   Your staff privilege to admit patients to Greenville
Mercy Hospital has been suspended pending completion of
all delinquent charts, as of the above date.

For the Medical Board
Karl Kleinert
Executive Director

. . . .

GREENVILLE MERCY HOSPITAL
GREENVILLE, NEW JERSEY

MEMORANDUM
TO: All Staff Physicians

There will be a regular business meeting Monday, October 19,
9:30 P.M.

It is urgent you be present at this time.
Topic for the evening:
Opening the Staff
Please be prompt—staff privileges revocable.

. . . .

GREENVILLE MERCY HOSPITAL
GREENVILLE, NEW JERSEY

Monthly Hospital Dues. $25.00
October, 1970—Payable at once or staff privileges suspended.

. . . .

GREENVILLE MERCY HOSPITAL
GREENVILLE, NEW JERSEY
OFFICE OF EXECUTIVE DIRECTOR: KARL KLEINERT

October 13, 1970

Dear Dr. Shoemaker:

May I take this moment from a very busy hospital day to congratulate you on arriving at a high point in our relationship. As
of October 15, you will have been a member in good standing at
the Greenville Mercy Hospital for fifteen years. This has surely
been a rewarding relationship between doctor and hospital, and
I am certain you can safely count on another fifteen years of cooperative relationships. Our growth is relative to yours, and the
future never looked brighter. It would be a less cheerful day
when Dr. Shoemaker did not grace our halls. Please, sir, continue
to be prompt to staff meetings, remit your monthly dues
promptly, and complete your delinquent charts.

Continued mutual successful relationships,

Yours fraternally,

Karl Kleinert

. . . .

SUBURBAN GENERAL HOSPITAL
GREENVILLE LAKES, NEW JERSEY
OFFICE OF EXECUTIVE DIRECTOR: PHILIP KOHN

October 13, 1970

Dear Dr. Shoemaker:

May I take this moment to offer my congratulations on your decision to join our newly organized staff. Progress has been more than satisfying, and we should be in position to break ground the first clear week in January.

You will be pleased to know, doctor, your name has moved to the top of the pile as per our telephone discussion. The Department of General Clinics is in need of a strong general practice-oriented physician. As you know, our main emphasis will be directed toward the G.P. and his hospital needs. The men on the executive board are aware of your persistent efforts in placing the G.P. in the proper medical perspective he so deserves. (Off the record, Johnny, they are also aware that you are a nut— about which we will talk.) Therefore, I feel you are to be well advised that your actions of the next several weeks may very well determine your acceptance to this special hospital post.

Keep up the good work, and come by and see me. It's that important.

Yours Urologically,

Phil Kohn

. . . .

Johnny Shoemaker fiddled with Phil Kohn's letter and absently touched his finger to his nose. It smelled of urine. Phil Kohn, now *there's* a nut, Johnny thought, a grown man spending his life soaked in urine and soggy prostates. And how about Lenihan—every minute away from the golf course in somebody's vagina. And Bergenholz—four-foot-five proctologist Bergenholz—up your ass. What do you call Pediatrician Abernathy, pukey kids around the clock? So who's the nut? I'm just nosey, I want a little of each complaint.

Maybe they got a taste of my molasses tonic I mix in Pop's old vat. Damn stuff works. Sally Mickel's hemoglobin went up from ten grams to fourteen in three weeks. Had twin boys a year later. This could be the big move, though: Director of General Clinics. Maybe Tom will reopen my case.

I know I'm a nut, but how do *they* know? Johnny opened his file drawer and fingered a torn newspaper sheet from last August's *Post*; there was a letter to the editor signed by J. J. Shoemaker, M.D., that said don't close down the Burlesque House on Charleston Street, where else can a person go today to see such natural beauty?

Maybe it was the art show at the Civic Center last May, Johnny thought. What could be wrong with a display of abstract sculpture made from surgical instruments?

Maybe it was the football. After all, how many doctors do you see nowadays with green and white goalposts in front of their office? Maybe, speaking of football, it could be Willie. Johnny had once been pictured in the *Post* with Willie holding him in embrace and it looked almost like a thing you don't do in a public paper. But what could they know of the thing that Johnny had for this Artuoro specimen? "He is a masterpiece," Johnny said out loud frightening himself, alone in his office, with only a gurgling fish tank to soften the stillness. A window shook, and Johnny made quick scribbles of clenched fingers on his doodle pad.

"We are aware you are a nut, Johnny...." So what else could it be? What makes a doctor think about his brethren doctor in such desultory tones? Johnny pressed his thumbs against the back of his skull, it made the pain go away. Hell's bells! I've got it. What else? It's the *1963 Buick*....

· ·

NEW JERSEY MEDICAL ASSOCIATION
OFFICE OF SPECIAL EVENTS

ANNOUNCEMENT

Put aside the first weekend in December. We're having a *golf festival* in *Jamaica*! Fly in on Friday, home for Monday hours. Tax-deductible convention special. Plan now. Full brochure on its way. Golf. Golf. Sun and Golf!

· ·

GREENVILLE MERCY HOSPITAL
GREENVILLE, NEW JERSEY

From the Office of
The Director of Intern Education

October 13, 1970

Dear Dr. Shoemaker:

We are returning your submitted paper, "General Practice," which you will present to the Intern Group at their
educational meeting on October 26. We are pleased with
your novel presentation and look forward to seeing this
program receive good attendance. However, you will note
several minor points which we have outlined at the conclusion of your paper and would appreciate your discus-
sing them with us prior to the meeting.

Yours very fraternally,

Charles W. Johnston, M.D.
Director of Intern Education

. . . .

GENERAL PRACTICE
A Paper by J. J. Shoemaker, M.D.

An unnamed reliable source has estimated that of the twelve
interns sitting here this afternoon, attending this session on
general practice, six of you will have been called away before
five minutes have passed. One to assist Dr. Hardenbach as he
slices away at his not-so-hot bellies; one to assist Dr. Kohn as he
passes twenty-gauge sounds into eighteen-gauge urethras; one to
assist Dr. Lenihan as he patty-cakes babies' rear ends; one to
assist Dr. Carliner as he makes white mud pies and pastes them
over cracked hand bones; and etc. Then there will be two of you
who will unconsciously sign off while you play hangman on
little white index cards. And two of you, concentrated brows
furrowed, hands folded chivalrously over heaving eyelids, wrapt
as if in astute attention, will be fast asleep. This will leave two
of the brightest interns in Greenville Mercy Hospital. You two,

whomever you may be, I welcome you to the most wonderful, most loving-kindness specialty in all of God's medicine—General Practice.

When I was a little kid I had the good fortune to be ill several times. A doctor who lived in the neighborhood—whose name I no longer remember but whose hand I still embrace—came to my room and made me well. I never knew where he went to school, who his parents were, what his wife wore to church, how much he charged, how clever his conversation, which car he drove. All I ever knew was, on sight, I was at once better. He wrote a page of instructions for my mother in an early medieval script as if he had been transported from some far-off mysterious land just in time to cure me alone. And he left for my father a single prescription toiled over with six separate Latin scribbles. And although my father was a pharmacist and he had concocted for me brews of unbelievable bitter strength, the doctor's scribbles, better or worse, alone made me well.

Now, boys, I am not for returning to the pre-penicillin and pre-tranquilizer days. Never. Not even pre-birth control. Hell, I am the first in the neighborhood to succumb to a new drug. You see, I am not so far-removed from my elixir-of-life-seeking heritage to let slip by the chance to cure mankind with a teaspoon of something or other.

Now, what I *am* for is something that old guy had that wasn't in his bag—that aura, scent, magic, witchery that made me better even as my mother put out the call for him. If I could instill this something, whatever it is, in just the two of you, and you cherished it, and embellished it, and bowed down to it as reverently as you do the listed signs and symptoms of pheochromocytoma, then I have produced the ultimate step in your ascension to that stateliest of all mansions, the General Practitioner.

But hark. Do not let anyone or anything deter you. You two who are going to be G.P.s, be alert, be proud. Alarmists brutally will denounce you. Liberals spiritlessly will pacify you. Conservatives shruggingly will ignore you. Specialists economically will eulogize you. But in our weeping world, there is a quiet hysterical need for you two who have remained with me.

If you were expecting a discourse from me on the science of

general practice and how I utilize the present-day methods of
the laboratory and the hospital as an aid in my daily medical
needs, then I am going to disappoint you. I couldn't possibly
offer you any new scientific tidbits—you know more of these
than I do. But I can offer you one gem. A week in my office
will place your entire medical education in reckless jeopardy.
You will find less than two percent of your work will be involved with what you have spent ninety-eight percent of your
time studying.

Your chief complaints will be Mrs. Fenster's running nose,
son Fenster's canker sores, daughter Fenster's menstrual
cramps, and pimples, and small breasts, husband Fenster's
backache and impotence. You will have a phone in one hand,
needle in another hand, pen in another, Band-Aid in another,
dictating machine in another, steering-wheel in another, handkerchief in another. There will be no end of sprained, pained,
bruised, snotty, vomiting children, sadly ignorant mothers,
measled (or is it chicken-poxed, Scarlet-fevered, virus-X, or
drug-reaction) bodies, bratty lollipopped sticky kids, tyrannical
teenagers, quick-marriage pleaders, screaming first mothers,
fainting new fathers, diarrheaed executives, sad jailed house-
wives, impossible young coronaries, sexy young widows, happy
old grandparents, sad old grandparents, and lots and lots of fat,
fat, fat everybody.

This, my boys, is General Practice. But I warn you, once
you have been bitten with the bug called the G.P., you will at
once become the disease that everyone is determined to cure.
You will have to fight for your lives every step of the way in
order to remain the carrier of this disease. You see, liberals,
conservatives, alarmists, and specialists cannot continue to survive if you continue to spread your magic. They cannot allow
your cures in cloudy mysticism in place of their deaths in
absolute science. You cannot heal the sick with your hand-
holding, they say. What you have cured, they will cry, is not
the disease but the person.

Are you two laughing? Laugh, boys, there is no way out

for you now. You had better start laughing and never stop this step out of your grave for, as I told you earlier, I have no pulsating scientific achievements to present to you this afternoon, no medical hamburg to rehash. But now, here is the answer I promised you: In my office there is an unframed canvas hanging in sight of my desk at all times. The canvas, smeared with a brilliant crimson background, has painted upon it in bold, white letters this little living message, the triumphant, wistful cry of the G.P.—"HA, HA, HA, HA, HA, HA, HA. . . ."

. . . .

Notes from the Director of Intern Education

1.   Retitle to: "General Practice—Whither Now?"

2.   Remove reference to interns leaving meeting to assist specialists—it will cause interdepartmental displeasure.

3.   Try to find name of doctor who treated you as a child, it would add credibility. (Also his college and hospital affiliation?)

4.   Don't mention father was a pharmacist—reference may be regarded in poor taste—or unethical.

5.   Remove word "hell"—Mercy Hospital will not tolerate reference.

6.   Are you claiming the use of mysticism and/or magic? Let us talk this over before Oct. 20.

7.   Don't underplay the role of the hospital and laboratory—spend much more time on this facet.

8.   Don't malign educational system by playing 98% and 2% statistics.

9.   Your finality of Ha, Ha, Ha, etc. is not understood by our committee.

Thank you for your fine paper,

Charles W. Johnston, M.D. (Chuck)

BANK OF GREENVILLE

We are returning the enclosed check and charging it to your account.

JOSEPH JACARDI Am't $6.00
INSUFFICIENT FUNDS

. . . .

2:30

```
GREENVILLE HIGH SCHOOL
        Est. 1917
```

The school had been updated several times over fifty years, but somehow the health facilities had remained unchanged. And so had Alice McGibbon, R.N. As if she had been born in this white-plastered basement room and had grown up out of the cracks in the cement floor, Mrs. McGibbon, with all her bumpy exterior of sand and gravel, was to this room like an indestructible, sweet-smelling weed.

She was at all times the champion of the child's eternal struggle to surface in a cement-covered world. The hoods, the delinquents, the goldbricks, the chronic hypochondriacs could find refuge at any time in Alice McGibbon.

"They are all dear, dear children."

Today was tenth-grade physical day for Dr. Shoemaker, a legal medical evaluation of the children's ability to walk into the nurse's room, remove some garments, say *ahhh* without choking, bend over without falling, and walk away unaided. Johnny wondered about his being replaced by a WEC calculator one day and smiled painfully. Son Tom's letter made no bones about it—he would be. His brother, Lem, had frequently referred to this part of the practice as a waste of time. But here he was, and somehow, McGibbon's protective attitudes had worn off on him and he held on in spite of the occasional foolishness and waste of his medical presence.

Mrs. McGibbon wore a white apron over her street clothes, and whenever she spoke would wipe her hands on the uplifted edges as if she were preparing to bake a chocolate brownie.

(She had trained for home economics, but changed her major at the last minute.)

"I had you scheduled for sixty today, Dr. Shoemaker," she told Johnny, wiping away at her hands, "but Dr. Leader wants to see you about Willie and this awful football thing." Everything that affected her children with possible disruption was regarded as an awful thing.

Johnny winced at the thought of a Leader conference. Probably wants to work out a deal. If he can play on Saturday, the kid plays. If not, not. No deals.

"He is a dear, dear boy, that Willie Washington," Mrs. McGibbon sighed, her apron wiping away at the corner of her eyes. Johnny hoped she wasn't going to cry. "And he loves you," she added emphatically. "They *all* love you, you know that."

Johnny frowned with embarrassment, but he liked to hear it said out loud.

"But to call in those people from Philadelphia," Mrs. McGibbon shuddered, her apron working double time on her hands, "just because you won't let him play. Well, my goodness, you *are* the doctor. I know these boys—if you say to Willie, you can't play, Willie won't play. He knows, they all know, the dear boys, how you care. They listen to you, Doctor...."

...Outside, just a few hundred yards back of the health office on a muddy practice field, Willie had just sprinted the hundred in nine-point-six. He had also just booted with his ripped sneakers six field goals, one forty-two-and-a-half yards off center. Earlier he had picked off four passes, had thrown twelve, averaged thirty-eight yards on target, had felt that flitting dull pressure above his left eye, and had spit at it each time it came over him. Once he thought he saw something red in the spit, and he kicked the forty-two-and-a-halfer then.

"Holy Chris'," Coach Bocca yelled at him, "whaddya holdin' back for?"

Willie ran out a fake Statue of Liberty, a Bocca oldie from his own college days, always good for a six-yard loss, and he hauled up alongside the fuming coach.

"You're holdin' back, Washington," Bocca spit white, clear spit. "Every day you go over to the Doc's, you come back

out here like a zombie. Doc maybe knows somethin' about
pretty muscles, but he don't know nuthin' about coachin'
football."

Coach Bocca was smaller than you would imagine a coach
to be, but he made up for it in width and belly, an alarming
declaration of Bocca independence. He consistently referred
to the fact that he was working his ass off, but neglected to
mention his gut. Also a nondeclaration of associated neglects.
"I'm workin' my ass off to get a scroungy bunch of stupid
kids to carry a leather ball a hundred yards in the right
direction so my kids won't go bare-assed, and *he* tells me my
business. Politics, all politics. Damn school job alone pays him
to retire." He cupped his friend's left butt gently. "Get out
there, Washington, and run your ass off. . . ."

Dr. Shoemaker had settled himself behind the drawn
curtain, his head shaking at the table of supplies set up by
Mrs. McGibbon. A box of wooden tongue blades, a notebook,
a pen, a pencil, a pen light, a stethoscope, a blood-pressure
cuff. Sterile gauze pads in three sizes, gauze bandages in four
sizes, Band-Aids, pressure pads. An eyecup, sterile water,
ammonia caps, zephiran sponges, alcohol sponges, tincture of
merthiolate, iodine, butterfly strips. A pan with sterile soaking
scissors, knife blade, syringes, needles, sutures, forceps,
probes, hemostats. A tray of cookies, a jar of lollies, a bucket
for throw-up, and a dingle bell. Fourteen years, every Tuesday
and Thursday at 2:30, behind the houndstooth curtain, Mrs.
McGibbon had set up this mélange. And at four she returned
all to its closeted space, less eighteen or twenty tongue blades
and—once in 1965—less one Band-Aid.

Johnny Shoemaker stared unbelievingly upon the treatment
table, then foolishly rang the ding-a-ling, and Mrs. McGibbon
prepared the first little one for examination.

"All right, girls, it's late. Now line up. Dr. Shoemaker is a
very busy man giving us his valuable time. Now take off your
sweaters and loosen your blouses, he can't see through your
clothes. That's right, dearie. Just unzip it from the back.
Never mind your hair. That's right—Mattie! don't stand there
that way—put your bra back on right now!. . ."

The first girl was tall and thin and pimply and smelled of girl.
The second was tall and thin and pimply and smelled of

girl. The third was tall, and thin, and pimply and smelled of Lysol. The fourth girl was squat and fat and smelled of grape juice, which also stained her shorts. The fifth was a giggler. Johnny touched the stethoscope to her back and she giggled; to her chest and she screamed with the giggle. Mrs. McGibbon poked her head into the curtain and smiled at the doctor. "Joann, act your age," she told the giggler, and Joann acted her age. Dr. Shoemaker touched her ear and she giggled.

What am I doing here? Johnny thought again. They don't need me here. Every year in May or June when this pubescent assembly line was all over, he thought it again. For the nine hundred and fifty dollars that rents us the house in the Poconos, I'll stay home. And every September, the day after Labor Day, in trudged Johnny Shoemaker, and the secretary heard the joke he had been saving all summer, and McGibbon cried and extolled the base innocence of youth and summertime. And Johnny shook his head at the medical table and touched the ding-a-ling and it started up all over again.

The sixth girl was short and dumpy, soft and floppy and had no recognizable smell. The seventh was tall and dumpy, hard and floppy, and also had no smell, unless it was that of fresh basketball. Number eight found herself in an unwritten letter to Arturo Artuoro. "Maybe this is what I am doing here, Professor Artuoro. Number eight is medium and firm and curved and clear-eyed and smooth-skinned and sparkling and she is gorgeous. Arturo Artuoro, you can count each of her six hundred and forty-seven muscles, each alive and wiggling. And she smells of mountain dew on a cool summer's night. Maybe *she* is why I am here. Maybe the next Willie will be a—Susie? Arturo, you never said no."

Johnny smiled at number eight. He paused in his rush to get through to number sixty and he smiled. Last year, number eight had had strange heart sounds.

"Hold it, don't make so much noise out there," Johnny had called, "number eight has strange heart sounds." Lub-dub, lub-dub, *lub-dub-a-lub,* lub-dub. Strange. "Mrs. McGibbon," he had ordered, "mark it down—get the family doctor—check it out—call me back. . . ."Later, Johnny had been contacted; number eight had a cardiac defect that nobody had ever picked up.

Johnny smiled at number eight, the scar across her rib cage

was pink and firmly healed, the hole inside that pump well cross-stitched, he was sure. Number eight was trying out for field hockey. Johnny gave her his OK, and she said "Thanks, Doctor."

Maybe they do need me here. *Lub-dub, lub-dub, lub-dub—* beautiful. . . .

. . . .

3:30

> Office of the Principal
> Dr. Henry L. Leader

Johnny Shoemaker liked to feel he owed allegiance to no living man, but favors—unfortunately—yes. I could tell McGibbon to call him and say there's an emergency in the office, Johnny thought, pointlessly, as he walked the old wooden section of the high school corridors on his way over to Dr. Leader's office. He knew as well as he knew his head ached already, not even halfway through the day, he knew he would spend the next half hour in Leader's den.

He touched the peeling mortar surrounding green-and-white banners prematurely proclaiming Greenville High as state champions. He patted a life-size papier-mâché of Willie pulling a pass out of nowhere and heard a resounding *Olé!* from a thousand voices inside his splitting head. Never carry a Darvon when I need it. Don't know if the damn stuff even works, but they all swear by it.

The half-rotting wooden floors smelled familiarly satisfying to Johnny. A loose board creaked under his weight, and he knew he had gained another two pounds this week. Making certain no hall monitors were watching, he went into his Canadian Air Force attention, high-jogged it down the corridor about fifty feet, panted to a halt, and felt relieved— not healthier, but better prepared for the Leader.

A boy passed him, showed a ticket allowing him three minutes in the john, and said, "Hello, Doctor." Probably my black bag, Johnny concluded. Most of the afternoon kids are from the other side of town. And then for no reason he could fathom, he suddenly felt good, just being here. His headache lifted, his spirits soared, and he picked up his feet, almost as if he were again on his way to class—how many years ago? Too many, he thought, behind the land rush invading the sleepy hills of Greenville. Now I hear there's going to be a *second* high school up at the Lakes. He hoped he could keep his kids in this one, unless Leader moves over, too. But he knew better: Leader's eyes were not on new local high schools, but on state capitol buildings and executive mansions, even as far off as Washington, D.C.

Dr. Henry L. Leader, an unbearably first-rank educator, had personally been responsible for the crusade to bring education to the school-starved migrants who had been rushing into Greenville from a hundred miles around, seeking the proper community for the growth of their future families. Leader, a fresh recruit from the Eisenhower administration's early committees on health and education, had come to them bulging with reputation for top-notch education reforms. And like it or not, in fifteen years Leader had managed a miracle of scholastic advance in Greenville—in his own strange and numbing way. It all involved a special credo he professed, "Anything can be done—*anything!*"

"I ran a hundred and two yards for a touchdown with a fractured pelvis and collapsed across the Air Force Academy's goal line to win the final game of the season." Leader grinned his trademarked expression showing half broken teeth and a bulging tongue. "I never played again, Johnny boy, but nobody ever forgot Henry L. Leader."

Johnny shook his head and heard the Naval Academy band playing taps.

"This is what I preach day and night to my students, and they go away from Greenville High with this ringing in their ears."

Leader's earliest papers for the education program in Washington emphasized the need for automation—with a single dominant figure with absolute control at a central command station, a person who could be in instant touch with every educational facility in the country. Then, through a system of checks and balances, he could readily systematize the learning programs in such a manner as to reduce teaching and learning error to its absolute minimum—plus or minus 0.001. This paper, along with several others involving segregation of the races and segregation of the colors (as well as segregation of the sexes), lay gathering dust in government archives in the Library of Congress. Several people in the know, however, had recently repeated comments from very reliable sources that after the November elections, Leader stood a good chance of returning to Washington and the dusty papers.

"You must impress," he grinned, "impress, impress. Their brains are still soft and receptive, and you must jam it through to them what they are, what they can be. Wait, Johnny boy, listen. If I wanted to, I could switch over to emergency control and broadcast the message right now." Leader leaned over to his intercom panel as if he were on the air. "Attention! Students and personnel of Greenville High School, this is Dr. Henry Lexington Leader speaking to you. Whatever you are doing this very instant, just drop it. Drop it from your hands, drop it from your minds. And now listen to what I have to say: From this moment on, anything you want is yours—anything. What is our credo? Repeat after me—*Anything can be done*"

He half grinned, then turned again to face Johnny, who foolishly returned the half grin and then hated himself.

"I could, you know. And I may at any time. I must control thirty-two hundred sputtering bombs from this desk. I keep them from igniting and exploding all at one time. Quite a job, but I do it. I don't believe there is another man in the state qualified to do what I have done in just fifteen short years. A backwoods summer camp is what they had here, four hundred farmers' kids. And now, today, the most modern, far-sighted, fair-minded educational system in all Jersey— possibly all the country." He grinned, half-tooth.

"It's all in the way you apply the credo. Johnny boy, didn't you have to learn how to apply it in spite of it all—your brother in that fire, your father ending up where he did, you in medical school with Mary and the kids? They were struggling years, and this was a fine opportunity for you, your association with Greenville High. I was very pleased, very pleased to be in a position to make this a fine opportunity for you."

This, of course, was the favor. Beneath his paste-up smile, Johnny had to admit he had a good warm memory of good warm early years at Greenville High. He had been apprehensive about returning to the old boom town with the affluence now twice removed from the comfort of its original ethnic implants. He had feared for his acceptance—the native son returning to the unfamiliar old town—clomping around in his big brother's shoes.

All the old-timers knew Johnny was a stand-in: Lem warmed over. Poppa Shoemaker had spread the mortar real thick, and Johnny came home and was a doctor with a ton of bricks on his head. The school job, though, was like a bulldozer. It ripped open the hardened Greenville-ites, and in the gap piled the new and the young and migrant hordes who saw on the football field, on the baseball diamond, on the courts, in the class, in the health service, Johnny Shoemaker, a doctor they liked to see. And so, Johnny remembered: Henry L. Leader, this is a favor you are owed. Now, after fifteen years, what do I do to repay it?

"Just a nasty little problem that you and I will solve by simply applying the credo," Leader assured Johnny. "It will be that easy. I know you live by the credo, and, of course, you know I do, so we certainly will not have any trouble coming to a decision."

Get on with it, Johnny screamed inside.

"We have here at Greenville, as you know," Leader eased it out, "a fine record of nonviolence and nonsectarianism. No color line. You surely know this, as our doctor. So, your little problem with Willie Washington is much too insignificant a one to jeopardize our statewide reputation. As I see it—if you will allow me—this boy is in an admirable position to win football games for us. Quite a competent athlete, strong, head like a quarry, I am told." Grin, teeth.

"Also as I see it, this boy stands to gain statewide recognition for our school if he plays Saturday. And also as I have been made painfully aware by a very angry and positive group this afternoon, if he does not play, we will be singled out for the first time as a target high school for race-riot potential." No grin.

"Now, in applying the credo to this, as I see it, we really have no problem." Big grin. "John, you have not said Willie Washington cannot play on Saturday. You have simply stated that as of *today* he cannot play. So, tomorrow—" grin, "Dr.

Shoemaker will announce through me that Willie Washington is going to be examined by a Philadelphia neurosurgeon—a good friend of Coach Bocca—and this neurosurgeon will give us an impartial decision, and so the fate of Greenville High no longer hangs on the decisions of its own affiliates.

"You see, my boy——" grin, "if the specialist says Willie may play, we remain heroes. And you, so to speak, are off the hook. If the specialist says the boy may not play, we are then all humanitarians. . . ."

. . . .

4:00

> N. J.
> MD-K885
> GARDEN STATE

The car stalled out at the circle. Horns blew, drivers swore, trucks bottled him up. It was the start of the evening rush. The automatic choke again, Johnny thought vengefully—as soon as you automate these things. . . .He pumped the gas and it turned over. . .*"the 1971's are creampuffs"*. . .I'll never make the calls, and I've got to get to the hospital. There's not enough time. I needed that Leader deal this week like I needed Tom's letter.

He pulled off Route 130 onto Barnhardt Street, and it was at once blessedly peaceful. He drew up in front of Jimmy Johnson's house and sat back for a second. His closed eyes burned, the insistent headache returning over his left temple. Lem came to Johnny and said: "Jonathan, you should do what Dr. Leader has said. He is a rational man who has offered you a simple, honorable solution to what could be a devastating problem. He has done well by you. I advise you to take up his plan and stay with it. Press your thumbs into the suboccipital fossa and hold for the count of ten while you breathe in and out rhythmically. The headache will go." And Jonathan, on the spot, took up Dr. Leader's plan and would stay with it. In ten seconds the headache would be gone. . . .

Lem came to Johnny more often in the Buick than any place else. It was never questioned, but if he would allow it a moment's thought, Johnny would conclude nowhere else was he more peaceful. And where else would Lem be more comfortable with him than in an old bag of Buick bolts? Isn't this where we would hide out when Poppa was looking for a delivery boy, or when Momma scrubbed the house and locked the doors?

The old Buicks—starting with the 1927 touring sedan with the jump seats—were always parked behind the store, covered with rubber sheets, blankets, and old burlap. They were aired and washed on Saturday and driven to church on Sunday and back home to Ephrata every July 4th. There was another in '34, and then the one Lem taught Jonathan to drive in, the '39. They sneaked it out one afternoon when Poppa and Momma were at a pharmacy picnic (the one other day of the year the store closed), and they drove out to Long Island to the World's Fair and saw the General Motors building and a girlie show.

The Buick was where Jonathan learned about things from Lem. Poppa sure as heck had nothing to say about life other than "Give the customer his fair shakes and you'll get your fair shakes in return" or "You got nothing to worry about, Lem will take care of us all."

And Momma, she buttoned her dress up to her neck on the beach. There was a baby sister somewhere in between Jonathan and Lem, but whether she died *in utero,* or at birth, or after birth, or what, nobody ever knew nor ever would know. When Johnny was finally old enough to dare to ask—his senior year in med school—Momma died and carried the secret buttoned up to her neck. Poppa probably was never sure about Momma and those things, except she certainly can make the fountain sparkle, she uses ammonia, you know.

So Lem seemed to come to brother Jonathan more comfortably in the Buick. There were times when Lem would move in and out of the office, quiet times, mail time, after-the-last-patient-closed-the-outer-door time. Lem came occasionally to Jonathan's bed, restless times, Mary-away or Mary-asleep times. Lem never came during active moments, like the middle of things, operations, office hours, sex. He never interfered with actual events, but Lem prepared his cases well and came only in peace. Once, a few years ago, however, during a neighborhood disaster, Lem did come to Johnny. The Clark's house, four doors down the street, burned helplessly to the ground, with two little Clark girls trapped in their bedrooms, and Lem came and held brother Jonathan back from running hopelessly into the impossible fire.

While helping Poppa Shoemaker clean out the cellar junk that had been saved for twenty years for his new office, Lem, then an intern at Greenville Mercy, somehow got locked in the furnace room when it blew up, and he was burned to death. The world, long used to multiples of death, holocausts, floods, famines, wars, exterminations where hundreds and thousands die, somehow reverses the neurons of disbelief, and when a single tragic catastrophe confronts it, reacts in petrified belief. Lemuel Shoemaker, Greenville's first native M.D., graduate *cum laude,* Mercy Hospital's intern of the year, one month away from the dream. Ashes. Tragedy. The town mourned his loss as it does many untried heroes, and the legend of Lem Shoemaker hung eerily over the reality of young John.

The call came to young John from his neighbor, Sam Sacks. It was several hours finding him over the transatlantic wire. A recently discharged serviceman cooling his flesh in Montmartre from two years of war doesn't sit by the phone waiting for a voice to say, "This is Sam, Johnny. You should come home now. Your brother, Lem, is dead."

Young John, after two years of labeling, identifying, and burying the dead, wanted a small taste of life before coming back to Greenville. He had now less than eight months' beard growth, a red beret, forty-seven dollars, and a roomful of unsold canvases, mostly of the Eiffel Tower with naked girls dancing around it. Immediately after his call from Sam, he slashed out a crimson and black abstraction which he called *Brothers,* and left for home. It was later sold by his friends and still hangs in a small Paris museum as an example of "infinite fire and perception, great strokes of love and hate, powerful and sensitive, despair and hope, a blend of human interrelationship not captured by any of our American visiting abstractionists. It tells a story of brotherhood in pleading strokes of raw color. And in the end it asks: 'Help me, my brother is dead.' "

.   .   .   .

4:10 House Call

> JOHNSON, JAMES #2982
>
> 927 Barnhardt St., Greenville—Age 5
> Grade School Ins.—BC & BS
> 9-4-64—Clear white skin, flaccid muscles, colorless eyes, unresponsive mother-clutcher...

—Oh, Dr. Shoemaker. Oh, Doctor! Are we glad to see you. None of us slept one minute since I read that. Hey, Jim! Comere. Just look at him, Doctor. I wrapped it up in Vaseline gauze, I didn't want it to get bruised. They said if it gets banged, it can bleed you to death. Doctor, we got Blue Cross and Blue Shield and Bulletin Insurance and my Andrew checked it out and we're covered for anything. Please tell us, where can we send him? Please, help us, he's the only one we got. *Jimmy*! You pulled it off! It's going to run all the blood from your veins, what did I tell you? Look at it, Doctor, it's enough to curdle your insides. What are you going to do? My God, Doctor, don't *touch* it! It's bad enough he sucks his finger all day long, and look what it did to him. Look, Jimmy, what you did to us—your father who smells all that gas so you can have the best medical attention, look how we will have to suffer....A *wart?*

. . . .

...Try to find name of doctor who treated you as a child; it will add credibility...

. . . .

4:30 House Call

> HOOKER, SILAS #1695
>
> 12 Willow St., Greenville—Age 75
> Ret. Carpenter—Widowed (3)
> 7-9-58—They say I'm the sixth doctor this year. Old Hook needs a total body transplant. He'll probably sing at my grave....

—Doc, I'm sure glad to see you. Uh. Wait till I get this old
carcass out of bed. Here, let me screw in a light bulb. Only
one left, kids took everything out. There 'tis. Hey, Doc, you
sure look good to me. You got to come see old Hook more
often. I can use you. Uh. This old belly just can't swallow
another morsel. It hurts all the time. You got some more of
them green pills? They make my water run better. Uh. This
belly, kids steal all my food. Can't get a hot meal cooked.
Sure could use a drink of whiskey. How 'bout just a little
porter, Doc? Damn, I lived seventy years before you told me
to quit drinkin'. How much longer you want to collect on
me? Let me be, Doc, an old man's got to have *some*
pleasures. Had a lady upstairs last Wednesday and it was
humiliatin'. She said to me, "Old man, lie down, you are
dead." You gonna give me the nature shot today, Doc? I felt
like a giant after one of them shots. Sure like to have a lady
come back. . .yeah—oh—yeah—good shot, Doc. It's like magic.
I can feel my nature surgin' in me already. Leave me a bag of
pills, Doc, them green ones. And thanks for comin' around.
Hey, boy, whyn't you drop by two, three times a week like
old man Washington's doctor do? Ol' Uncle Medicare is payin'
for it now, he told me, is that right? He told me he's
collectin' two ways, one from Uncle Sam and one from the
Welfare. He's no good, that black man. We know him around
here. He's the kind makes it bad for the rest of us. Don't let
him put no scare on you, Doc. Willie is a nice boy. Willie's
got a place out there that none of us had. We want to see
him make out, but we sure don't want him to get hurt, the
way his old man does. We know him, he don't care, but with
us, whatever you say goes, Doc, you are our boy. You won't
let our Willie get hurt, no sir. You are our boy, you hear?. . .

. . . .

". . .I wouldn't go out there alone. They're all alike, seventeen
or seventy-six. All alike. . ."

. . . .

It was ten to five and Johnny decided to skip Laurie Lee.
What more could he do for her today? Resurrection would
help. "Not as much as a diaphragm," Lem said.

He had time for Gertrude, just a shot of cortisone into the boggy knee. Gertrude was painless, a day full of Gertrudes and Johnny could throw away the Tums.

At five to five he pulled into the hospital parking lot.

. . . .

> GREENVILLE MERCY HOSPITAL
> Founded 1919
> QUIET ZONE—NO PARKING
> PARKING FOR DOCTORS ONLY

—Hi, Doc. Pull it in next to the Chief's Caddy. You been stallin' out again, Doc, it smells bad. Say, before you go in, Doc, I got this pain under my right shoulder bone. . . .

. . . .

> RECORD ROOM—Mrs. Katherine Chrizsowski

—Well, I *am* sorry, Dr. Shoemaker, but a letter of forewarning *did* go out to you last week. And *I* personally *did* call your nurse and advise her of your delinquent charts on Monday. I run a very rigid room here. My girls are all hand-picked encoding experts, each and every one. A mistake is untenable. Why, I could summon up file number—just pick any number, seven hundred and twenty-two? My girls could locate any bit of information down to the last aspirin tablet ordered, and seven hundred and twenty-two goes back, you know, to 1920. May seventh. I *am* sorry about that letter of suspension. Mr. Kleinert was just saying to me today, Dr. J. J. Shoemaker, negligent on hospital charts, not *my* boy, J.J., I'll have to write him a fine letter today. I am happy to see you here, Dr. Shoemaker. Mr. Kleinert said you would be. There are only a dozen or so to do, you can do them zippo. Let me pull them out for you. . .*girls,* do any of you know how four of Dr. Lenihan's charts got into Dr. Shoemaker's file? . . .

It was already five-fifteen. "I'll never make it," Johnny said. "Leave the damn charts until Saturday. I'll run in after the game and get them done."

At five-seventeen Johnny dropped in for a wave and a belly pat to Clarice Burns, seventh pregnancy, told her not to run up stairs (ha), and to check the baby's circumcision, and wrote out the discharge. At five twenty-one Johnny listened to Otto Hawkins' chest and wrote an order for a bronchoscopy. At five twenty-five Johnny discontinued the I-V fluids for the Michaels' baby, noted the vomiting had stopped for twelve hours, and ordered a liquid diet.

At five-thirty (dinner was being served in the Shoemaker house on Lake Drive) Johnny got to Surgical West where Reba Gold was waiting.

"Oh, is she waiting," Mrs. Jason, the floor nurse, expediently offered.

Dr. Shoemaker knew she was waiting; he had known it for two days.

"How come you keep your patients waiting so long, Doctor?" This was Ron Klinger, G.P. from out of Merrybrook section. Sixty percent Welfare, forty percent Medicare. "What you need is a partner, Johnny. Since I took on a partner, everybody gets seen, even if I don't see them. We're looking for a third man over at Merrybrook, we can't even rubber-stamp the forms fast enough. Any time you want out, there'll always be room at the bottom."

5:35 <u>Reba Gold</u>—Rm. 220—Bed #2—Adm. Diag. Dysmenorrhea/ Dysparunia

—Oh, darling, darling, let me kiss you. I've been waiting for hours. Where were you yesterday when I needed you—I know it was Wednesday, but it's me, darling, *me*.

I put on these jumpers just for you. It's only twenty-four hours, don't I look wonderful? They can't get over me, the nurses and the doctors here, they think I am just fabulous. I redecorated the nurses' station, and I put curtains in the interns' rooms.

They all love me. Even during the operation, the way I looked they couldn't stop talking about my hair. I wish you were there like you promised. I know, darling, you're so tired. Here, sit, sit down, I'll bet you didn't eat yet. Have a cookie, my kids baked them for me. Have I got great kids. The house is spotless while I'm away. Who needs girls when I have such beautiful boys?

I want to tell you *everything*, step by step, exactly how it happened from the minute last night they gave me the needle. . .darling? Dr. Shoemaker—now you wake up, come on now. . . .

"*. . .Wake up, John, come on, you'll never make it, you're on the early shift this week.*"

At six forty-five, the sun just cracking the bleak October sky, intern Johnny Shoemaker had wheeled his boy's bike into the hospital parking lot and dumped it in the first open space.

"Hey, don't park it there, Doctor, that's the Chief's place. How do you keep that relic moving? Looks like it's a hundred years old. Say, Doc, before you go in, I got this pain under my right shoulder."

Mary needed the car again—substitute teaching was getting to be full time. Johnny couldn't complain: With his forty dollars a month, and Mary's sometimes hundred, they were making it.

He had found Klinger asleep on an empty labor room cot. "You know there is no goddam place left to sleep in this hole? They even got patients in the solarium. This is going to be a great town, Shoemaker. We stay in this town we got it made. I got a deal to buy an office over in some shitty neighborhood called Merrybrook; Doc Stone, he's getting ready to die with cancer of his prostate. He shows seventy-five g's a year on his books. He's going around the world and figures he'll be dead by India. One hundred percent Welfare. Got a druggist down the corner, he already introduced me, who says in ten years I could retire. Couldn't you work something out with your old man?"

He couldn't. Klinger gave the report. There had been three deliveries through the night. One Klinger had handled alone, and didn't call the doctor until she was crowning. For the other two, he cut sutures. "This guy, Lenihan, is a comer, he does a sweet job. When he's done, he slaps their behinds and kisses their bellybuttons. They die."

A DOA, a coronary, a nosebleed, and a fly in an ear covered the Emergency Room. On Meds, Tillie pulled out her I-V twice. The third time Klinger stuck it in the mattress. Pflauzer in Surgery pulled out his catheter and Klinger stuck it back and blew up the balloon in the urethra. Everyone awake past one had Seconal grains three, except Kantor who couldn't stop coughing—he had Vicks. "Couldn't make a wave with Kelly, she says there's too much screwin' around, and don't I bump into her working over old Manuel down in the furnace room. That's hospital life. I'm off for two days. Think I'll go down and buy a yacht."

At seven-thirty Johnny had boiled himself two eggs and eaten breakfast with the kitchen crew, one who had a chronic hack, the other an armful of boils. Johnny told them to go home, but they laughed, and asked him if he was going to make up the hundred trays.

Johnny had morning surgical service. There was much to learn, if you could get a hand in it, but the surgeons were wont to divulge little more than didactic bits and pieces and ask you when you were opening your office in the area.

So, at eight Johnny scrubbed with Klauber (ENT) for a routine tonsillectomy and was allowed to hold a retractor on the right tonsil.

At eight-thirty he scrubbed with Cassidy (GYN) for a routine D&C and was allowed to hold a retractor on the upper cervical os.

At nine Johnny scrubbed with Kohn (URO) for a routine prostatectomy and was allowed to hold a retractor on the left descending ureter.

At ten Johnny scrubbed with Albertson (GEN SURG) for a routine hysterectomy and was allowed to hold a retractor on the left Fallopian tube.

At eleven Johnny scrubbed with Taylor (GP) for a routine removal of a supra-clavicular mass and: applied the anesthesia, incised, drained, shelled out the tumor, scraped the wound, cleaned, irrigated, closed up—twenty minutes, skin to skin.

Johnny made notes in his little black memo book about the great men who go into general practice. At noon Johnny had lunch with the doctors.

Klauber (ENT): I told her I could straighten her nose—she told me if I got a hairpiece. . .

Cassidy (GYN): She's not even seventeen. I told her a hysterectomy is out of the question. Maybe we'll go to Sweden.

Kohn (URO): What we need is a place to work where you can make up your own mind.

Albertson (GEN SURG): What we do need is more interns who can hold a retractor on the left Fallopian tube without getting an erection. (General laughter.)

Taylor (GP): Hell, boys, if things don't work out, you can always take a few courses and go back to practicing medicine.

Intern Shoemaker had afternoon general hospital service. There were six new admissions in his file when he got to it at one o'clock—three surgical, two medical, one pediatrics. Checking the admitting diagnoses, the age and sex, and the referring physician, Johnny sorted the afternoon's work and set up his attack. Grab off the medical cases first before old Grawtch gets here. Once Grawtch shows, I'm stuck on medical rounds, and all my diagnoses go down the drain.

Grawtch enjoyed sadistic medical management. Symptoms, and signs, lab reports, et al. to the contrary, what Grawtch said was gospel. He controlled sixty percent of the medical beds.

Johnny shuffled the history sheets and came up with patient A. C., Room 110. His approach to a new case was almost sensual. Freud would have chomped his chops at a Johnny Shoemaker, to whom each new case was a nonorgasmic orgy. He was Scotland Yard, he was Marconi, Houdini, Arturo. He was Lem Shoemaker.

His surgical greens had been discarded now for the barbershop whites. He always felt foolish dressed this way, as if, scissors and razor in hand, he should announce, "Next, please." His pockets bulged with crib notes on how to examine and treat a patient. His biggest fear in his latter years of college (first years of practice?) had been how to call to mind the information on what to do next. In his quiet moments of panic he had often devised in his head—even once architecturally scaling a model—elaborate spy methods of hidden closed circuitry in his consultation room where a pushed silent switch would eject a book into his lap and find the answer to Mrs. Oglethorpe's pink mottled bellybutton spots. In more realistic moments he planned his full library in an adjoining master closet to his consultation room, where at the end of an examination he would cough viciously, excuse himself for a drink in the closet, and return with the dramatic cure.

He entered now into Room 110, bare of all these accoutrements, armed only with Lem and Arturo.

Patient: A. C. Rm: 110 Adm. Dr: Grawtch
Admitting Diagnosis: Thyroid Adenoma
Chief Complaint: "I'm having a tough time swallowing."
Findings: Distended superficial neck and thorax veins, obstruction of the superior vena cava.
Bulging mass lateral to the sterno-thyroid.
—Absence of diastolic bruit, severe systolic bruit.
—Pulse 40, long-sustained.
—Enlarged heart.
—Cyanosis.
—History of positive Serology.
Impression: Aortic Aneurysm
Rule/out—congenital malformation
Rule/out—syphilis

Beaming, intern Shoemaker went on to his second medical Grawtch.

Patient: B. R. Rm: 114 Adm Dr: Grawtch
Admitting Diagnosis: Multiple Sclerosis
Chief Complaint: "My left leg shakes and I lose my balance."
Findings:
—All neurological tests negative.
—Spastic shortening of the left Achilles tendon.
—Anatomical left leg shortening.
Impression: Congenital Short Limb Syndrome (Suggest ¼" heel lift)

Arturo beamed with intern Shoemaker. Lem congratulated them both. They went on to Peds where Patient L. M. was to have his tonsils removed in the morning. Johnny went over him cautiously and noted alongside the miniature tonsilar tissue, a history of one sore throat this past year and a gray-white boggy nasal turbinate. He wrote a note for an allergy survey, but made a mental note to be on hand at 8 A.M. to be ready for the retractor on the left tonsil.

The surgical admissions were less challenging to intern Johnny. "Most cases," Dr. Albertson would tell him, "are cut and dried," which was his joke—but it did hold water.

Unchallenging or no, intern Johnny enjoyed shaking the boat for just a ripple or two so at least surgery would know he had passed on through here.

Patient P. B. for a Cholecystectomy *did* have an unvisualized gall bladder which was some indication for surgery, but what about her husband's fist marks at J. B. Murphy's point, right above the gall bladder?

Patient C. L. for a third inguinal herniorrhaphy repair *did* have a bulge hanging out of his crotch like a pomegranate, but where in this watery muscle shell of a man were you going to hang the thing this time, Albertson?

And Patient G. L., age twenty-two, scheduled for a left salpingo-oopherectomy, *did* have a mushy lobule in the lower left quad and a chocolate mousse intermenstrual discharge, but hasn't she had recurrent gonorrhea since age fourteen and chronic PID forever after? Take it *all* out, Albertson. Who's boss of this case, you or the board of trustees?

At the supper hour, on his early evening indulgent return from what he would like to think was a successful day, intern Johnny whistled softly, shuffling his happy white feet through the briefly quiet corridors, thinking contentedly: What dumb, dumb luck to be here.

"Shoemaker!" the message was loud and clear. Grawtch had stayed on longer than anticipated. This man, who looked like a porcupine, used each word sharply and professionally like a quill, digging for what had to be his nourishment—intern blood.

"Dr. Shoemaker." He walked Johnny into a wall and surrounded him with his prickly barbs, "you examined my new admissions, and you made despicably poor diagnoses. I have had many of your snide antics removed from my charts, but these last two I believe I shall hold and present at the next intern meeting for Mr. Kleinert's resourceful handling. Do you know you could be released from your service here? You are not a child, Shoemaker, you have a wife and several little ones waiting for your support. Well, young fellow, let me tell you, at this rate you are not going to make it. I think

it is about time you realized we have had enough of this
soft-soaping of you because your brother was a special person
to us. You haven't made it, Shoemaker, you never will. A
quarter of an inch heel lift—God, man, that poor soul is on
the verge of a neurologic catastrophe. Your brother Lem
would have seen it at once. Your brother. . ."

. . .Johnny had blanked out. It went on and on and on, but
soon it would be done and the quills would retract and the
fur would soften and the light of destruction would leave the
porcupine's eyes. And soon he would smile. . ."So let us say
bygones will be bygones. You've a few areas of roughness, but
after all, that's why you are here, and that is why we have
you, to take up the challenge of intern training and see to
it you *do* have those rough edges polished by the time you
leave. And let me tell you, *any time* you are having even the
most miniscule medical problems, you can count on me.
There will always be a bed for one of young Johnny
Shoemaker's problems."

He crouched tackily down the corridor, avoiding touching
the walls or other passersby lest they rub his crusty fur and
expose the nerve endings, and he disappeared into the men's
room. He did have a secret medical problem involving his
bladder or some associated area, so Johnny excused him. But
at the same time, he felt that recurring twinge of guilt. Surely
he had a wife and children at home to soon support, and
surely he was no match for Lem, he felt he was adequate,
maybe a little more—he just felt that.

His head ached and he wished he could go home. Why
don't I go home and tell it all to Mary? Mary, I had this case
today, I'll tell her, and I'll explain to her how I went through
thirty-two neurological tests and not one was positive. And
I'll say to Mary, see, see what a great guy I am. . . .Maybe I'll
come back tonight and talk to Jonesy. . . .

—. . .And the next thing, they got the nerve to tell me it's all
over and I missed the whole thing. All I remember is they
were all kissing me. You doctors are just too much. Your wife
must die, just die every time you leave the house. . . .Hey, J.
J.—Johnny—*Dr. Shoemaker*—don't go yet, I didn't tell you
everything—don't go—you didn't kiss me! . . .

.   .   .   .

6:00   THE SHOEMAKERS
                              692 LAKE DRIVE

                              ———————————
                              WELCOME
                              ———————————

*See the doctor house. See the lawyer house. See the
accountant house. See the executive house. See the church,
the temple, the church, the church, the school. See the big
doctor house. See the grass. See the weeds. See the doctor
frown and shake his head. See the doctor sad.*

Tom used to do a good job; he never left the last cutting
go past September. Edges razored clean, each blade tapered to
a three-quarter-inch quill, peat a level two inches and a half,
shrubs mulched three inches with coffee grounds, the mimosa
packed ankle deep in last-grass clippings.

Johnny missed Tom on more than one level. Charles? High
school son, Charlie? *Everyone* has a gardener. Don't they
come with the house? The rusted lawnmower down the
basement has gotta be a joke. Pop never really cut grass. Back
in his day the wheels were still square. I would do it right
now, Johnny muttered in defiance to the four cars already
parked around the office entrance. I really would. A little oil
and some steel wool and I could get that relic chugging away
and I could have this place looking like the old days. Damn
gardeners. Tom alone did more in one afternoon than a crew
of them do all day. Like everything else, a day's job, a week's
pay, catch me if you can.

Another car pulled up to the office. Hannah Hardy! Her
appointment's not until six forty-five. Johnny thanked God
for the old mimosa, and dropped his head under the low-flung
branches that had dutifully blocked off his house entrance.
Hope the kids have eaten.

Johnny pushed open the unlocked, burglar-proofed steel
door, smelled baked ham, expectantly felt his stomach twinge,
and eleven-year-old Jennie was first.

—I'm first, Daddy. *Me—me* first. I have to tell you first. David
was first yesterday.

—We waited, John. . . .

Recently Mary had waited. If there were any chance at all of
Johnny getting home, Mary waited. Her husband's distressed
gastric juices had long ago entered the discontinued column,

along with other thankless concerns. She waited now, because
she was concerned, reproachfully, with her own gastric juices.
—Eat your green beans, everybody—eighteen green beans
each...
—In gym today—*Daddy,* listen to me—in gym today I ran the
six hundred and I couldn't breathe. I mean it, there was no
air. You ought to talk to them. My chest hurt and the nurse
wouldn't give me an aspirin...
—I ran the six hundred too, and my leg is killing me...
—Jennie, fourteen more green beans...
—And it hurt me all afternoon. I couldn't take a deep breath
until Carrie gave me a pill...
—What kind of *pill?* Ten more, David...
—Ma, I hate the stuff, What's it good for? ...
—It'll get rid of your pimples. John, can't you do any more
about David's pimples? ...
—What can an old country G.P. do? Send me to a university
skin specialist...
—*Cosmopolitan* had an article where they are using a cream
made from green vegetables...
—Gimme them beans, Mom. I'll smear them all over my
face...
—My chest hurts when I swallow...
—Eight more. If your father doesn't care, I do...
   Father sure as hell cared, but for what? On what level does
your care begin and end? And for whom do you show it at
which instance?
   Johnny the father deeply cared, but like his patient Rose
Selena, the act of nonreaction was as powerful an emotion as
he could dig up in his defense of interfamily survival. He felt
as he had when Grawtch had quilled him to the wall and tore
down his medical pants. He deeply and profoundly cared, and
he declared it by his silence. How else do you show you care
in a hopeless ailment? Johnny Shoemaker would just shake
his head in cursory understanding, finish his salty ham, and go
off to work where his caring was protectively sectioned into
time-trapped understandings.
   Johnny knew he had a role to play: Father. He worked at
it and it held up. The kids loved him as they were supposed
to. He was a visiting uncle who also happened to be a doctor

as well as a relative, and they took no more advantage of him
than did many of his patients. As before, the demand for
units of his time was handled adequately by Mary. She moved
in and out of his time slots like a well-trained referee, and
Johnny, knowing this, played his role with equivalence. The
game went on, the score never quite indicating the strengths
of either team. To Johnny it was a time between Time. There
was never time, but there was always Time. He never
originally planned it that way; but, neither had he originally
planned to be a doctor. . .
—Every time I raise my arm it hurts. . .
—You said it was your leg. . .
—It's my arm *and* my leg. . .
—Green bean seconds? . .

Johnny chewed and swallowed, chewed and swallowed, and
found it hard to imagine he was even there. He once spent a
summer on Uncle Adolph's farm, and now Mary and Jennie
and David and Charles and Jonathan were a barnful of brown
and white cows, heads clamped shut between rotted wooden
planks, bowed into mounds of straw, chomping away at their
mash, while hollow hands drained them disdainfully dry.
There was a time when food was king, and Johnny had paid
homage in stately manner. But now, discover me a pill to take
the place of all this wasted time, he cries, and I'll say
someone deserves knighthood and a bagful of gold.
—Charles, you've eaten only two pieces of ham. . . .It's too
salty, isn't it? It's never good any more, is it? John, you've
only touched one. . .
—Not your fault, Mom, he had missionary for lunch. . .
—It's so hot in here. Jennie, open the back door. . .
—Try the yellow pills, Mom. . .
—You left one green bean, Pimples. . .
—Shut up, Skin. . .

There was something eerily familiar to Johnny about the
whole scene. Naturally, it had happened before on many
levels (Johnny missed Tom on more than one level). But there
was something about the raw scratchy screech of the
childrens' voices, the fading in and fading out of recognizable
patterns and topics, the colors, the auras, the blurs and the
blips. It was like the old shaky television set in the bedroom.

A few edgy tubes, a condensor or two burned out, a picture
tube with loose crystals. Screechy sounds. Blurry pictures.
Too bright, too dark. Sudden brilliance. Great reception, then
blur. Screech, blip, blackout.
—*Sports Illustrated* had an article last week that said Joe
Namath ate a pound of green beans a day. (Brilliant.)
—I'll betcha Willie Washington don't eat green beans. (Blur.)
—I'll betcha he eats hawg chitlins. (Blip.)
—That's Pop's boy, Charlie, keep it cool, man. (Blur.)
—I got a buck and a quarter riding on the game, Pop. Is it
true you're going to let him play with a cracked head?
(Blip.)
—Lots of loose talk around school about a Black Saturday.
(Blur.)
—What's the scoop, Pop? Gotta cover my bet. (Blur.)
—Leave your father alone. Can't he have a few minutes away
from his business? (Brilliant.) One more bean for you,
Charles, (blur), two for you Jennie, (blur), and six for you,
David (blur).
—*Six?* (Blip.)
—Or there's no dessert. Look at all that ham, all that food
left over. Your father works so hard to buy this food, and
nobody eats a *thing!* (Screech.)
—I'm saving mine for the starving kids in the ghettos.
Everybody make up a bag and I'll deliver it over to
Merrybrook. . . .
   Blackout.

   Willie's ma piled on the greens.
—Read someplace, son, O. J. Simpson eats two pounds of
greens a day. . . .
—I'll eat four, Ma, I'm twice as good as he is. . . .
   It smelled good in the Washington flat. Plank steak
smothered in mushroom gravy, home fries smothered in white
onion sauce, greens, lots of greens, smothered in bacon fat.
And Ma Washington piled it on smothered in love, lots of
love.
—Green stuff is good for your head, son. . .
—Only thing good for my head, Ma, is hittin' it against a
Centerville goalpost with a ball in my belly. . .

—Don't you worry about that game, boy. Your old man has got Saturday set tidy. . .

—Ida and Isabelle, you see what your big brother is eatin'? He's goin' on to college. You eat up your greens like good little girls, you go on to college. . .

—They don't have to worry, Ma, I'm gonna take care of everybody. No stoppin' any of us now. . .

The new high-speed train drowned out the television, but it came through that on Saturday there was a sixty percent chance for rain, seventy percent Sunday.

—If it rains, Willie, don't go slippin' into mud holes like you did las' week. Nearly lost us a game. . .

—Nothin' happened to me, Pop. . .

—Your doctor friend don't think like that. . .

—He worries about me. . .

—He worries 'bout himself. . .

—He's OK. . .

—He's no better'n any of 'em. . .

—He's OK. . .

—Not a one, boy. You believe experience, not a one. . .

Ma Washington told her husband to kindly shut up in front of the girls—that's how you start prejudices—and she reminded him of the scholarship papers Dr. Shoemaker got up for Willie.

—Makin' it look good. . .

—And callin' down the State scouts for Saturday? . .

—Cover up. . .

—He's OK, Pop. . .

—They got a plan, boy. . .

—Only plan they got is to win. They need me. . .

—They won Saturday without you. . .

—Not against Centerville. . .

—They're pullin' Graham out of junior varsity. . .

—He's a shell. . .

—He's gonna play in your place. . .

—Shells can't play in my place. . .

—They don't want you up in their State College. . .

—Doc says it's all set. . .

—He's gonna cross you. . .

—Not Doc. . .

—He's gonna. . .
—He's OK, Pop. . .
—He's white. . .
—Washington, you're a bigot. . .
—White is white. . .
—He don't see color. I know, he told me. . .
—Crap, they all see color, they all no good. Ain't a one good one. Don't I know? Can't keep a job more'n a couple weeks. They find some shit reason to fire me. . .
—So, what're ya hittin' me for? . .
—Leave the boy's head, Washington. What you pushin' him for? You all right, son? You *really* all right? . .
—If Doc says so. . .
—Now you face it, boy, what's he care? What's he *really* care? . .
—He cares. . .
—It's a black head, boy, he don't care. You see any of Doc's kids playin' football? . .

Mary spooned the last green bean into David's plate. Had she prechewed it and deposited it into his puckered mouth, it would have affected Johnny no differently. Dimly he remembered how Tom swallowed his eighteen green beans unheralded, how he ran ten miles a day, cut grass, chopped wood, swam twenty lengths, pressed two hundred pounds, and drowned in milk. That was during freshman summer in high school. In September he came to his father and said, "I'm ready, Pop," and he was ready. Johnny didn't need a Willie, Tom had done it to him years earlier. I'm ready to go out for football, Pop," he smiled, his new-capped teeth breaking upon Mary's summer watch of unbelieving indifference. Now it was September, and her ninety-seven-pound weakling was transformed into an After, from a Before. "I'm ready, Pop."

"Over my dead body," Mary said.

At six-twenty Service called Doctor. He had forgotten to check in, there were four calls. Also on the line was an emergency from Coach Bocca.
—*Doc,* that you? Listen, Graham got clobbered this afternoon again. The knee, it bends backward. We couldn't get him on his feet. His old man is on his way to the office now. Fix him

up, Doc, he's my only backup for Washington. And hey, Doc, thanks. I talked to the Leader and I just want to thank you—for the wife and my bare-assed kids, I want to thank you. Take care, Doc. Get some rest, I understand you look like hell. Maybe we'll get together in the gym? Swap medicine balls, hah? Good boy. . . .

Johnny swallowed a half cup of cool coffee—it didn't matter, kept him awake—rinsed his hands, ran a wet comb through his remaining hair, washed out his mouth, smelled under his arms, and stepped rapidly through the enclosed patio to the office door.

—Don't forget my chest. . .

—Don't forget my leg. . .

—Don't forget my buck and a quarter bet. . .

. . .And Mary, don't forget Mary. Johnny pecked her cheek goodbye. Don't forget Mary who could have added her voice and said, "Don't forget my uterus." Don't forget Mary who could have told you about *her* day. Who could have told you the colored girl didn't show today, the wrong day—just the day she had to be at the new hospital luncheon and be attractively seen so that Dr. J. J. Shoemaker remains in first rank for that new clinic post. She could have told him she tried four dresses before she could zip one closed; or that she came home to get dinner started and the smell of food made her throw up. She could have told him she cried, and then she laughed, and then she sat in your rocker and it felt good. Yesterday, she would have told him she was committing suicide if she doesn't get her next period. Tomorrow she might tell him she is taking him along with her. Today, she looked at him forlornly at the dinner table and chose not to tell him. As he walked out of her timeslot, a whisper nudged itself into her thoughts, and she allowed herself the passing pain/pleasure of accepting it as new business. She half-waved to the doctor; a half-smile making the whole. Maybe, the whisper said, if I *were* pregnant. . .

. . . .

At six twenty-five Johnny ran George Graham and his old man through the side entrance, a well-traveled door used by the afternoon injured. Difficult enough battling the silent daggers in the waiting room thrown by the *legit* six-thirty appointments. George had neglected (sic) to have his ankles and knee taped before practice, stepped in a cleat hole, and felt like a truck hit his leg. The knee actually bent backward. Torn medial meniscus.

"Torn what?" the old man asked suspiciously.

Johnny explained the supporting structures of the knee, drawing little line diagrams showing how the inner membranes can tear under stress, especially sixteen-year-olds', and the resultant possibilities of lifetime damage if not attended to properly, and even *if* attended to properly. He taped the wobbly knee together and let them know George was finished.

"Whaddya' mean, 'finished,' Doc?" the old man demanded suspiciously.

And Johnny explained the knee structure, drawing little line diagrams showing how the meniscus can tear and how a kid would end up a cripple unproperly attended, and the first step is taping for immobilization.

"You gotta let me play Saturday, Doc," George cried the standard-bearer cry. "I'll get right off it after Saturday."

No play.

"Shoot some medicine into it. They shoot medicine into the pros and they get right out and play."

No medicine.

"You're lettin' Willie play?"

"Yeah, Doc," the old man asked suspiciously, "you lettin' Willie play?"

"It's *only* my knee."

"Yeah, Doc, only a knee."

"It's Willie's *head*."

"Head."

No.

"Send me to a specialist. You're sendin' Willie."

"Yeah, Doc, the kid wants a specialist."

And Johnny reexplained the structure of the knee, drawing little line diagrams showing the origins, insertions, actions of the full supporting mechanism and how tearing of fibers heal. A specialist would have him on the operating table tomorrow; Johnny was offering him the benefit of a few days conservative grace.

The old man looked at Johnny suspiciously. He had long since tuned out.

"We're goin' anyway, whether you send us or not, Doc. This kid of mine's been waitin' two years for a crack at Washington's job. Now's his chance.

A pent-up father/son venom shot out, grown apparently especially for this suspicious occasion. "Rip off that tape, Doc, we're seein' a specialist tonight. Heard about you and that nigger. . . ."

. . . .

Evening
6:35

JONATHAN J. SHOEMAKER, M.D.

LAKE OFFICE

DOCTOR IS IN

NO SMOKING

NURSE ON DUTY: MISS GEORGIA JAMES

. . . .

She was the antithesis of Frances Cooper. Allegorically night and day. She was a blonde with blonde roots, a Revlon box cover. Adored by the men, tolerated by the women, they saw in her the naivete and creamy pure virginity they would wish for in their own little daughter. And somehow simply and innocently, with a three-month course in speedwriting, office management, and Power Words, she parlayed these qualities into an efficient office aide. Johnny looked forward to his nights; to him they were like a regenerating tax refund. She made him smile. However cautious he was to subdue his enjoyment over her malapropisms, lest they disrupt her accuracies, she and her Scarlett O'Hara drawl made him smile. —Why good evenin', Dr. Shoemaker, you beat me to work again. Two years now and I can't get used to your northern nights. Down Birmingham it is still burnin' sunshine at this hour. Schedule is full, I see, and I sure like a full schedule. Lucky, lucky bunch of people. Come in draggin' their floppy tails between their legs, time they leave you tails as stiff as a hundred-dollar studded mare. I would certainly like to be a fly speck on your wall. . .sorry, sir, we do have to get on with it. Service had four calls. One was an appointment for a Salvatore Cooper? Says he is your daytime nurse's husband? She sure hides her husbands well. What's to hide? I'm only twenty-three, been through two and workin' on three and four. Momma says I'm lovable—sorry, sir, we have to get on with it. Here's two calls I couldn't handle. It should be a delightful night. All these sick little cuddle bears just waitin' for you to rub their fallow fur and make them orgiastic again—sorry, sir. I'll send someone in soon's the light goes off the phone. Keep up the good work. . . .

. . . .

—Good evening, Centre Pharmacy, Marvin the drug addict speaking—when you buy drugs from me I addict to my bank account. Oh, oh, it is you, Dr. John. I waited all afternoon with hot chicken soup spiked with penicillin just in case my old mother was lying again. You said Essie Howard was through. She sashayed in here for her pretty twenty yellow pills with an Rx from your pretty foolish hand. You got more years in school than me, but we'll both get even up in the cell block. You'll come by tomorrow, Doctor? It's only like downstairs from your cash register. I'll have a real gourmet surprise for you, old-fashioned Hungarian goulash à la Zsa Zsa. That's my mother's maiden name. . . .

. . . .

—This is Clara, Doctor. Look, I can't help it. I told the girl to never mind the call, just put me down for *anytime* tonight, even if it's after midnight. You got to see her. I wouldn't even wash it off until you examine it. You know how I am with her and dirt. Well, she not only has dirt on her knees from crawling on the floor—and how she got out of the playpen before I spread Lysol around—but, my God, she ran right for the dog's bowl and stuck both hands full up to her wrists in the Gravy Train. She is stained brown, and chunks of meat and sticky gravy are just hanging there. If she puts her hands to her mouth, I will throw myself out the window. God knows what kind of disease she might already have. I swear I will kill my stupid husband for bringing home a dog at a time like this. I couldn't get you. It always happens at supper time, and I called the vet to ask him if Lisa is poisoned yet. Shall I wrap her up and bring her right in? ...

. . . .

Backed up already fifteen minutes—*"It is inevitably written —you are already two days behind"*—Georgia sent in the first scheduled patient and Dr. Shoemaker began his medical scribbles that at evening's end would only begin to tell the story. . . .

. . . .

Progress Notes - Thursday Eve., Oct. 15, 1970—Lake Office

6:45 HANNAH HARDY—Weight #156. ½ pound loss. 7 pds/6 mos. Very Poor Loss. She says it must be the scale (make note to have Bureau of Wts & Msrs in for √-up). Says it's air. "You know my adenoids, when I sleep I swallow air."

6:55 RUDOLPH GARRONE—BP 160/100. Heart sounds distant. Pulse irreg.—78. Lungs clear. Pro-time 27%. Voice shaky. Problem w/wife again. Watches him "like I was a Roosian spy." He looks out a window, she says go on over there to bed with her. He sits in toilet, she busts in and says whatcha doin' so long? He says he's only there long enough to take a leak. (Make note to call wife. Uses coronary as excuse against sex.) "She says it's bad for me." He knows better. Man's got to live by more than digitalis. "Even when I'm on her, you gotta excuse me, Doc, the way I gotta talk, you bein' my family doctor, but even then she says you done yet, you done yet. Now, you know, Doc, that ain't no way to be." (Make note to call wife and tell her at certain times just to keep her mouth shut.)

7:05 DANIEL KATZ—BP 145/85. Wt #155. Loss 20/2 months. Fine finger tremors, wheeze. Left exopthalmos. Hair brittle. Balding, scaly. Bronchogenic CA (?). Thyroid adenoma (?). He says its the fault of his wife Millie (!). Goddam pills. She acts like a rabbit locked up for two years. Says her weight is bullshit. She *likes* fat. *Wants* pills, makes her sexy. He needs help. Weak, failing. Tail dragging. Can't cover territory. Got to keep going. "I got broads I been taking care of on the road for years, already label me dead." Ultimatum: Get her *off* the stuff or put him *on* . . . .

7:15 <u>BETTY BROWNLEY</u>—Good kid. Lacerated thumb on rusty skate key (kids still use *skate keys?*). Spurting. Eight #00 nylon. Tet. tox 0.5 I.M. Tet. fluid 0.5 I.M. PCN 800,000 I.M. Furacin dressing. Grape lolli. . . .

7:30 <u>JANE REGAN</u>—Nose surgeon recommended pierced ears. BP 135/85. P. 110. Edgy, sexless, sad Sally. Needs full face job. Passed out cold with one ear hole. Grape brandy. . . .

Memo from Georgia:

I'll keep Molly Pitcher lying down awhile 'fore I let her go on home. Hate to say this, but the earrings make the poor girl's nose look longer. . . .Got Mr. Mawson's EKG done. I see no problem, he pinched me twice. . . .

7:40 <u>MERRIL MAWSON</u>—Anterior wall infarct. Elev—ST

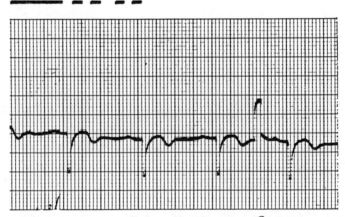

SANBORN VISO-CARDIETTE *Permapaper*

seg. Lead I & V, Q waves. Guy is out of his mind. Drove home from Baltimore w/sweats & chest pain. Felt better *climbing the stairs* to my office. Hosp./Grawtch service (have Georgia contact wife/ambulance/lawyer/priest/Coreen (Poochy) in Baltimore). . . .

Memo from Georgia:

Sorry about that, Chief. Ambulance on its way. Phone—you'll never guess. Who owes you $142 and we said no more appointments? She says tell him to get to the telephone right away, it is desperate emergency. You won't talk to her. You will talk to her. . . .

—He raped her! He raped her! This little girl, she is only fifteen years old. The dirty old bastard Garrone, he raped her. I told them, I told them, he keeps looking out his window at her. Dirty old man. *I'll* give him a heart attack this time. We will *kill* him. Stop your *screaming*—Doctor, they are carrying on like lunatics and screaming and crying. I swear she is spoiled. We are all coming right over! . . .

. . . .

At eight o'clock (TV station break) Dr. Shoemaker responded to a knock on his side door and handed through a Band-Aid to Jennie, who also asked how things were going.

. . . .

8:05   **COOPER, SALVATORE #1705**

> No Address—Crane Operator—Age 27—
> No Ins.
> 5-19-58—No comment. Fifth amendment. Husband of nurse.

—Surprise. The bad penny comes up heads again. Doc, it's good to see ya! Miss me? My little lady did. She flipped when she saw me, but you can see she's scared, you know. It's her old man—a tyrant. Keeps her locked in at night. All he wants is her dough. She's scared he'll kill us both, wouldn't put it past the old Polack. She's crazy about me, but she's scared he'll really start shootin'. All right, so I hit her once, but he shouldn't of called the cops. A husband's got a right to slap his wife a few times, right, Doc? Sure as hell can't let 'em take over a man's job. Gotta be a man, Doc. Hell, how many times you belted your old lady? Nobody's gonna call the cops on a doc, huh, Doc? One good belt. . . .

"...My God, you hit me." For the first time in four years of marriage, Johnny Shoemaker hit his wife, Mary. Not a big hit, really, just kind of a face slap. A witness would have to admit there was cause, but it was a hit. And Mary did get finger marks that did turn yellowish after a few days, but then, Mary had that kind of sensitive skin, and bruises came out in places where she never remembered bumping or hitting.

Mary remembered this hit. The yellow faded, but the nerve endings would key in a full set of memory patterns on cue. It was in essence just a little more than a little hit, therefore, enough so that after this things were different.

"We can't, we just can't have another one now." This was final to Johnny. Four more years of school, then a year at Mercy coming up, and then—who knows what after that? One child's enough. This was final.

It would be no trouble at all. Johnny had filed away an old formula of Pop's, you just soak a big wad of four by fours in it for ten minutes, then pack it deep into the cervix, and in a few hours, kerplop, into the toilet bowl it comes. It was easy to dig up the chemicals in the lab, and just as easy to walk off with a uterine forceps in clinic. There would be no delay. The longer you wait, the lesser the chances of—they never said the word—"aborting." Johnny called it a TTMI—Therapeutic Treatment for Menstrual Irregularity.

Up until the actual moment of insertion, Mary had passively accepted the finality of her husband's decision and never questioned him on procedure. In truth, she had disbelieved he was serious, and moved in and out of her daily chores half-listening to his plan. As she understood it, she would take the soaked pads from him one night and she would adjourn to the hall toilet, push the pads in place like she did her vaginal cream tampon, and then sit on the john awaiting the arrival of the fetus.

Within two nights of their original discussion, Johnny announced he was ready. He waited until he heard little Tom breathing in the rhythm of a child's absolute sleep before he began preparing himself for surgery.

With the precise certainty of a freshman medical student, he went about his cleaning and draping of the kitchen furnishings as if he were an OR supervisor. He explained to *her what would be done. She was to spread herself across the kitchen table, lithotomy style, because here was the only high and hard surface with good light, and he would pack her with a double wad to be certain. It was over two months, he reminded her, and you can't tell with some of these solid pregnancies.*

Mary, knowing herself to be fertile, found herself agreeing with him. After all, hadn't Tommy taken hold after their very first *time, and in a car? And even though John hadn't insisted on it, she had gone to Dr. Kronin and had three shots, but Tommy still held tight. So, Johnny, impaled with brother Lem's death, embraced the opportunity to have his very own child, and to her awkward joy, he married her as rapidly as she could be fit into a bridal gown.*

After Tom was born, although she knew Johnny would never completely let go, she gratefully saw his obsession with Lem's loss slacken. But eccentrically, the devotion transferred took on an unreal relationship. Johnny would spend hours over baby Tom's crib, just talking, mostly about daily events, college, sports, anything that came to his mind. When finally a word or two of simple reply was formed, Johnny pushed deeply into developing his son's conversational acumen.

At age two Tommy and Johnny discussed elemental chemistry and physics and Johnny read his experiments and term papers aloud to him seeking a brief, smiling "bravo" for acceptance, or a grunt of "nyet" for rejection.

At age three, Tommy had personally copied the Hippocratic oath from Lem's framed scroll hanging over his bed, and presented it to his father as a graduation gift from Lebanon.

At age four—now that Johnny was in med school in Chicago—Tommy had already been to two Arturo lectures on General Practice, and after one lab period of dissection, he could pick out the humerus and radius, and after the third, differentiate the seven leads of the Brachial Plexus.

"You're going to do it!" Mary cried out, her first acknowledgment that it was really happening. This, when she saw the kitchen table being draped with blankets and sheets and the Chicago Tribune. *She held her hands clamped tight over her mouth for fear of awakening Tommy, or—not that it*

would be new to this place—attracting other roomers to the cracks in their door. They were known to pile three deep at the first signs of catastrophe, and to dissolve as rapidly in the face of emergency; only one other medical couple lived here now, the rest almost derelicts who had taken over the once handsome Georgian house in South Chicago where Lem had once lived in ebullient style.

Johnny had visited him one Thanksgiving in his freshman year, bringing from Momma the full holiday feast wrapped in wax paper and coffee tins. When he received his acceptance, Johnny wrote at once for Lem's old room and was exhilarated to find it empty and waiting. They moved in with the prepared grandeur of youth and adventure, and after six months of stink and sputum and saddle-back roaches, John admitted to error, but was committed to the lease. So they scrubbed it, and Lysoled it, and plugged up the roach holes and carried newspapers to the hall toilet to cover the seat, and lived again—not in grandeur, but assuredly in adventure.

Mary, on call, climbed upon the news-covered table, clad only in the old faded rose-covered robe given to her by the girls of her sorority the day she announced she was pregnant and getting married. She deeply disbelieved what was happening, and felt that because she was naked, only covered by her friends' roses, somehow she would then be pure again—and purity rises and floats to the top, and she would exorcise herself from this hard table top leaving a substance below not belonging to her, and from a safe distance she would observe a strange phenomena of a man, apparently her lover, poking poison barbs into a hollow tube and extricating from this tube a pulsating mass of love's labors lost. From her vantage point she would then be able to laugh at this silly sight, and when it had gone away, on command she could snap herself back into the body mass and go about once again preparing it properly for her bed and her lover.

The soaked chemical pad seared her insides like vinegar on a raw cut. The formless figure on the table muffled a cry. Tommy cannot awaken. John doesn't like Tommy to awaken. Her face, always flushed a shiny McIntosh red, drained of color, and beads of moisture dripped oil into her already tearing eyes, moments ago laughing incredulously, now staring blankly.

—It really is happening. He really did it. My God.

He told her to just get down now and go about her business as if nothing had happened, but she simply sat in his rocker, unchanged, her face distorted with sickening reality, and rocked and rocked, and rocked apathetically.

Three hours later she felt the first contraction. And it rapidly advanced to grabbing, acute spasms of the entire lower abdomen. Twice she vomited, then, in one last massive overturn of her lower gut, holding back a precipitive scream lest Tommy wake up—lest this anger his father—she dashed for the hall bathroom. It was in use. At 2 A.M., who the hell was in there? It wouldn't stop. Mary held tight, but it pushed and twisted and pushed and she could not retain it. She fell to her knees and rolling on the filthy hall floor she squeezed out a bloody clot, then a bag of a grayish formlike mass followed by more clots, as Johnny scooped up the mess in newspaper and pots and pushed Mary back into the room.

It was done.

Mary, piled on the floor like a heap of oil-soaked rags, could not contain herself any longer. She burst into a raging fire, and then proceeded to put herself out. She rolled around on the rug crazily kicking out at the walls, banging over the chairs. She pounded on her head, she beat her breasts, she punched and gored at her empty belly, and she screamed loud and long and joyfully, and she said selfish, selfish, selfish. And the cracks outside the door darkened with bodies, and she said selfish, selfish, selfish, and she pounded her breasts and she pummeled her belly again and she glared hatefully at her husband who twitched manfully at her side.

It was not until Tommy appeared sandy-eyed in the doorway that he hit her. He hit her four-fingered across the cheek in the middle of a pleading cry from her that Lem should stay dead, but whether this was why he hit her, or because Tommy had awakened, or because he had finally decided the time had come for that kind of manly action, he never did know. But Mary knew.

"Momma, Momma!" she cried, a different kind of a cry. "My God, you hit me."

...Takes a little time, Doc, they get over it. She wants me back—don't they all. It's not easy. I been sick down the Shore over a year. There's no work for a sick guy on a crane. Shit, you could kill a whole crew. She knows, I stopped the booze. She's ready for me, but it's her old man. If we could just take off one night, we got a spark even his spit won't put out once I get it lit. . . .I don't want to take up your time with my crazy troubles. Just take my blood pressure, Doc, that's all I'm here for. Gets so low I gotta have a shot, and then some jag pills. I hate the crap, but it keeps the pressure up. And you charge me for the visit, Doc, regular price, no favors, you hear. I'll pay you soon as I get up in that crane. I make damn good gelt, you know that. . . .Still low, huh? Just gimme the shot, and don't give me any of your samples, just an Rx for the pills. I can get it filled, I got a friend. Make it for a hundred, will ya' Doc, so I don't have to bother you. And look, Doc, if you could put in a word—you know, to Fran you're the God—just tell her I'm dead serious and sober. If we could just get away one night, a dinner and a motel. . . .OK, thanks Doc, you are a real gem. Doc, hey, look, I'm going to need a ten spot to put this over, just until the pressure is up. Hey, sorry, Doc cat . . . .

. . . .

while I continue to keep this oath inviolate, may it be granted To me to enjoy life and the practice of the art, respected by all men at all times, but should I trespass and violate this oath

8:15 <u>JOHN GRUBE</u>—B.P. 180/100 P. 100 irreg. Pulsus alternans. Wt 210. Kid in Vietnam. Angina better. Kids plugging toilets with Kotex and bobby pins don't bother him any more. Trouble with broken lockers, floods in boiler room, OK now. Watches war on TV news, pains worse than ever. . . .

8:25 <u>WILLIAM MORTON</u>—C. W.'s son. Exec. VP WEC. Wants letter for draft board. Kid had butt hematoma falling out of bleachers 3 years ago. "Dammit, J. J., we don't buy this war, Billy and me. What the hell, J. J. You'll find a way to keep yours out. Just a letter is all we need, in triplicate, explaining in *detail* his back problem. . . ."

. . . .

—Georgia here, Doctor. Two calls. Black and white. Line two and one. Keep up the good work. . .

. . . .

Line one. Dr. Shoemaker, this is Roger Barnegat over at Meadow Park Medical Center. I just examined your little boy, Graham. I'm afraid he has a torn medial meniscus all right, and we're going to have to open him up first thing in the morning. Sorry to take away your best little shortstop, but I guess that is the name of the game. . . .

Line two. It's Willie, Doc. I had to call you. Sorry I have to butt in on your night hours, but maybe I won't get to see you before Saturday. You know they're sendin' me over to Philly to see this guy, supposed to be some kind of big-wheel doctor. Well, hell, Doc, you know how I feel about doctors, you're *It*. But you got a softer spot in your cranium than I got, you know, when it comes to us guys gettin' hurt. We're young kids, Doc. We're tougher than you old folks seem to imagine. I just don't want you to worry. I gotta play Saturday, you know why—we come too far to stop now. I just want you to know. I appreciate your interest, but sometimes a white man, close as he gets to us, can't make it to the end. . . .

. . . .

8:55 <u>ALICE V. GLEASON</u>—BP 110/75. P. 80. Hrt & Lungs OK. Wt 188. Gain 40 lbs. Father died two months ago. Claims she still cooks as if he's here and eats his food. . . .

9:10 <u>CHARLES HALLOWAY</u>—Hallelujah. A cold, a real runny-nose cold. Wants shot of PCN. Give *aqua distillata*. Feels better. So do I. . . .

. . . .

—Georgia here, Doctor. *They* are here—en masse. Father, mother, aunt, the little lamb, and the holy ghost. I'll buzz you in five—make it ten. . . .

. . . .

At nine-fifteen Mr. and Mrs. Samuel Belotti, their niece Roseann Martucci, and her daughter, Bernadette Martucci, came into the office. Bernadette was fifteen, unmarried, in a special school for backward children (probably a birth injury or an attempted abortion—*if they only would use Pop's plugs instead of coat hangers*). No one ever spoke a word except Mrs. Samuel Belotti. She spoke like the memory of an ethnic Tugboat Annie.
—Now all of you, shut up. I'm the girl's aunt. Her mother is too prostrated to talk. Here, Bernadette, you get up on that table. Doctor, it is stinking, an old man like him. You can see the momma can't even talk. And she, just losing her husband, he took advantage of that. If her husband was here, he would rip open the liver of that old man and hang him up by his—Bernadette, shut your ears, what kind of upbringing you got? Listen t'me, Bernadette, now open your mouth, *tell* him what you told us. Stop twisting your mouth—damn old man, he made her get another attack. Doctor, give her a needle. Now, Bernadette, you *stop* that and tell us what that dirty old man did to you. He knows she gets an attack and her mouth gets all twisted so she can't call out. Every night, from his window, he's been watching, that old bastard. His wife, God save her, she told us he would do it. I yelled at him, *Garrone,* you damage my crippled niece, we will kill you. Her father will come up from the grave and cut off your—Bernadette, shut your ears, what kind of house you live in? Bah, we will give him a heart attack, he will rot in hell. Now—*Doctor,* examine her and tell us. Bernadette, what kind of upbringing you got? Open up your legs like you did for that dirty old man. . . .

Dr. Shoemaker buzzed Georgia, and together they examined the young, petrified child and found an intact and undisturbed vaginal opening, pink and virginal and sweet-smelling, so much so that Georgia said to Johnny, "Doesn't it just make you nauseous?" . . .

—Whaddya mean? I don't believe you. What do you know? *We* know. Come on, Samuel, Rose, Bernadette, we owe this poor doctor some money so he sticks up for dirty old bastards. You wait until tomorrow, Dr. Shoemaker, we will have enough to pay you your stinkin' money you need so bad. Bernadette, get your ass off the table and pull your dress down. What kind of upbringing you got? . . .

. . . .

—Georgia, Doctor. Call from Dr. LeRoy, says it's personal. . . .

. . . .

—J. J., close up shop early tonight. Shoo them all on home, take a stiff drink, get into bed with Mary and make it last, boy, make it last. Frank Jessup won't have the chance, he just had a massive coronary and never got to the door. An office full of patients. . .some of them still complaining as they left. Forty-four years old, three kids, and all that tear-jerking rot. Thought you'd better know. . . .

. . . .

—Georgia checking out, Doctor. All files in order, letters typed, lights out, money's in the safe, made progress notes on three shots, dear little heinies, I love them, two diathermies, four insurance forms, six Rx renewals, and fed the fishies—an extra shake for the pregnant one, you know. Don't know *when* they get around to it, I'm watching them all the time. . . .You sure you going to be all right with that insurance carpetbagger out here? He looks at me like it's a sin being alive. My Poppa never believed in insurance. When he was going to die, he said to Momma, "Now, Lulu, you go look downstairs alongside the coalbin and there's a loose brick on the floor, and as soon as I'm gone, you stick your hand in this hole and you'll know what livin' with you for forty years has meant to me. He was still warm when she was down there scratching out this brick and got her hand caught in the biggest rattrap you ever did see. . . .

. . . .

Jerry Albert, energetic young tax and trust attorney, legal aide, professional management counselor, and general entrepreneur—better known as accountant Larry Albert's kid brother—spent nine-thirty to eleven with Dr. Shoemaker. This was a second meeting and possibly a last one before the final documents would be prepared.

Worksheet for Trust Agreement and Last Will and Testament
Name—Jonathan James Shoemaker
Age—45
B.P.—USA
Profession—Physician (M.D.)
Address—Home—692 Lake Drive, Greenville Lakes, N.J.
　　　　　　　Office—1555 Centre St., Greenville, N.J.
Wife—Mary Hollister Shoemaker. Age—42; B.P. USA
Children—
　　Thomas—Age 21—Medical College—1 yr.
　　Charles—Age 17—High School—Sr.
　　David—Age 14—Jr. High School
　　Jeannette—Age 11—Elementary School
Gross Annual Income—$51,000
School Physician Salary—$1,400
Income from Stocks—$33
Mutual Fund Value—$2,500
Income from Business (Wash. Mach.)—Loss $2,800
Net Income—$28,000
Real Estate—692 Lake Drive—$35,000 (Mort. $18,000)
　　　　　　　Office Addition—$15,000 (Mort. $8,000)
Pontiac Station Wagon—1968—$2,600/encumbered $800
Buick Sedan—1963—$500/encumbered -0-

Jerry Albert never made points quietly, but he gave them out cautiously. Some he gave away as samples. Others he sold you at your request only. Those he could not profitably turn over he filed away, and you would find them turning up in chatty newsletters he would send you quarterly. There were those few items he could not classify, good only for a yak at a convention meeting, or a smoker. With Dr. Shoemaker he could not wait until morning to see his brother Larry, there were several items too hot to sleep on.

Item (to Larry)—A 1963 Buick?

Item (to Larry)—$33 from stocks?

Item (to Larry)—Is he hiding anything? Stocks under the kid's name, cash in an oatmeal box, business deals under an assumed name, a numbered account in a Swiss bank? It's all been tried, you know. These doctors are quite a bunch. Blondes? Brunettes? Is he telling it like it is?

Item (to Larry)—Make sure he has a good doctor. He better live it out, 'cause if he's dead tomorrow, his family will not make it. He thinks he's in great shape, but the wife better be ready to go to work in a mint that gives out free samples. I told him, remember Dr. Jonas Carlsdorf who died just a year ago today. He left an estate with property in Philadelphia, and stocks and bonds and holdings to put this piddling estate to shame—his wife is out now looking for a job in a dress shop.

He did tell him, "Whatever you do, Dr. Shoemaker, I tell you it won't pay you to die."

Item (To Dr. Shoemaker)—Big real estate holdings? Take for example, your office. Fifteen thousand dollars, tricky figure. You know what your wife with a few tears thrown in could get for all this junk—maybe two thousand from the scavengers, maybe one. If you were lucky like Dr. Felix Strohmeyer, you would die in July, a very fine humane gesture to your beloved ones. Plenty of available ripe young interns, and residents, hot to get hold of some action in the disease market. Die in October and you are poor dead. You can't afford it, even in July. Phil Reagan, the dentist, $65,000 gross, his estate poorly managed, fumphitted around for an extra month—kerplooey, the practice melted away like the old proverbial snowball where he was. Brain tumor, you know, ate it away like ants at the picnic cheese. He went cuckoo.

Item (to Dr. Shoemaker)—Age 45. Net $28,000. You have had it. Just when you are ready for a chunk of life, your income will begin to kaput. A few more hey-hey years, a few extra medicare checks, and soon you're collecting your *own* medicare checks. Keep working, hang on, whatever you do. After the kids get out of college, you may make it. Take care of yourself, work less hours, slow down, relax, find some hobbies, see a doctor. But by all means, you must *keep up your gross*. Without it, you'll never make it, alive or dead. . . .

.   .   .   .

11:55   Mary had already gone to bed when Johnny came up. The TV was off, no doubt the Tonight Show had a replacement for her other Johnny; she didn't bother watching replacements. "I've got two Johnnies in my life," she would say, "one I *laugh* in bed with—."

While he undressed he told her of the awful shape he was in, Jerry Albertwise.

"No matter what his statistical source, John, *I'm* going to die first. The whole thing isn't worth your time. And don't bother insuring me, because it's going to be a suicide leap from Frank Lenihan's OB table when I go there tomorrow and he tells me I'm pregnant."

She sat up in bed for a minute and pinned up some loose red hairs. She was covered with a layer of cool perspiration, only since John had come into the room. She *phewed* and tossed her hair aside, wrung her pillow as if to release the heat, fanned her sheets, said, "Did you turn up the thermostat?" and laid back on her side.

After a minute of quiet: "For a few hours there when you went into the office tonight, I thought, well maybe if I *were*. We somehow make it better when I am, don't you think? I remembered how great we were when we found Charles had held on that awful night in Chicago, he was still in there—only Carla had aborted. Could I make twins again, John? . . .Uh, uh, Casanova, don't you dare. Just turn over, you and I have had it. What I went through with your monsters tonight between homework and television, and dirty underwear, and shoes all over the floor, and hair in the sink, and ironing, and shut up Skin and kill Pimples, and he's touching me, tell him not to

touch me, and the heat, the awful goddam heat in that
kitchen....Until I get the word from Frank Lenihan, your
credit card in this department has been voided. I'm serious,
John, dead serious, and I'm scared, I really am. How could
you fool with your own wife and that pill? Didn't we
learn?...Open a window or turn on the air conditioner or
give me a shot. ..."

Mary was asleep. Once John got home she could go off to
sleep in the middle of a word. Eleven, three, five, it didn't
matter—once she heard the key in the door and the click of
the alarm system, she was asleep. When John reached over to
kiss her goodnight, he tried not to see it, but it was there, he
wondered whether only he saw it, but it was there, he was
sure, four livid fingermarks across her cheek...

. . . .

FRIDAY

1970	OCTOBER				1970	
S	**M**	**T**	**W**	**T**	**F**	**S**
				1	2	3
4	5	6	7	8	9	10
11	12	13	14	15	16	17
18	19	20	21	22	23	24
25	26	27	28	29	30	31

16

OCT. 1970

. . . .

Fri., 11:30 P.M.

Dear Tom,

I've been counting time all day awaiting that peaceful moment when I would settle down at my desk and write to you these four little words: "Your new ideas stink."

And don't think they didn't—up until an hour ago.

Here in the office, with a cinematic dash of drama in the raw, a person held a gun to my belly and, propitiously, your evil written words became brazen, thoughtful truths. I still cannot buy your total death knell of the G.P., but I may very well have to put a down payment on the demise of <u>one</u> G.P.

Although the day moved on in the same old slapstick way you so aptly described, it still, like old Charlie Chaplin, made a lot of people laugh, smile, cry, forget, and maybe even hope for a better day. Out of fifty or so that treadmilled through (and, hell, don't I <u>know</u> they treadmilled through?), I felt I had played a valuable role in the lives of thirty. Twenty? Ten? One? Whatever, I was doing my thing; at worst, none were harmed. Arturo said, "Practice as you will, but so none will be harmed."

These are commendable thoughts. They keep me going in spite of the unconscious wails that prod at me like the melodramatic tragedian: Tom <u>may</u> be right. However, there is in that unconscious a membranous layer of protective cells that keep me spirited and certain, and the dialogue of a lifetime acts as an impermeable filter against the rupture of that onionskin wall. Tonight, with gun at my belly, that wall split apart, and I passed through the thin line. Now I am fearful that maybe my son Tom's thoughts about my kind of medicine are <u>not</u> foul play. Still, however, there does hang over this entire abomination a caustic, sick smell. But perish and hark, the rotten truth says, the odor may come from, alas, within me, not you.

You see, sixty minutes ago, when this apparently routine night was about over—(my nurse, Georgia, of tender mouth, called it a "shitty evenin'" maybe because of poor Albert, who had a juicy epileptic fit all over the waiting room floor)—at about this moment, a young man came into the office and held a gun to my belly. Obviously he was insane, I thought nervously, and, having read enough morning headlines, I knew that tomorrow I would be a statistic. I counted myself dead. The gun, aimed directly at my belly for a full three minutes (this is <u>long</u>), while a puffy, ratty-looking figure of a man—not even a man, still with unproductive fuzz along attempted sideburns— held both Georgia and me immovable and dead. . . .

10:30 P.M.

"Remember me, Dr. Shoemaker?" The boy with the fuzz on his face flipped the old German Luger nervously from hand to hand. "Of course you remember me," he said, "how could you forget? I must've put on forty, fifty pounds from them insulin shocks, but it's still me, Harry Steele."

Yeah, Johnny remembered, a scrawny kid about three years ago, went berserk, broke two cops' arms, threw his wife down a flight of stairs, smashed a toilet seat over an intern's head, and went out like a light when I slipped a needle into his arm.

"When you're a hero you remember the night, huh, Doc?" The fuzz face twitched peculiarly. "Three years go by fast when you're a hero, but not when you're the villian. Slow as cold tar."

Georgia, made unrealistically mute by the night caller's presence, for some reason moved several steps away from Dr. Shoemaker and the boy smiled respectfully at her.

"A good idea, honey," he said. "It's only the Doc I got to get squared up with."

He stepped closer to Johnny and toyed for a moment with the weapon. Then he said bitterly to his old doctor, "How does it feel, Doc? You can write 'crazy' on a piece of paper and a guy gets shoved in a padded cell for three years?"

Johnny tried to think how it felt.

"Do you lose any sleep? Do you ever throw up a meal or two? Three years, you must have made a bundle. Three years. You know what I got? A dollar twenty-three." The boy scratched at his fuzzy growth, "Damn place has bedbugs as big as flies. You ever been out there, Doc? It would do you worlds of good. It might make you think another few minutes before you write 'crazy.' "

Johnny hated to write out those commitment forms. Who is to know who's crazy? The pen could be in *his* hand.

"I'm cured, you know," the boy said sacredly. "That's why

I'm here, so I can pay back some of the old bills and stay cured."

What went wrong with him, Johnny tried to remember? His wife and a couple of hoods beat him out of some money. He tore them apart, and they put him away.

"The wife ain't there no more," he said. "I went straight over to the old place. The kid, he's eleven now, he and the grandmother gave me a meal, some pot roast and chicory leaves, and then I went right upstairs to the bedroom and behind the loose panel back of the old dresser, I found the gun. . . ." He stuck the barrel deep into Dr. Shoemaker's belly and Georgia let out a grotesque gurgle. She knew what her Poppa would do: kick the guy right in his crotch and then hammer-chop his neck and—Georgia made a move toward the gun. . . .

"Uh-uh, pretty girl," he smiled gently at her, "not for you, for him. You know," he looked down at the barrel pushed an inch into Johnny's belly and he sighed satisfactorily, "all the time I kept thinking it would be gone, and she would have it, or one of the kids would have it. God, what a relief to find it."

He took the gun from the belly and examined it like it was a ransomed jewel cache, and he shook his head and he sighed again and said, "What a relief. You got no idea, Doc, what a relief this is to my mind. Now I can rest easy. You know, it was *loaded*. I already shot two. Can you imagine the trouble if the kids ever found it? Or how about the police? I'm a lucky guy. I been lucky for three years, from the minute you slipped me that shot. A guy can go along messin' up his life then suddenly—he don't even know it—he can get lucky."

The gun moved from his hand and was carefully placed on the doctor's desk. Four separate cartridges were placed alongside it.

"I want you to know, Doc, that I am grateful and humble to you. I want you to take this gun and give it to the police. They'll understand it comin' from you." The kid sniffed water back into his nose and scratched at the fuzz.

"I'm going to call you after things settle down and make a regular appointment instead of bargin' in on you after you had such a long day."

He took Johnny's hand and shook it hard. "Stay with it, Doc, and God bless you. . . ."

God bless you? All day long I hear it, Tom. Have I really blinded people that they God Bless Me all over the place? I sign Mrs. Costande's medicare forms, God bless you. I pull a pencil eraser out of Craig Anderson's ear—God bless you. Sue Menolli, I call Abortions Anonymous for her—G.B.Y. Charlie Clark, I write a note to his boss and say no more two-hundred-pound panels without help—G.B.Y. Willie Washington, I send him off with his X rays that show nothing so he'll play ball—G.B.Y. I hear it all day long. "God bless you" comes out of their mouths like sugar-free gum juice, in one ear and out the other. Empty shell words. God damn you would be better, that's more like it.

It took Harry Steele three minutes to deliver his sermon, and you know what happened to me in those 180 seconds? Forty-five years—click, click, click, what did I see: Jonathan J. Shoemaker, promising young successful suburban doctor, a man at the height of his most productive years, enjoying life's overwhelming gratifications?

Bullshit.

There he was, J. J. Shoemaker, g.p.—lower case—a disillusioning blur of a drowning doctor.

God bless you, he said. What does it mean to me now? In minutes I would be dead. Truth now: What am I, what is there to bless? I wink and see only a hapless lifetime rush by, and I hear a father laugh (". . .An artist? An artist, you say? That is a laugh. It's a good thing this family has Lem. God bless Lem."), and a brother pledge (". . .Keep trying, Jonathan, pull out the choke. Now pump, pump hard and turn it over. Good boy, Jonathan, don't panic, I won't leave you."), and a son resign (". . .I'm not going into General Practice with you.").

What's the use, who am I kidding? God damn you, pull the trigger, now's the time. Didn't I get the word in the mail today from the Andrew Jackson Longer Life Clinic? Quote: ". . .We, (Franklin G. Shrevelove, M.D., and his associate staff of twenty-five specialists) after a two-months in-depth study of Dr. J. J. Shoemaker's chief complaint of head pain, have come to the following conclusion: . . .a reevaluation and a rearrangement of life's stresses with emphasis on cutting the overall daily load will aid the patient's present complaints."

(". . .Keep up your gross, keep it up.")

For the twenty-second time today I reread your letter that counted me out before even the eighth round of a fifteen rounder. Hadn't you split the last nerve to survival when you hit the nail right through my head—only God knows how many of those poor souls I touched today would be better off touched by more youthful or expert hands?

The full day clicked through my mind to illustrate the rawness of your truths. There were twenty, maybe thirty progress notes I had to reread. They were awful, just awful. These patients had all left blessing something or other, and suddenly their charts were confessions of a Pied Piper in disguise. One, two, three, twelve, thirty—all of them may have done better elsewhere. I read them, reread them, and grew weary and bleary, and ran them through the Xerox to send on to you. (See, I do use Xerox, and EKG's, and electric typewriters, and electric pencil sharpeners—your old man is not a complete horse and buggy.) These progress notes have something hidden away in them. As I Xeroxed I read again, and it is in there someplace. One of us is right. One of us is wrong.

But it won't surface. I know something is there, because this damn midskull pressure is unrelenting. The message wants to come through, it's somehow related. I had this pressure the day I saw the Stine kid with a runny nose, and the next day he was down with encephalitis. I had it when Otto Brown saw a few drops of blood in his stool and the next week his bowel burst with a mesenteric adenoma. It's the pressure I had when they took Poppa to the hospital and cut off his leg the next day. It's that awful midskull pressure I got when Sam made his transatlantic call, and before he said it, I knew Lem was dead.

What a blessing if the insane one had pulled the trigger. Pull the trigger, the pressure screamed from inside my head, I don't like tomorrow. No, he said with a saintly smile and a finish from an old late, late, movie. Here and God Bless You, he said. Ach! I said—when I am unnerved I say ach, as did Lem—Now I must return to the task.

What kind of task? Since when a task? A challenge, an uncertainty, a mishmash, a labyrinth, of course; what isn't that has at its center the reward of rewards? But a task? Never!

I thumb through the Xerox sheets and otherwise, I sit quietly. It is in there, and I listen for the answer. The music that played unheard all day now suddenly I hear, and it is a memory of a peaceful summer soft rain, falling on the old slate roof of the mountain house. The door to the office is latched closed, the files locked in order, the lights—all but the one over the bubbly fish tank—out for the night. The vitamins permeate the air with the smell of instant strength. The telephone, that two-headed monster (one spilling out money, the other bitches) now is quiet. But only with the quiet of a pregnant, laboring belly preparing for the next contraction. It will rise up again, of this you can be sure, but oh, in the moment of calm, how generous the Lord can be! And so I sit here between con-tractions and complaint, between monsters and monies, between right and wrong, and prepare a letter to you, the would-be doctor, and prepare to tell you not to be so goddam smart so soon. But suddenly I am drowning in my own smart juices, sweating and hurting. And the thoughts I am thinking are from another life, not mine. And the desires I have are another's, not mine. And I think, maybe if I run out into the Buick and talk with Lem. . .but, no, it is you I must talk with, Tom. I'm tired, really tired. It's been a shitty day. You think I have really reached the end of Doctorsville? Have I really been fooling my-self that I have some valuable niche to fill in this world, and am I really totally replaceable at any given moment by a wacky WEC machine? Here, son, take a look at the Xerox's. They're just as they fell. No retouches, just the way it was today. . .the answer is in there. . .just the way it was. . . .

.   .   .   .

Progress Notes—Friday A.M., Oct. 16, 1970—Downtown

9:00 NICK GOLOPAS—PCN 1,000,000 IM. #7. Three more and "Old Moneybags" is off my back. Won't have Mrs. Cooper give him the shot. Says Fran's husband, Sal, was picked up last night, armed robbery, candy store, sixty-three-year-old lady owner claims rape. He wasn't booked for some reason. They're watching him—bigger things (?). Nice guy.

Fran late. Mixed up with Sal? Phone driving me berserk. Picked up a few. . .

Tele-Memos: √ Patient didn't give name. Thought it was Service.
                     Call back when Fran gets in.
                  √ Patient exalted. Trying to talk to me for days.". . .
                     About that itch from my cat—"
                  √ Patient shocked. "Is it you?" Wants to discuss
                     charges. Will call Fran.
                  √ "Doc, that you? Where's Legree? This is Hatfield,
                     can you make an appointment?"
                  √ "Doctor? Oh, never mind. . ."
                  √ "Sorry, wrong—is this Doctor? . ."
                  √ "Doctor? . ."

9:15 MEMO: From Frances Cooper—
I *am* sorry, but there are a lot of bastards in the world. . .and
please, keep it moving. . . .

9:20 MARCIA HENRY—Wt#97—8 lb. loss. Better than expected. Too
thin. Says she *must* stay under a hundred. Looks like teaching
model you hang from skull. "Husband thinks I'm ravishing at
105. Now you know we can't fit more than twelve in the
station wagon."

9:25 CONSUELLA DOMINIQUE—Lumbo-sacral sprain. Looks like
a weight lifter. "Kid from the football team helps me with
the boxes, he said you could do it. I tried everything, plasters,
heat, liniment, gin." This gal is a rock. Bent a 23-gauge needle
in her lumbars. Threw my back getting her up. (Got to start
jogging again.)
". . .Sure I know how it happened. I run my own place and
had a busy weekend. I'm a funeral director. . . ."

MEMO: From Frances Cooper—
Dracula X-rayed. Took down her address. I may have business
for her.

9:40 RUDOLPH GARRONE—Sad. Cried the whole visit. B.P.
210/120 (up 50 from last night). P. 110. Lungs congested.
Guy could have a stroke right here. Sad. Doesn't look like he
would touch a turnip, let alone poor fifteen-year-old
Bernadette. "People are crazy, Doc. What is it with women,

Doc, when they get older they get crazy?" Says they want you to stay with them when they get older, ". . .and all they think *you're* thinkin' about all the time is their breasts and their privates, and all the time it's *them* what's thinkin'." Never touched Bernadette's privates, he says. They hooked him. Sad. "My own kind, they give us a bad name." Says he goes over there to play with her, makes her laugh. Makes his chest feel better. "They treat her like a prisoner. She never laughs. She looks like a bulldog, but I tell her she's pretty and she lets me rub her stomach 'cause you know how good it feels when someone rubs your stomach. And she likes me to lay in bed with her and feel her around. Well, the poor little kid got nobody who will play with her. Do you see any harm in this, Doc? You're my family doctor, and if I can't talk to you? . . .They say I done something to her. They screamed at me, and they swore, and my wife when I came home kicked me in the privates. I gave 'em a hundred and twenty-five dollars to shut them all up." (Make note—if Belotti pays $125, return to Garrone.)

9:50 <u>WILLIE   WASHINGTON</u>—Magnificent/pompous/frightened/ child. Says he feels great. Ripples like a cobra. Slapped his rt. latisimii, sprained my left pollices, be a week healing. B.P. 120/80 Ht & lungs OK. Reflexes neg. Eyegrounds neg. ENT neg. Neuro neg. X rays neg. Clean as a textbook. Awful pressure in the center of *my* skull. Why do I love him? Black is beautiful. Willie hugs me. I'm his boy. "You're up tight, Doc. Gotta play, gotta go to State and get away. Gotta, Doc, gotta. . . ."

10:00 <u>SUSAN LEADER</u>—Trouble. Read it every time. "Anything can be done," she says. Looks like she's done it. Missed period 3 months. *"He* didn't send me, that's for sure. He won't let McGibbon lie the girls down when they come in with cramps. Has 'em run around the track." This is suicide stuff. Hers or Leader's? "If he ever finds out," she says, "he'll scream foul. It wasn't foul, it was the fairest of fair. The boy wants to marry me." Can hear Leader switching on the command station asking for volunteer confessions. . . .

10:10 <u>GUNTHER HABER</u>—Wt 210 P. 84 Hrt. & lungs neg. Wants vasectomy (dig out lab report). "Is this gonna hurt?" The big ox looks like he's going to cry. "I get swollen balls I'll clobber you." Wife can't take pills. Pregnant every year. "Eleven years, nine kids. Jesus, Mary, and Joseph. I don't understand, Doc, I get plenty stuff around town, never got one knocked up. The wife, every goddam year." I told him to go home, he nearly hit me. "What the hell you *mean* the laboratory says I ain't got no sperm?"

10:20 <u>DOROTHY SARGENT</u>—Second drippy sinus visit this year. "No wonder you doctors get rich. Which room did I build? . . ."

10:35 <u>JOHNNY ORANGE</u>—Musician. Green pants, red *blouse*, orange shoes. "Always wear orange shoes, Doc. Otherwise, who will know it's Johnny Orange." Phew. PCN 1,000,000 U. IM. "Hey, look, Doc, word gets out to the boys, this could *ruin* me. There was this party after the show, I must have gotten looped. Must have, sure as hell wouldn't be caught by my worst friend in *her* house." Slide shows intracellur diplococcus. Loaded. "Burns like hell." I'm sure it does. (Make note to remind Tom about Pop's cranberry-juice cure). "Hey, look, Doc, any of the boys come around, I haven't even *been* here. The worst part of it is, I hear she's a lesby. . . ."

Tele Note—Clara called. Says it is a *dire* emergency. Says the baby is doing it *right* now, right in front of her. "Like a well-paid prostitute, giggling, laughing out *loud*. *Playing* with herself, Doctor." Clara says she'll wrap her up and bring her right over. "You know my great grandmother was an out-and-out admitted Lesbian?" . . .

10:45 <u>STEVEN PORCHOW</u>—I don't believe it. 526 lbs. Can't weigh him. "Last time I got weighed was at the Philadelphia Market on one of the truck scales. Five twenty-six, an ounce or two off one way or another. I had my clothes on, don't forget. Shoes must weigh three pounds alone." Been to eight doctors, "All quacks." Three specialists at $25 per. Got the regular tool case full of pills. Ate them like candy, gained regularly. "I feel it around my waist when I gain. I'm like you, it all goes to my belly." No pressure, no heart or lung sounds. Can't hear a thing. "Nobody does. Can't even weigh me. They used to tie hammers on the scales to try to balance me. I broke the floor in one guy's place. You wanna try your luck, Doc? I hear you got guts." Laughed so hard he split his pants and broke my side chair. Said he was going to sue. (Make note to check malpractice with Jerry, or is it Larry?)

10:55 <u>MATILDA EDISON</u>—Health nut. Gotta be. Looks sunflower-seed gray, sunken eyes, underweight, handshake like a steel trap. "It isn't that there aren't any good doctors in Ocean City, but I was told by my sister's landlady if you want a real doctor, go to Dr. Shoemaker. If he can't help you, he won't hurt you. (Make note to hurt somebody and spread the word around.) "Most doctors just don't have time for me. While I talk to them they are usually scribbling notes, and between phone calls and conferences in some back room and nurses' buzzes they manage to listen to my heart and one or two have taken my blood pressure." Most doctors lose interest when she compounds her good health. Allowed her a full five minutes on raw nuts, molasses, chickpeas, and garlic juice. Also a three-minute dissertation on why they have no hospital insurance, Blue Cross, or Blue Shield. Wants no shots or medicine. Wants me to be her family doctor. I said what for? She said just be there. (Make note: There is a key here.)

11:10 <u>CYNTHIA ALMA HOLLOWAY</u>—(Willie's married sister). Un-like lean and smooth Willie, she's round and bumpy, a studded snow tire. "Willie says you take care of Cynthia Alma from the day she is born and we got a international beauty queen in eighteen years." Baby looks like the spare in the trunk, studs, et al. "She's an angel. Never had one like her. Number six and it's as easy as breathin'. Sleeps, pisses, eats, and shits." Explicit. Second look, she's beautiful. Xct health, good wind, great swimmer coming up: "Don't waste your valuable time on this one, you're a busy man, but you gonna pierce her ears today? . . ."

MEMO: From Frances Cooper—
Laurie Lee called to tell you all the kids are blowing green bubbles from their noses. Don't order anything—she'll use up what she has around. Sweet husband went hunting. I'll give him Sal's address. If he can shoot as straight out of bed, he's hired.

11:25 <u>KATHERINE AULTMAN</u>—Wt #163. BP 110/75. Hrt. & lungs OK. Feels lousy. Gained 6 lbs. Wants answers. She brought a two-page list of questions. I played emergency game with Fran at top of her second page. She told Fran she'd leave list and I could mail her the answers.

11:35 <u>ANN HAWKINS</u>—Wheezing worse. Lungs wet. Sinuses juicy. Hrt. sounds poor. BP 165/95. Wt. 123. Explained to her she was on the border of emphysema. Showed her the hardened alveoli in her chest film. Showed a compar. of a clean plate and a dirty one. One year at most she'll be breathless invalid. "I got to smoke. If I quit I'll gain weight. My husband runs around enough with little nympho 100-pounders." What's more important? "I'll take my chances. . . ."

Tele. memo—Call from Marvin. Good morning, he said, this is Marvin, your corner light in the window, coming to you over an intricate device of a monopolized network of hidden wires. His complaint was (complaint #0073006) Mrs. Cardowski says I am a no-good doctor because I wouldn't renew her prescription over the phone and don't I know what a bad cold the baby has. "You are in league with a bunch of money-grabbers," she told him. "For your further info," he told me, "she has had this Rx renewed four times over the telephone by four of your non-money-grabber colleagues." His problem was, does he or does he not unsmurch my name? (Make note to look up medical ethics and malpractice regulations on tele. Rxing for pts. not seen within a two-year span.)

11:50 <u>MARIE CONNELLY</u>—Urgent. Total verbatim: "I want to explain why I am here tonight. For one thing, I don't like doctors. They are all arrogant, bossy, unmindful of our true needs, economically and morally selfish, shockingly inept, ungrateful, and above all, intellectually stagnant."
      That would be enough but there is more.
"I have been to four doctors in the past year, and each in turn has disillusioned me to the point of active nausea. My complaint is simple [sic]. I have a headache. You would think American medicine with the scientific acumen to transplant

one kidney from body to body, with the ability to ascend into space, you would think the medicine working man behind the leather-ingrained [sic] desk could come to a curative conclusion on a little throb behind the rim of my eyes. Doctor number one gave me codeine and I flew, but the headaches stayed. Doctor number two gave me speckled aspirins with a fancy name, and I got a bellyache along with the headache. Doctor number three shot me full of hormones, and for each headache a nosegay of hair grew over my lip. And Doctor number four gave me shots of pink vitamins for which I gained eleven pounds and the head has never been worse. And you are number five."

Apparently she is much improved with me.

"I must say you should wear a button because you do try harder. You probed, and picked, and X-rayed, and washed out sinuses, and flushed out bowels, and emptied my uterus and changed my contact lenses, and talked to a Dr. Lem about me. But until last Tuesday at 7:30 P.M. the headache persisted unmercifully as if in laughter to your pummeling. Now at 7:35 on this same Tuesday, I miraculously lost the pain, and to this moment it remains among the missing. I only came for my visit this morning to so advise you, Doctor, that you may *act* wiser than the first four, but you are an equal imbecile. Last Tuesday at 7:30 I visited a chiropractor. . . ."

11:55 SONNY JAY—Pothead. "Don't knock it, Doc. Remember the constipation? A whole year, now every damn morning like punchin' a clock. Remember I couldn't get it up? A whole year, now I can't get enough. Remember the headaches? A whole year, now clean as a virgin nipple." (Make note to try pot, chiropractor, or virgin nipple.)

12:05 EVERETT WASHINGTON—(Willie's brother). "Just tired. Just all-out tired." Like Willie is all-out dynamo, he is all-out dredge. BP 80/60. Hrt. sounds weak. Mitral regurg. Moderately jaundiced. Reflexes sluggish. Splenomegaly. Hepatomegaly. Lab reports in: RBC's 2 mill. Hb 8 gm. Retic. 40%. WBC 23,500. Ser. Bil. 12.4. ESR 22. Crescentriced cells w/sickling effect. Poso. sickle cell anemia. "I'm only twelve now, but I got a great arm. You wanna see me throw? I threw Willie a twenty-two-yard pass just last night. Wore me out but he caught it, and man was he gone. I'm gonna be better'n Willie when I get into high school. And, man, he is great. He's goin' to State College. That's where I'm goin', man, what a way to go—gotta go—gotta. . . ." (Have Fran make *immed.* appt. w/Art Brookfield at Eastern. Gotta, gotta. . .)

12:20 <u>JOAN MCKAY</u>—Advice for friend. "You see this friend of mine, well, she's afraid of doctors. She works with me you see, and I told her I heard about you and that you were OK and would do a girl a favor." This one doesn't read like that. "No, it's not sex or anything like that. You see it's hard for me to understand, because I don't have any problems." Husband's a doll. Brings home his whole paycheck. Children are angels. Mother-in-law sweet. Job perfect, life is beautiful. "But this girl, see, her husband runs around and see, she picks her face, all the time, see, and it bleeds and gets infected. It looks terrible and the boss says he will fire her if she don't clean it up." Works in candy, wants salve, husband doesn't bring home money, and she needs job. Cries a lot when husband runs. "If you could give me something for her, like for her nerves, boy is she a mess. Sometimes I guess people don't know how lucky they are. . . ."

MEMO: From Frances Cooper—
What the devil does that girl do to her face? It looks like scratched shredded wheat. . . .

　　Well, ol' Doc, you made it. Want me to call off your house calls? None of them are even important—take a nap. Don't check me—I feel *great*. Whatever was in that pill you gave me, I'll take home a barrel. Sorry I was late, and also a sonofabitch, but Sal met me at the bus and I nearly threw him under the wheels. But you know, he called a while ago and whatever he said sounded good. How come? Who knows? But he's lonely, the poor guy, and I'm lonely, so what else is there? He says maybe—you know—give it a try—who knows? You want to borrow one of my pills? . . .

　　Got memos on all the shots & stuff I gave. Myra Sacks here with your lunch—Bye. .

12:45 <u>MYRA SACKS</u>—"Don't start with me, I'm no patient. Eat

your *fahcockta* corn beef with white bread, you think you'll
live as long as me?" Myra left Sam in the middle of a
businessman's lunch. She is sick. "Don't start with me." B.P.
220/115. Hrt. sounds arrhythmic. Long, low-pitched diast.
murmur. Maximal Int. left sternal border. Blowing rough aorta
systolic murmur. Aortic insufficiency? Myra Sacks, syphillitic?
Mazel tov, Sam, you lived dangerously. "You started with
me—so, finish. It hurts. Every time I pick up a case of milk it
hurts." So? "I couldn't let *him* pick it up, with his truss. All
you doctors, looking for business." Explained to Myra the
thin-walled balloon she was carrying around inside her chest
and outlined a program of future treatment. She listened
intently and said, "Give me a shot of penicillin and let me go
home." (Make note to talk to Sam when he comes up
Monday.)

· ·

Hospital Notes

fternoon

2:00 Monahan, the parking attendant, wants to know when I'm
going to trade up. I told him, when I get the message. He said
his shoulder hurt.

2:05 Kiley, the OB nurse, sold me a ticket to the Halloween Ball.
Said I didn't have to go if I didn't feel up to it. (Make note
to look into sun lamp.)

Hollman, the surgical scrub, wants to be last patient. Doesn't
matter, eleven, twelve. Long talk about *him* again. Anything
new for ocular hematomas?

Ainsworth, the medical nurse, wants husband Joe's workman's
comp. forms. No checks in three weeks. Arm still hurts.
Wants him to slip in tonight for a quick shot.

Carr, daytime supervisor, reminded me when it was Albertson,
me, and her against the whole damn hospital. Can't be fifteen
years. Damn. "I had six nurses, you must've had six hands."
Stitch a little head, pull out a little baby, pound a little chest,
open a bag of pus, wrap a little finger, write a hundred charts.
"Now I've got seventy-three nurses, twelve interns, nine

residents, a traffic jam in the halls with practicals and ladies' aides, and candystripers, and I can't get a day's work done. What do you think's going to happen to medicine when we old folk die off?" Her sinuses are still blocked.

2:20 REBA GOLD—Rm. 220—Bed #2—A.D.—Dysparunia.
Called me sonofabitch for coming an hour early. Didn't even get on her wiglet. Didn't want me to look at her. Complaint: Nobody kissed her today. Interns, doctors, et al., stayed away. Feels there is a nurse conspiracy. Warned me they are jealous and not to believe a word they say. Plans to call a staff meeting and straighten it out. Made big error—forgot to examine incision. I don't love her anymore. Get her out of this hellhole. Her husband is home dying for her. Exit. "Hey, don't go, you didn't kiss me. . . ."

(Note to call husband. No sex for six weeks. Call pharmacist for tranquilizer—for him.)

2:30 GENEVIEVE LOWREY—Rm. 242—A.D. lung tumor.
Looks tired. Bronchoscope positive. Schedule Surg. Mon. Says how come they won't let her smoke, afraid it might give her cancer? Wants action. "Don't mess me up, Doctor. Cut it out, get me back to the pinochle game. The girls are holding a special prayer meeting. I told them, don't pray, keep up your Blue Cross. . . ."

(Talked with family. Explained full picture. Total encroachment of oesophagus and entire left bronchus. She may not make it. They understand. I don't.)

2:50 MALDEN R. HASSINGER—Rm. #250—A.D. Incisional hernia.
Intractable hiccoughs. Incision ripping. "Where the—hic—hell you—hic—been? I told them—hic—surgeons, if they want to find out how to cure—hic—me, to call my—hic—doctor. Big surgeons—hic—they can't even stop these god—hic—damned hiccoughs." Says come on, Doc, wave your old magic wand. Ready to stop when I say the word. I said WORD!—never stopped.

(Order consult for phrenectomy and two ounces of Irish whiskey every 4 hours.)

3:10 Meeting with Karl Kleinert, Administrator GMH.
How good I dropped by. Look prosperous. Why not? Very
deserving I am. All the boys look prosperous. Why not?
"Don't they deserve it? Don't they all have the rights and
God-given graces for the oft-thankless tasks they perform to
be prosperous? Of course they do. And your prosperity
reflects upon us here at Greenville Mercy Hospital, and we
bask in the light of your success. Where would each of us be
if it were not for the other?" He remembers when it was me
and Albertson and him against the whole hospital. "What a
fine job we did together. Fifteen years, how time flies, as I
always say. And as it flies, it catches up the particles of life in
its hands and molds the lives we are to live in its circle of
minutes. This is what I always say. How grateful we should be
in looking back and *erahna, erahna, erahna, erahna* . . .and
now in our fifteenth year together, we can humbly see the
stupidity, nay selfishness, of those who attempt to rob us of
our birthright—yours to be a staff member in good standing,
ours to be the only general hospital in Greenville. Let us
renew our pledge made fifteen years ago—and made each new
year—that our allegiance to each other shall remain indivisible,
with liberty and medical justice for all." The word was out.
Make note to cue in Kohn, et al. Kleinert means business. All
renegades are without staff privileges as of Jan. 1. ". . .Drop
by any time, John, onward, upward, into the Golden Jubilee
year of Greenville Mercy—and remember me to Mary and
those four needy children. . . ."

. . . .

House-Call Notes

3:45 LAURIE LEE—A mess. House filthy, kids snotty, smell of
garbage. Dog fighting, Laurie reading. "What's gamma globulin, doctor? Shouldn't my kids get gamma globulin? It could
have saved the baby. It says so in *Redbook.*" (Make note to
ask Mary what it said in *Redbook.*) "How about her antibody
titre? Did you do a titre? Did she have a sweat test or a
spinal tap? Electrophoresis?" Examined kids, all sick with
inner rot. What to prescribe? Euthanasia? Vasectomy? "I was
up all night listening to them breathe. Once Andy stopped
breathing and I blew air into his mouth. Then Kathy coughed

and it sounded like inside an empty barrel, and I ran and dialed your number. You know you can't get you after midnight? The girl said she would try if it were an emergency. What else at two in the morning? I said the hell with you, let them all die in their cribs. Doctor, when you get a heart attack at two some early morning, try calling your friend's number from the telephone book—if you live that long. . . ."

. . . .

4:15 <u>ELIZABETH STONE</u>—Not home. Discharged from hosp. 3 days.
Post-hyster. Kids said she had a beauty parlor appointment.

. . . .

4:30 <u>ARTHUR CARPENTER</u>—Willie's uncle. Amputee. Blood Sugar 328.
Warned him about losing other leg. Warned me 'bout losing Willie.

. . . .

5:00 <u>RUDOLPH AMSTATT</u>—County jail. Knifed wife dying of cancer. Police officer says he was found carving body into geometric figures. No resistance. Exam. Xct. hlth. Neuro-intact. Apparently stable. Sign commitment papers. "I am as sane as you are, Doctor, when you cut away a *piece* of the malignancy. Why don't you come away with me?"

. . . .

Progress Notes—Friday P.M., Oct. 16, 1970—Downtown

6:00 —Service Calls
√ Mrs. Carpenter—Mrs. Lowrey's daughter. Wants to know if she can bring her cigarettes.
√ Clara—She says you know Clara who. Lisa is flushed and do you want her to wrap her up and bring her right over?
√ Raymond Cardone—Phila. call. Mr. Jacardi's lawyer. Wants you to be alerted for trial date Tuesday.
√ Mr. Stevenson—New pt. Wants to know if you specialize in general practice.
√ Laurie Lee—Says after you left, all the children started vomiting.

√ Mrs. Podalsky—Your nurse's mother. Says that it's urgent. Daughter went to shore with husband. Tried to get you but you were en route. Should have phone in car.

√ Sam Sacks—Says thank you. Myra took the day off. Says it's better than any medicine—for him.

6:30 Memo from Georgia:

Notice you do not have on a happy face. My Momma used to say about my Daddy—if the old goat has a worn tire at seven, look out for a blowout at eleven. Six to start. Three no appts., incl. Belotti with father & son. You want to get the blowout over with right off? Charge *all three* of them, you hear. . . .

6:35 MARIE BELOTTI—Frightening. She says I signed an oath and I cannot be a hypocrite. Slips the $124 in my pocket and says, "You gotta see me. A lousy hundred and twenty-four dollars. You piss away twice this on a weekend between gas for cars and whiskey for your belly. Big doctor needs my little money. OK, work for it." Wants weight control. Fat as a pig, belly like a sewer bottom. "Give me a *couple* bottles of pills and don't be so cheap, fill them up to the top. And my back is killing me, give me a bottle of pills for that. No prescriptions, you got plenty samples for your friends. And give me some of that oil your old man left you with for my hair. He made stuff like in the old country. Big doctors, all you know is money. Give me two bottles, don't be so stingy." She'll be back each week. Now for Poppa. Looks like a picture out of a Fellini movie. "Give him some hormones or something. Damn old pig sits all day in the rocking chair on the beach and plays with himself. Fill up the bottle!" And Mario, sweet Mario, looks like a leftover from the St. Valentine's Day Massacre. "Look at his mouth. He had a fight in school. He called a kid a smart Jew, and the kid was a tough wop. You give him a *full* examination. We got time. . and don't go writing on your card three visits, this is *one* visit—doctors are the cheapest. . . ."

Memo from Georgia:
You marked only two visits. .

7:00　<u>KEVIN KEITH</u>—Freshman football. Little kid. How did I ever pass him? Looks like he would disappear into the turf. "It just hurts at the tip of the spine. Nothing broken, is it, Doc?" The old college try. Says when he falls they all sit on him and if he cries, he gets the razzes. "It's only a bruise, huh, Doc? I can keep playing? I played all last year in the midget league with a broken finger. Only me and my Pop knew. And I played last month with a sprained ankle. Pop says a kid shouldn't get hurt if he's smart." Clint Keith, all-state tackle, 1948. Now Keith's Super Transmission Center, East Greenville, "He says he played six years and never saw a doctor once. The coach says I got to see you, but I'm not hurt, huh, Doc? Pop takes the afternoon off to see me play—please, even if it *is* broken. . . ."

7:10　<u>CYNTHIA BOARDMAN</u>—Sweet. White, long, straight, Wasp hair. 15/16. Uncomfortable. Mother: "We have our little spats, but Cynthia has come to regard me as her real mother, and she and I do talk but we do agree that some professional advice is in order." Mother died 3 yrs. Fthr. remar. 2 yrs. Ran away once. Slit wrists twice. "It's her menses. You know, even though we do speak on an adult level about these very private things, we do agree that some professional advice is in order." Last menst. period, 3 months. Menarche age 11. Dur. 5 days. Cycle 29. "We do agree, Cynthia and I, that missing a period at her young emotional age is quite normal. But Cynthia seems to feel that I have not placed sufficient emphasis on what is actually happening." When asked, Cynthia seems to feel that it is not an emotionally missed period, but Cynthia seems to feel she is pregnant. . . .

7:20　<u>ALBERT BROWNLEE</u>—The kid with "no problems." Turns out it's Susan Leader. Yesterday, sullen; today, hateful. "He's a real bastard. They got wardens at State Pen with more feeling. He's a phoney and she knows it. She wants to walk through his halls pregnant, but she knows he'd kill her first." Wants a sure cure. Said I didn't know of any. He knew a guy, but it costs plenty. "How about *you*, Doc?" Said I didn't know how. (Head pounding.) "Hell, Doc, don't you feel bad for her? Me, I don't count, but don't you feel bad? You know this old man of hers. You're a doctor. You always have to live by a book? Don't you ever want to break out of jail, Doc, and just do something that's right 'cause it's right, and the hell with the book? . . ."

7:30 OSKAR & KARLA RUDOLPH—Virus, both. Temp 101.2°, both. Tonsils infected, both. Harsh lung sounds, both. He wants a shot of penicillin. She says, "Whatever you give him, give me. I use his glasses."

Memo from Georgia:
Backed up into the hall. Would you like to come out and have them stare at you? Call on line one. Line two ringing. . .

Tele. call: Joanne Wells, Laurie Lee's sister. Four kids all down with something. Coughing, sneezing, snotty. Baby croupy. "Like Laurie's kid before she died, y'know." Doctor's on vacation or gave them up. Wants call after hours. "Anytime, I don't care. . .oh, oh, hold one. . .never mind, Doc, one of the kids just ran through the storm door and he's bleeding all over. I'll take the whole gang to the hospital. . . ."

Tele. call: "Come quick, Doc, we must be poisoned." Death rattle, so help me. Says kids are rolling on the floor. "Belly feels like fireballs." Mushroom soup from grandma's. "Hurry, Doctor—oh, this is Mrs. Harrigan, you don't know us. We live—oh, no—doctorrrrrr—"

7:40 BEATRICE FAIRLEE—"You sent them all to Mercy Hospital? Good luck, I warn you, whatever you find wrong with me, *you* are taking care of right here in this office, even if it's a hysterectomy. I'll squat down on your bathroom floor." R.N. GMH 15 yrs.

8:00 CAROLINE JOHNSON—and kids. "I started out for your office by myself, think I could do it?" Bunny says she's tired. Bertie says his throat hurts. Bugsy says his stomach hurts. "What'sa matter, Bugsy, you feel like throwing up? Here, here, baby, into Momma's handkerchief—no, not in the doctor's sink where he sterilizes." Six hot dogs in whole pieces. "Can I dump this into your sink, Doctor? It was clean hot dogs." Check Bunny. Eats junk. Ten-year-old shell. Anemic. "Is she anemic? You know she's ten, and I told her it could happen any time. Bunny, you feel your period might be coming on?" Check Bertie. "We can't get near him, his breath knocks us over. He's only a child. My dog had the same thing, we took out his tonsils." Decaying hypertrophic tonsilitis. "How much will it cost? The vet charges thirty-five dollars." Bugsy throws up on desk. Charles, the husband, reads comic book. Mother forgets why she is there. "Bunny, you feel sick too? It's not your period? Bertie, you look green, you have to vomit? How many times I told you not to use that vulgar word—oh, dear, that's why I came. I feel sick myself. Your sink? . . ."

Memo from Georgia:
Momma had this problem with Poppa when he came home from the butcher shop, but this is a doozy. It's like they were all boiled in a vat of skunk. Take calls in back, I'll spray something around. Mind if it smells a little whorey?

Tele call: Friend of Dr. Kohn? "It is difficult getting through to the doctors. I'll be brief. I am working for the County Hadassah, and we are preparing our annual Charity Ball souvenir book. . . ."

Tele. call: Clara! "Fooled you, didn't I, Doctor? This is Clara. I'm at my neighbor's house and used her number." Urgent. Neighbor child age twelve babysits Lisa. "Never for more than a few minutes." Urgent. "Neighbor just told me her daughter got her first period today, and I have to go out marketing tonight and so I'm wondering if there is anything catching. . ."

8:20 <u>BERTHA SCHMITZ</u>—OB. GR I; Para 0-0-0-0; BP 145/85. Hrt. & lungs neg. FHB 140. Fundas 3 fingers above unbilicus. Term. Wt #235. "How come you let me gain ninety pounds? Don't you know better than to let me gain ninety pounds? My girl friends all go to obstetricians and they don't gain ninety pounds." Explain to her that her girl friends don't eat six meals a day and sit on their fat cans drowning in chocolate and beer. Explain to her like nine times before there will be a price to pay. "You're right," she says. "My husband says we have any trouble with this delivery, we could sue you. . . ."

8:30 <u>SHIRLEY RENLO</u>—Embarrassed to just call. Made a visit of it. Needs tranquilizer for X-country trip. "Dog's a poor traveler. . ."

8:35 <u>STANLEY STRAHER</u>—Caught finger in door last Thursday. No damage. Needs forms filled in. "Got one for *Inquirer*, and one for the *Bulletin*. Hell, I been payin' for three years." One for Milwaukee General. "They like theirs in triplicate." Workmen's Comp card. Shipyard local. "Just mark me a note dated Nov. first. I'm going down to visit the folks in Miami. Take your time, I'm in no rush. . . ."

8:45 <u>HELEN HARPER</u>—Wants brief $\sqrt{}$-up & Rx. Brought bag of pills. Old doctor left for service. War is hell? "Some of the labels washed off, and I switched bottles so I could carry them to work. I'll just spread them out on your desk and you can just give me new prescriptions. You don't have to waste your time examining me, God bless you, you are *so* busy. . . ."

8:55 <u>ANDREW & CAROLYNNE WHITMAN</u>—As it happened:
—Andrew, you go first.
—No, dear, age before beauty.
—Andrew has a keen sense of humor.
—From living with a sharp-tongued girl for thirty years.
—We feel, doctor, because of our age, actually Andrew's age. . .
—You're a child, dear.
—He is so kind—we feel we are, well, advancing a bit in years and tend to overindulge, probably rich foods, a cocktail or two—
—Or three, or four, or five, dear.
—He is humorous. Well, at any rate, we are both aware of the need for diet and weight control. . .
—She listens to Jeremiah Crumple's show every day and he puts the damndest ideas in her head. Damned woman's been giving me dried figs till they're coming out of my ears.
—Doesn't he have a rich sense of humor? I felt with all our drinking, we'd best have some added enriched foods.
—I haven't caught up with you yet, darling.
—So, we have decided to put ourselves in your hands, being actively interested in building young bodies, we feel a vitalizing program from you——

—What she means, Doc, is—we both drink too damn much, and screw too damn little, and what the hell can you do about it? . . .

9:10 OLIVER LARK—"I just want them removed, that's all. There's no pain and no bleeding, but they are there. And I read where hemorrhoids interfere with your sex life. . . ."

9:15 CALVIN HARDENBERG—"It's just me and the wife, and our bachelor son, he's a A&P manager, he worked himself up from a fruit clerk in eight years. He's a nice boy. We're all suffering from the same thing, so I came and you can examine me and tell me what we can all do. . . ."

Tele. call: Marvin. *Stat* call. How come I didn't cue him in on Willie? "Now make your diagnosis more accurate. Is he or ain't he playing? I got two dollars riding on this. I don't have that kind of stuff to throw around. I got no corral to keep the restless cattle. Sounds like a rustling stampede going up those stairs. Are you sure you know what you're doing? If you miss on Willie, what about Susie or Jimmy—or *Marvin*? Don't let me disturb your evening, but let the words of that sage and flower of the mortar and pestle, Marvin the Unbeliever, ring hollow through your jammed waiting room tonight—it is better to have saved a bundle, than never to have saved a life at all. . . ."

9:25 SIDNEY KATZ—(Millie's son). Age 19. College, home for weekend. Wracked up car. "Hell, no, my old folks knew I was here they'd ground me for a month. All you got to do to get their bowels loose is say 'money.' You know my old lady, is she forty if she's a day? Dresses in hippie boots and wears her hair down to her navel so I can feel like I belong when I come home. Old Daniel just got a toupee makes him look like Tony Curtis' grandfather. If they hear I wracked up, I'm in Vietnam." Kid is a dealer. Trading a piece of land in Mexico for his Cadillac, going to grow pot. "And I hadda go wrack it up yesterday." Whiplash, legit. Kid'll collect a million in insurance. "Hey, Doc, this thing keep me out of the Army? My marks stink. One more semester I'm on my way. Hell, I got qualities to be somebody. I could be a doctor. What's it take to be a doctor? I don't have to go to Harvard. Some back-door school, what the hell, who reads your diploma? Write me a letter, Doc, you got your son in." Told him I would discuss it with his father. Being a doctor somehow starts there. "Thanks, Mr. Shoemaker. . ."

9:35 <u>ALBERT GOODFELLOW</u>—Looks better. No attacks 4 weeks. Working dishW. Another chance and he'd be a white Willie. Great body. "I'm gonna make it, Doctor. With God's help and you I'm gonna make it." Happiness is hope. "I got the guitar. Skipped lunch for a month, but it's all electric with chromium and leather things. I can follow along with most of the country-music shows now. I can really whomp it up between nine and four when the other boarders are out. I do as good as them dirty hippie kids. I got inner qualities none but you and Oliver know about."

BP 125/80. Hrt. & lungs neg. Eye grounds neg. Reflexes neg. Big change. Stay w/new medicine. "I wrote words for some of my songs, makes me cry when I sing 'em. You're the only one I ever said that to except Oliver, and sometimes I wonder if he's really listening." Roommate, supports him. Good? Bad? "He don't ask much of me, but he gets awful mad if I say I'm going to leave here and head down to the Gulf and see where I can hit it. We lay awake in bed and I talk to him about what I once was before I met you. He cries when I tell him how they used to beat me when I got the spittin' fits. They wanted to put me in a nut house. It's a funny thing about Oliver, when he cries he wants to hold me, and I don't know, but he says it's all right, if he holds me, and he's been good to me, so I let him. But it's a funny thing I'm gettin' to notice, whenever I go into one of my spasms and pass out, I get so disgusted when I wake up, I've been playin' with myself. And this is happening more and more when Oliver holds me." Wants meds for Oliver so he won't have to hold him or maybe leave him. "You see, Dr. Shoemaker, you're the only one I really love. . . ."

Tele. call: Hospital. Larkin/intern. Mushroom family—3 dead. "Blown up like toy balloons. Baby only about a year so she didn't get much. Called in Ped. resident and he's handling her for you. Know all about you busy G.P.'s. This other kid who went through the storm door, no sweat, ten years from now when he gets sliced apart by the Vietcong, no one will notice the forty-two stitches across his forehead. . . ."

Memo:

Albert has epileptic attack in W.R. Ogling Georgia, he touched her hair, and went into chicken-with-throat-slit dance. Cleared W.R. of standees. Georgia sprayed whorey stuff.

10:00 <u>ARNOLD SALZBURG</u>—WEC Exec. SOS. "Your system stinks, Shoemaker. Anyone running a business this way would be out in the street in a month. My appointment—whatever *that* is—was for 8:45. I was here at 8:40 and there were five ahead of me. Now, please, Shoemaker." WEC calculator would solve it, he says. I say the only thing that will solve it will be less sickness. He says WEC Executive here one week would make me shape up or ship out. Someone can't make it in our business, then look around for a new line, boy. "I counted eleven people in and out while I waited. Now that's more than you can see *honestly* in an entire day." I say when does WEC start its subsidy system. He says if it's money, boy, raise your fees, see less, give more. If I'm going to entrust my family's life to you—" B.P. 155/90. Says how come. That's only 3 less than last week. Only fifteen in two months. That's less than 2 points a wk. Got to be faster. Call in help. Don't hog. See less, charge more. (Note—Georgia says he complained about bill. One visit overextended—chg. $7 instead of $6—said he'd bring it to Med. Griev. Com.) "Speaking of service, where you going to be this weekend? Hunting, fishing, golfing, or some such Christian endeavor you doctors do while my wife and kids might just as well die? Now if you're being given the responsibility of our family and you are our family physician, I want to know where you are at all times. A WEC System will do that for your patients." (TOM!) "So, just give me your home number if you expect to be our family doctor." Wants a gynecologist's number for wife's odor, dermatologist's number for kid's rash. Wants an otolaryngologist number to pierce daughter's ears. "I think that about clears it up." Comforts him to know he can get me pronto 3 A.M. Man's need for confidence in a doctor is imperative in this rat-infested world. "If, therefore, you can supply us with that real old-fashioned warm friendly medicine, we want you as our family doctor. . . ."

10:30 Wrap up. Georgia says we made it an hour early thanks to
Albert. Twenty-two tonight. Forty-four dollars. Avg. 2 each.
Doesn't that grab you? Can't say it wasn't fun. Fran called
from shore. Georgia working a.m. in place. Wants to go to
football game—rah, rah. Is he or ain't he playing?

He is playing. *He is, he is, he is. . .*

. . . .

. . .And then, Tom, in comes Harry Steele and the gun in the
belly and click, click, click, a dissolving lifetime—and this
is where you came in, Tom, this is where you came in. . . .

It is now five of twelve—just about Saturday, the day
it all seems to be heading for. I get up and I walk about the
semidarkened office, only the Gro-Lite from the fish tank
to shadow my steps through the asphalt-tiled halls. And I
thought how many thousands of nights have I walked these
musty doctor-smelly old halls, and felt the comforting chilly
warmth and breathed in the hangover odors of a day well
spent? In the total analysis of the day, it mattered only
passingly if one was lost, and one mislaid, and one stolen
away. It mattered briefly only in the total if one was ragged
and one was soiled and one was lavender and lace, if one
ran pus and one ran blood and another ran not at all. At
the day's end they all formed that masterful abstract
pattern splotched indelibly into the record book. As old
Sammy Sacks says, "a bei gesundt," as long as you are well
and have done your job honest, what else matters? This
was it: Wrap up your old bag, take one last look at the old
walls; sneak out the back and head home to your mother and
the horrors of her day.

But tonight, damn headache, it wouldn't come out that
way. Tonight for the first time in my life it came out what
Sam called "geharget"—smashed, garbaged. And I did
not want to wrap it up and saunter on home. If she tells
me tonight one more tale of woefulness where the kids don't
hang up their coats, or take out the trash, or leave their
glasses in the sink, or that she is pregnant, I think I would
just as well slice out her prattling tongue and let it join the
ear you're sending me—for all the good either is doing me.

So, what is it, Tom, my electronic doctor wizard? What
is it that makes tonight different from a thousand other

nights? They haven't invented the tubes yet that could come
up with the answer I came up with. Tubes are geniuses sealed
in glass, and what I came up with is stupid, stamped in
wood. Such self-analysis I really did not need, but need it
or not, like projectile vomiting, I found it there, spilling
all over me.

You went over the Xerox? It is there. Make it a game,
like we used to play: "Tonight is different from a thousand
other nights because. . . ." Complete this statement in
twenty-five words or less and you win a prize.

Someplace from Nick Golopas to Harry Steele, is the
answer. Marie Connelly, the one who told me I am an imbecile? Not really, I tried a chiropractor. . . .The Belotti
menagerie? Belottis are cured with Gelusil. Clara? Someday,
but not yet. Harry Steele? Funny, what I came up with is
more frightening than a gun in the belly.

Coach Bocca? Warm. Kleinert? Coming up fast. Leader?
Top contender. A final clue: Friendly nonpatient male—
Right, our old friend and neighbor, Marvin, the Joker.
Somehow, tonight, out of context or in, Marvin made no
big joke, but he made the mark. I will repeat the telephone
call from memory:

9:20– . . .Is he or ain't he? . . .Are you sure you know
what you are doing? If you miss on Willie. . .

The answer unavoidably is Willie Washington. You know
Willie, he is the one I chose when you were counted out
by an unimaginative mother, the one without whom Greenville High will never make it—and without whom there may
be race riots for the first time in Greenville's history. And
without whom your father may be—as you predicted, but
not why—finally counted out.

You see, I told myself, Willie is the final pure abstraction of all the cases that have passed through me—not only
Golopas to Steele, but File #1 to File #4478. Willie is the
standard-bearer of what is left of my rights to practice as a
G.P. What happens to him, happens to me. If I am right about
Willie, I can go on, and nothing, no matter how you spell it
out, will change me. If I am wrong about Willie, then the
whole structure of who I am collapses and I enter into the
limbo that you have painted for me.

Willie embodies the privileges and sanctions of my G.P.
mind. Here is a case: a seventeen-year-old boy, head bashed
in the third game of the season, out like a light for a full
three minutes. Then he arises (like all the Willies do) and he
demands his freedom. His coaches and his fans and his aunts
and his uncles and his poppa demand it, but little G.P. me
out on the field says no more play today. So, a week of
rest, X rays, neurological studies, etcetera and Willie is tip-
top like a bull. Absolutely no signs of distress, like he was
never hit—as I would expect from Willie. He can make Greenville High champion of the state, give himself a scholarship
and a life no one ever imagined for him, but the asinine
unrealistic G.P. school doctor says no. Now why? The X rays,
smooth and firm, sharp and clear, say yes. The eyegrounds
and the reflexes and the Arturo body say yes, and today, so
did the specialist neurosurgeon.

Pandemonium: The school is in an uproar, the hero is
returning unharmed. The poppa signs the release and tomorrow Willie plays ball.

But lo, where has the schnook G.P. gone? He is still
whispering no, but he is on the sidelines, not on the starting team this week. He stubbed his toe, but he still mumbles
no. Overwhelmed by authority, smothered in facts, he
continues with his no. Now tell me why.

Aye, now here is the rub. I say no—now get this—because
I feel something. This itty-bitty doctor feels something.
Foolish—but this is the way it is. This is the way it was when
Carla Gorbecki ran a subnormal temp and everyone said
faker and two days later she was dying with pneumonia.
This is the way it was when Harry Samuels had a normal
graph and Harry said I'm going back to work and I carried
Harry to the hospital where Harry threatened to sue and two
days later the graph showed a massive occlusion.

I have no right, you say, to practice such pseudomedicine?
Ah ha, but that is the right! The right and the plume of the
family doctor. To sense, to suspect, to feel. How in hell
can you expect an ivory-towered specialist to look into my
Willie's eyes and see what I see, feel what I feel? He feels
nothing, but I do, and by God, my way of life lives or dies on
that premise.

Tomorrow afternoon. . .

Tom, I'll finish this tomorrow. Right now I have to go
out on an emergency. A call just came in. Seems old
St. Nick Golopas has returned to the early scene of his
disease. He is a bit panicky. Seems his Trojan is caught in
his bed partner's posterior fornix and her husband gets
home at one. . . .Now tell me, son, what should I do here,
transfer the call to a gynecologist? . . .

.   .   .   .

SATURDAY

1970	OCTOBER				1970	
S	**M**	**T**	**W**	**T**	**F**	**S**
				1	2	3
4	5	6	7	8	9	10
11	12	13	14	15	16	17
18	19	20	21	22	23	24
25	26	27	28	29	30	31

17

OCT. 1970

SATURDAY, OCTOBER 17, 1970

• • • • • • • • • • • • • • • • • • • •

Morning

6:10 —Doctor, this is Service. Mrs. Dusharme just called, said her contractions are every four minutes and she's not waiting. . . .

6:40 —Dr. Shoemaker, this is Calloway, OB intern on duty MGH. Mrs. Dusharme was just admitted under your service. Contractions pretty strong, q.3 minutes, dilated 4-5 cm., station –1, bloody show, membranes intact. She's screaming for you. Coming over? . . .

7:05

```
┌─────────────────────────┐
│          N.J.           │
│         MDK885          │
│      GARDEN STATE       │
└─────────────────────────┘
```

Route 41

It was going to be an old-fashioned football Saturday. The sun stood ready to deliver the day. Early warmth beat into Johnny's eyes, lulling his chilled expectancy to the task ahead. (*But a task, never!*) Independent of Willie, a Saturday morning in October was wrought with enough raw nerve endings to activate psychiatrist Bloomquist's shock machine. This morning Johnny would have to settle for a 400 mgm Miltown, the only thing that didn't put him to sleep.

Several years ago he had a case with a quarterback. The kid had acute bronchial asthma, was better only when he played but worse after the game—worse to a point where he was often hospitalized for several days. But if he didn't play, he went into status asthmaticus from acute depression. The choice, naturally, was to let him play. One week the boy's father had died, and the decision to let him play was made by Johnny on Friday. On Saturday Johnny took a 10 mgm Librium when he awakened and a 25 mgm Benadryl before the game. They found him asleep on a bench in the locker room.

The Buick chugged along Route 41 and Johnny wondered if he or it would conk out first. Never should have gotten into the squeeze. Willie should not play and that is all there is to it. The muffler being ragged the way it was, it was convenient, Johnny could yell his head off and not be picked up as a public nuisance. So he often yelled in his Buick. *Never! Never! And Leader is a sonofabitch. And Bocca is a punch-drunk ass. And Willie is a beautiful boy.* They are going to kill him. *They* are? *I* am—He is all I have left and I am sacrificing him—for what?

Lem came to Johnny and said, "Jonathan, it is all right. Just press your thumbs up under the occipital bone and it will be all right. Willie is all right. Have confidence in your decision, Jonathan. You examined him, your X rays were negative. The neurosurgeon has removed any doubt. Everyone knows how upset you get on Saturday. And now you've got a job to do, a girl is screaming for you in the hospital. It will be all right, Jonathan. Believe me, have I ever led you wrong?"

All right. . .

7:15

GREENVILLE MERCY HOSPITAL
GREENVILLE, N. J.
DEPARTMENT OF OBSTETRICS   EMERGENCY PARKING

LABOR ROOMS—HOSPITAL PERSONNEL ONLY

—I'm Calloway, Doctor, OB intern. Do you deliver or do you want me to? I had two years as an extern in Philly and delivered six on my own. I used blades once, and I got it right the first time. The baby had only a little dent over the left ear. The mother figured it was a birthmark. I do midline episiotomys, never had a problem. The boys tell me you are very cooperative. You can get back to your office in time for morning hours, I'll call you when she's in stirrups.

No trouble at all. . .

—Ohhh, Dr. Shoemaker, Dr. Shoemaker, this is terrible, *terrible.* Dr. Lenihan never let me suffer like this. Please, I'm sorry, I don't want to compare, but these *pains.* I feel like my skin is ready to burst open. What did you explain to me about breathing? I forgot. I forgot everything you told me to do. Who can remember when these things grab you like an octopus? Ayyy—here's another, here's *another*—let me squeeze you, *squeeze* you. How can you breathe easy when it feels like it's coming out of your throat? This is for the natives in Africa, not for me. Dr. Lenihan would have had me under. Please, Dr. Shoemaker, forgive me. Am I in trouble? Tell me if I'm in trouble. I never had this trouble. Will you have to call a consultation? Ohhh, another. Aren't you going to give me *anything?* Ohhh, Dr. Lenihan. . .

Orders for Mrs. Dusharme
1. CBC—STS—Urine
2. Cleansing enema
3. Prep for delivery
4. Atarax 50 mgm IM Stat

Progress Notes:
This is a white female, age 28, Gravid 2—Para 1-0-0-1, admitted walking in active labor, contrac. q.3 min., strong. Exam: cerv. dil., admit 2 fingers, station- 1 membranes intact, transverse presentation. Sedative ordered. Consult considered.

—Calloway again, Doctor. Are you considering calling in Dr. Lenihan? I don't see why. I've seen them turn around and slip out in a matter of minutes. I'll watch over her, you go on back to your office where the action is. You won't need Lenihan. He gets them all after a while. Must be pretty discouraging to a G.P. to finally realize he doesn't do enough of anything to get to master one of them. . . .It sure bugs guys like me. I don't know what I'll do when I get out. I've been on this service three weeks and can't get my hands on one full delivery. You know, you actually have to shove the doctor aside to even touch the kid when it's coming out—just to see what it feels like, warm, you know.
What the hell am I going to do when I get through in July? People think you're an expert as soon as that shingle goes up. I'm scared shitless, to tell you the truth. I'll probably stay on for a residency, just to give me another few years to loosen up. Even then I hear some of the guys always run scared and send everything out, like traffic directors, never really sure of their own decisions.

How do you *know* when you know? Hell, I'm top dog when they wheel in the coronaries into the ER. I can pull out most anyone from an infarct. Never miss an IV. I diagnosed a Pheochromocytoma on a clinic case last week and old Grawtch bawled me out for that. Now that's bucking for top medicine, but what do you do when they have sinuses that drip poison and they never get better? And backaches that always ache? And eyes that are always crusty? And a stomach that is always sour, and cramps that get worse each month and no matter what you give, it never helps? Don't you want to get right back into school, or wish you were smarter, or someone else—or does it matter? You've been at it fifteen years. You got the answers? And how come I hear you're such a gungho G.P. and you're thinking of quitting and going into the new hospital to head up General Clinics? . . .

. . . .

8:15

Alexander Kohn, M.D.
—UROLOGY—

—Now suddenly you're anxious. I've been at you for five years, and now suddenly you got to know today. It can't be now. Monday night is the wrap-up meeting. It's either you or Harris. My money is on you, you know that, but who can tell. Do you still have those goalposts out in front of your office?

Alex Kohn was Johnny's long-time friend in the hospital. When he was an intern, Alex let Johnny peel out his first prostate, binding them together in some kind of professional camaraderie forever.

—Johnny, you look like hell. Drop your pants and just squat down, over the table. So the gang at the A. J. Clinic came up with the same thing I did. Took them six weeks and a hundred and ninety-three dollars and thirty cents. Well, serves you right. Phil Lehman did the same thing. All you G.P.'s are alike, and where do you run when you're sick? And don't give me the bullshit that Mary made the appointment. I told you six months ago either you're screwing too much or not enough. That's the whole thing with you soggy prostates. All right, bend, won't hurt a bit—

Johnny pulled up his pants and said he wasn't so anxious, it's just that he would like to know in case today he had to make some decisions.
—Don't worry, we want you, Johnny, we need your good non-Yiddish *cup,* and we need your money. Come February first we'll be digging dirt, and running business by this time next year. At your age, with your cholesterol, you need to deliver little babies? With your *feshtunkena* stomach lining you need those brats throwing up on your desk? You need coitis interruptus for some neurotic night call? *Be* anxious, screw the decisions. Come on, Johnny, you're forty-five years old and coming on weak to fifty. How much longer you think you can net thirty grand?
Johnny heard echoes of Larry—or Jerry—Albert. "You got four kids to see through college, one to marry off." It's a good thing I didn't marry Ilse Goldstein, Johnny remembered gratefully, or I'd be having Alex's headaches today. In a few hours he'll dump eight grand on his little Sammy's Bar Mitzvah.
—But at my gross I can make it. A year from now you could make it, too. Think about it, Johnny, tonight when you're full of my booze and dancing with some other guy's wife and the call comes in you're wanted in delivery. Think about next year: ten to four, three and half days a week, two weeks to Jamaica in the winter, three in the summer to wherever *goyim* go—Cape Cod or someplace. Weekends in New York, Caddies in the garage—anxious?
Anxious.
—All right, kid, depend upon me. For now, just zip up your pants and go out there and smile at the people. Me, I'm on my way to getting stoned. Today, my son, the thirteen-year-old doctor, is a man. . . .

". . .My son the doctor? His name is Lemuel S. Shoemaker. My other son, Jonathan here, I don't know what's going to be with him. Tell Mrs. Goldstein what you are going to be."
When he was thirteen, Jonathan, knew what he wasn't

going to be. Hells bells, the last thing I want to be is a doctor. *A doctor was somebody who smelled of ether and was caked under the fingernails with old blood and lived in the back of the office on bread his patients baked for him and on pot cheese from people like Mrs. Goldstein. I don't understand—Jonathan shuddered to think about such a calamity—how such a good guy like Lem got roped into such a life. Wonder if he knows how much money Dr. Kisserling has just* owed *to him. (And how Mrs. Kisserling owes Pop twenty-seven dollars over three months now.)*

"Lem," Jonathan asked his brother on Lem's first summer home from pre-med, "how come? Do you really *want to be a pillpusher?" Lem, now almost nineteen, with ten years behind Pop's counter as pre-pre-med, had slipped naturally into a smooth delivery suitable to all occasions. "A born bedside manner," Pop Shoemaker beamed.*

"Say something in bedside," Jonathan would mutter behind the fountain, and sip a Bromo-Seltzer. Lem had years ago developed a deep, resonant, lyrical voice that melted the starch from all the lady customers' blouses. Jonathan always figured Lem would end up as a minister, or at least a radio announcer—"Ladies and gentlemen, Easy Aces. . ."

In spite of his recalcitrant desires, Jonathan was magnetized to Lem. There was something deep and mystical and comfortably warm about his total being. To look at him was the cure. Whether it meant a time when he extracted a two-inch wood chip from Jonathan's butt with his teeth, or simply sticking his head in the door when he was shivering with fever and saying you look better already, Lem was a natural. Whatever he said—and he often said things that Jonathan never understood, and maybe Lem never understood—it always came out sounding final. Lem says so: Fact.

So, in this, the thirteenth year of his life, Jonathan wanted to know from this fool who could just as well be a radio announcer, "How come you really *want to be a sawbones, Lem?"*

And Lem answered his brother thusly: "Is there a choice? You are what you are. If in some strange fateful way I would have been a mountain climber, or a wood carver, or a diamond cutter, or a cheese salesman, I would still have been a doctor. It would not matter if my body had moved up a mountain or my hands had molded a head, or cut a stone, or sliced a cheese—inside would be the doctor, begging, screaming, choking to get out like a strangling unborn fetus. Some beg and scream and choke a lifetime. The wood is carved and the diamond is cut and the cheese is sliced, but the doctor never gets out. When you know what you are and it is in your throat and you are eating it and someone makes magic over you and suddenly you Are, what else is there? I am eternally a doctor, and if I were to die, I would go on being a doctor.

"Jonathan, you must promise me this. If I die, I must go on being a doctor. I could not scratch and paw and dig an endless cave. Don't, please, don't keep me under the ground. If I die,—don't let them bury the doctor. I could not go on through eternity roaming the endless pit. You hear me, Jonathan, you are all that I have, you hear. It will be up to you when I die. . . ."

. . . .

9:00   JONATHAN J. SHOEMAKER, M.D.

DOCTOR IS IN—PLEASE BE SEATED

NO SMOKING

Georgia had arrived before eight and had made the office into a green and white football stadium. Crinkle paper shakes hung all over the bookracks, white banners with scribbly green letters cried *Beat Centerville, Yea Groundhogs, Greenville is #1, Support Your Team Doctor, Yea! Yea!* Pictures of football in action dug out of *Sports Illustrated* and *MAD* hung from the walls. The fish tank was a swirl of green and white stripes made from crepe paper, the water and fish dyed a deep green from some vegetable color Georgia had dumped into the tank, the bubbles looking like Happy New Year with a green Guy Lombardo. It had been years since the office had had the spirit. Johnny used to keep in time with posters and scoreboards and banners, but in recent years Fran had discouraged his efforts by misplacing the material or maligning the purpose. "Is this an office or is this a locker room? It's bad enough that it smells like one. Maybe it was all right when you were a young, struggling G.P. looking for a few extra points in the community, but you don't need this any more. They take more from you than you could ever gain, and they smell on top of it. I won't have my office cluttered up with this garbage."

Johnny could have kissed Georgia.

He never had gotten over his frustrated dreams of playing star quarterback on *any* team. Through his association with the kids, he had made the mystical transposition of carrying that ball down a treacherous field to the winning score, running the hundred in 8.5, intercepting the tying pass in the end zone; and then being carried arm high by his screaming teammates and dumped into the shower, a soaking body of glee.

But this was not first. First were the kids, not the game or the glory but the scroungy little pawing kids. In the kids Johnny had found a touchable tranquilizer, rest, pleasure, a schism from the rat-running doctor. In the kids he found what was probably his only real purpose. Through them he was able to satisfy the scratching and clawing and begging of something inside him to get out. Through the kids he had found peace.

And he could now have kissed Georgia.

Georgia had dressed herself in a Greenville cheerleader costume and every few minutes would jump to the sky shouting Groundhogs! Groundhogs! G-R-O-U-N-D-H-O-G-S! Yea, Yea, team, team, team! [Scissor jump.] Yea!

She looked at Johnny sheepishly and said demurely, "Yea team? Nick Golopas first, yea?"

9:05 **GOLOPAS, NICK #7**

1217 Park St., Greenville—Age 29
Police Officer—Married—Ins.—Pol. Benefits (BC & BS)
7-12-54—This 29-year-old cop has a recurrent Wasserman. . .
10-17-70—New dose last night. May be total resistant. Start
on new series PCN 2 mill U. Check out contact. . . .

—You going to report her? You got to be out of your mind.
Her husband's a judge. Big report you'll make out on her.
Ouch—damn you, Doc, it wasn't such a hard favor I called
you for last night. You could have stayed, she asked you to.
You looked twice, don't give me that crap. You doctors don't
make night calls for the money. Have a good weekend. One
helluva life, two days on a golf course. You need a
partner? . . .

.   .   .   .

—Georgia here, doctor. It sure is an exciting morning. First
Saturday *morning* I've seen in years. So many *kids* piling up
out here. Looks like the pill never caught on in old
Greenville. Marvin on the phone. Yea. . .

.   .   .   .

—Ho, ho, ho, green doctor, what's new besides you're going
to jail without me? What the devil is with this nurse of yours,
the daytime one? She's waiting at the door this a.m., suitcase
in one hand, a big lunk with a three-day beard on the other,
and she renews all the pills. She just got them two days ago,
and you're not in yet and she says they are late, so I fill
them. After all, *your* handwriting, *your* help. Have you
looked at her eyes recently? . . .

.   .   .   .

9:10 **TILBERG, DONALD #4133**

1214 Southern Parkway, Greenville—Age 17
H.S. Student
10-17-70—Sallow. Wet hands. Crusty eyelids. Lower lip
quivers. Smiles like he is crying. Makes me want to hug him,
or kick him.

—Am I all right? They ask a lot of questions on these forms. Did my parents answer them all right? I get a feeling sometimes everybody knows I have some incurable disease, and they've been told to fake it and just let me live out whatever is left of my life as normal as it can be so I wouldn't know. Can I see what you wrote? I *am* normal, you said so here. Gee. Is this the way you're sending it in? My mother called you and told you not to tell me. . . .

. . . .

—Your wife, sir, on line two—yea, yea, Groundhogs. . .

. . . .

—You have it planned very cozy, don't you, dear? Tiptoed out of here this morning before I had a chance to tell you my latest. I've made up my mind that I *am* pregnant, and when you get up for those 3 A.M. feedings, think about me. I will be in Las Vegas, or wherever the other rich divorcees go. . . .Listen, dear, I know you have a lot on your mind, but do you remember tonight is the Kohn Bar Mitzvah? I'm going to the Temple this morning and will pray in several languages for your pill. The kids expect you to take them to the game, so drive carefully because we'll—as if I'm saying something new—have to use two cars tonight, I imagine. And work very hard, very, because I'm thinking about the most luxurious maternity wardrobe you ever saw—so I'll look ravishing when they lay me out. . . .

. . . .

9:30 —It is *late,* Doctor, and we are not moving. I have the Phillips family out here. Four kids for measles vaccine, then there are the two Gleason kids for polio. Then the Stanleys—three—for boosters. Then two kids from school for working papers, and two arms in splints, and one for college entrance exam. Can I work steady Saturday mornings? I haven't been so heavenly eye-raped in years. Yea, yea, Groundhogs—let's get on with it. Sorry, Doctor. . . .I put Sue Ann in the back room, take a quick look—emergency. . . .

. . . .

Sue Ann did not panic readily. She had seen a father through Hodgkins' and a mother through uremia, a brother through a brain tumor, a child through an ulcer, and a husband through bankruptcy.

"I'm pushing the panic button," she howled as Dr. Shoemaker came into the room.

She had forgotten her pill last night.

"First time in two years. What do you think, Doctor? You know what they say after a couple of years."

Johnny shrugged as if to say, can you call back yesterday?

"Hell, I wouldn't care, but you know Cliff, he never asks questions, and last night after eight beers—well, I must have twenty billion sperm floating in me."

Dr. Shoemaker agreed, she must have.

"Well, what do I do, just sit back and wait? Now you know I can't do that. Come on, Dr. Shoemaker, what would you do if I were your wife? . . ."

· ·

—Calloway from OB, Dr. Shoemaker. Your girl's just about slowed down to a squish. I checked her a few minutes ago. Station 0, 4 cm., and holding. You go on to your ball game, I have it A-OK here. If she acts up, I'll just say you couldn't be reached. Dr. Lenihan is gone for the day, his two delivered. I cut the cord on one, sucked out the nose on the other. You go on, don't worry about this end, I'll stay past my duty time. Maybe I'll practice some more on the plastic model they have set up for the nurses. . . .

· ·

—Georgia, Doctor. Say, is this Dr. Calloway cute? Sure would be fun having an obstetrician for a boyfriend. . . .Sorry, sir—yea? . .Well, the Fishers are here with all their pretty little heads covered with fish nets, they've got nits *en masse,* all four of them, and Momma and Poppa. And the Spencers are here, three runny noses and one runny ear, and Momma has a discharge. And a Mr. Berman just walked in says he can't wait, he's a neighbor and his Theodore has an upset tum-tum. . . .

· ·

10:40 BERMAN, THEODORE #4134
                    412 Superior Rd., Greenville Lakes—Age 9
Elem. School (Friends)
10-17-70—Fam. Dr. Sam Carlson (Pediatric) out of town.
Kid has chronic belly. Looks like a miniaturized old man.
Spastic colon, pruritis. Und. Testicle. . .

—Holy Chris', J. J., how do you stand all those kids so early
in the morning? You could open a circus. Always people who
shouldn't have 'em, knock 'em out like popcorn. Irish, huh, J.
J.? Another hundred years it'll be all green and black, but
what the hell, we won't have to see it. A good move we made
out to the Lakes, forty percent Hebes, sixty WASPs. Kids can
grow up *free* in a community like this. Not a care in the
world. Swimming pools, car pools, sex education pools,
conveniences that make the cities look like snake pits. Our
kids have the world by the. . .uh, take Theodore here, my
only kid. His own playroom with billiards and Ping-Pong and
basketball, his own color TV, his own bathroom and shower,
his own wing of the house actually. Total privacy. No
interference from any family gatherings and hell, J. J., you
know us when we put on a brawl, sure as hell ain't no place
for a kid. This kid lives in his own world, free to come and
go. Ever hear of such a thing in your day? My old man,
wham! right across the mouth if I ever left the house without
saying where I was going. So tell me, J. J. you're a doctor,
tell me why the hell does a kid like this wake up each
morning he's got a tum-tum ache? . . .

. . . .

):50 JOHNSON, FRANKLIN #4135
                    418 Superior Rd., Greenville Lakes—Age 34
Married—H.S. teacher—School Ins.
10-17-70—Fooler. Borderline yellow. Handsome. Willie
toned down six shades. Bellyache. Hx. old ulcer. Black stool
2 wks. ago. since. . .

–Thank you for seeing me this morning, Dr. Shoemaker. I know you have a tight Saturday schedule, but I don't think I could get by until Monday. This pain has me hanging on, I'll tell you. Like, unbearable. I'll give you several hot clues and you can take it from there. I've made a few good investments that have paid off. Teach history at Greenville High, also double in Guidance. This is a bellyache at times, but the real live one started two weeks ago when I moved into the new house at the Lakes. My neighbor just left, Mr. Berman. He didn't pay no neighborly greeting to me, that's for sure. When he walked past me in the waiting room, that torpedo in me just zeroes on target, kaboom! It's like that in the morning, every morning. It's that recurring dream, you know, that Mr. Berman is burning down my house and I awaken with it burning a hole right through the middle of my belly. By the time I get to school it is easier, but certain choice items key it in again like it has been computed. For example, I am your friend Willie Washington's guidance counselor. Dr. Leader likes to keep everything neat and orderly. Willie has a special problem, one that is closing in on me, and that problem, Dr. Shoemaker, is you. He is scared silly you are going to discover his head isn't right and you will lay him to rest in a field of black clover while the team drops number four and the State scouts laugh at him all the way home. His head hurts, but only he knows and only I know. He won't come to you, and I am not to tell anyone either. Not until after today. Today is Willie's day—*only* today. Forty-eight minutes out of today, actually. You see, Willie *must* make it today. He's being scouted, and if he makes it, his chances for moving into a Lake house like mine one day—although remote—come closer to the American Dream than Willie will ever come in a lifetime. The problem is, we both know the medical consequences if he plays today like Willie must play. So what kind of advice do you think his friend doctor gave to Willie? A quiet no, so cross him off. His counselor, his black counselor, *he* now says to Willie, "Willie, you play, and you play with all the black guts you got inside you. And don't you stop playin' until you get to State—or until you drop dead." So maybe Willie gets killed trying. So what about it, another redskin bites the dust. But ah, if he makes it, and he sure as hell can—you know that body better than me—if he makes it, the move into a Lake house is just over the hill. All right, he may not slide in as smoothly as me with my pretty clay color—he's a real black boy, you know—but what the hell, if a guy like Berman made it, why not Willie? Now why not? . . .

You got something to say about my bellyache, Doctor? . . .

. . . .

—Georgia, Doctor. I cut off your schedule at eleven like you said, but there's a Paul Seaburg says you *always* see him when he comes in. He says he's from Philadelphia and says nobody but "his boy Johnny" touches him. . .

. . . .

11:05 SEABURG, PAUL #3

Chancelor Apts., River Dr., Phila.—Age 30 Divorced—Artist—No Ins.
7-8-54—Pauly Baby. Cannes, Paris. Paints. Girls. Talk, talk, talk. The original freedom kid. Can't take more than 10 min. or I am on my way. Needs shot, — ? — . . .

—Johnny Baby, it's me, your boy, Pauly Baby. I know, I know, it's kiddie day today and the big doctor is going to the big football game and run his big ass off. Jerk. Listen to your boy, Pauly Baby, and give up all this trash and come with me to Mexico where you will suck on hot enchilladas and paint horny pictures of bulls in heat. Come alive, Johnny Baby, you only got one move left—time is running out. Man run, run while you got legs without varicose veins. Run away with me, Johnny Baby, and we will paint skies of angels' titties and rivers of flowing semen. How many would die if you ran away with me for a year, for two? Nobody would notice. The sky would fold you in and the space would be void and the Man would erase the spot and there would be no more you. They would all go on living, but *you* would live, live, *live.* We did it before, Johnny Baby, but this time we'll cut the wires, this time it is for damn well good. Come away now, I tell you now, *right now*—don't you dare think, out the door, into the

car, and fly, fly, *fly*. Together we will paint nude on the
beach by the light of a torch held by two horny Mexican
slaves. Don't say no, don't say no, because you lie. You want
to run and you lie. You lie, you *lie*. . . .

. . . .

—Georgia, Doctor. We're *free!* Just a message from Clara, she
says Lisa stepped on a rusty spiderweb and should she wrap
her up and bring her right over. And Laurie Lee called and
said she might be having a miscarriage. I turned them both
over to Dr. Peters. I cleaned up the toilet—it was full of
bubble gum. I patched up the magazines, nailed together two
chair rungs, put a window shade roller on hooks, dunked out
the lollipop sticks from the fish tank and called Service to
check out to lucky Peters. I am on my way home to feed
momma some hot bean soup and fish heads, then on with my
green Pucci slacks, my green beret, and my white sweatshirt,
and yea, Groundhogs! I'll be at your house at 12:30. What a
glorious, exciting day, and what a glorious, exciting way to
live. Did you ever stop to think that you are the luckiest man
in the whole world? . . .

. . . .

Afternoon
12:30   **THE SHOEMAKERS**
                                     692 LAKE DRIVE

                                     ――――――――

                                     WELCOME

                                     ――――――――

   The mimosa was hung with green confetti. Georgia and the
kids had tossed bags of crinkly stuff over the balding
branches. The ranch wagon looked like a float in the Irish
rebellion. A horn blast vibrated through the house, an
announcement for all fans on deck. They came at him from
the basement, the attic, the bedrooms; Judy, a neighbor,
struggled from the toilet, her pants caught between her boney
legs.
—Daddy, can I take Judy with us?

—Oh, no, Pops, are you going to take their fidge friends?
—I put green and white paper on the mailbox, is that all right?
—No, it's not all right, Skinny, our colors are lemon and lime.
—Daddy, can you get us in free?
—Pops, can I sit on the bench?
—Daddy, Judy's sister Annie called, can she come?
—Oh, no, Pops, I'm taking Kippy and Harky, there's no room for fidges.
—I asked first.
—I'm older.
—You're stupid.
—Shut up, Skin.
—Hey, Pops, grab a piece of chicken and let's go.
—What's taking you so long, Pops? We've been waiting all morning.
—Don't sit down, Pops, eat in the car.
—Hey, Pops, I got two-fifty going now that Willie is in for sure. He *is* in, isn't he? The whole school looks at me like I'm from Centerville. They say you told Willie no, and some big doctor said yes. How come? I thought you were the boss?
—Daddy, is Willie the black one?
—Shut up, Skin.
—Hey, Pops, I heard they were going to tear the park down if you didn't let him play.
—Daddy, he's the one who always makes the touchdowns. How come you don't want him to play?
—Cause he hates niggers, Skin. . . .

12:45

> ### GREENVILLE ATHLETIC STADIUM
> ### —OFFICIAL PARKING—

It was Andy Hardy revisited. The policemen at the gate smiled brightly and said, "Good to see you, Judge." The parking attendant smiled brightly and waved him into his place. The kids piled out and scrambled into a parade of chums with green shakers and white teeth, and they all marched off singing a Metro-Goldwyn-Mayer original victory march sounding much like "Old Cayuga Waters." The sky was charged with California sunbeams, and into each cheruby face it reflected technicolor delight. The stands were a roar of apple cider and doughnuts. Red-cheeked Mr. Purty led the Greenville High School Championship Band or Chamber Music Group across the green-and-white striped field in an original Purty pretty called *Centerville* (Coatsville, Millville, Pennsville, etc.) *we think you're Grand, but Greenville is Grander.* The trainers and the bucket boys joined heads in a barbershop chorus of poor little sheep who have lost our way, and the bare-legged MGM chorus girls née cheerleaders jumped up and down testing the tenacity of their soft rear ends and/or their new strapless bras. And the mayor greeted Johnny with a broad, gold-toothed grin and reminded him of his duty to vote in two weeks and waved to the stands as they roared "Down in front."

The sun always shines on Andy Hardy's football game. It beat upon Johnny's corduroy jacket and his mittened hands and he wondered if he dared disrobe. If the sun had shone last week, he thought, there would be no problem, Willie wouldn't have slipped in the damn mudhole and had his face stepped on. What do we know? Weather can change the whole course of history. Ask Napoleon, ask Joe Namath. But it was now, and it was so, and it would soon be over, and it was certainly a day for the game, and that black boy of mine has got muscle fibers no one has even *used* yet. He'll make it. *Damn headache.*

Johnny rubbed his eyes, getting lint in the corners. Damn Mrs. McGibbon. Last football game she went to was Penn/ Yale 1922, last day of October, temperature twelve degrees, she froze her little heinie and knit the gloves in remembrance for Dr. Shoemaker. But today it was sixty-two degrees, balmy, delightful, a winner's day if there ever was one. And in spite of the gnawing in his belly as Johnny stood alongside the bench readying his bag, he was nowhere else but here, nowhere else but home. The growing threat of misfortune that had reached its boiling point with Franklin in the office just a short while ago was cooling, and with each new minute closing in on one o'clock, although it beat time in the pit of his belly, his head lightened and the peace of Andy Hardy was with Johnny Shoemaker. . . .

Enter the villain(s).

Off to the far end of the wire fence separating the field from the stands was Sam Washington and a representative group of Sam Washingtons.

"Hello, there, Doc," said Sam Washington to Johnny.

Johnny said hello back.

"See my boy yet today?" asked Sam Washington.

Johnny admitted not seeing him. He usually did not interfere with the pre-game tapings and conditioning in the locker rooms.

Sam said to just wait and see how great that "sick" boy looks. "He got four touchdowns in his legs. *Four. I* put them there. You just watch that boy," Sam Washington said to Johnny, "and you just think real hard to what you nearly done to us folks."

Johnny wished them all luck.

And Sam Washington answered by saying not to be so condescending—but he said it like, "Shit, you say, we know what you think of us. Now you hear this, Doc, I got a lot of touchy friends out here today, and they don't like to see their friends treated unfairly, you hear? So you just keep your *eyes* on our Willie, not your *hands,* you hear, and you watch them four touchdowns."

Johnny wished him well, and wished Willie would do well.

And Sam Washington said to Johnny, "If you are so snotty, you want to make a little gentleman's wager? I'll betcha your Cadillac to my Cadillac. . ."

Ten minutes.

The school superintendent shook hands with Johnny and said he was glad to see him and hoped he didn't stir up a hornets' nest there, boy. The chairman of the school board shook hands with Johnny and said he was glad to see him and hoped he didn't stir up a burnt stew, young man. The PTA president shook hands with Johnny—glad to see him—and hoped there hadn't been any hurt feelings there, Doc.

Dr. Leader arrived and reminded Johnny of their great fortune in following the credo, and as he could see, anything *could* be done. He pointed out to Johnny that he had taken care of everything with the superintendent and the school board and the PTA, and they understood how these things can happen. He emphasized how he had fought a battle until midnight, how he had literally taken Johnny down from the wall where they had pinned him, and how all was now as well as could be expected. He did say that they were after *someone's* neck, and he had literally removed Johnny's from the noose.

And as he said neck, Dr. Leader could not resist mentioning his desire to peck Georgia on her bared silky sternocleidomastoid, and exclaimed joshingly how he must *taste* everything that looks so appetizing or else he would just wither away and die. It was part of the credo that *anything* can be done. And he added as a final whimsy that if the board knew that Johnny was hiding such a pretty young thing as Miss Jones in his office, maybe they would reevaluate whose neck would give them more pleasure.

Georgia waited until Leader had wrapped himself in a khaki hood next to the girl cheerleader's bench. Then she laid it on.

"Dr. Shoemaker, haven't you heard just about enough? I been listening to all this talk about Willie, Willie, Willie until *I* have just about had it. What does it take to make you shovel a little back at them? You told me just last night about a boy out in some Kansas high school who had his neck broken and died, and you told me that Willie Washington is not any better off than that.

"Now I been workin' for you only a short time, and although I am only a young girl in years, I have been and have lived with men and I know when one is in deep, deep, trouble. I know you long enough to know you don't give a hootin' damn what that school board thinks, or what that weird sex-maniac principal says. But you are actin' like someone who sees a handwritin' that no one else sees. There is somethin' that has made you back off on this Willie thing. This is not really you. And you are actin' like a possum playin' dead, hopin' the shot just goes over his head and away he will run. You are upset, that is for certain. You certainly can't completely go dead cold, you're talkin' about somebody you think could be your own son. I'm from Birmingham, so you got the wrong party for sympathy, Doctor, but even the die-hard ol' nigger-haters where I come from wouldn't do what you're doin'. Unless there was a reason much more penetratin'. Like you are havin' trouble with Mrs. Shoemaker? That's got to be the only one reason a man starts actin' like you are, it's a vendetta. Go shoot up a town, kill off the blacks, rape the women. Damn you men, you got love troubles and you take it out on the world."

Five minutes.

Howard Crankshaft of WGRN shoved a padded mike under Dr. Shoemaker's chin and explained to the radioland folks that this was the team physician for the Greenville Grounders. He would like a first-hand report from the doctor on how the team prepares for a game—medically, that is—how a doctor sets himself up as a "team physician," and where the qualifications come from, and what about Willie Washington?

Johnny explained about pre-season workouts, body building, running, contacts, scrimmages, food, basic health laws, etc., etc., and the announcer said, "Do all the boys take part in this?" And Johnny answered, "Those who care." So the announcer got back to qualified leadership and dangers of injury and, "Shouldn't they be made to care?" But at once with all the turmoil on the sidelines, and the screaming in the stands and Mr. Rosy-Cheeked Purty playing the Greenville victory march because the team was running onto the field, the dissertation Johnny had prepared about there being not enough time or help or money or interest to conduct acceptable medical screenings and follow-up care was smothered. The announcer thanked him. "And just so long as here comes Willie," he said, "I guess that answers the last question." He then stuck his cushioned mike into place for a few words from Coach Bocca, who spit and said, "The boys are ready. If the wind is right and if it don't rain, I can make a winning team of these scroungy kids so's *my* kids don't go bare—" The mike clicked off and the announcer stood at attention.

"And now, ladies and gentlemen, the "Spar-Stangled Banner. . ."

.   .   .   .

4:00   **JONATHAN J. SHOEMAKER, M.D.**

DOCTOR IS OUT

NO SMOKING

Medical Report: Greenville vs. Centerville. October 17, 1970.
Dictated but not read by Dr. J. J. Shoemaker:

Pre-Game

Coach Bocca and trainer Larry Hesel reviewed week's injuries:

1. Cal Klemper—Fracture 4th metacarpal—3 wks. OK to play/Dr. Arthur Finnegan, Orthoped.
2. Andy Ralberg—Sprain collateral knee ligaments. OK to play/Dr. J. J. Shoemaker.
3. William Lipsky—Hematoma, left deltoid. OK to play/JJS.
4. Arthur Krockheimer—Nasal bone fracture. OK to play/Dr. Arthur Finnegan.
5. Clayton Moore—Laceration right gastrocemus. No/JJS.
6. Willie Washington—Concussion syndrome. OK/Dr. Fletcher Snyder, Neurosurgeon, Phila., Pa.
7. Philip Key—Jock strap itch. OK/JJS.
8. Albert Kornfeld—Low back sprain. OK/JJS.
9. Kyle Orthobothum—Infectious mono. No/JJS.
10. James Spatula—Sprained shoulder girdle. OK/JJS.

1st Quarter

1. Cal Klemper—Refracture 4th metacarpal—out of play.
2. Sam Ragucci—Lacerated right thumb—out of play.
3. Jeff Seamone—Fracture 4th & 5th right ribs—out of play.
4. Howard Lobel—Sprained ankle ligaments—OK.
5. Albert Kornfeld—Low back sprain—OK.
6. Pete Robinski—Possible hip fracture—hospitalized.
7. Oscar Kryzskaczki—Sprained right small finger—OK.

2nd Quarter

    1. Arthur Krockheimer—Refracture nasal bones—out of play.

    2. Albert Kornfeld—Low back sprain—OK.

    3. Sheldon Piccone—Winded—OK.

    4. Franklin Halbeisner—Possible concussion—out of play.

    5. Oscar Kryzskaczki—Sprained left small finger—OK.

3rd Quarter

    1. Albert Kornfeld—Low back sprain—OK.

    2. Oscar Kryzskaczki—Sprained left second finger—OK.

4th Quarter

    1. Albert Kornfeld—Low back sprain—out of play.

    2. Sheldon Piccone—Winded—out of play.

    3. Donald Tilberg—Bloody nose—out of play.

    4. Clayton Moore—Opened laceration—out of play.

    5. Philip Key—Jock strap itch, acute—out of play.

    6. James Spatula—Shoulder dislocation—out of play.

    7. Oscar Kryzskaczki—Compound fracture left radius, ulna, and humerous and tibia and fibula—hospitalized.

Post-Game

    1. Albert Kornfeld—X-rayed at office—OK back sprain.

    2. Clayton Moore—Laceration repair at office—OK.

    3. Philip Key—Jock strap itch—OK—treated at office.

    4. James Spatula—X ray at office—shoulder strapped—OK.

Other injuries advised to see family doctors. Hospitalized cases referred to Arthur Finnegan, Orthoped.

Copies to: Board of Education/Dr. Henry Leader/Coach Bocca.

FROM THE DESK OF—JONATHAN J. SHOEMAKER, M.D.

This will be my final report. As of the conclusion of the Centerville game I request your permission to be relieved of my position as team physician for Greenville High School. I will submit to you the names of several men in the area well qualified for the task.

Thank you,

Jonathan J. Shoemaker

5:30

GREENVILLE MERCY HOSPITAL
GREENVILLE, N. J.
DEPARTMENT OF OBSTETRICS   EMERGENCY PARKING

LABOR ROOMS—HOSPITAL PERSONNEL ONLY

Labor Rm. #3—JEANETTE DUSHARME—Age 28. M. Gr. 2. Para 1-0-0-1. Adm. 10-17-70—Dr. Shoemaker. Station -1, dilation 5 cm—membranes intact—contractions q. 15 min, 20 sec, weak. Enema given—poor results—Prep. BP 130/80—FHB 40-30-30-40.

—I'm a problem, Dr. Shoemaker, I've been a problem from day one. My mother had eight before me and three after. I want this baby. How come I don't feel it any more? When there's pain at least I know I'm trying. Dr. Lenihan made me have pain. He said it was good for me. I want some good pain, I want it to *hurt.* Is it all right? I know you look at me like I'm a liar. Maybe I became pregnant for another reason, but I want it now. Can't you do *something* for me, Dr. Shoemaker, instead of just standing there? Throw me down a flight of stairs. Anything. I've got to have this baby, nobody but me knows, I've got to—Do you know if Dr. Lenihan is coming back tonight? . . .

INTERN QUARTERS—OB
NOTICE—QUIET! Tired, overworked, underpaid, oversexed doctor sleeping.

—Yeah, yeah, I'm Calloway. Sorry. Yessir, sorry, just been catching up, sir. I've been awake thirty-six hours, sir. We have a unit system, me and the other fellows. I owe four units, so it's my long weekend. From Friday noon to Monday A.M., it's not bad. All you got to hope for is no night deliveries and a sexless RN on duty and you can sleep through most of it. Yessir, your patient, your patient . . . Mrs. Dusharme, I checked her just recently—nothing, nil, she is stopped cold. How about if we rotate her? When I was an extern in Philly I once helped rotate one, came down in three minutes. A great delivery, the doctor told me. He said I'd make a great obstetrician, gave me five bucks, went home and let me sew her up, she was torn right through to the rectum. Dr. Shoemaker, trust me, I come from a good family, my father is a bank vice-president. Go on to your party, have fun, I won't sleep another wink. I'll make out for you, trust me. Look, my old man calls up every Sunday and says, "Tell me about your deliveries, son." For God's sake, what do they expect from us here? I haven't had a delivery to myself in six weeks, and this is my last night. Have a heart, Doctor. Christ, don't you remember when you were me? . . .

"*. . . Good work, Shoemaker. Now just pull down and twist, back and forth, back and forth. Yeah, good. It's coming. Now, wind it like a watch. No, the other way. OK now, back and forth, back and forth, get that ass out. OK, pull down. OK. There's a shoulder. Grab it. Cord—unwrap it. OK, fine. Now, up, up, pull up the chin, watch that neck, down, rotate, left, left, OK, slow, here it comes, hold on—yeah. Nice, nice job. Suck it out, suck it out. OK, take your time, get that cry. Get that cry. Fine, hold 'er up. Hey, Mrs. Schultz, hey, you got another goddam boy. A hanging boy.*"

Lenihan laid the wet, sticky baby on Schultz's belly and blew her a kiss from under his mask. "Good show, Schultz. When you get better I'll show you how to make a girl."

That Lenihan was a real comer.

He had turned over a third one to Johnny—actually three

*deliveries on one service. Dr. Frank Lenihan, senior OB resident,
saw to it that each boy had at least one, no more than two. He
planned to open his office in the neighborhood, so why should
the G.P. know any more than fundamentals? He would always
be available. Why knock yourself out with technicalities?
You've delivered one, so what's the kick later? But it's like
playing the violin, no instrument for an amateur. "The less the
kids know, the better. How far will I be?"*

*Johnny liked delivering babies. He was, in four years,
Lenihan's only* three *man. "You get under a guy's skin,"
Lenihan told him after his second one. "You make it look like
you're enjoying it. With the other damn kids there's sweat
running down their balls and shit in their pants. They should
shoot penicillin the rest of their lives. You got a touch for a
little more, Shoemaker, maybe I'll slip in a third."*

*Delivering a baby was the closest Johnny felt a person could
come to Deifying himself. Arturo had included in his dream of
the Ultimate the continual retouching of life's first breath. To
Johnny, the miracle of the newborn was in a class with the
miracle of a Willie. Next to delivering a Willie, delivering a baby
was the closest Johnny felt a person could come to the
fulfillment, the Thing. It was not a patchup, or a mockup, or a
makeshift, or a transfer, or a shell—it was an Absolute, the only
cure medicine had to offer. The rest was make-believe.*

*And Johnny had had enough make-believe. The squeak of a
baby's first muffled sound became to him the only redeeming
factor in a world of medicine known best for its repair work,
not its creation. Therefore Johnny delivered lots of babies.*

. . . .

6:30 On the way home the Buick stalled out twice. Johnny's head
dulled, and all the cars that passed him were Cadillacs.

The day had changed. The early morning brightness had long
since disappeared into bleak pre-November grays. A pearly mist
hung over the road, and the Buick seemed to be grasping its way
home. Johnny turned on the defroster but it didn't help. He
wiped away the fog covering his windshield and turned the
heater up. He was chilled and hungry. He reached into the glove
compartment for a candy bar and came up with an old used
lollipop. It would have to do.

Fog covered the highway in pieces, traffic had dissolved under a veil, Johnny felt disturbingly alone. He never felt alone in the Buick. He switched the radio on, heard a blast of rock music, and switched it off. He was relieved to find his tape set under the seat and switched on to Arnold Webster of the University of North Dakota Medical School describing the loop of Henle and its importance in electrolyte imbalance. If it was a bit of a bore in school, it was a total wipe-out here. Switch off! He cleared the window again, revved the motor and shot ahead, testing the fog. He blew his horn. He called out, "Willie! *Willie!*" He shrugged and said simply, "Lem, Lem."

And Lem came to him. But when Lem came on call it was often not the Lem who came willingly. Jonathan felt grieved to think his move away from the team would be agreeable to Lem. Not too soon, either, Lem told him, and suggested he get to the affair tonight bright and early and move fast on making the General Clinics of Suburban Hospital his new baby. "Jonathan Shoemaker's time as the old G.P. is running out," Lem said, and he predicted that after today, Jonathan would never again be the same.

Johnny winced at his brother's adverseness. He had expected battle, never condescension, from Lem. And pressuring attitudes in a direction he had fought vehemently from the beginning? "General Practice *is* medicine,"—if one had a credo, this was Lem's—"all else is the money game." The voice Jonathan was hearing was familiarly Lem's, but the affirmations were strange.

Johnny shook his head. He would not listen. He switched on the car radio, but it did not work. It sputtered, and Lem continued to talk above it. Jonathan cupped his hand over his aching eye and Lem expressed strong doubt whether he would ever get rid of those headaches.

"Never could buy those feelings of yours, Jonathan, you always were a bit of an actor. I imagine this is part doctor, also, but it's not part good doctor. A doctor *knows,* he does not feel. He *daren't* feel. Your feelings are as unreal as the gassy belly of a fake pregnancy—hot air, no life."

Who was talking to him? Johnny felt the fog on the road had seeped in through the cracks of his side door and had enveloped him as insidiously as it had the cars groping their way along the

road to some kind of homesite. Lem sounded like Tom. For a
while there he had been able to replace Lem with Tom.

"Today it was proven beyond doubt. Your 'feelings' are
simply subterfuges for your inadequacy. If I can't tell you, who
can?"

It was Tom.

Now I have more to say to you, Tom, and I am going to
finish that letter tonight. . . .

*"Jonathan, bring down these bandage rolls to the cellar. And
don't put them too close to the furnace. And check on the
medicine cartons, I heard a few corks blow. Move them over
against the wall. Another year I'll have enough for him."*

Poppa, where are you, Poppa?

"You are not the doctor, Jonathan, *I* am."

Lem had never said that. At least never out loud. Why
now, why are you saying that, Lem? "Because you need
me, now more than ever. Without me you are nothing. Don't
you know that yet? After all these years, hasn't it sunk in? You
are not Dr. Shoemaker. I am Dr. Shoemaker. Does it have to be
spelled out in blood?"

Jonathan sucked at his finger, ripping away at the thumbnail
until blood trickled to the corner of his mouth. Now he would
feel. But it was like a trick was being played on him. After the
Lee baby, he could not feel.

*"Draw me the origin insertion and action of the hand
muscles, the nerve and blood supply, and the bony skeleton.
And when you are done, show me how these material
substances can feel so deeply and so profoundly that a brain can
be made to expand into genius or collapse into imbecility, or
that a heart can be made to weep."*

Arturo, Arturo, tell me more. I feel.

Give the origin insertion and action of feel.

I don't know the origin insertion and action. I just know, I
know.

"Without me," Lem cried out at him, "you are still a dreamer
roaming the streets of some dirty foreign back alley looking for
the cure in art, in visions, in abstractions. You will roam in pain.
The head will always ache. The answer will never come in guilt.
I am your salvation. You must come to me."

"You must stop riding around on square wheels when the world is floating on compressed air. . . ."

The tapes spun at double speed and Dr. Arnold Webster mashed potassium through the loop in falsetto. The radio sputtered back rock. The Buick coughed pollution. Johnny shook his head trying to conceive what he was, where he was, trying to feel: pain, remorse, anger, hunger. He wanted to be home. He pressed harder on the gas pedal.

"One day, Dr. Shoemaker, along will come the gladiator, the lion . . . the absolute truth of what your practice could *be. . . ."*

Don't go away, Arturo. Only you seem to know the truth.

"I love you, Jonathan. Don't let them bury my soul, you are all that I have, Jonathan. You hear me, I cannot go on through eternity. . . ."

Jonathan pawed for the switch on the tapes and turned them off. The radio had caught on and the dashboard rattled with violent thing sounds. Jonathan placed his hands over his ears; in maddening terror he screamed, "Willie! *Willie!*" And at that moment came the crash.

Had it not been for the way they made cars back in those days, and the fact that the fog had slowed the traffic to a jog, the damage might have been mortal. As it was, the front of the Buick was bashed into what might be a couple hundreds' damage, and the rear fender of the woman's Cadillac was folded into her back seat.

A blur of incidents followed, including hysterical women, indignant motorists, calloused police officers, ambulance sirens, tow trucks, a telephone call to Mary, a hamburg at Gino's, and a parking attendant at the Fine Arts Museum in Philadelphia who had a sore shoulder.

At eight o'clock Saturday evening, when he should have been arriving at the Kohn Bar Mitzvah, Johnny Shoemaker found himself roaming the halls of the Fine Arts Exhibit of the Andrew Wyeth Jubilee Collection Series. He remembered receiving in the mail a few days before a notice that the exhibit was to open, and he had filed a memory pattern to try to get to see it. That he was here he accepted and enjoyed. Why tonight, and how, he pondered as he walked the quiet halls.

He was glad he had come, he thought, and he would be full of cheerful sentiment when the experience was digested. It would allow him to reduce the recent chaos and step away from himself and see things as they were, be what he was. Here he would find himself . . . . Whatever.

He crossed from room to room, examining at length the vast and satisfying work of the master. The never-ending fields, the infinite skies, and the constant countryside, the sleepwalking character of the central theme, all gave to him the quality he felt he so intensely desired: A return to the peace and quiet of a way of life he had long ago lived and now had irrevocably cut away.

He relaxed. He knew he was here because he had to be here. He felt as he had not felt in a dozen years amidst this air of simple sadness and humble truth; he felt at last, this day, at evens with life.

On his second tour around, Johnny remembered there was one painting at which he had stopped and smiled, then moved on. At none of the others did he smile. He made note to return to this painting. And again he smiled. Now whatever happens, Johnny thought plaintively, that causes an artist to suddenly make such a statement after thirty or forty paintings? Painting after painting, rows and rows, room after room, wall upon wall, umber, flesh, sallow gray, white, cold, bleak, hay, straw, walls and walls, room after room.

And at once brilliant, majestic blue. Icy cold blueberries. Eight, ten, twelve, in an umber bowl, on a straw table, in a cold, bleak room. Brilliant, majestic blue.

What would come over an artist, a lifetime out of a single silent tube, suddenly an exclamation, a *proclamation*—Look at me, I am also somebody else!

Johnny stepped back, stared in hypnotic admiration, and smiled. He said, "*I* am also somebody else." He said it, however quietly, mostly in grays. Johnny was mostly gray; he knew this, but apparently this was as he had chosen some time ago. The last time he was more than what he was, he had splashed a mass of raw colors on a canvas and had called it *Brothers*. As if he had purposely created this effect by not waiting for underlayers to dry, he had worked over the colors of his life until they were mud, using a brush he had never washed. And although his life was constantly splashed with color, the panorama he allowed to appear on canvas was indeed dull, without as much as one brilliant blueberry.

Johnny could not at this moment remember one single element of joy, one moment of satisfaction, or even condescension. He only knew he was without cause or reason, without memory or pattern that could otherwise be involved in the simple, normal satisfactions of what he was on the surface—a doctor. He could not even be convinced, nor could it be suggested to him at this moment, that a Dr. Shoemaker was who he was. He knew there *was* a Dr. Shoemaker, but faintly recalled there was someone else so-called. He was, for all intents and purposes, Jonathan, the younger son whom God only knows what will become of.

He sat on a bench across from the blueberries, his legs aching for rest, his back crushed, and he bit upon his nails and sucked at the flesh and sensed blood trickling into his throat and he tried again to feel like he was known to feel. He could not even question why he did not; he did not and so it was. I wonder, did the artist feel the blueberry? Did he taste it? Did he know what it was like to hold it, to squeeze it, to watch the blue water wash down his wrists? Did he feel it in his belly? Did he feel it in his head? If I could taste one, just one. They must be a magic kind of fruit for this artist, room after room, wall after wall, suddenly to give to us. Eat one and you will be what you are. You will be what you *really* are. Johnny stared beggingly, hopefully, into the umber bowl, and the blueberries screamed out at him and said look at me, I am somebody else. And Johnny answered who, who am I?

And the terrible images of his patients and his friends and his children and his wife rose up and strode before him, and each in turn dabbed on him a duplicable spot of blue, majestic blue, until he was a mass of blue photoelectric dots. And he felt himself falling into the mouth of the giant WEC MED CALC and tumbling and tumbling and tumbling until he was spit out the side slot. And where the blue had been painted, punched-out holes appeared. He was Zap. Zero.

Hells bells, he exclaimed, I am annihilated. I am not even recognizable to WEC MED CALC. I am not.

THE KOHN BAR MITZVAH
A PLAY

As the curtain goes up it is ten o'clock at the Greenville Country Club. The time is October 17, 1970. We are in the Baron Hall Mezzanine where such affairs take place regularly. The setting is lavish. We see on stage several tables magnificently decored as is expected in an eight-thousand-dollar party. Dozens of other tables seated with well-dressed people and decored decoratively give the illusion of an enormous room jumping with gaiety and abandon. Left stage the Tommy Taylor Band is playing and a sample group of couples are dancing to a wild South American rhythm. Waiters and assistants in white gloves enter and leave regularly, bringing in and taking out enormous platters of food. The table right and front stage is the center of our interest. Seated in circular clockwise order briskly chewing and swallowing in between occasional bursts of forced laughter are: Dr. and Mrs. Jonathan J. Shoemaker, Mr. and Mrs. Arnold Katz, Mr. and Mrs. Karl Kleinert, and Dr. and Mrs. Frank Lenihan.
[The air reeks of heavy cigar smoke.]

Dr. Lenihan: (*He is a disappointing man for who he is—Chief of Obstetrics at MGH. He is small, portly, a mass of red blotches over his face. But a mane of silver-gray hair distinguishes him in some redemptive way. His voice is mellow, deep; that, on command, it could be sexy is apparent, but now with six or eight gins and water, it is heavy and phlegmy.*) Dammit, Katz, if my old man had thrown a party like this for me when I was thirteen, maybe I wouldn't have turned out to be such a bastard. (*He turns to Mrs. Kleinert, seated next to him, and kisses her neck.*) For you, sweety.

Mrs. Kleinert: (*Smiles.*) Frank—

Dr. Lenihan: It took me thirty years to work out the traps so that the world brings me money and kisses my ass, and here this kid gets it all before he even has wet dreams. (*He turns to his wife, squeezes her cheek, and drops a roll of paper money into her plunging neckline.*) Patty, I want you to send that thing you have at home to Jewish school and buy him a Bar Mitzvah.

Mrs. Lenihan: (*She pulls out the bills and scatters them over the table.*) Don't waste your money. He'll marry a Jewish doctor's daughter, and you'll get the same party.

Millie Katz: (*She puffs incessantly, her mouth taking big, wet drags from her cigarette. She is actually an attractive woman, but she is not at her best in her see-through shimmering silver pants suit and her stark white, heavily painted face showing only two black fanning eyes. She places herself in unabashed defiance of the youth she could have with considerably less effort.*) *I'm* a Jewish doctor's daughter. I saw my father *four* times in my whole life—

Arnold Katz: Millie—

Millie Katz: Once I saw him when I had my tonsils out. He looked into my room and grinned and said, "How's our little sore throat today?"

Arnold Katz: Who gives a damn—

Millie Katz: The second time was when my mother died and he looked into my room and grinned and said, "We must be brave little soldiers—"

Arnold Katz: Come on now—

Millie Katz: Third when he married his anti-Semitic nurse and he looked into my room and grinned and said, "She reminds me of your mother."

Arnold Katz: Millie, for Chris' sake—

Millie Katz: And last when he was laid out a year later. Anyone for a drink?

Mary Shoemaker: (*She is a sweet-looking girl, simply dressed in a high-necked, black-ruffled gown. She blows air on herself often, fanning with her menu.*). Is anyone here hot?

Arnold Katz: (*He is a one-time sensitive curly-haired Jewish boy who through years of battling out in the territory has taken on the settled, paunching, balding-with-side-curls look of the suburban male who has made it, but with caution. His main stock-in-trade is an endless parade of new or remodeled jokes, and a predatory sense for a hot-line investment.*) And how's business at the old butcher shop, Kleinert? Hear you're raising a bond for a two-hundred bed addition. A fellow doesn't know where to put his tax deductions lately.

Karl Kleinert: (*He sips ginger ale through a straw, but not because he wouldn't rather have gin. This is one of his prices for running a major hospital and running it well. Kleinert is sharp, reads through Katz, answers him Kleinert classically.*) Put it in brand names, Mr. Katz. The return is guaranteed.

Arnold Katz: I just got the same deal from a few friends who will go unnamed, but sure put on a great Bar Mitzvah.

Karl Kleinert: Although the pasture of hay on the hill has a vision of abundance, the field of clover in view has the most accessible nutritive return.

Arnold Katz: For Chris' sake, Kleinert, tell it like it is—If you had a few thousand bucks stashed away, which deal would you drop it on?

Karl Kleinert: That which is, will always be. That which is not, may never. A bird in the bank account is worth more than an egg in a hat. Put them all together and you spell Greenville Mercy Hospital, the *real* doctors' paradise. Am I right, Dr. Shoemaker? You have been at Mercy for fifteen years. Tell your friend, Mr. Katz, where to put his money

Dr. Shoemaker: (*He is apparently not listening too intently. What he says seems totally irrelevant.*) Into blueberries, Katz, into blueberries.

Tommy Taylor: (*The leader of the band, Arthur Tomaczefsky, steps from his podium and motions everyone to be seated.*) And now, brothers and sisters, uncles and aunts, grandpas and grandmas, friends and relatives, and, ah, yes, *doctors*. We have present tonight, I have been told, Greenville's elite corps of doctory. In fact, an announcement appeared in all of tonight's *papers and on local radio and TV that the entire community* should take two aspirin and sit quietly until morning. . . . Now, I have been asked by the man who pays the bills—so actually I have been told—to make the following rearrangement in the program. Insofar as this has been a Reform Bar Mitzvah, and the poor Bar Mitzvah boy never gets a chance to make a speech like his orthodox father did sixty years ago, it has been arranged for your dining pleasure to have Kenny Kohn give you a belated Bar Mitzvah speech tonight. And so, without further ado, he needs no further introduction, I give you the star of the show, Kenny Kohn. . . .

[General applause and glass knocking.]

Dr. Lenihan: (*He has in the last few minutes downed several more gins and water. His speech is now close to slovenly.*) He looks like a midget Alex—poor kid. I wonder if he knows his father plays with penises for a living.

Mrs. Kleinert: He's cute. Looks like our Peter.

Dr. Lenihan: (*Kisses Mrs. Kleinert's cleavage.*) Glad to hear you agree, sweety. . . .

Kenny Kohn: (*He* does *look like a smaller version of his doctor father, who stands by grinning foolishly, waving nervously to friends. His voice is at first shaky and high-pitched, and the sounds of the room drown out his opening remarks about how happy he is to have all of them here and how grateful he is to be here himself. But most of all, and his voice takes on strength and the room quiets for him*—Most of all, I am thankful on my thirteenth birthday for my father, the doctor.

Dr. Lenihan: Hear, hear.

Alex Kohn: Ssh. Quiet, this is the good stuff. Go on, Ken.

Kenny Kohn: (*With vigor.*) How many of my friends can say this on their Bar Mitzvah? I often used to think what a shame all boys couldn't have for a father a doctor. . . .

Mary Shoemaker: Can you hear your boys saying that, John?

Kenny Kohn: . . . And I felt sorry for my friends, or even kids I didn't know. But now that I am a man and I can think maturely, I have even reevaluated this premise and can only be grateful that of all doctors, my father is a *specialist*. . . .

Dr. Lenihan: Hear. Hear.

Kenny Kohn: . . . Otherwise, would I have the fishing reel and be able to go out with him to the lake every Wednesday and Sunday in the summer? Or would I have skis and boots and be able to go out with him every Sunday and Wednesday and Saturday in the winter? Or would I have him home with me nights working on my model trains or my hi-fi? Or would I have him for breakfast and for dinner, for the Phillies or the Eagles games? Would I have him at my Blue and Gold Scout Dinner? . . .

Mary Shoemaker: Hear! Hear!

Kenny Kohn: . . . On this my Bar Mitzvah day, I thank God for making me thirteen and the only son of a prominent urologist. Amen. . . .

[The party moves on, the eating comes to a climactic halt with an orgy of cholesterol-laden desserts. On the dance floor, Kenny's friends gyrate to even the Viennese waltz and the Jewish national anthem. The relatives form circles and make great perspiring efforts at youthful recollections. At ten

forty-five Tommy Taylor knows he must make this next move.]

Tommy Taylor: Grandmas and grandpas, boys and girls, swingers, I know you're having a good time. But, my friends, the doctors, how about you? Don't just sit there and watch your wives Boogaloo and Alley Cat. Show us that inside your sterile and stainless-steel trapping roars a lion writhing to get out. I've dug up a group of songs for all of you doctors who are really a jumping bunch to play for. God forbid I should need a doctor, not a one of you could make it to the stand. Come on, docs, we've run out of aspirins, so grab your bag, you've got to make this a live call. OK boys, a-one, a-two, a-three . . .

Mary Shoemaker: We did dance once at our wedding—or somebody's wedding, didn't we, John? I'm going to the ladies' room, I'm sure you'll be here when I get back. Millie, you want to go? . . .

Millie Katz: Somebody might ask me to dance. (*Mary exits, fanning herself with her scarf.*) Now's the time, Johnny Shoemaker, we're dancing. . . . (*She pulls him, not so reluctantly, onto the floor and they dance.*) Come on, Johnny, move in, no girdle, eight pounds since Thursday. Feel the difference? Six more pounds and I have it made. All the old clothes. You're an angel, I love you. (*They dance closer.*) Feels good, doesn't it? Come on, boy, enjoy, you look like a lovesick teenager. I can spot 'em at forty paces. You are prime merchandise tonight, Johnny. (*She moves in on him, sensing agreement.*) Phyllis Kohn has two rooms reserved for anyone who wants them tonight, and the key for one is in my bag. No one will miss us. Mary is in the john cooling off. We'll be back before her sweat dries. That sad face of yours will never be the same, this much I can promise you. (*They dance close to the hall doorway.*) Come on, Johnny, I'm going to get you, you are ripe. (*He continues dancing, moving a bit away from the door.*) Johnny, come on—you are a *fool.* I'm more than you ever dreamed you could have. Johnny, I'm going out that door—*now.* . . .

Tommy Taylor: Telephone for Dr. Shoemaker. Dr. Shoemaker, telephone, please. . . .

[Johnny picks up the phone at the Service table.]

—Dr. Shoemaker, this is Mrs. Crabtree in OB. You better get over here, *stat.* Young Calloway is in mucho trouble and he's not about to call you. And if Dr. Lenihan is there, she's screaming for him. . . .

—CURTAIN—

11:00

N. J.

MD—1OB

GARDEN STATE

Route 41

Johnny drove Lenihan's car. That's the only way the Chief would have it. He admitted to three or four drinks, but Johnny lost count at nine. However, the cold night air cleared away the fuzz and left him well-lubricated, but aware enough to know that Johnny had better drive.

"Beautiful ride, huh, J. J.? It's a '71, first on the road. How long you been in practice, J. J.? Fifteen years?"

Johnny said sixteen, counting this year.

"And you still haven't had your first Cadillac?" Lenihan's blotches erupted with his perturbment at Johnny's simple, nonverbal shrugged answer.

"What are you afraid of?" he asked.

"People talk," Johnny answered.

"People talk if you ride a Buick."

"My old Buick gets me there."

"So would a *bicycle.*" Lenihan bit the dead end of Alex Kohn's cigar and puffed smoke, voluminously clouding the windows. He flicked a button on the dash and instantly the windows cleared and the smoke vanished. "Take it from me, J. J., your patients *want* you to drive a Caddy. They *want* you to be spoiled rich. After all, you're their choice of doctor, wouldn't they be the first to yell if you went back to spittin' tobacco juice and riding a horse and buggy?"

"There's a place for that guy," Johnny muttered.

"Come on, J. J., snap out of it." Lenihan pushed a button on the dash and warm clean air filled the car. "You've been dreaming of the old days so long and look like Paul Muni looking like Louis Pasteur—'Believe me, gentlemen, there are such things as germs, and in the next reel I will kill myself to prove it.' "

"So," Johnny mumbled, "where would we be otherwise?"

"Exactly where the hell we are now—alive and in a world that doesn't damn much care." Rain had begun to fall, and Lenihan pushed a button and silent wipers came up and cleared the windshield. "What you need, J. J., is a few more asses under you. Do you worlds of good."

Johnny looked ignobly from the corner of his eye at Lenihan, who caught and accepted the look.

"Hell, J. J., save the look for your PTA sex classes. I know what they say about Frank Lenihan, but remember, it never hurt me one bit. Do you see me in chains? The truth is there isn't a one of you noble doctors who don't see it my way a dozen times a day, but you all tail it home with your swollen prostates hoping your wife isn't menstruating or faking it."

Smart sonofabitch, Johnny said to himself.

Lenihan sat back against his headrest, pushed a little button, and the seat reclined. He puffed smoke and it disappeared. He was enjoying his ride and his captured audience.

"I know who I am, I don't hold any false promises for my salvation. This is me, I've been horny all my life. I screwed every kid on the street, every nurse in school, I aborted more uteruses when I was twenty-two than you ever have examined. But that doesn't make me any less of a doctor. I'm the best OB-GYN man in a hundred miles, and you know that."

Johnny assured him this was not in jeopardy, but he had to admit his approach to his patients was, to be sure, different.

"Hell," Lenihan said, "I don't expect you to be me, one's enough," and then he added intolerantly, "but at least be *you.*"

Johnny offered him the shrug of, then who is me?

"You got it written across the top of your face like a neon sign. 'Escape,' it says, but escape to where? You don't know where the hell to run. Escape to the Katz broad? Escape to Kohn's new big hospital deal? Lenihan laughed until he coughed up a plug of phlegm. He pushed a button, the window slid silently down, he spit out, and spoke clearly, the quality of his voice now the somber mellow quality he was credited for in local bridge and Mah-Jongg circles.

"Some big deal they got for you, J. J.," Lenihan said contemptibly. "Chief of General Clinics, whatever the hell *that* is. Don't be a jerk, don't give up the ship that got you there for one that never left the dock—Karl Kleinert. And you better believe he has made Mercy one of the best hospitals of its size in the East. You think hard before you leave us."

Johnny assured him he had thought.

"A few bad days," Lenihan said, "and a wife who thinks she's pregnant, and you're ready to cash in as the neighborhood sawbones."

Johnny asked what about Mary.

"She cornered me. You know Mary. Another good example—stick to your pills and I'll stick to mine. I don't know if she's pregnant, but she's not happy with my ginned-up tableside diagnosis."

Johnny said neither was he.

"Good show, J. J.," Lenihan smiled, puffed smoke into Johnny's ear, and said, "If that's your problem, you came to the right store. I'll tell you what I'm going to do—you turn over all your OB cases to me, and I'll see to it that Mother Shoemaker has a quiet, unburdening D&C. . . ."

11:15

GREENVILLE MERCY HOSPITAL

———

PRIVATE OBSTETRIC PARKING

LABOR ROOMS—HOSPITAL PERSONNEL ONLY

Estelle Crabtree, R. N.—Night OB Supervisor

—Just throw on a gown, boys, and save that mother—the baby's already dead. . . .

. . . .

Saturday, 11:50 P. M.
Hospital OB Lounge

Dear Tom (continued)—

When Jeanette Dusharme's mother was her age, she had already had six children and six more to go. Jeanette has already had two misses and has probably as of tonight struck out. She is not yet aware of her debenture on life, but soon I will be called to notify of same.

I'm writing to you now only in the hope of relieving a growing numbing glob in my head. Today has just about blacked out in me whatever whiteness might still be part of the life of the ol' family doctor. The death of Jeanette's baby is in itself not the tragedy. Babies do die; I have taken part in several. But the past deaths were of unmistakable cause and effect, and doctor or no, they were to be and were. Jeanette's baby should not have died, and my negligence is a direct cause. You will be happy to know that I did have at my side a masterful technician, and Jeanette is alive now only because of him.

We arrived together, Dr. Frank Lenihan and I, just about forty-five minutes ago, knowing well we had a transverse lay on our hands with a C-Section imminent. But what was neglected was the fact that I complacently left in charge of this tricky pregnant belly a raw, unthinking, greedy, but honorable and understandably anxious young intern. Just prior to our arrival, as the clock was closing in on him and the desperation to be for that moment a real doctor, he ruptured her membranes and made a manual rotation he observed once from a gallery and had read of once in a classroom. It worked. The infant came full around and decided to deliver stat. It strangled on its cord wrapped three times around its neck, and failed ever to open its eyes on this bright, blameless world.

We arrived as he was in his twelfth minute of resuscitation, sweat pouring from his every crevice, tears running from his swollen eyes. Thank God for Frank Lenihan. Jeanette was torn wide open, gushing blood like a broken faucet. Frank was unbelievably calm. His repair, single-handed—I cut sutures—was from the fingers of an artist. To have ridden with him moments earlier and to have sat by his side in the operating room was to have lived two separate lives. One door opens, another closes. The doctor is devil; the doctor is God.

I'm too tired and too full of nitrous oxide to explain that to you now, but it looks like your give-me-general-practice-or-give-me-death father is ready to phase out as predicated.

Dr. Lenihan is in cahoots with you, who have somehow formed an alliance with your poor, dead uncle Lem. You are all against me, but I cannot fight for me, because I cannot find "me." Could everything I have ever envisioned, everything I felt I had been spared for, the dream of the lovable old family doc who stands by your side in every hour of need—could this be the myth, and the real doctor be Frank Lenihan?

This is just about what you say, Tom. The days of the G.P., arc thcy really shadows in a fading sunset? Am I too stupid to dare to want to hold on in the face of writing so flagrantly slapped in my face?

Willie Washington scored four, you know. Laughing all the way. Never got a scratch.

All my patients apparently will do better in other hands than mine. *This* is the tragedy.

What is there then for me? I don't know, I really don't know.

For you, maybe you will make it so that at the end of your five years you will be a doctor who is not yet. How you will do it, what is the key, I have no fatherly or doctorly (sic) wisdom to offer you at this moment. I have been at this hour on Saturday, October 17, 1970, a moment before midnight, already turned back into a pumpkin.

I hope Lem will forgive me.

May God guide you as I feel (Lord, there it is again!!). I cannot.

Heaven help me, I am lost.

Love and hope from all,

Dad

P.S.–Tom, didn't I once take you to the Blue and Gold Banquet?

.   .   .   .

SUNDAY

1970	OCTOBER				1970	
S	M	T	W	T	F	S
				1	2	3
4	5	6	7	8	9	10
11	12	13	14	15	16	17
[18]	19	20	21	22	23	24
25	26	27	28	29	30	31

18

OCT. 1970

Morning
9:00

> ### FIRST CHURCH OF CHRIST
> ### GREENVILLE, N. J.
> Rev. Charles W. Ableman
> Sermon: "God, Sunday, and Doctors"

When Jonathan was ten years old he saw Reverend Ableman strike a boy with the Bible across the back of his shoulders, throw him to the ground, scream defamations of devilish origins at him, and order him out of his religious classroom forever.

With his own two hands Reverend Ableman had placed stone upon stone, plank upon plank, to build this church in this new and uprooted world, and no one man or boy was even by word to disturb a single flake of cement in its structure. His hellfire and damnation sermons roared through his small band of sin-struck congregants like a Nebraska twister, sweeping the weak and the bloodless to other churches—and from the tenacious and the willful who were able to hold on, he built one of Greenville's most indestructible congregations.

As his following grew and the times were good, Reverend Ableman's sermons mellowed, his hellfire became sparkles of peace and love, his damnations philosophical reflections. The newer members knew of him only as their most gentle and loving minister.

Not until this very morning did Jonathan see again the wrath that once was his Reverend. And Jonathan felt, with Reverend Ableman's glassy eyes bearing down upon him, as his long-ago friend in religious school must have felt—starting first with a sharp hammering pain across the back of his shoulders. . . .

—Congregants, I speak to you today of the loneliness of God, of God's lost people, and of his sadness. I speak to you today on a subject which permeates your daily living more vividly, more realistically than the word of God himself. As you know, two weeks ago my youngest brother in Cleveland, Ohio, was taken from us, and through your graciousness I was able to visit his wife and four young children, where my stay was of imminent Christian need. This young, vital lad, not yet in his fruitful years, was delivered over to God by one whom we have become to believe to be His right hand, his family doctor.

Joseph, my brother, was an artisan in a book bindery, an occupation in which he excelled and in which he found great pleasure. On Friday, the last day of his workweek, he entered the shop to investigate a complaint. One of the presses was sticking. Would he help the men release the metal wheel that had jammed? He found caught within the iron meshes a large binding copper staple, which he proceeded to pry loose. In so doing, he jabbed his palm with the sharp raw edge of the staple and proceeded from that moment to die.

The cut went unattended on a busy family Saturday. On Sunday he awakened with a high fever, a swollen hand, and dastardly pain. Several calls to his family doctor went unheeded. Finally his desperate young wife convinced the answering service it might have a very sick man on its conscience and the doctor's home was contacted. The doctor's wife stated the doctor was unavailable. A stand-in young resident from the local hospital was suggested but, when called, he begged off because he was "covering" for nine other doctors and was overwhelmed. He did promise he would put him on his list. By seven that evening he arrived. My brother, whose fever was now 104° and whose arm was fiery red, was given a shot and some antibiotic.

Assured of healing, the family patiently awaited the morning. By Monday morning the boy was delirious with fever and thrashing with pain. The family doctor was called in his office and his receptionist stated he was with a patient and would call back. At noon the doctor returned the call, stating his sorrow for the delay. However, his office was getting too busy for him and he must do something about it soon. At three that afternoon he visited my brother's home, and at four my brother was hospitalized as an acute septicemic emergency. At nine my brother was dead of what has been recorded as bacterial encephalitis.

God will forgive me in my grief for what I say, for it is His grief also. His right hand has been cut away. He no longer has for His right hand the reverent family doctor, for God has been blasphemed by this onerous group of men, and the Devil has taken on the lot.

Surely, you say, this is not *my* doctor of whom you speak. Not my kindly, sympathizing, attentive, fatherly, saintly doctor who has seen me through many of life's sorrows. Surely, if all the others have sold out to the Devil, mine remains true. Yes, in our very congregation we have eleven physicians and their fine families, several of whom have been with us through the pains of our early labors and have seen us delivered from the womb of the high school gymnasium to this, our humble new sanctuary. There are others of you who have been with us less time, but offer your kindly financial and moral support unhesitantly. But members of our congregation, to the very faces of these men, I must denounce what has become of them. They have passed out of God's reach and as assuredly as the word of God cometh through Jesus Christ, His Son, they have fallen hand in hand with the Devil himself.

Am I saying that my brother's doctor acted as dictate from the Devil? Am I saying that he is not an honorable man who entered into a life with honorable purpose? Am I saying that he purposely refused to heal my brother? Am I saying that my brother's doctor should not have a day of rest? Did not his God have a day of rest, you will answer? But, ah, herein lies the devilment. Is this man a God? Is any man a God? Who says that he is to rest from his chosen work? And who says that on Sunday he is to sign away his responsibilities to God for a man's life, and in its place choose not to rest, but to play? Where was my brother's doctor? At rest from his wearying load he had chosen to carry? No, not at rest where he could be summoned for the emergencies he had signed a covenant to protect, but at play on a private golf course, with all communications blocked by well-planned devices of the Devil.

Am I saying that my brother's doctor does not deserve a day of rest? That he has not toiled hard and long and with depleting consequences which necessitate this day of rest? Only my brother's wife and my brother's children can best answer this question. The day of rest God took only when at last his work was done. The doctor, who has openly made agreement to enter into the blessed profession of the care of the living and the dying, has made that covenant with his God that he *cannot* rest until that work is done. He cannot "sign off." He cannot turn his responsibilities on and off like an electric sign. He has signed a contract in the eyes of God with his patient from the moment he accepts to listen to his first set of complaints. And the contract says until death do us part seven days a week, twenty-four hours a day, Sundays and holidays, come hell or high golf.

There is no substitute for God in deciding who is to live and who is to die. My brother's doctor, in so arranging his life to suit his own devilish purposes, has assumed this role—and from my pulpit today, I denounce the entire profession of medicine for being so arrogantly, and ignorantly, and pitifully assumptive. . . . May God have mercy on us all. . . .

.   .   .   .

10:15

> ### GREENVILLE MERCY HOSPITAL
> ### OBSTETRIC PARKING ONLY
> ### MATERNITY—GRACE NEWLEY, R.N. ON DUTY

—She's all right, been sleeping on and off all morning. She cries a little, but between her husband and her mother, I'd be in hysterics. They've all but burned down your hospital in effigy. And her brother-in-law, a scurrilous-looking character, he's waiting for you in the lounge. Says he'll wait all day. . . .

The brother-in-law *was* a scurrilous-looking character—thin, haggard, as if he had not eaten in several days, and seeming many years older than his voice gave him away to be.

"Shoemaker? How do you do. Clarence R. Paltzinger here, LL.B., County Selectman, attorney, and brother of the anguished and despondent husband of Mrs. Dusharme, and father of the late George M. Dusharme, deceased now ten hours and forty-five minutes."

Dr. Shoemaker prepared himself. These were usually telephone bits, rarely face to face.

Paltzinger nervously flicked ashes from his serge suit, a spark making a hole in the collar. He spit on his fingers and made a pinch closing over the burn like he was used to this as a daily occurrence.

"I have been a practicing attorney in the southern sector of Philadelphia for seventeen years"—Johnny figured seven—"during which time I have administered legal aid to thousands of suffering men and women damaged by the cruelties of society and inequities of the law." He paused for a loose, phlegmy cough, flicked more ashes, and went on scurrilously. "However, in all my contacts, Doctor, with the ravages of man's inhumanity to man, the incidents leading up to and finally befalling my innocent sister-in-law far and away surpass any of the umbrages of any client I have ever had —" ash flick, pinch closing, phlegm cough. "This includes several dozen rapings, abortions, and intents to kill."

He shakily lit another cigarette and Johnny withheld his life-saving instincts to shove it down his precancerous throat. Instead, he hung on for the lawyer's sum-up.

"I have exhausted eight hours of interrogation," he mumbled through a mouthful of wet tobacco and smoke, "including that overworked and benevolent young intern, Calloway. The answers, my dear doctor, that I have come up with, lead me to only one irascible decision:

"I am filing for my clients, my anguished and despondent brother and his depressed wife, a suit of malpractice against Greenville Mercy Hospital, Dr. Frank Lenihan, and Dr. J. J. Shoemaker, in the sum of one million dollars. . . ."

. . . .

11:00   **THE SHOEMAKERS**
692 Lake Drive

Doctor's Entrance
THE DOCTOR IS NOT IN

Johnny, before going into the office, closely examined the Buick for the first time. It sat exhausted in the driveway, protected graciously by the weeping mimosa. A smashed left headlight, a wrinkled left bumper, a shoved-in radiator, a bent license plate, a scratched MD emblem.

What to do?

Could fix it up, make it like new, only a hundred deductible. Lucky if they don't cancel me, Johnny thought. Maybe better to write it off. I'll call Larry or Jerry. Have to tell them about Paltzinger. A guy could make a living going from hospital to hospital. There should be a million or so every day to be found.

Well, Johnny thought, got to get on to the golf course. . . .

THINGS TO DO TODAY—SUNDAY

1. ~~Hospital~~
2. Mail—Saturday
3. Blue Shield forms for—Cavendish, McKay, Holland, Turk Greenberg, Frankel.
4. Insurance forms for—Cavendish, McKay, Greenberg, Kirk Mahoney, Isaacson, Phillips, Washington.
5. School insurance for—Whipple, Stewart, Washington, Goldstein, Harper.
6. Medicare forms for—Abbott, Aronson, Chaucer, McKay, Frankel, Lionel, Roberts.
7. Lawyers letters for—McKay, Carlisle, Phillips, Greenblatt.
8. Report X rays to doctors—Sorenson, Brown, Kelly.
9. Letters to draft board for—Killian, Brownstein.
10. Prepare info for quarterly employees tax for acc't.
11. Review trust agreement and will.
12. Review medical report from Jackson Clinic.
13. Read article from Post Grad Medicine—"Retirement and Premature Death."
14. Repair tape recorder.
15. Repair X-ray cassette.
16. Repair toilet drip.
17. Repair signpost light.
18. Unpack United Medical supplies.
19. Record inventory narcotics, barbiturates, amphetamines.
20. Clean fish tank.
21. See Poppa Shoemaker.
22. Complete painting lesson #5.

.   .   .   .

12:00 RANDOLPH CARSON—690 Lake Dr., Greenville Lakes—Age
Noon   44—Married—Engineer WEC—File #2390—April 2, 1960.

—Hey, J. J. you in here? Mary said you were in the office.
What the hell you doing in on a day like today? Damn
doctors, never find them in on a day like today. Holy Chris',
you need some organization. Look at all them damn papers.
Don't they teach you fellows how to expedite these things?
We got machines at the office will do this stuff in four
seconds. Just call in one of our men, I'll send someone over.
Look, I don't want to bother you on your day off, but Holy
Chris', trying to get you during working hours is for the
peasants. Your police officer on the telephone says come take
your chances. In my business nothing is left to chance. So it'll
only take you a minute now. The relaxation is good for you.
Anyhow, I got a problem. Maybe you can learn something from
it, two other guys messed it up, maybe you can benefit
from it. Hell, a neighbor is a neighbor, and if I can't do you a
good turn, who can I turn to? Now, Doc, it's a long story.
This pain comes on about four o'clock every afternoon, it
starts right up here. . . .

. . . .

. . . Hey, Pops, it's them Puerto Ricans. They brought you
two baskets of apples and in the car outside is about eight
heads. They won't go away. They know you're here. . . .

. . . .

MIGUEL PEREZ and family—Pasture Road, Morganville—
Produce Pickers.

—She say she no wanna go no place else. She like you. We go
to hospital last week, she no better. She say only you. She
trust you. You see her, please, Doctor. We bring you new
apples. Very good. I go get her . . . . Hey, Mamma, all
right . . . . She say her head hurt bad. And she can't no
swallow too good. And she so hot, I can't no sleep with her
one night. You know you make her feel good, I pay you
anything. You don't worry about money. You fix her. She is
my wife. She is all I got. She sick all week and don't cook. I
got thirty men in the apples. They got to eat. She no cook all

week. I cook, and clean, and wash the dishes. You fix her, I pay anything. She is my wife, you know, and I still love her even if she look like she dead now. Here—hey Mamma—take off dress. Doctor, you look at her good. I excuse you. . . .

Thank you, thank you. You are a good doctor. I got my daughter in the car, she come all the way from New York with her kids. I don't know, so sick. You see them. . . . Hey, Melita . . .

. . . .

1:30 —Hey, Daddy, you're wanted on the phone. I don't know who it is. It's somebody. . . .

. . . .

—I swore on a stack of Bibles I would never do this, but Dr. Shoemaker, he *is* an old man. And this young kid you have taking your calls, well, I don't know. It's just he's visiting today and for him to ask for a doctor, well, he has got to be a sick man. Can you imagine, he is eighty years old and he still has his appendix. But if you could just run over. I figure what are neighbors for. . . .

. . . .

—Hey, Daddy, you're wanted on the phone. I don't know who it is. . . .

. . . .

—This is Finley in the ER, Doctor. We have a patient of yours here, she's going to fibrillate to death, but refuses treatment unless you are here. Now Dr. Grawtch is standing by with the cardioverter in his hands, but she says call my doctor. . . .

. . . .

—Hey, Daddy . . .

"Marvin, here, seven days and seven nights, that makes a week, man. You get that old doctor, a weak man, like a play on words, week, *weak,* man. Oh, well. Speaking of man—man—our boy Willie is on the glory road. He is like flying around here, putting in two days work in one afternoon. You must've bet heavy, you old sonofagun you. Give the kid a handful of speed and bet heavy—man. . . . Oh, yes, prescription for Katie Kelly, isn't that sweet. Like I can see her when she wore a tulip and I wore a big red nose. Renewal for number 18 *diaphragm.* They still use those things? Have a nice day, what're you doing in? . . ."

—Someone at the office door for you, Pops. Says it's personal. . . .

—I was driving by and saw both cars. . . .

.   .   .   .

—Hey, Pops, Mom says come out of the dungeon, Uncle Mac's here with Zelda. . . .

At two-thirty Johnny greeted his swinger brother-in-law with a pinched smile. The brother-in-law was in stocks and bonds and real estate and fraudulent bankrupt deals. Rich, very mucho. Johnny remembered the first stake for twelve hundred dollars, and wondered how to get it back. . . . Nine years, now. The family held him in awe. Son Charles said: "That's for me. High School dropout, world traveler, big money man. Marries a girls' underwear model. Hell, Pops, somebody just dealt you a bad hand, the way I see it."

Brother-in-law was here for a purpose, he never just *came.* Johnny was broke—and Mary knew it. "Let's get that Eagles game going, kiddo," brother-in-law said. He was used to saying let's get something or other going, kiddo. Johnny was relieved. He had worried about missing the game.

The Eagles were having a rotten year. They were in Cleveland today. Brother-in-law said what a raw deal, he could have flown in and caught it live. "But no," he said, "I got to come sit in front of a sixteen-inch set with too much red in it and watch a game. How come you can't get a twenty-four inch without red in it, Johnny? You need cash? Come on, kiddo."

Johnny was relieved. When b-in-l made a jesting offer, momentarily he was not in need—although he wasn't offering either. "Why am I here, instead of there—dammit, this guy Williams is as bad as Kuharich. Who the hell has he got at tight end—fumble, *fumble! Get that damn ball.* Shit. Handle a ball like it's a greased pig. I should be there. What am I doing here? Ask her," he said, "ask your sister-in-law, Zelda, why I'm here." She was in the other room trying her new mink on Mary.

"I says to Zelda," b-in-l said to Johnny—"*Bradley, you bum, run, run*—three big yards—I say, Zelda, for a Jewish girl who married out of class you sure got yourself a reversible goy. Mink coats. Cadillac cars—Johnny, please, let *me* buy it for you, you'll pay me back at five and a half percent, where could you get it at half today? My sister, the wife of a doctor, riding around in a eight-year-old Buick, now with dents. They'd laugh me out of the Boy's Club. You need a deal?"

Johnny assured him he needed no deal.

Bill Nelson of the Browns tossed a thirty-seven-yard touchdown pass and the Browns led 27-6. B-in-l cursed Leonard Tose, the new Eagles owner.

"I could've had that club, two more guys back me up, I could've had it. Johnny, you need a deal? You can tell me, I'm like flesh and blood. You got hot money stashed away you can't spend? I'll give you a piece of property I just took an option on in Center City, the whole package is yours for forty grand, cash. That you got under the refrigerator."

Johnny assured him the refrigerator was without his monetary help.

"Wherever the hell you doctors keep it, Chris', Johnny, *I'll* buy the car. I'll *lease* it to you . . . *stupid putz!* Guy can't even kick a football thirty-two yards over the goal. *Send him back to Canada.*" B-in-l cursed the entire Philadelphia back-field.

Johnny was not enjoying the game. He watched Cyril Pinder run broken field and get clipped from the rear and eight men pile onto his sunken body. But he *saw* Willie Washington's number 3 green and white jersey tear-legging it past all contacts and once, twice, three times, four times, plunge over that end zone to the ecstatic glee of the whole damn stand. And he shivered to think he was not equally gleeful. Rather lonely and glum. He had pressure, hard inside, deep pressure again.

He watched Snead short pass to Woodeshick and watched

the bulky back get smeared and the ball bounce crazily over near the end zone, and watched Dave Lindsey smother it for the Browns. But he *saw* Willie Washington pick it off the ground like a ragpicker would snap up a paper bag, and he saw Willie fly ninety-seven yards to the other end of the field. And he heard the stands go ape, and he waited for Willie to thrust him into the sky. And he found himself behind Miss Georgia Jones and found he didn't come out until Willie went back into the game.

The b-in-l had just cursed the entire Philadelphia team.

"I should be there," he said. "I could be there spitting on those bums. I could buy and sell them. She knows that, but no, she wants me to come here today. What more does she want from me?" He outlined the cars and the minks and the swimming pools, the vacations in Bermuda and the vacations at the Concord. "She wants 'something' more lasting, she says. Now, Johnny, what is more lasting, I ask you, than a thirty-two-foot Chris Craft? You got something more lasting? Yeah, yeah, big thing, a seven-foot '63 Buick."

Johnny could read it, like he could read the young girls with missed periods, and the men with the clap. One look and he could read the brother-in-law. It was coming.

"Three kids," b-in-law says. "Can you imagine, she tells me she never enjoyed making one. And what about the two-point-five times weekly us gentile lovers are supposed to partake of? Never once, she tells me, does it ring the bell. Why? Ask her why?"

Zelda was in the other room trying her bracelets on Mary. The Browns were in field-goal position.

"Block it, you bums, block it."

Nobody blocked it, nobody even tried. Johnny remembered why he gave up the Eagles' season ticket. In pro football you don't try to get killed. You are over twenty-one, and the name of the game is Survive. To the kids in high school the name of the game is Kill. You play with relentless, blind, joyful spirit; the spirit says Kill, and the game is good. Johnny liked the abandon of the high school game. He liked the play for Kill, and wondered why. He wished he could leave the room and cry, and wondered why. He reached into his memory bank for a slide of Willie racing downfield clutching his head, falling to his knees, wretching in pain. Quiet on the field: no such slide. He wondered why.

Brother-in-law was now entering the last call for help. He was no different now than the seven forty-five appointment on Friday, only it was Sunday, and you got right in, and it was free. But in the end it was the same: Help me—I don't need anyone, but help me.

"You know why she wants me here today? Let me tell you. You take a girl off the streets and you never get her out of the gutter. You give a poor Jewish girl from the back of a fruit store a twenty-carat life and what does she want? She wants you should circumcise me. . . ."

Al Nelson went forty yards off right end for a score. Browns 37, Eagles 17. B-in-law cursed the entire city of Philadelphia. . . .

.   .   .   .

5:00   "I'm Mary, John, remember?"

Mary didn't come to John very often. In this office rarely ever, now.

"We're eating in a half hour. Going to join us?"

John crossed out 8, 9, 10 and 11 on his List of Things to Do Today, threw away Post Grad Med article, rescheduled 13, 14, 15, 16, and 19, for next Sunday, and greeted Mary with bland acknowledgement that he would join them for dinner. Sunday dinner was bearable. The elements of table life remained as disparaging, but time allowed for a kindlier flow of digestive juices. He would eat Sunday dinner.

Mary, he knew, didn't come to invite him to dinner. She unpinned her curlers and let her soft amber hair fall to her neckline. John noticed and wondered why he didn't kiss her neckline.

"You know, I guess, that I'm not pregnant."

"I know." Johnny also knew for some ungodly but advantageous reason she really wanted to be pregnant. Women are crazy, he heard Garrone say, they want you to hold them, but not too tight, and not too long, and not too often. They want you to know that sex is *your* thing, but theirs when they are ready. John wondered if she was ready. He was not.

There was a time on a Sunday when Mary would come to

the office and he would be ready. She would step in; he would hear a muffled click of the lock, and Mary would stand in his doorway shadowed by late afternoon sun, very pretty. And Mary would crease up her forehead, and purse up her lips, and begin to berate him for working his life away over those people. It came out like Instant Replay of Complaint Standards. . . .

"... *My God, John, you've been hibernating in this cave for four straight hours. Can't we do something together?"*

And John began the countdown. "Five, ten, fifteen, twenty, twenty-five, thirty ..."

And Mary, quietly with pokerlike elation, continued her plugged-in diatribe.

"You missed lunch, like you planned to miss it. You missed David telling Skin to shut up, Skin telling Pimples to drop dead, Tom dropping his weights on the table. You missed Jennie not answering to Jennie, it is Jeanette *nowadays. Life is passing you right by, Doctor. You weren't even present to see your little girl step from Jennie to Jeanette. . . ."*

And Johnny was up and at her soft-scented neck. He could not at this moment name the origin, insertion, or action of a single neck muscle; he was counting ... forty, forty-five, fifty, fifty-five, sixty ..."

Mary backed into Treatment Room Number Three, the one with the four-inch foam-covered table. And Mary switched on, "I will not lie for you on the telephone again. I want to crawl under a rock sometime. They know I'm lying, and I could never stand anyone knowing I'm lying. Even the kids have learned to say 'My father is not home' with you sitting right in front of them. . . ."

John held Mary propped against the X ray box in Room Number Three. It was black in here with the door shut. He flicked on the pale, cool X ray light. He liked his wife reflected in pale, cool X ray light. He held her face in his, her hair highlighting formless shadows from the flat boxed light. His count had skipped rapidly ... "seventy-five, eighty, eighty-five ..."

Mary said, "Something is missing in our life. . . ."

"Ninety ..."

Mary said, "Something is . . ."
"Ninety-five . . ."
Mary said, "Was . . ."
And John said, "One hundred."
The table and Mary and John were soft and the light was
soft and love was soft—and warm—and good on a Sunday
afternoon.

John was not ready on this Sunday afternoon. He knew
there was deep trouble brewing, and he said so to Mary. Mary
shook her head; she knew. John said to Mary, it is
menopause. Mary said to John, it is John. Neither said the
truth.

"Shall I leave you?"

"No one will leave anyone," John said.

"It's no way to live."

"It's life."

"Don't talk to me in saintly riddles, I am not a patient."

"Don't act like one."

"I am a person."

"I know how persons act."

"Not this one," Mary said.

"How true."

Mary said, "We don't communicate."

"About what?"

"So what's left?"

"Life."

"Whose?" Mary said.

John said—hesitantly—"Ours."

Mary cried; John waited. Mary turned to leave. She didn't
like to cry, or to be seen crying. She opened the office door.

"I'll be in for dinner."

"Why?"

John wondered why. Mary waited for an answer. The
telephone, the hateful, omnipresent, omniscient telephone
rang, and John was happy.

The voice made him chill.

It was Sam, the death messenger. Myra Sacks was dying in
her store. Come quick.

. . . .

5:45

> SACKS' DELI-LAND
> ... Through These Portals Pass the
> World's Most Beautiful Salamis...

Dinner hour. The store was packed with hungry Green-villites. Sacks' was a good place to go. They gave a good meal, they cared. Now Myra was gasping for a longer stay because she cared. Johnny looked at her purple-ballooned face begging for air and he wondered what the caring was all about. Where would she be for lunch tomorrow?

It was evidently the aneurysm. It was seeping—if it had burst, she would be dead by now. At best on her last breath. Either way, Johnny got right to work on her on the kitchen floor, saying nothing. Sam talked.

"Dr. Johnny, oh, you're a God, a real God. Who else would I call? Go ahead, work, she's hardly *breathing now*. Every-body look out, he's a *doctor*. Get out. Go back into the store. Such a busy hour she picks. . . . *Gottenu*. Doctor, open your bag, give her something."

Johnny finished his examination and opened his bag. He gave her two needles. She screamed out with each one. "You're killing me!" And then she went back to gasping, clutching her breasts.

"What are you giving her? Doctor, you know she's allergic, careful what you give her. *Another* one. *Gottenu*, she must be sick. Myra, beautiful Myra, don't worry, breathe, *Mommenu*, breathe, here is Dr. Johnny, he'll make you breathe."

Johnny pulled open her apron and ripped apart her dress. She was not responding. He pounded on her sternum.

"Doctor, what are you doing? You close up her dress, you hear? She is a very modest woman. To this day she never exposed herself to me. Thirty-nine years last Tuesday, we got only another year we get a party from the kids. Eighteen grandchildren, Doctor, eighteen. Myra, you *hear*, a big party."

Myra did not hear. She had stopped breathing. Johnny pounded on her chest. Sam reached to pull him away. "You're hurting them," he screamed. "Those lovely breasts, they fed six healthy babies. Stop hurting them." Johnny kept pounding. "Myra, breathe, breathe, please breathe."

Johnny opened his bag and extracted an airway. He jammed aside her spastic tongue and shoved the plastic piece into her throat. He began a rhythmic breathing into her mouth and excursions upon her chest.

You don't die on me, old girl, he said to himself. Haven't I had enough? You just don't dare die. I told you were in trouble years ago, now I have to pay *your* price? Breathe, damn you.... She did not. You don't tell Myra Sacks to breathe and expect her to listen.

Sam got up. "Leave her alone, Doctor, you know she is dead." Johnny kept breathing and moving her chest. "Oh, Myra! *Gottenu!* Six o'clock Sunday dinner, such a time you pick to die...."

Myra, as if in total humiliation, breathed once. Then twice. Then three, then ... rhythmically. Her purple became blue, then gray, then white, then peached out. Johnny had someone call the rescue squad.

They hadn't talked about it, but when she was packed into the ambulance, Johnny automatically said, "Greenville Mercy, I'll follow her over."

It was then Sam said, "Uh-uh." It was all right, he said to Dr. Johnny, when you got pneumonia, or when you got everyday aches and pains, but after all, a girl who was just dead? You send her to University Hospital in Philadelphia, I'll call my brother and he'll get the best specialist.

Johnny said, "*Sam!?*"

"Look, Johnny, *boychick,* don't I love you? Don't I send you patients you can't find room for? Who else would I trust but *you?* But, Johnny, this is my *wife.* Would you do different for *your* wife? ..."

. . . .

6:30   Number 21 on the list was See Poppa Shoemaker.

Once a week, sometimes less, Johnny made the pilgrimage to the nursing home. Poppa had been in extended care for six years. A year after Momma died everything fell apart: He lost a leg from diabetic gangrene, the store went to Marvin, and senile arteriosclerotic changes forced Johnny to make the son's final agonizing move for his parent.

It was a little ride into the country, and Johnny welcomed the fresh smell of October corn, the memories that came with crackling leaves. The brisk evening air poured into the car and beat color into Johnny's washed-out face. He shrugged his shoulders, shook his head, and made comment to himself as to what was happening all of a sudden to his life. A man comes and goes, serves his time, offers up his life, spills his blood, and in the final analysis is marking time alone. For fifteen years Sam Sacks' personal, but *personal,* doctor. Myra all right, a tough patient, in and out, couldn't pin her down, but you are his doctor, his confidant—he said it himself, his *God.* And like you switch off the TV, you switch off the God. Send her to University—call a specialist. She's alive, but she's dead. Get a big name—*big.* "He'll bring her back. He'll come running out in place of his dinner and he'll pound her chest and suck her saliva and bring her back. Sure he will. . . ."

"Lem, you hear that?"

But Lem did not come.

"Lem, Lem?"

The sun suddenly was gone, the air chilled and damp, night was moving in. Johnny reached over and rolled up the windows. He was cold, his skin moist and clammy. He pushed shut the vents, but cool air kept flowing over his legs. Damn accident probably blocked the vents. The Buick coughed and stalled out. He pumped and choked and got it going again. "It's inevitable," he said out loud, "it's got to be. Doesn't a guy have a choice?" His voice took on a bedeviled shrillness as if it were not himself, but as if he were outside talking in. "The car is next," he said matter-of-factly. "What else? Bowl 'em all over. Strike! You're next, car. You're next."

Hey, Lem, the Buick's dying. I need you now, you stupid ass, where the hell are you? What have I done? Why don't you come to me? Lem—please—come back—I need you—I need . . .

Johnny found himself in the nursing home parking lot. How long he had been there he didn't know. He knew his stomach was caught in a grinder. He knew his head was eight-feet wide and expanding. He knew his fingers were bloody. He looked into the rear-view mirror and was stunned to see red-rimmed eyes. Crying? Ridiculous! He pulled up his jacket collar and entered the Home, where he would find solace, comfort, credibility, life as it is. Here is a place where you are needed. Here is a place where you will be what you are, more than what you are. Here you will find a fading life commodity. Here you will find ancient warmth.

> WILLIAM R. BROWN
> ADMINISTRATOR

7:00   Billy Brown looked more like the receiver than the administrator of services at Greenville's latest addition to the bulging nursing home community. Even sitting down, he was taller than Johnny, freakish behind his desk like a sideshow thin man. A bend in either direction would break him like a dry twig. Only three or four years ago, Johnny remembered, Billy Brown, was a fat, sweating G.P. running a factory office where people would come and stand in line, spilling over onto the porch and down the sidewalks waiting for three and four hours to get in to see him, even in the rain or snow. Now his bony face and ghoulish-cast eyes and maloccluded jawline and scratchy voice made Johnny uncomfortable and uncertain in his presence. He could see himself five years from now behind his Director of General Clinics desk, and wondered how it would feel to be free like Billy. . . .

—This is my life, J. J. *Anything* is better than general practice. This is no place for weak livers, but I psyche myself. These people are dirty and smelly and cantankerous and bitchy and sick with every damn disease. And if they're not sick and dying, they're crazy and alive. But they're my buddies. I stick my head in their doors, smile, wave, listen to a heart or a lung once in a while. Nothing bothers me. I don't even smell the place anymore—my sinuses are rotten, it's the best damned thing ever happened. But they're a good bunch. I get attached, like owning a dog. I hate to see them die, but there always seem to be more. I'd build another one in town if I could get enough help. The turnover of nurses is ridiculous. A girl can take so much wet beds and shitty sheets. The biggest problem for me is keeping up. I can't get a doctor to spend any time here. Now there's a good deal, J. J., there's a fortune in it. I got Medicare billings going out each week that would turn your bank account green, but I need help. This could be your answer, J. J., you look like hell. Don't I know, didn't I go through it? I used to wake up in the middle of the night and find myself freezing and bawling my eyes out. I haven't missed a night's sleep in five years. Lost a lot of weight, but hell, money-counting takes a lot out of a guy.

Tell you what, J. J. You come up with twenty grand and you're a full partner in the new place. I need cash. I'm billing a small fortune out of this place, but the damned Medicare keeps knocking me down. Now, if there were two of us, with a little cash surplus, you got a second chance, J. J. How many in a lifetime get a second chance? Buy yourself out of purgatory for only twenty grand. . . .

. . . .

7:15 JOSHUA SHOEMAKER—Age 72—Widower—CVA—Diabetic— Rt. leg amputee.

"Hello, Jonathan. Is it Friday again? I just closed my eyes and you were here, and now I open them and you are back. Did you bring the kids?

Jonathan hadn't brought the kids in three years. They just felt cringy coming here, and after a few battles they stopped coming.

"I would like to see the baby. Just a few months old now, she must be quite a rascal. Keep her warm and give her regular physics. I believe in physics, they keep the mind pure."

Jonathan remembered the cascara seeds and senna leaves and podophyllin pods and rhubarb root and flaxseed and chamomile tea, and his belly growled and his rectum puckered. He felt sick.

"You look fine, son. How are you doing? All your customers come in today? Treat them nice, smile, even if you're sick and tired of them, give them honest measure and they'll come back. Wipe my mouth, son."

Jonathan wiped his father's mouth. It drooled like a teething infant and ran down the corners and over his ragged beard and settled there making crusty, foul-smelling indentations. Jonathan remembered a sparkling cherry jellylike face with a hand-brushed homburg atop and a razor-edged Vandyke below and the smile of a happy fool in between.

"Marvin should clean the fountain with ammonia. Syrup stains won't budge unless you use ammonia. Your Mom takes care of that anyway, she'll keep Marvin straight. She always does me. From the first day we took over that store, I knew your mother would take us places. She certainly makes a clean fountain, and if there's anything a person wants when they come into a store—say, Jonathan, why isn't she with you?"

Why isn't *Mary* with me, Jonathan thought.

"She could break away one night just to straighten my blankets. Nobody could straighten blankets like your Mom. You kids when you were tucked in, God forbid there was a fire, you'd never get loose. Son, there was a fire once, wasn't there? There *was* a fire. . . ."

Every time, Jonathan thought, every time I come. Dammit, *every* time.

"I told you to keep them boxes of cotton balls away from the furnace. I told you. Now see what you done. . . ."

Poppa, please.

"He would have been Lemuel K. Shoemaker, M.D. What a fine doctor! . . . You ever need any help, son, you just call on Lem, he has it born in him. And he is a good boy, too. I think about him a lot in the fire when my eyes are closed."

I do, too, Poppa.

"Oh, God, Jonathan, I am glad I have you. You just keep working at it, son, you ain't no Lemuel, but you can be a damned good doctor. Don't you worry, son, Lemuel'll make you the best damned . . . Jonathan, how's business? Don't ever be too proud to talk to your father. I know what it is in the early years. You need any money? You know it's no snapper with three little kids and a new practice. Town's pretty small, but hold on, son, don't you pay me no rent for a few months, you hear, until you get started. You can live in back of the office for a few years, it does you good. Didn't you kids do it? Made you both great doctors . . . both. . . ."

Jonathan fed his father corn soup and ground-beef hash with mashed potatoes, weak tea, and a butter cookie soaked in milk, and gave him his nighttime meds.

"Where'd you get those pills, Lem? Are you dispensing *in your office?* Rotten, ungrateful kid! Jonathan, tell your mother to come see me today, I must talk to her about Lemuel dispensing in his office. You think Mom will come today? I miss her. She smells from ammonia, that woman, but it's cleaner and cheaper than that French junk your wife wears—and it cleans out my eyes."

Jonathan had to leave. He had no place to go, but . . .

"Don't, Jonathan, it's so quiet here all week—no kids at the fountain blowing straws, so quiet. Can I come home with you? I won't be trouble. I'd like to be around kids again, they make me laugh. You think Mary would mind if I came? . . ."

. . . .

At seven forty-five Johnny sat in the Buick a full ten minutes before starting her up and heading her home. He had been ravaging his mind's memory banks for a clearer picture of incidents leading up to the fire. He tried piecing together a visualization of the actual, horrible moment when his brother was enveloped in the sacrificial flames, the exact moment when he himself was entangled in some floozie's lace panties. He was sick over his father's constant references to the cotton balls and the furnace, sicker over the possible truth of it. He was sickest over the flash thought of lace panties and fiery death.

That's why you're not coming any more? "Lem!" He screamed into the hot Buick air. "Lem! Come on out, wherever you are, Lem, it's dark in here. Hey Lem—I'm scared. Come out, come out. . . ."

". . . wherever you are. Come out, come out." The best place to hide was behind the old medicine boxes down in the furnace room.

Little Jonathan crept into the back storeroom making sure he was out of Poppa's sight, because Poppa said never *go down those trap-door stairs without somebody holding on to you. It's dark, and dangerous, and to make the pledge stick, he said, the rats will eat you alive.*

Other than an occasional country mouse, Jonathan and Lem had never come across any of the larger varieties, but they allowed themselves few defiances. Playing in the storage basement was one.

The favorite game was Ghost. You hide from each other, then make eerie noises, throwing your voices and keeping your hiding place a secret. The object was one is Big Ghost and one is Little Ghost. Lem always seemed to end up Big Ghost and Little Ghost had to go find him.

Jonathan hated this game. It was frightening standing in the middle of this rat-infested, black room loaded down with strange medicine bottles and strange, eerie sounds. But he played like we all play, because the discovery of Big Ghost—although scary at the instant his hand creeps along your neck—ends in resolution, and like in a bad dream, you say, "Now that I am about ready to die, I will awaken." Lem's hands at his neck made his innards loose, and one time he actually lost control, sending Lem into squeals of laughter and sending Poppa down after them with a length of rubber hose. But after the cold, eely hands came, then Little Ghost was able to grab hold and hug Big Ghost and all was safe and good again. They would tell weird stories to each other, and they would tickle each other and would laugh and laugh until tears came into their eyes.

This one day Big Ghost never came out. As usual, they pulled straws for position. As usual, Lem won and went off to hide. Somehow or other Little Ghost knew he was alone. The dankness of the room crept over his petrified body. Rats were swarming at him from all sides. Lem had snuck out. He hadn't wanted to play. He had just about outgrown this game and he had a girl down the street he would run off to see. He even told Jonathan he once saw she wore lace panties. Fearful of the absolute black darkness, fearful of being eaten by rats, fearful to cry out because Poppa would hose him, Jonathan ran around in circles, flaying in all directions for some hope, some glimmer that Big Ghost had not really left him alone. A touch, just a touch on the neck, scare me, make me jump out of my skin—"Big Ghost, please, Big Ghost," he whispered as loud as he dared. "Please, Big Ghost, you know how scared I am. Come out. Come out."

Lemuel was gone. Jonathan, now aware of the truth,

attempted to pick up the boxes he had knocked over, but the darkness and the desperation made him stumble and fall and he scraped both hands and, holding them up in the dark, he felt them bleed and he cried out loud, "Lem, Lem, I hate you, Lem...."

And Lem came to Jonathan in the Buick at this final moment before panic, and he said simply to him, "Thank God Poppa is senile. If he were to know how you botched up your life. I have given you twenty years, Jonathan, and you're still the Little Ghost crying in the dark. You need some advice? It's very simple. You haven't made it, and you never will. If someone is kind enough to offer you a job, take it; you're lucky. That's all. And stop calling me, I'll come when I want."

And Lem was gone.

"You left me in the dark," Jonathan screamed. "I hate you, Lem. I *never* liked you. I hope you are still burning in hell!..."

. . . .

8:30

> HERMAN M. BLOOMQUIST, M.D.
> —NEUROPSYCHIATRY—

Neuropsychiatrists make very few Sunday calls, but Bloomquist came at once. He was in the hospital when Johnny arrived. Bloomquist was out to cure all G.P.'s, explaining that any doctor who punishes himself so stoically is suffering severe guilt and needs the cure.

He had other doctor syndromes which also needed curing, his favorite being that any doctor who continues to eat in the hospital cafeteria after he has completed his internship is obviously psychotic. Although the men wouldn't dare chance his cures for themselves, Bloomquist was the recipient of most of their referrals. He got results. Where others failed, he turned out neuropsychiatric cures like one would lance a boil. He didn't believe in wasted years of analysis, and if he couldn't work out the cure in short order, he was secure enough to label it incurable.

His approach—which frightened away the doctor, not his patient—was often way out. He was known to put patients naked into wooden boxes and let them stay locked in it for several days. He injected little-known chemicals into their veins and played back their trips to them on home video tape. He held group experiments, all in the nude. He lectured women's clubs on sex play and was known to be the cause of four neighborhood partner swaps. He gave sex-education courses to fifth-grade boys and girls, for one season only.

His latest revival was shock treatment.

"One or two milliseconds, Johnny, my boy, and *whatever* is wrong, at least you are given a fighting chance. We're living a shocking type of existence today, so, fight fire with fire. An electrode here on the frontal lobe, an electrode there, and—click, click—you are cured! Who wants to listen to your infantile toilet habits?"

Johnny had come in desperation. To allow Bloomquist even an opportunity at him was a humiliation, but he could not go on. He had fought his way back to the hospital battling the voices of Arturo, Willie, Marvin, Poppa, Kleinert, and Leader, and he threw up in the parking lot, but it didn't help. You could throw up your guts, but up there in your head they keep poking away at you, hot, fired-up pokers at your brain. Words. Words.

"Everybody hears voices, Johnny," Bloomquist said after a closely attentive period following Johnny's recall of his recent accident and the voices. "Psychiatrists would be out of business without voices. They're all around us. Some hear them all the time, some at special times. Who knows how many discoveries and inventions, as well as international decisions, have been made from voices? From the moment we are born, maybe before, voices and words and sounds make indelible imprints on our nerve circuits. They may key in at the strangest unrelated time later, sometimes much later on. So, John, it seems you're not so crazy after all. I worry about the guy who *doesn't* hear voices."

Doctors had the nasty habit of putting down other doctors' complaints, but Johnny was too sick to be put down. He explained to him that it was only his brother Lem's voice he heard for many years, but now they were all bombarding him. Dead, alive, or not yet born, they were all closing in.

Bloomquist made funny little noises with his cheeks, puffing them out and poking them with his finger, blowing air into the room like the nervous, semi-silent expelling of gas. He was deep in thought over a new treatment for voices.

"Strange you should come to me at this time," he said to Johnny, gratefully. "I have been working on a group shock plan where all similar reactants are joined together through multiple electrodes attached to a single switch and—click, click—interchange of nerve energy—*unshock*—reduction of nerve interplay. You are locked into other brain energies and must be deployed from them like uncapping a hot bomb fuse. Our first group meets Wednesday. You must bring with you as many reactants as you can: Arturo, Kleinert, Leader, your wife, Lem—"

Johnny was not satisfied. He explained to Bloomquist that he had been happy with Lem. There was no problem here, he accepted his comings and goings, he looked forward to them. He asked for them, he *needed* them. But suddenly, as if all the other voices have frightened Lem, or influenced him, or changed him in some way, it was not working out.

"Wednesday," Bloomquist stated.

Johnny said it was not that easy. It is not that he wants to get rid of *all* the voices. Just the others.

"All or nothing, Johnny."

"They're so persistent now," Johnny told him. "And so defiant. They run me down. They disagree. They undermine whatever framework I ever had to live on. And worst, they must have gotten to Lem; he agrees with them. I scream at him. I never scream at people. Never at Lem. I told him I hate him. Bloomquist, I am ashamed."

Bloomquist told him there was no other answer. Shock. Shock and—*unshock*.

"Enough of your jokes, Bloomquist." Johnny screamed at him as if he were locked into the Buick. "I am a sick man. I am coming to you for medical help. I went to my friends, they say go to a specialist. Specialist of *what?* Where can a doctor go? I can't even go to my minister, now. Bloomquist, help me, don't treat me like I am a child Don't give me your quack ideas."

Bloomquist, hurt, got Johnny's message, but he was still Bloomquist. "Sorry, boy, but I am right, and you are wrong."

"That's what it is," Johnny cried out. "They are all right and I am all wrong. Did you hear about Willie? Scored four laughing all the way."

"You need help."

"Goddammit, Bloomquist, I am finally getting through to you."

"You are suffering from a list of psychoses as long as a Chinese dinner menu, Johnny. You have one column of paranoia, you have another column of schizoid, one column manic, one depressive, two columns hysteria—but most of all, what really matters is you are a person who is very, very unhappy—this is what really matters."

And to this Johnny had to tearfully agree, and so he cried. It was not a real cry like when his brother Lem died, or at Mom's funeral. It was more like when Mary announced she still had another baby in her belly after he had aborted the one. It was a cry of guilt, and remorse, and relief—mostly relief. Someone understood.

Bloomquist told him his brain cells needed a shutdown. Now shock would do it, but again there are other ways. There are drugs, put you out for a few weeks. There are gases, there are wooden boxes.

"But it has been my experience," Bloomquist said, puffing his cheeks into the air, "that all you doctors need is a little of your own medicine. So this is what we do. You take a brand new bottle of aspirin, now it must be a fresh, unopened bottle. All right so far? Remove two aspirin from the bottle every four hours. Place the aspirin on a red linen napkin. Fill an amber glass, *amber,* three quarters full of distilled water with a quarter teaspoon of Arm and Hammer, *Arm and Hammer,* bicarbonate of soda. Drink it down slowly, taking a full five minutes to finish it. Get under your covers and stay there for a full twenty-four hours. All right, Johnny boy, got it? Now, if that doesn't shock any doctor back to reality—then I will see you on Wednesday. Our group meets at eight thirty-three sharp. . . ."

.   .   .   .

10:00   THE SHOEMAKERS
                            692 LAKE DRIVE
                            ─────────────
                                WELCOME

   Johnny laid out on his night table the new bottle of
aspirin, the red linen napkin, the distilled water, the amber
glass, the Arm and Hammer bicarbonate of soda, and fell
asleep crumpled over the last lines of Things to Do Sunday.

21. ~~See Poppa Shoemaker.~~
22. Complete painting lesson #5.

.   .   .   .

MONDAY

1970	OCTOBER					1970
S	**M**	**T**	**W**	**T**	**F**	**S**
				1	2	3
4	5	6	7	8	9	10
11	12	13	14	15	16	17
18	19	20	21	22	23	24
25	26	27	28	29	30	31

19

OCT. 1970

• •

Morning

8:00   Johnny was awakened from a dream; the alarm, a silent
voice deep inside his head. He rested there in his shade-drawn
room, light cracked through the edges cutting across his eyes.
They blinked and he smiled in its warmth. I'm alive. It was a
dream. He shook. Damn dreams are getting closer to home all
the time. When I tell Bloomquist the asinine prescription he
gave me—

An arrow of light pierced amber glass and bounced waves
against the paneled wall. It shattered Johnny's dream. There
were other shatterers. The new bottle of aspirin, the Arm and
Hammer, the red linen cloth. The alarm inside jangled
insistently and Johnny obediently filled the amber glass three
quarters with distilled water, threw two aspirin back against
his dried-out tongue, and sipped slowly.

He remembered. His last dose was 4 A.M. The note he
wrote for Mary was propped against the bathroom plumbing.

Mary—

Don't awaken me. I'm staying in bed today.

I'll explain later. Keep the kids out.

Good girl. The curiosity-seekers' parade was aborted. Pop's
in *where?* She held it to that. Good girl. Wanted to leave her
twelve times. I'd have to be a full-blown madman, not just a
Bloomquist toy, to try this thing all over from zero. I'll stay.

Bloomquist's Rx was already working.

He dozed.

Mary awakened him with a disturbing nudge **on** his
shoulder. There was a special delivery *registered* letter from
the hospital.

He tore it open and read it while Mary marked time
puttering around the room.

GREENVILLE MERCY HOSPITAL

GREENVILLE, NEW JERSEY

Office of Executive Director: Karl Kleinert

October 18, 1970

Dear Dr. Shoemaker:

The Board of Trustees, the Administration Department, the

legal staff, and myself have been at work all day today attempting to clear away the kindling of a very urgent matter before it burns away unnecessary property.

As you know, the task of hospital administrator is oft strewn with the debris of its members and its physical working plant. To surge to a surface and keep the institution out of contaminated waters is a thankless and deenergizing job, but a job which must be done for the ultimate safeguard of not only the immediate hospital family, but for the community which it is dedicated to serve.

Precisely, our problem today is to act upon an untimely event which occurred in our OB department Saturday night in which an infant's life was sadly lost. We have received word that because of negligence on the part of some, we are now involved along with you, Dr. Shoemaker, in a million-dollar litigation.

Of course, this is not a new experience to hospital officials. The elements of chance and death hang heavy over our house at every moment, but apparently this instance involves a lot more. The attorney for the neglected mother has chosen to make this event a banner which he intends to wave in support of a new local hospital. And, of course, you know only too well, Doctor, how our Board feels about this Brutus-like act.

Therefore, after careful study and evaluation of the facts as garnered through thorough midnight-oil burning, we have come to an irrevocable decision.

Enclosed with this letter you will find a notice which is self-explanatory. As of Saturday, October 17, 1970, your hospital privileges were under suspension due to an infringement of hospital policies, re: record and chart completions. Therefore, your obstetrical privileges were similarly infringed upon when you entered your patient, Mrs. Jeanette Dusharme. Therefore, the act which occurred Saturday night was without hospital approval and without Chief of Staff's acknowledgement. In fact, our Chief, Dr. Lenihan, did respond to the night nurse's call for emergency aid—which is hospital policy— and indeed saved what might have been a second tragedy.

In short, Dr. Shoemaker, you will assume full responsibility for the delivery of a dead infant.

We are sure you will understand that this procedure, as agonizing as it appears on the surface, will obliterate the force of the opposition's scurrilous attacks, and the issues represented will then fizzle to a simple malpractice maneuver.

At the completion of the legal action against you, of course, the Board and Dr. Lenihan will reconsider your application to return to the obstetrical staff of our community. . .

Johnny's head pounded.

He dialed Bloomquist. Then he hung up. He dialed Kohn.

"They're all the same," he said to Mary. "The enemy is the same person. He is Kleinert and Leader and Lenihan, the same person. I swear, he changes clothes and puts on a plastic mask and smiles through it and calls himself Kleinert or Leader or Lenihan or—Tom or Willie—the enemy is one and the same—a whole lifetime he is the same—"

Mary did not understand. She saw no enemy. She saw her husband in hell, and she suffered with him. She was not an enemy, please—enemies suffer, but not *with* you.

Kohn answered.

"Alex," Johnny called into the phone, his husky half-sleeping voice unrecognizable to Kohn. "It's me, Johnny, J.J."

Kohn asked him what he was shouting about, and it was all over the hospital about the dead kid. What the hell was the matter with him?

"Alex," Johnny whispered to Kohn hoarsely, "I want the job. Absolute, positive, no strings. Full time. I *want* it, you hear?"

Kohn told him to be at the staff meeting tonight and he personally would deliver him the contract. And he added whimsically, "Stay away from this hospital today, don't talk to anybody—and don't be seen dancing with Millie Katz."

Johnny, self-satisfied with his bravado, explained the progresion of events to his indignantly impatient pillow-propping wife. He knew she was indignant by the way she punched little holes into his pillow. Another time he would have clammed up and carried her indignation to work with him, telling himself little stories of indignation about her and working up a full-blown program of indignation to use on her

that evening before bed. But seldom did it come off
indignant—more like apologetic. Today time for cure was
short, he didn't have room for her indignation. He would only
be in her way one day. When was the last time he had
interrupted her propping routines? Once, he remembered,
about twelve years ago, he had shaken with the flu so badly
he couldn't shoot a needle—so he had gone to bed for one
day. She was sympathetic then. She said he looked sick and
she took his temperature and he ran a fever and she *fluffed*
his pillow and she put him to bed. When you run a fever, you
are sick. Mary came from stark stock. Today he had
considered warming a thermometer and showing it to her, but
he didn't—Bloomquist's prescription must certainly be working. He just said the hell with you, Mary, I'm staying in bed
at 98.6°!

He related to her his experiences of yesterday, including his
demoralizing moment with Sam Sacks, his ultimate end on
Bloomquist's couch, his eventual move out of GMH, the
school resignation. And he added, "Don't worry, I'll make it."

Mary worried only about things Johnny hadn't given
thought to: Tom, David, Charles, Jeannette.

John promised her that today he would find time to think
about them. After all, this was the purpose of Bloomquist's
prescription, to find time to think about things that haven't
been thought about. And not to think about things that
have been thought about. To *unthink*.

Mary agreed, kissed his forehead—with shaky lips, he
sensed—and said she would be around. John watched her
spreading butt disappear from his puttered-around room and
wondered why he did not care, really.

9:00   Johnny called Fran Cooper and explained to her the reason
for his absence, leaving out the parts about Bloomquist and
substituting Grawtch, and leaving out the new bravados
and substituting reorganization.

He was frightened of Fran. All these years he was
frightened of her. After the initial male desires to lock into
her body had dissipated (it took about a year), he slowly
began to despise her commandeering of his office. Mine
enemy is a voice. Fran had been lined up with the enemy,

and her capabilities as an office general denied Johnny of his opportunity to *be,* even in his own castle.

He delivered her the following orders:

Call everyone you can and reschedule. And don't overload me. They'll come at *my* convenience.

Treat whomever you can—collect—including Golopas' shot.

Tell all the salesmen we'll be back in a month and take all the samples they've got.

Turn all emergencies (ha) over to Peters. Don't send anyone to the ER.

Vacuum the rug. Feed the fish. Clean the sinks. Wash the medicine bottles. Unpack the drugs. Clean the X ray tanks. Dust your desk.

Fran said yessir, she was sorry he was not well, she would get everything done and call him before she left, and by the way, the new drug she was using was great and Sal loved her and maybe doctor should try some.

Although he was exhausted, even after eight hours sleep and a half-hour catnap after Mary's breakfast tray, he sat himself on the toilet seat and peered into the overlit mirror and shaved. He could not be less than clean, the elements of sterility control remained an insistent energized command. Dirt meant wash, hair meant comb, beard meant shave. He rubbed the whining hand machine like a pumice stone over his face and thought why the hell can't they invent a less cruel manly procedure, or give us all hormones when we're thirteen. Sex stinks anyway.

The light caught his face in such a way he appeared yellowed. All I need is jaundice, he thought sourly. Artie Powers was yellow one day and dead the next. Hell, dying isn't so bad, it's living that's giving me my headaches. He pulled down his lower lid and examined the conjunctival margins. Viral concretions. *Viral?* I even tell *myself* it's a virus. If you fool the customer long enough, you believe it yourself. It's a medical mirage. There is no virus, there's just junk. Junk we manufacture because we're so stupid. Live like beasts, eat like pigs, think like machines. Disease is crap coming out of our pores and out of our mouths and noses and vaginas and assholes. We're so full of crap somebody up there keeps opening up the holes to let it run out until it plugs up so bad even The Guy can't help and we're dead. Virus? Bullshit. We're just all full of crap.

Johnny opened his mouth into the light and examined his throat. Red, injected pillars, palate mottled with white elevated dots, teeth half-capped half-filled half-bridged, gums pale and boggy. No chance, Johnny said solemnly, no chance. We're all empty shells. Cracks in the walls are coming on like mad, and soon I'm going to crumble like a saltine. Only one giant, only one—Willie Washington, you sonofabitch.

Johnny shaved under his neck and patted up the falling chin line. He opened and closed his jaws like a plier head, stretching the flagging skin until it hurt, hoping in back of the survival center in there someplace that it might miraculously tone up, regenerate, get hip, be twenty again. Thirty?

Johnny ran the electric stone over his face and had a hundred thoughts. They tumbled through his head like the winds of March—senseless, sensitive, annoying, frightening, relieving. Thoughts that were there/always/fleeting/forever/ mutants. Frozen in apogee. The graffiti of the mind:
—How many friends will I pronounce dead?
—I know the period dates of all my friends' wives.
—Millie Katz doesn't wear pants.
—Genevieve Lowrey is going to die.
—So is Rudolph Garrone.
—Willie Washington?
—Me.
—How many patients needed me during the night?
—Flu shots don't work. What do I give them?
—Water works. Why don't I give more?
—I wonder about penicillin.
—The Buick is a lousy car.
—Mary is getting old. Wonder if she'll die first?
—I know the girl friends of all my friends' husbands.
—Tom, Charles, David, Jennie—I have thought of all of them.
—The artist portrays life with more truth than any other professional.
—If we could cut out adolescence and menstruation and menopause, life would be one big ball.

—Mary is lonely, tired, soft, and loving. Why don't I love her?
—Mary is bitchy, aging, unforgiving, stupid. Wouldn't let Tom play football.
—How many doctors even care?
—The doctor portrays life with more truth than any other professional.
—Old Pops fried thorn apples never made a hemorrhage in anyone's brain.
—How many patients are *rushed* to the hospital?
—Now what the hell does jogging really do?
—Doctors are old Jewish mothers—instead of food they stuff pills.
—How many hours a week are wasted on talking patients out of house calls?
—Thank God for Alex Kohn.
—Director of General Clinics! Great day.
—Now, what the hell is Director of General Clinics? . . .

. . . .

At eleven o'clock Marvin called.
—The top of the mornin' to ya, and saints and begorra, lad, but this is Marvin O'Swartz callin' to cheer your day and to congratulate you. First on bein' the only doctor I know who is smart enough to go to bed at 98.6°. And second on bein' elected by the Erin Trucking Corporation as the doctor most likely to keep the wheels rollin', you are. Shmuck—you can't hide under the covers, they're coming to get you. They picked up this morning your Rx for your nurse's husband's speedballs. He's selling them to the truck drivers at a dollar a shtick. They got one in Plainfield, another in Atlantic City. Mine's the only original. The others were forged for one hundred pills per. . . . In case you're interested as the day goes by, I'm stocking leeches. . . .

. . . .

Mary told John he must take this call: Fran said the police cut in on her line.
—My God, Doctor, *oh* my God, I tried every way to get you. This is terrible. It's Lisa, her ears. They must be killing her. She's been trying to tell us somehow about this for weeks, but I just caught on. It's frightening. Here's a poor innocent

kid with an ear ready to rupture and she has a stupid mother and a doctor who is out of town. This ear, I think it's only one, but you know how when a kid gets the hiccups and you try to get rid of them by scaring her? Well, we always say boo. But Saturday when I yelled boo she put her hands up to her ears and cried. I must have ruptured her eardrums! I'll wrap her up and bring her right over. . . .

. . . .

Dr. Peters, the covering doctor, called.
—Hey there, Dr. Shoemaker, I asked Grawtch about you and he said he didn't know you were sick. He couldn't go on, tears streaming down his rosy nephritic cheeks. He thinks you went to another doctor. Ran into Bloomquist, he used the same jazz on my old man last year. Worked like a charm. He left my old lady, married the other girl, and they both use the cure every second Monday. Stay with it! If you want to get away for a few days, even a few months, I'm available. Fourth year now, I can't get set in my own place, can you imagine? I feel like a medical peddler, all I need is a panel truck. Maybe one of these days I'll make the plunge. But I see some of you guys, and I wonder. . . .

Anyway, not too much for you this weekend. Little blood, but people with lots of guts. It's cutting down, though. People don't even bother to call nowadays on a weekend, they make up their minds they'll be sick on Monday. Or else they wait in line at the ER like they're giving away dishes. Competition from your own kind. They think they're getting free community medicine, and by the time they leave with a shot and a Darvon, they've dropped fifteen bucks in Kleinert's bag.

It's getting pretty rough out on the street. Three paid, and three gave me forms to fill out. Only one you need to know about, a Shari Lee, mother says her newborn just died. This one swallowed a bottle of aspirin. I took her to the ER myself. The mother looked like she was going to abort. The other two kids had fevers, so the old man called up another sweet guy and they went off hunting. Oh, well, maybe when I grow up and become a big doctor, maybe I, too, can have your enviable, felicitous practice. . . .

. . . .

Mrs. Podalsky, Fran's mother, called.

—I would *never* call you at your home. You deserve a whole *week* in bed, but you can't leave her alone. This is the *worst* time for you to stay home. Dr. Shoemaker, you listen to me very careful, this girl Frances is in serious trouble. I don't know what she is telling you, but this guy has got her hypnotized. She didn't get home until five this morning. They come in like they were teenage lovers, gigglin' all over the halls. Disgustin'. But I tell you after he left, she stopped her gigglin' and she cried all the way up the stairs and didn't stop cryin' until she went off to work. All the pill bottles you gave her, they're empty. And doctor, you got to get back there so you can watch her very careful—that gun is gone. . . .

. . . .

Calloway called.

—I *am* sorry, sir, but they gave me this number. This is Calloway here, sir. You remember me? I assisted you in that unfortunate delivery the other night. I learned a great deal from that experience. Learned a G.P. has no business in OB. I guess you learned that, too, didn't you, sir? You sure learn your limitations in this business. I see it now, I'm going to spend another four years in hospital service. Maybe go into a specialty like dermo, or radiology—nine to four, fifty g's, no nights, nobody cries, nobody dies, no emotions—that's for me. I can't stand seeing all these people screaming with pain, and throwing up, and bleeding all over the place at five dollars a throw. There must be a better way. I'm going to hang around until I find it. . . . The lady checked out early this morning, with her brother-in-law, the lawyer. Say, Doc, how come you ordered a Post on this kid? You know as well as I it died out of neglect—what are you looking for? . . .

. . . .

11:50 Ten minutes before twelve Johnny could wait no longer. He filled the amber glass with three quarters water and downed two aspirin with slow sips. Something was happening. He thought, Bloomquist's prescription was working. He laid back and sighed. It might work, it just might. . . .

. . . .

12:30 Johnny was hungry. He called down to Mary for some lunch
and dialed his office for Fran's report. Busy signal. Dialed
again. Busy. Waited a minute. Dialed. Busy. Damn doctors, he
said, never can get them when you want them. He laughed.
Maybe I'll call Bloomquist and tell him I'm cured. He just
laughed. He dialed Fran again and she answered.

Fran's report:

Contacted most day cases, rescheduled with expected
problems, most everyone understands—people are beautiful.

I could only contact a few night cases. All at work, or
someplace. Georgia will have to take over. She's a doll baby.

Mr. Calvin, attorney for Jacardi, says case is scheduled
tomorrow. He's sending over files.

Sorry about Clara's call. Poor dear.

Three salesmen, all have a cure for you. Scotch. Bourbon.
Gin.

I renewed everyone's medicine. Medicine is beautiful.

Shot for Golopas—he made a pass, and I bent the needle in
his rear end.

Therapy for the football kids. Sweet bunch.

I cleaned, dusted, sang to my wild Irish mother. It was a
great, beautiful morning. He loves me and the new pills are
beautiful, and I'm sending over the mail with a sample bottle
for you. Hurry back. We miss you.

.   .   .   .

Johnny made a double-spaced two-inch indelible note on
his pad—TENSIG. He must check it out with Bloomquist.

Mary's lunch of chicken noodle soup and crackers with
Swiss cheese arrived. Very few words were spoken, neither
having it to say. On the tray of lunch Mary had left three
magazines with infolded pages.

The Journal had an infold on the "Confessions of a
Doctor's Wife."

Redbook had an infold on the "Truth About Your Wife's
Menopause."

Family Circle had an infold on "Doctor, Heal Thyself."

Mary said she must leave/shopping and things/can't disrupt
the schedule/she'll be back soon/forget the phone/if the kids
get home before she does tell them to take milk/they never
eat anything/don't know why she shops. She half smiled a

mumbled goodbye, flipped her loosened hair away from her
eyes—for a flick John saw sex—then she was gone, and he
wondered why it didn't matter.

2:00 Johnny tried anxiously to sleep. It did not come easily,
but just lying there totally diminished in feeling was so great.
This was a great prescription. He couldn't remember the last
time he lay in bed in the afternoon. The sheets felt cool and
comforting, the blanket warm and relaxing, the big brown
teddy bear cuddly and safe. *The big brown teddy bear?!*
Johnny jumped from the bed and shook loose the sheets and
the blanket, pounced upon the mattress, scrambled under the
bed. There was no big brown teddy. Hadn't been one in forty
years. Now how in hell did that feeling get under the covers?
Feeling? He bit open his hangnail and waited for blood. It
oozed and he worked it over and bit deeply into the loosened
flesh until it ran real red. He waited. Not a thing.

Johnny crawled back under the sheets and tried a trick
from "Doctor, Heal Thyself." Yoga style he flattened his
body against the force of the mattress, removed the pillow,
stretched his six hundred and forty-seven muscles until he
could separate each one in position, and then started the
process of count-down. He commanded:
Gala aponeurotica—softer, softer, peace . . .
Frontalis—softer, softer, peace . . .
Orbicularis occuli—softer, softer, peace . . .
Occipitalis—softer, softer, peace . . .
Orbicularis oris—softer, softer, peace . . .
Triangularis—softer, softer, peace . . .
Sternocleidomastoid—softer, softer, peace . . .
Trapezius—softer, softer, peace . . .
Platysma—softer, softer, peace . . .
Scalenii—softer, softer, peace . . .
Serratii—softer, softer, peace . . .
Rhomboids—softer, softer, peace . . .
Abdominii—softer, softer, peace . . .
Deltoids—softer, softer, peace . . .
Triceps—softer . . .

Johnny slept. A deep, deep, softer, softer, peaceful sleep.
Many muscles sooner than the article stated he would
sleep. But Bloomquist was right: There was a deep need to

break the pattern, reverse actions, shock and unshock. Johnny needed this off-scheduled sleep. He was, according to the article, to think only beautiful thoughts, dream only beautiful dreams. To Johnny—who had been for the past several months awakening with cold sweats from poorly recalled nightmares, although they all smelled of death in some way—to Johnny this sleep was closer to the cure than he could believe. No dreams, no sweats, no death memories, nothing. Only that he had sometime earlier shut his eyes and sometime later opened them. Somewhere he had read or over one of the tapes heard that good health was being alive without being aware of your body, sleeping without being aware of sleeping. At this single moment he felt he had made it.

Hells bells! he called from his flattened position in bed, I'm going to be all right.

It was at that moment that Jonathan J. Shoemaker, M.D. decided that he was going to chuck it all. General Practice stinks, he said to himself. If this is what it does to a guy, it stinks. The air is saturated with the word, the rats are leaving the ship, the old G.P. is sinking fast. What the hell kind of nut am I to go down with the tub? You think Clara or Golopas will save me? Or Sam Sacks? They all knew—Tom and Kohn, and all the WEC men and Pauly Baby, and how about Frank Jessup, who never made it through Thursday night hours? He knew, but what does a guy do? Mortgage, kids, lawns, plumbing, dresses, cars, green beans. What does a guy do?

. . . .

4:00 Type Double Space 3 copies—Rush
(Submit to Editor *GP—The Family Physician*)

WHY I AM GIVING UP GENERAL PRACTICE
by Anonymous, M.D.

No, Virginia, there is no general practitioner, and whether you read it in the *Times* or the *Ladies Home Journal* or see him on television, that dear old doctor is as dead as the docile dodo. And if your mommy and daddy insist that he still lives in that house on the corner with the lamppost and the sign, you just look right smack into their devilish eyes and you tell them that they are fibbing.

They are keeping alive a myth.

You know what a myth is, Virginia, a doctor myth? This is a story a mommy and daddy tell to their children when they want to win a ticket to Heaven. You know why, Virginia? Because it was mommy and daddy who killed that doctor and if they want to keep from getting caught and sent to Hell, they tell you there *is* a doctor on the corner. And they bring you to him for your baby shots and your school shots and your measles and your mumps, and your earaches and your gym sprains and your high school physical and your college physical and—well, that's about it. Then *you* will be a mommy and you will carry your little one to the myth on the corner with the lamppost and the sign. But, you know what, Virginia, all the time, like the emperor who rode naked on the streets, you will know he has no clothes on, and the doctor on the corner is not there.

Now, Virginia, let me tell you how he died. One day your daddy came into his office. Your daddy had a big belly and tattered pants and he said, "Doc, I need to win this big contest and if I don't win this big contest, I can't replace these tatters and my kids will have to go without pants." Now just after your daddy came into the office another daddy came into the office, a very, very Big Daddy, and he said, "This contest must be won," and he was a highly respectable daddy and the doctor believed what he said and he wanted to help him real badly. Now these daddies sent the player in this contest to another Big Daddy and this daddy also says this player can win the contest. And so do hundreds and hundreds of other daddies and mommies. It is important for all these daddies and mommies to be happy and pleased. It is important for the player of the contest to be happy and pleased. The doctor was anxious. He is always anxious to please and make happy. This is what a general practitioner does, he pleases and makes happy. But a real doctor should not please and make happy, a real doctor should cure and make well. The general practitioner is a travel agent. The real doctor is in Spain or Majorca. The G.P. will arrange for you to get there. Happy.

At any rate, Virginia, the contest was won. The player lived. And in his place the doctor died. Who was me. And who is now dead.

But don't feel bad about your mommy and daddy going to Hell, Virginia, for aren't we all? I'm a daddy and I already have killed off my share. What daddy has not? When I was your age living in a small town with trolley tracks running down the middle of the street where my daddy had his drugstore, my daddy said to me, "Be a doctor. There isn't nothin' else for a son of mine to be." And so, Virginia, this is the way one daddy first sharpened the knife.

There were other mommies and daddies who completed the plunge of that deadly tool. The learned professors of medicine who assured the doctor of the validity of his judgment on matters of life and death. The charming wife who, bare-handed and often bare-footed and oft bare-chested, carried his banner higher and ever higher until even he could not run fast enough to read of its virtues. His cloaked colleagues who, year after year, day after day, moment after moment, defended their rights to the throne upon which they perched, they joined the resounding clamor which echoed with the vibrancy of their saintly resplendence. And then, Virginia, the teachers in your school, the nurse in your infirmary, the attendant in the parking lot, the waitress in the restaurant, the cop on the corner, the boy with the ball, the body on the slab, all in unison, all in rejoicing spiritual accord, sing Hallelujah for the doctor on the corner. The doctor is dead. Long live the doctor!

Virginia, don't go to the corner doctor any more. I give you fair warning from my grave, he is lethal. He is reacting to the myth of his existence, and will strike back at you for keeping him locked in his corner cage like a stalked lion. He will jab you with needles that have barbs on them. He will smile sardonically at you and tell you he is presenting you with an elixir of life, and instead he has filled you with hot air and cold water. And he will roar inside with humiliating laughter as you kiss his feet and God Bless him for saving your life. Ha! Ha! he will say, another, send me another. And another.

Run, run away from him, Virginia. Go instead to the doctors across the street in the big, shiny, new brick building with the elevator that sings. Go to them. They, I promise you, will not even look at you. Fear not, they will not kill, for they are sterile and cannot themselves be killed. They will place you in their box of buttons and they will command the buttons to be pushed and the lights will dazzle you and the sounds will be those of heavenly chords and you will emerge *Virginia the Vivacious,* lusting for life in a chromed and plastic shell which he has cast upon you. You are now impervious to life, and he on the other corner in the new, shiny brick building with the elevator, he has it for you. He will enter the world of the Hollywood whore who can earn millions a year and win golden awards for virtuosity. Your daddy and your mommy will no longer put their pins and needles into their doctor dolls. Your daddy and your mommy will emerge in the new world and themselves will build the sterile pedestal and happily and sanctimoniously will pave the new doctor's path with loving gold.

They have done their job well, Virginia, the daddies and the mommies, but fear not, whatever they are building to replace the myth on the corner, be at peace, dear, they verily do deserve . . .

Addenda: To my colleagues in General Practice, hear ye, I am not yet dead. I am still very much alive in my new post as Director of General Clinics in a new hospital. Amen. Thank God for the daddy and mommy pogrom. General Practice—bah, humbug!

. . . .

5:30 Hell's bells! Forgot the four o'clock meds.

Down the pills, down the Arm and Hammer, and down the water. No damn better than the patients I bawl out, he said to himself. You forget one dose, then another, then the symptoms build up, then you call up and say, "Doc, this medicine stinks, I feel worse."

Johnny really felt better. His mind was clear, decisions easily catalogued. No gas, belly felt flat. Head pressure not yet gone, but surprisingly dulled. The future looked brighter than it had in days. Bloomquist's methods worked.

Now, regardless of Pop's thorn apple juice and flaxseed poultices, Johnny Shoemaker was nobody's fool. He knew he was on a queer kick, and he knew Bloomquist was playing him for a cure in a strange way-out way, but he also knew up Bloomquist's sleeve was pure professionalism. Johnny was treading on parting waters, but he also knew he was feeling better. From Pop's earliest days he had learned that there is only one truth in medicine: what works. Johnny was not many years separated from Poppa's two-dollar amulets and silver mystery boxes the old chronics came in for by the dozens. And he watched them outlive the emergency surgeries, and the twelve-fifty pharmaceuticals, and the twenty-five-dollar specialists.

Johnny Shoemaker, after fifteen years of working medicine, had no man to bow to. He had studied hard, continued his post-graduate courses yearly at some local or city hospital, belonged to his county, state, national, and world medical societies, attended meetings, read three journals a week, listened to two medical tapes, read one *Reader's Digest* article a month, and in all "kept up."

However, what he kept up with at times smelled anti-Establishment, and it was this part of Johnny Shoemaker that allowed him the privilege of feeling better with Bloomquist's cure. For instance, Johnny didn't hesitate giving Hassinger a shot of Irish whiskey for hiccoughs prior to a pending phrenectomy. It worked. When Momma Shoemaker was opened up for a lower laparotomy and found stuffed with CA and closed over again, Johnny never hesitated running her to Salt Lake City to see the controversial Dr. Daley and had her shot with a dozen vials of his underground cancer vaccine. Momma Shoemaker certainly wasn't cured, but because of Johnny's off beat effort, she lived peacefully without pain for a year longer than the best of them had predicted.

But someplace along the line the ass had lost his stability, his cool, his confidence in that which he was and could still be. Just like Brown from the nursing home had said, some night he had awakened in a cold sweat, eyes red-rimmed with nightmarish fears, and he had exclaimed aloud into the dark, "I'm only a doctor because of my brother Lem!"

At six o'clock David and Charles and Jennie filed in, each carrying a bowl, each bowing graciously and presenting to their King his called-for supper. Then each in turn proceeded to enlighten him with their catastrophic day.

David had a sore foot from a kid who jumped on it in gym and he wanted two notes, one to skip gym, the other to jump on this kid's head. Father heard him out, wrote out the note for the former and expressed his philosophies on nonviolence concerning the latter.

Charles would be seventeen Monday and everyone knows you get a car when you are seventeen. Father heard him out and wrote an "IOU, Charles, one car" when you (1) fix the lawnmower, (2) mow the lawn, (3) trim the bushes, (4) clean out the cellar, (5) take out the garbage, (6) finish one year of college, (7) eat all your green beans.

Jennie only wanted him to know she was now Jeannette. Father heard her out, watched her walk across the room, flip her auburn hair away from her eyes, and become Jeannette.

At six-thirty he notified Georgia and set her to work reorganizing the night schedule. It was right here at the Lake Office and plenty will see both cars. Georgia said, "What do I do with anybody who just walks in?" And Johnny smiled and said, "Tell them they have a helluva nerve. Would they walk in on their specialist? But if they want to wait, I'll be back Thursday. On second thought," he said to her, beaming, "I'll check with you at nine, because I'm going out to the hospital staff meeting, at which time I may never come back at all."

. . . .

8:00 Willie Washington delivering a get-well card from Marvin asked if he could see the doctor. The kids, the first time a black boy had been in their house, particularly *this* black boy, formed an honor guard up the stairs and as he passed them by, each managed to brush or touch him and each made his individual face of stolen delight. Willie impressed them. He was lots bigger than he looked out there on the field running wild all over them other guys. He was huge and hulking in fact, but his stride up the stairs was sensitive and quiet as if he were holding back and a full down step would come crashing through the stairwell. He was well-dressed, smelled of a new deodorant, and thanked each one cordially for their help.

Johnny, cleanly shaved and dressed for the meeting, greeted his friend coolly, his head pressure dulling up several decibels.

Exchanges, surface hello, how are you, thanks for coming, glad you're out of bed, etc., etc. Then Willie said, "They signed me for State today." And Johnny said, "That I would expect."

"Hope it works out."

"It's *their* gain."

"I don't know."

"Believe me."

"It's a long way from high school."

"*You're* a long way from high school."

"Because of guys like you. 'Specially you."

Johnny wanted to touch his friend, wondered why, and didn't.

"You'll make me cry, Willie. I got this sickness, I cry when I'm happy and don't know what else to do."

Willie said, "Jump up and down. Jog around the block. Punch a bag."

Johnny said, "Lift a guy in the sky."

Willie sucked air. Dr. Shoemaker *had* missed it. He knew it. He knew it.

Willie said, "I want to apologize, Doctor, for scoring those four touchdowns."

"Apologize? My God, man, you were sensational."

"It's an awful feeling I got." Willie sucked air again as if he were working at keeping alive. "But somehow I let you down and I can't put my finger on it."

"You're on your way, Willie, you don't have to look back."

"I never picked you up once."

Johnny said to himself, you never picked me up once, you must hate me you sonofabitch. He said—

"We're getting older."

"No," Willie said, "that's not it. I just didn't do it. I saw you. I looked straight at you from behind those goalpoasts each time I went over. I didn't see no one else. I said, gotta get to Doc, love that guy, gotta get to Doc. Then I didn't do it."

Johnny shrugged, once for Willie. "It's the thought, Willie, times move on, we change. I understand."

"Uh-uh. Most times you do, but not this time."

"You were tired. You played a full game. I understand the strain."

"No, you don't. No strain ever stopped me from grabbin' hold of you. Only one thing stops me—bein' scared you would say to me, 'How are you, Willie? Feel OK? Everything OK, Willie?' "

"It's part of my act, Willie."

"Uh-uh. If I came to you this time there wouldn't be no act. I hurt like hell. I knew if I came near you, your damn ESP or whatever the devil you use to suck these things out of guys, would know. It just hurt somethin' awful."

"We went over that, Willie. You went to a specialist. They took that out of my hands."

"Shit, damn head never hurt. That don't hurt since Friday. Head's fine. Never nothin' wrong with my head. I told you that all along. It's my back, it hurt like all hell, burnin' and achin'. Can't even take a full step it hurts."

Johnnie's head pulsed. "What are you talking about? *Where* does the back hurt? Does it *still* hurt? Let me see. Damn you, Willie, what do you want to do, kill yourself?"

Johnny had Willie pull off his shirt. He examined his back. He asked the boy to place his palm over the painful spots, and Willie put his hand full over the left flank alongside the eleventh and twelfth thoracic and first spinal lumbar. Johnny had penciled that hand on a thousand memo sheets. Beautiful hand.

Johnny ran his fingers briefly over the affected muscles, then returned for a specific investigation of individual groups, then single strands and fibers. Willie's body was a textbook of anatomical drawings. Johnny never could find anything wrong with Willie.

Willie explained how he got stepped on two weeks ago. It hurt then, but the head seemed to be what everyone was interested in, and he figured a back is a back, everybody gets a backache in this game.

"And it hurt all the time?" Johnny yelled at him.

"Yeah, it hurt all the time, but I sure as hell wasn't startin' up with you on this—I had enough with my head."

"How do you feel?"

"Lousy."

"What do you mean, lousy?"

"Just lousy. No energy. Didn't practice today."

Johnny grabbed hold of Willie's arm. "Let's get down to the office!"

At the same time, he looked at his watch, and it was eight-twenty and his head pounded intolerably. He sat himself back on his bed and poured himself three quarters of a glass of distilled water, downed two aspirin, shook his head as if attempting to remember or forget, and stared at Willie wildly.

The boy was visibly shook. His doctor, his friend, had played a weird cop-out. He finally said, "Hey, Doc, what's *with* you?"

And Johnny explained to him how sick he had been, and about Bloomquist and the medicine and his brave new decisions and his overwhelming cure. And he told him he would not be able to take care of him.

"I'm not going to be your doctor anymore, Willie," he said, his eyes burning with cure. "I'm going to be Director of General Clinics in the New Suburban Hospital. But I will see to it that your back is taken care of."

Johnny shakily wrote out the name on a card and handed it to Willie.

"It's Dr. Applewhite. He's an osteopath, good friend of mine. If anyone can take care of your back, he can. Call him tonight and tell him I sent you. He'll see you. Now don't neglect it, you hear. Tomorrow might be too late."

Willie shook his hand and Johnny counted his fingers to make sure he still had five—a little joke—and the boy said thanks for things and left.

Now what did I do that for, Johnny said to himself, now what did I send him to Applewhite for? What difference does it make anymore? Backache. Think I give a damn? Kid can drop dead for all I care. . . . Kid can drop dead. . . . Johnny's head split wide open.

. . . .

9:00 Georgia reported.

Johnny heard her say things about patients missing him and all that crap and how many shiny heinies she shot tonight, and there was a call from Clara, Lisa ate an M&M and there was chocolate on her hands and should she rush right over, and Marvin called and said something funny but she couldn't remember—he always says funny things but she seldom knew why.

Everyone's gone except Millie Katz, Georgia said. Don't know what I'm going to do with her. She calls and I tell her you are out and she says I don't believe you and she is here. She says both cars are out there and I will be the last one. If you find her here in the morning, you'll know I failed you. Good night, and get better, we miss you and all that jazz. . . . Hey, you should see sexy Millie out there. I swear she's naked under the mink. . . .

. . . .

9:20

> ### GREENVILLE MERCY HOSPITAL
> ---
> ### Founded 1917

> **Hospital Quiet Zone (No Parking)**
> **Doctors' Parking Only**

—Here for the meetin', Doc? You're the last one. Gonna cost you twenty dineros. Enough to buy me and the kids a week's milk. Better run or it'll cost you twenty-five. . . .

> ### DOCTORS LOUNGE AND MEETING HALL
> ### QUIET—MEETING IN PROGRESS

"... And if it is so discovered, we have been authorized by the Board of Trustees to fine the staff doctor severely. We cannot tolerate crossing hospital lawns recently seeded. This resolution accepted, the ayes have it, the nays, no sign. The meeting was adjourned with a motion from Dr. Thailor and seconded by Dr. Charles."

—Gentlemen, you have heard the minutes of the last meeting. Any corrections or additions? If not, the minutes stand as read. In order to facilitate the especial purpose of tonight's meeting, we will dispense with committee reports, other than

Good Cheer and Welfare. Dr. Jones, you have a report from Good Cheer and Welfare?

—Yes, it was my sad duty this past week to visit the widow of our late friend, Dr. Samuel Cader. His untimely death under the wheels of an overturned golf cart moved us to a point of great unhappiness and, therefore, we of the committee felt it would be a gesture to present the widow Cader with an engraved gold golf cart in memory of her brilliant, beloved husband, Dr. Samuel Cader.

—Thank you, Dr. Jones. I'm sure all of you will agree this was a stellar action on the committee's part, and it only adds to our growing feeling of comraderie at Greenville Mercy. It is a warm feeling to know that when tragedy stalks, there will be a Dr. Jones and committee to work out a suitable plan of remembrance. And now, we will enter immediately into the grand purpose of our monthly meeting and open the floor to all members, full-participating, general staff, associate staff, and consults. We want to hear your gripes, your sentiments, your deep need for Greenville Mercy to serve you better. I, Karl Kleinert, your chairman and hospital administrator, will answer any and all from the old clavicle, that *is* near the shoulder, isn't it, doctors? . . . Yes, Dr. Green.

—I am an associate staff member. I have been for five years. I pay regular monthly dues. I refer patients to all the consulting men. Why can't I park in the special-key parking lot?

—Dr. Green, you *can* park in the special-key lot. We have never refused any member on any level this privilege. However, fire regulations do not allow more than sixty-three cars in the lot, and we have just sixty-three key members now. The moment there's an opening I will send you the very next key. . . . Yes, Dr. Frankfield.

—I have been trying to get a patient into the hospital with an obstructive jaundice. Admissions tells me now for eight days there are no beds. But Dr. Carl Mayer, our surgeon chief, just admitted two obstructive cases today. I pointed this out to Admissions, and they said the two cases were for emergency surgery. I don't want my patient operated until I've had adequate studies. How do I get the bed?

—Very simple, Dr. Frankfield. Dr. Mayer will meet with you after the meeting and I'm sure you and he can come to some amicable solution. . . . Dr. Clarke?

—I had one patient on a Diabetic 1000 diet, and another on a Diabetic 1500 diet. And they both got the same meal. This happens regularly. How do we change this?

—Simply by complaining, just as you are now. We have a dietician who checks every dish as it leaves the kitchen. However, with the rising cost of food we have asked her to reduce the number of special diets, and no doubt she made a compromise for you, so saving your patients' calories and our treasurer's budget. . . . Dr. Delany.

—Where the hell did you get this crop of interns? One speaks Dutch, another Portuguese, and a third Esperanto. Not only do I end up doing all the footwork nowadays, but I have to act as an interpreter. I say either fire the lot of them or get a gang of student nurses in.

—Dr. Delany, the intern training program is in high gear. These boys are all hand-chosen, not only from some of our finer schools of the continent, but we also have two from the North Dakota Osteopathic College who have turned out to be just fine. They speak a very fluent English. After all, it's only October. By July they will all be first rate. . . . Dr. Spewack.

—My office, as you know, is in the neighborhood. Now, if I'm not around, most of the new people moving in or even my old patients, they run over to the emergency room for service. OK, fine. It comes in handy. But when they end up hospitalized under Medical Service, or Surgical Service, and I find out three weeks later on the street from an unhappy relative, what do you say to that?

—Dr. Spewack, Dr. Spewack. This is a sad moment for Greenville Mercy Hospital, whose only purpose of existence is to have mercy on your patients—

—That's horseshit. The only purpose of Greenville Mercy Hospital is to make money on the Dr. Spewacks—

—Dr. Kohn, you are out of order—

—It doesn't matter. Boys, all your questions will *never* be satisfied by Greenville Mercy, or by Karl Kleinert, or by any board member. You may as well know it and face it, you are a captured audience. . . .

—Dr. Kohn, you will be removed—

—Mr. Kleinert, as of tonight, I *am* removed. Not only *I* but better than ten of your consultants, and if you're wise, boys,

better than most of you poor shnook G.P.'s who are being disgraced by a humiliating association with this backwoods institution—
—Dr. Kohn!—
—Boys, this is it. I formally announce the opening for staff membership to the new Greenville Lakes Suburban Hospital. Membership applications are available in my office, where a board meeting is in progress right now.
—Doctors! This meeting—is—adjourned!!

. . . .

11:00

┌─────────────────────────────────┐
│   ALEXANDER KOHN, M.D.   │
│   —UROLOGY—   │
└─────────────────────────────────┘

—Johnny, sorry you had to hang around all night for this, but they had to. They had no choice. Up until this morning it was you. Would I lie to you? I fought like hell for you. You know how I can scream. But what could I do against legal advice? You're a class-zero risk. We need the insurance companies now like we need oxygen to breathe. With you they would figure someone is standing on the hose. One shaky department head and we end up no loot, no hospital. You know, for the want of a shoe, and all that crap. Until this million-dollar malpractice *chozzerai* is off your neck, you are not our boy. Bennie Harris got the job. . . .

. . . .

11:30   THE SHOEMAKERS
                           692 LAKE DRIVE

                           ───────

                           WELCOME

                           ───────

Mary was reading when Johnny came into the room. She had taken to reading in recent years—not anything deep, but short stories, mysteries, popular magazine stuff on how to live with yourself, and the world kind of pop sociological commentary. Marrying early, cutting out of college after one year, pregnant with regularity, Mary felt cheated. John's knowing, especially in recent years, made her feel a sense of insecurity far beyond the real gap between the two. She was attractive, well-spoken, enjoyed by her friends, intimately active and concerned with community affairs, envied and satisfyingly hated by John's female clientele. Mary really had no cause for concern, except possibly the fact that John came home later each night, spoke less, slept later, and left earlier.

She was reading the *Redbook* article on menopause and looked up at John vindictively. She had just read that not one man in several million understands his wife at this precarious time in her life, and the seven-year itch becomes the twenty-year boil.

"You usually call after eleven," she said to John.

He said it was too complicated to explain.

"You might try."

He was not in the mood. He looked for a way out of the room.

"You're getting worse than a politician."

John said he was hungry and he would come back.

Mary said, "Why bother?"

And once again they were incommunicado. Johnny took off his tie and put on his slippers and robe and moved to the door. "You want anything?" he asked.

Mary was amused. "You giving me another chance?" she said to him.

He said he never remembered discontinuing the first.

"When you stopped calling," she reminded him.

"Oh," he said, "some things lose their importance."

"There was a time," she said, "you would call in the middle of a delivery. Share it with me."

"Time," he said.

"Lonely time," she said.

"We were young."

"Gets lonelier. So the article says. Gets lonelier."

"Keep busy."

"Only until night time. Then it's lonely again. . . ."

... There was a time, Mary thought, looking at her husband, one foot poised at the door, escape written desperately over his drawn face—there was a time you would drop everything in the middle of hours and I would see that door fling open and you would wrap me up and say to hell with the patients. I would shove you back in and remind you of the shoes your kids needed and pray you would say to hell with shoes, feet are supposed to be bare. Come back, John, I would cry inside, come back. Bleed on other people's time, I would scream at your patients. This is my John, not yours, mine, you stupid fools. He's just using you to buy shoes. But he uses me for whatever else there is in life. You never did come back in. I certainly won't complain the stupid wail of the doctor's wife. If I felt a neglect, it was one of pity for your day, not mine. I never was much of a doctor-type wife anyway. I never felt that was our relationship. I felt more I was Johnny Shoemaker's wife, Johnny Shoemaker, the catch of all Greenville, the boy the girls whispered about in locker rooms and over party lines. He is going to be a doctor, you know, girls, and you know what that means. Go get him, he's fair game. And what game. My, you were a handsome boy. That's what they all said. I couldn't quite see it. Your hair was too light for my taste, and your face was square. Never liked square faces. But I didn't analyze, because I never had a chance anyway. My mom always said, "A sort of plain girl like you, Mary, ought not to set her sights too high." When I missed my first period you said you would marry me. If I never loved you before, I did then. And somehow did more and more, in spite of the fact that I knew you never loved me. Not then, anyway. A guy like you does right by his Nell. So you did right by me. Could I complain? Plain Mary Hollister and handsome medical student, catch number one, Jonathan Shoemaker, married today in the First Church of Christ. . . .

"Did you ever love me, John?" Mary said softly.

"What did you say?" John heard, but it did not penetrate.

"Did you ever learn to look at me without seeing a big belly in your way?"

John shrugged bewilderment at his wife.

"I don't think so," she said. "Lucky you got very busy in the office and were able to hire help. Then I was *really* out. That seemed to be the end of whatever need you had for me other than Alex Kohn's orders to get your glands drained regularly."

"Come on, Mary, for God's sake."

"But sad," Mary went on, "I never once while we were together felt I was any more than a mechanical reactor."

"You read too many magazines."

"They don't make it change. Sad is sad."

"So sad," John said. "For whom? Me or you?"

"I'm sad for me," Mary said. "Somebody has to be."

"Who's sad for me?" John said. "Who? Tell me who?"

"Bloomquist cured you. You told me before you left, Bloomquist cured you."

John told her of the night. Bennie Harris got the job.

Mary was quiet. She was sad for John, she told him so. "Why didn't you call me?" she said. "I would like to know. Don't you know I would like to know?"

He said, "And if you knew . . . ?"

"It might help."

"My problem is me, not you. I'll work it out alone."

"Alone is a death sentence," Mary said.

"That was Bloomquist's cure."

"That was twenty-four hours." Mary paused, placed her magazines aside, brushed that strand of hair from her face, and looked out of very alone sorrowful eyes. "Try," she said, "twenty years."

John was listening.

"You have *never*," Mary said, "been alone. There was always the office, the hospital, meetings, school, calls—Lem."

No comment. John thought fleetingly of Lem. First time today. Bloomquist was fading.

"John, you know," Mary said, "this is the loneliest room in the entire world. It is a lonely time waiting here. You wait for a door to click, for a phone to ring. And all the nights you wait you roll the hair and it gets thinner and you grease the face and it drains color, and you exercise the sagging skin and you pull up the drooping breasts, and you bicycle the purple-veining legs, and you sit and you count the new liver spots. It is lonely, Johnny, here in this room at age forty-three, and your only real claim to fame is out forgetting to call, or not even planning to anymore. And you know it, and you fight it by getting flabbier, and veinier, and bitchier, and your belly goes sour, and the room gets hot, and you scream out to nobody, you scream out war is hell, war be over, and you know you could just die if the fighting was done, if only for the moment of armistice. . . . What are we going to do, Johnny? What are we going to do?"

And Johnny reacted as a well-trained doctor should. All problems reduce to their basic denominators. Fever means infection means penicillin. Loneliness means lovelessness means sexlessness.

John approached Mary automatically. He placed his hands around her neck, sunk his head to her chest, and kissed her breasts.

Mary slapped her full open palm upon his cheek and rolled away spitting.

"Oh, for God's sake, John, get the hell away from me. What is wrong with you? Don't come *near* me, you damn fool—don't *dare* pity me. . . ."

. . . .

At eleven forty-five Johnny opened and closed the refrigerator. He was not hungry. He sat at the kitchen table and saw he had ·bitten into his nails again and they still bled. He was alive. That is a laugh, he said. He looked over his mail. It was something to do. He wouldn't sleep tonight. At least not in his room. He would go into the office, the back room has a table with four inches of foam rubber. He remembered and thought yes it does, doesn't it. His mail was heavy. He threw aside the samples, the bills. Some of the ads looked promising. He opened his mail.

. . . .

LAW OFFICES

Seligman, Jerome & Wagner	964-7777
400 Centre St.	Cable
Greenville, N.J.	Seljerwag

October 17, 1970

Re: Susan Jason

Dear Dr. Shoemaker:

We represent the above client in a divorce proceeding. A

hearing is scheduled for October 23, 1970, in City Hall. Mrs. Jason has referred us to you for information regarding her sexual abuses at the hands of her estranged husband.

We will be sending Mr. Wagner, our junior partner, to see you in a few days, and would appreciate your going over your files on these abuses so you can properly demonstrate them to Mr. Wagner.

Yours very truly,

Frank Jerome, Esq.
Seligman, Jerome & Wagner

FJ/cst

. . . .

Dear Doctor:

Enclosed are four separate disability forms to send out for me to my insurance company. Please date them four weeks apart and send out on dates. I still have six weeks coming to me. The weather down here is great. Caught a 200-pound marlin.

Your patient,

Bill Boyd

. . . .

GREENVILLE TELEPHONE DIRECTORY
...H - I - J - K -
Kelly
Keaney
Kandle
Kathy
Katz, James R.
Katz, Mildred 27 Erie Drive **667-4023**
......**667-4**—

. . . .

STANLEY SERVICE - A free classified advertising manual for physicians. Prepared monthly as a service to our friends, the doctors, by the Stanley Pharmaceutical Corporation, Los Angeles, California.

FOR SALE

Land

40-acre ranch, twenty miles from Honolulu. Low price. Interested in doctor for retirement living. Ideal for raising horses, or for gun or game club. Year-round stream, fish abounding, deer, quail, pheasant. One thousand dollars an acre. Write Box 720 Stanley Service.

Corner lot facing golf course—unobstructed view toward western sunset. Excellent residential area in Southern California. Will trade for Eastern home in suburban area. Write Box 721 Stanley Service.

New Hampshire—35 acres of woods and fields in the lakes and ski areas. Near Squaw Lake. New red farmhouse. Retire or practice quietly in secluded area. No hospital, just old-time medicine. Write to owner, Dr. Luke Jones (age 84), Box 7, Squaw Lake, New Hampshire.

Offices

Medical office and house combination for practice or investment. Sixteen rooms, small estate, plus swimming pool and guest house. Tired of the humdrum? Come to Arizona. Write Jim Trolpe, Box 12, Yuma, Arizona.

Practices

General Practice for sale. Well-established. Golf, hunting. Good gross. Leaving for residency.

General Practice. Lucrative area. Race track nearby. Leaving for specialty.

Very busy G.P. Fully equipped home and office. Family breaking up.

General Practitioner's home and office—residency—

General Practice—leaving after sixteen years. Modern office fully equipped. Reason for leaving: family problems.

General Practice—$60,000 gross—getting too old—wife and kids gone—any offer.

General Practice—leaving.

General Practice—family.

General Practice—

G.P.—

. . . .
. . . . . . 667-40—

. . . .

RX GOLF AND TRAVEL
The Sports and Leisure Magazine for Physicians

Articles

A Mountain of Mine
Dr. X takes you to a hidden mountain resort he has purchased. Meet the man who successfully fled the "rat race" to find life.

Great Bear for Great Fishing
Read about two young doctors who fly north every year to find an Arctic paradise for fishermen.

Hawaii—Retire or Run Away
Jim Noxon tells you how he made it after selling out a $50,000 practice. Poi oh Poi!

. . . .
. . . . . . 667-402—

!! MEDICINE IN REVOLT !!

Support our protest against traditional, outdated, and outlandish medical ' customs.
   Subscribe now to—MEDIVOLT
   The voice of SHO—The Student Health Organization
   Brace yourself, doctor, be prepared for the shockwaves of tomorrow's medicine. The explosive impact of young American doctors is alive and well in MEDIVOLT.
   Read in this month's issue:
   •Make It or Leave It
   •Commitment Is Nine-Tenths of the Law
   •Medical Education Is Adolescent
   •The GP Is Not Our Bag
   Send your contributions to MEDIVOLT and blow your mind. . . .

. . . .

... 667-4023

Hello? Hello ... who's there? Hello? Now who the devil is calling at this hour? Hello—someone's there, I know it. Now, dammit, hello—hello. ...

. . . .

It was midnight. Johnny remembered it was four hours. He returned quietly to his room. Mary was sleeping. He gathered the stuff from his night table and carried it into the bathroom. He rolled the amber glass in the red linen napkin and dumped it in the trash. He poured the aspirin and Bloomquist down the hopper, flushed the bowl, looked in the mirror and saw his thinning hair, his draining face, his sagging skin, his sunken chest. He found his purple-veining legs and he sat and counted his new liver spots. His belly was sour, the room hot. He looked again at his face in the mirror, and he swore across his left cheek were four faint finger marks.

. . . .

TUESDAY

1970	OCTOBER				1970	
S	**M**	**T**	**W**	**T**	**F**	**S**
				1	2	3
4	5	6	7	8	9	10
11	12	13	14	15	16	17
18	19	20	21	22	23	24
25	26	27	28	29	30	31

20

OCT. 1970

· ·

Morning

7:05 Millie Katz called on the private line, "Just to say it was nice of you to call last night, you bastard. You and your simpleton face. I told you you were ripe, Johnny Shoemaker, I'll see you tonight. . . ."

7:35 A try at breakfast and the kids didn't work. This was going to be a hard, long day. The office bell rang while he was shaving and still in his pajama tops.

"It's a patient and a little kid," Jennie told him. "Are you home?"

Jackie Kane had her eight-year-old by the wrist and it looked like if he moved a fiber the hand would come apart in her fist.

—I tried, honest to God I tried, I did everything you said. Would I come bothering you before breakfast? But you got to help me get this kid to school. . . .

He was a mess. Black and blue marks all over his arms, both legs scraped to the skin, his eyes swollen, practically no mouth.

—He's got to go to school, I can't take it anymore. I listened. I swear I listened to you. I turned my cheek. Then my other cheek. Then my back. Then my whole damn self! Your advice nowadays isn't worth a quarter. You're out of touch. . . .

One of her kids had peed on the floor, the other one rubbed peanut butter and jelly in his hair, the other one heated a curtain rod and branded his sister.

—You gotta be kidding, doctor, you not only can't turn a cheek, you can't blink an eye. There's only one way to handle kids today, you beat the shit out of them. . . .

8:20 Susan Leader called. "This is me, Dr. Shoemaker, the all-American girl, principal's daughter. It's a different kind of call this morning, Doctor. My father, the leader Leader— thought you'd want to know—he beat the shit out of me. . . ."

· ·

9:00   JONATHAN J. SHOEMAKER, M.D.

DOCTOR IS IN

NO SMOKING

NURSE ON DUTY: MRS. FRANCES COOPER

—The pills are slowing down, or something. All of a sudden everything is different today. The world smelled of roses yesterday, today it just smells. As high as I was, that's how low I am. What do you make of it? Shall I take more? A bigger dose? I tossed in bed all night. He wants me to go away with him, and all of a sudden I'm scared again. It's not like it was Sunday. He's different again, all business. Never touched me once last night. All night he never laid a finger on me. I was dying to have him touch me. What is it with me, two years without, then once I get started it's like I need a fix. Said he had too much thinking to do. What do you do, Doctor, when you know you need this thing so bad? My big kid says to me, "Here, Mom, take a drag, you won't need him." If I had a gun last night, I swear I'd of used it. I don't know on who—me, him, the kids. I hear voices. You ever hear voices? Should I double up on the dose today? I can't go home, please don't send me home. He's going to be here at noon. I'll be all right. Let me go to work. I'll be all right.

Tuesday A.M. OCT. 20, 1970—Schedule—Centre St. Office

9:00	Nick Golopas	I		
9:10	Essie Howard	GP		
9:20	James Spatula	TP	Andy Rolberg	TP
	William Lipsky	TP	Moore	TP

9:30	Sam Washington	GP	Abel Zucks	ECG
9:40	Christine Burns	GP		
9:50	Dr. Frank Jewell	GP	Mattie Kahn	XR
10:00	Charles Wise	GP		
10:10	Carolyn Anderson	GP		
10:20	Elizabeth Finley	I		

11:00 Doctor scheduled in court—Jacardi case

12:00	Sal Cooper	GP	

9:05 <u>NICK GOLOPAS</u> #7—Police Officer—Ins. Pol. Benefits—Age 29
—Hey there, Moneybags, a few more hours and there it is
Wednesday again. Where the hell were you yesterday? Don't
leave me alone with *that* one. She's like all the rest of 'em,
wasn't for the next patient walkin' in she would've raped me.
Her old man's hot, your whole damn office is staked
out.... Damn you, Doc, whatever you did yesterday didn't
make you any better....

. . . .

—Marvin on line one...

. . . .

—Gendarmes around the building. But he is wise. He made his
purchase with a legit Rx, and he hasn't dumped them yet.
He's onto the bluesuits. If they drop in on you, you don't
know anything, only what you read in the medical journals—
unless you're sincere about leaving medicine....

. . . .

9:15 HOWARD, ESSIE #14
                     217 Parkway Drive, Greenville—Age 30
Married—Ins.—BC & BS
11-13-55—Sharp-looking, soft-spoken, chronic hypo. Must
be addict. Can't be so many painful places. Wants codeine.
Nothing else works. Pain unbearable without. Tried everything. Last doctor did...

—I spilled them in the garbage. I don't know what's happening to me. Last week they just rolled out the car door, the week before I heard my daughter walking up the stairs and I panicked and dumped them in the toilet. I don't think I've had three for myself in four weeks. Don't lecture me, just write, please—these headaches are unbearable, I can just about see some mornings. I don't understand what's the matter. I lay there most nights just dying inside and he's there like he's a dead fish.

Now you're about as fair a man as I know, what do you think? Wouldn't you be looking for some out? God almighty, I don't know how it can be otherwise, *any* out. Now what would you do if your wife just lay there cold fish each night and you with an idiotic erection? ...

· ·

—Laurie Lee, Doctor. Stupid women should castrate their husbands the very first night. It's our only chance for sanity. —Doctor, what'll I do? I just got out of the hospital and you didn't see me. I lost the baby. It's only two days and Andy came home from his hunting trip and came into bed with me before he went off again. I just started vomiting. Can I be pregnant? ...

· ·

:25 <u>JAMES SPATULA</u>—High school football—Special—Age 16
—The strapping you put on Saturday is killing me. And I need a note to get out of gym. Bocca also wants you to check me over, he says I got the energy of a glass of day-old beer. ...

· ·

—Doctor, there are three boys out here from the rah rah team, but Spatula says you're not seeing them anymore? You're not giving up those sweet-smelling flowers of American youth, are you? Better if we castrate them the first year of high school. Say, when you have other bits of good news, let me know in advance, I could use a laugh. Took two pills—seems to have turned me on. Here comes the next laugh—Mr. Sam Washington, the hero's father. The insurance still owes us for Willie's last injury. ...

35 —Sam Washington must have had a lean life. With a heavy

corduroy mackinaw his total weight couldn't be over one-twenty. His full muscle mass would fail government inspection for low-fat content. Everything about him was as dry as powdered skim milk. He spoke as if every word would break apart as it left his mouth.

"I don't want to take up too much of your valuable time, Doc," he said, straining to hear himself talk, "but I got somethin' for you from my boy, Willie—you know, who scored them four winnin' touchdowns—just ribbin' you, Doc, that's all. We didn't mean no harm down there on the football field. What harm can an old rheumatism-struck man be to somebody like you?"

Johnny assured him he understood there was no harm meant.

The old man said between the ten of them down there, not a one could of raised his arm above his waist, "All got rheumatism."

But that wasn't why he was here. "Willie gave me a check a couple of weeks ago he said came in the mail. It was for the injury, time he hurt his knee?"

They spoke of his knee and how Willie over the years not only hurt a knee, but a shoulder and a foot and some ribs and a nose. "But whatever it was the boy hurt," Washington said supporting his toppling frame on Johnny's desk, "I fixed him up. Nothin' could stop this boy. I know this all my life. So no matter what it would be, I wouldn't expect anybody on the outside even though they mean right, I wouldn't expect them to understand my Willie and his needs. Cracked knee, or cracked shoulder or foot, don't make no difference, a father knows what's in his boy's heart. I fixed him up and he played."

Washington eased himself into Johnny's chair and made faces like he was tearing apart.

"Willie said I should see you," he whispered through his tense lips, his bony arms still suspending him a few inches from the seat, the final drop allowing a rattling grunt from his spread nostrils. "I guess he wanted me to thank you for referrin' this money to us, it sure came in handy. Rheumatism can strike any of us down with no warnin', summer or winter. Sure hope the check for his head injury comes along soon, it's going to be a cold winter."

Then with inconceivable effort he dragged himself out of the chair and toppled into the doctor's arms, at which point Johnny expected to be left with a handful of old bones, the body never to be seen again. But he pulled himself together and drew upon his scant reserve and shook Johnny's hand respectfully.

"God bless you, Doc, keep workin' on them young boys—ain't many around like you who cares. . . ."

. . . .

9:45 BURNS, CHRISTINE #4138
                                  12 Nelson Rd., Greenville—Age 78
      Widow—Ret. Medicare—Overseas
      10-20-70—

—Now, I don't mean to tell you your business, but God knows I have had doctors in my time. I've lived in Jersey for sixty years and had doctors who graduated from Harvard and Princeton and others who had mail-order diplomas from Oswego. It doesn't seem to make any difference when you finally get here. In spite of the raw liver juice I got from the mail-order doctor who was a dear boy, or the compounded prescription that was imported from Boston from the Harvard doctor, who was also a dear boy, I survived. Neither one made me much better or much worse. And so I believe it goes. If you're going to make it, you do. Doctors nowadays seem to hold themselves in awe of themselves. But hells bells, sonny, fifty years from now your miracle medicines will be ancient history, and those that make it will make it in spite of you. . . . Don't bother with my Medicare number, sonny, I'll never spend fifty dollars a year. . . .

. . . .

—Doctor, Laurie Lee's sister is on the line. She says she knows you're not her family doctor, but she can't reach him on Tuesday. He goes to New York for psychiatric studies, or did she say treatment? . . . I'll be in back lying down. Suddenly I'm not feeling well at all. . . .

. . . .

—This is Molly, you know, Doctor, Laurie's sister? Look, Doc, I'm pregnant, you know, about three months, and I think my three kids are all coming down with the German measles. None of them had the shots. Now, if they get it, I'm gonna need some gamma globulin. I didn't have it last time and I think the baby is retarded or something because you think a kid eleven months old should make any sounds yet? My doctor never gives me an answer straight. He's sick or something, always smiling at me when I ask him questions. He never talks, just mumbles. But *bus-y*. Comes out to my house four in the morning. Just starting his house calls, he says. I read in the papers today more doctors commit suicide than anybody. Hey, Doc, hey—you there? . . .

. . . .

10:00 JEWEL, DR. FRANK #2883
                            12 Erie Lane, Greenville Lakes—Age 48
Married—Research Chemist—WEC Ins.
7-8-64—SOS—WEC Head—Wants BP checked and kept at
128/74. Won't accept substitutes—Accepts me? Hx;
married, sex 2.7 weekly, children 3.8. . .

—I cannot believe that you have no explanation for my pressure going up over 128/74. In my field if there was a need for a piece of cloth that must be dyed a hundred colors in one dipping, I assure you one of us would come up with the formula. So, in a field apparently of more importance, the human structure, there is a need for a chemical to reenergize my dying cells and so reduce the charge on my rising blood pressure. You mean to say there is none available? Ridiculous. I want my pressure to stabilize at 128/74. Now you just allocate monies, analyze the need, and come up with the answer. How can you continue to practice your art or your science or whatever, as a puppet? What do you do, wait until someone rings your bell and deposits on your doorstep the immaculate bag of chemicals? My God, what a stupid way to live. You call this doctoring? What do you do here all day long other than listen to drivel and feed it back in spoonsful of chance? My God, man, don't you feel like an idiot most of the time? Have you no cure for *any* of my ills? Are you sure of nothing? When I want a vermilion crescent on a chartreuse swatch of silk chemise, I know precisely that a 12.3-second dip will produce the exact impression I want each and every time. My God, man, how can you live with yourself otherwise? . . .

10:10 —Just a few minutes of your busy day, Dr. Shoemaker. We know how busy a doctor's life is, God bless him. No pitch, just a few boxes of goodies from Robert J. Sweeney & Co., makers of *PIT,* Pregnancy Intrauterine Tampon, the first device used for *assuring* pregnancy with every act of love. *GOB,* Girl Or Boy douche, the first absolute solution to predetermined sex. And lastly, but *heaven's,* never lastly— *HOPE,* Homosexual Preventitive Elixir, the first oral contraceptive specifically for those who *really* care. . . .

. . . .

—Doctor, sorry about that one getting in. I've been upchucking my weekend. I feel a little better. Sorry—head's clearing a little. I'll send in a soul lifter. . . .

. . . .

10:15

WISE, CHARLES #3095

1112 Newton Rd., Greenville—Age 68
Divorced—Retired—Medicare
11-3-66—DOA in ER. Bluer than a band leader's shirt.
Came back with a chest pound and a prayer. Left wife,
says she killed him once, never again.

—Ha! Doc! Ha! Get up out of that chair and grab me. Here. Feel this muscle. Ha! Shuffleboard. Dead, am I? Ha! You ever see anybody more alive than me? Four years. You still got my death certificate? Half signed. Well, you just frame it. I'm gonna sign *yours,* ha! Hit me in the chest. Hit me harder. What you need, Doc, is your first damn heart attack. Get it early, get it over with, makes you feel like a million bucks. Look at me, best damned thing ever happened to me. Got rid

of my stupid crying wife, have *three* women down in my
house in St. Pete. You want to feel something *really* hard?
Doc, I swear, if you want to get away from it all and really
live, have your heart attack now. It's the best damned
medicine in the world. . . .

. . . .

—It's your lawyer, says it's urgent. . . .
—Johnny, what the hell is this? A million-dollar suit? Who
carries your malpractice? You can't be covered for over a
hundred thousand. What the hell did you do? Did you really
kill the kid? This shyster Paltzinger, he's a shrewd ball
breaker. Christ, Johnny, you gotta be more careful nowadays.
They'll sue you if you pluck out one extra eyebrow. You
better lay low, no hospital cases, no deliveries, no surgery, no
questionable drugs—just lay low until I can contact your
carrier. Christ, Johnny, maybe we can claim insanity. . . .

. . . .

10:25 ANDERSON, CAROLYN #1648
19 Clarke St., Greenville—Age 38
Married—Housewife—BC & BS Rider J
5-31-61—Needs GP. Moved from Calif. Had spec. for kids,
self, husband. Wants specialist care at family rates.
Problems from dandruff to ingrown nails. Time. . .

—I've been coming here nine years, did you ever once in that
time *suggest* an electroencephalogram? I don't want to be
unappreciative, after all you've done for me. Between the gall
bladder and the hemorrhoids and the arthritis and the
pneumonia and the migraines you had enough. And I didn't
forget Harold and me and our goddam battles you sweated us
through at plenty of two o'clocks in the morning. And I
didn't forget Sally's passing out all the time and how you
straightened her out and got her married and pregnant and
delivered her RH negative baby. But here I been telling you
time and again about this pressure in my head, you know
how it makes me act so crazy and we can't get to the bottom

of it, and here you send my neighbor, Mrs. Philbert, for an encephalogram after her third visit, and me, I've been with you over nine years and all I get is the two-aspirin bit. I don't mean to be unappreciative, but someone else could consider this a cause for malpractice. . . .

.   .   .   .

—Whatever that double dose does, I want to do it again. I feel *great,* even caught myself smiling at a patient. Can't wait for that sonofabitch to get here. How did I ever get into this mess with this guy? Sex is a rotten leveler. A feel of a breast and a wet lip and your whole life goes into a sewer and out to sea. Well, whatever is in those new pills, Doctor, sell 'em by the bushel, I'm cured. I never felt so goddam cured in my life. Oh, my God, when he gets here . . .

.   .   .   .

At ten-thirty when he should have been on his way to the courthouse, Johnny agreed to see the Tensig salesman.

"Not only have we received the OK from the Food and Drug Administration to go ahead on the fifty-milligram tablet," the black pin-striped suit said, "but doses up to two hundred milligrams a day are now acceptable."

Johnny told him Frances was taking double doses.

"She's a sweet kid," the white oxford shirt said. "While you've been too busy to see me, I've been slipping her enough samples to keep her on her toes. Never worry, the FDA says it's OK, you don't come by that easily."

Johnny asked about the newspaper articles.

"Do I have to tell you about newspapers?" the gray silk tie asked of the doctor. "We have a litigation going right now against the four major chains who ran the pictures of the mutilations."

What about the litigations of the families against Swanson Labs, Johnny asked the square-cut face.

He outlined to Johnny the worldwide research on this new psycho-energizer and flipped through a four-inch notebook stuffed with papers from great men of medicine, really honorably university-seated great men. The drug was undeniably a new mental miracle, and when used in expert hands had been changing schizophrenics back to normal practically overnight.

Johnny remembered the wasted bodies he had seen in the coverage of the Tensig scandal in last year's newsmagazines.

"After all, Doctor," the lacquered black hair said to Johnny, "you know the lowly aspirin in excess can cause psychoses, even death."

Johnny told him thank you, and not to leave any more samples.

The black wing-tipped shoes turned solemnly from the office and said in leaving, "Need a few starters for yourself? . . ."

. . . .

—One more and away you go. But Betty says this is urgent. I don't believe myself, but I *believed* her . . .

. . . .

10:45 FINLEY, ELIZABETH #2412

Cottage Apartments, Greenville—Age 34 Widow—Secretary (Leader) Greenville High School—School Insurance 4-9-62—Chronic inflammatory lip ulcers. Husband died four years ago. Suspect contact dermatitis. Make note to check out Leader one day. Rx cortisone. . .

—He has finally blown his cork, the school is like under martial law. He has removed every free regulation and has restricted any free movement. No more club meetings, no more school plays, no more student government, no more interscholastic sports—nothing that will allow interrelationship of the sexes.

He is segregating classes and reorganizing schedules so that only boys are in the halls one hour and girls the other. He won't allow a boy and girl on the same school bus. He looks like he's aged fifty years overnight. His telephone is on his ear every minute, he is dictating a dozen letters at a clip, he wants

a new school built immediately. He has had the school board
call a special meeting. He wants temporary quarters at once
for separate classes for boys and girls. He is going out of his
mind, and he's taking me with him. I had to run over. You've
got to give me a shot or something, and you've got to get in
there and see him. He has your letter—my God, Dr.
Shoemaker, are we all cracking up? . . .

. . . .

11:15

GREENVILLE COURTHOUSE
Room 28—Judge Schickal's Chamber

—You're Dr. Shoemaker, right? I never miss a doctor, they
always have that . . . doctor-look. I'm Attorney Calvin. Sorry
to get you down here on such a busy morning, I tried calling
but I missed you, your nurse said you had just left. Sorry
about that, doctor, but the case was settled just ten minutes
ago, and you won't be needed. One of those legal setbacks
that you don't read about in the papers. Poor guy, out of
work two years, over forty-seven hundred dollars in doctor
bills alone. They had a file of pictures on him they showed
me in some barroom brawl over some dame—him with his
misplaced disc. They played me a piece of tape they bugged
in your office way back when he first came to you and you
said you couldn't find the ruptured disc. Look out for smiling
agents with too many pens in their pockets—miniature mikes,
you know. Dirty pool, eh, Doc? Not like the old Hippocratic
gang, suave, genteel, soul-searching, honorable men of the
community.

Look, Dr. Shoemaker, I am *really* sorry to get you down
here on a wild goose chase. You'll be paid for your time, but,
hell, poor guy's got beans. There's just about enough for legal
fees. You had a bill in with us for about six hundred. Two
years of work, that's fair enough. You should see some of the
bills from crooks who saw this poor slob only once or twice.
Six hundred is fair enough. Well, with what he's going to get,
poor shnook, after all expenses are deducted, if we can settle
for ten cents on a dollar we'll be lucky. How does that sound

to you, Doctor? This poor slob, he probably will never get out of debt. We cut our fee from one-half to one-third. We'll mail you a check as soon as it's cleared. Don't worry about us, Doctor, our professional contacts are valuable assets, and you'll be protected. Thanks again, Doc, you can take the morning off. . . .

.   .   .   .

Johnny remembered in his grinding stomach pit he had bypassed breakfast. It was eleven-thirty, he could stall a half hour in the Courthouse Coffee Shop.

"Black coffee and jellied English?" the big dark lady with the pancake-face smile placed his order in front of him. "You're Dr. Shoemaker?"

He didn't know her, but that was not unusual. How many times did a strange face come up to him out of nowhere and say, "Remember those green pills you gave me, should I keep taking them?"

"You see my no good husband," she reminded him, "and my kids. Me, no time for me. I got two jobs to hold down. Six days a week here on my wobbly legs, they got veins in them look like Mississippi worms. They are fat, juicy worms." She laughed a fat, juicy laugh and shook her head remembering another day. "Other job is at six o'clock, I go make pretzels at Bendleman's. They are good Jews. Give me all the pretzels I can eat. I save myself three dollars a week on suppers."

Johnny stuffed down his first half of a muffin, expecting possibly the grain to turn immediately into action-packed dextrose and he would have the energy to just get up and leave.

"You still don't know me?" the chuckling waitress upbraided Johnny. "Naw, you wouldn't have no cause to see me. I sit home all Saturday afternoon and I pray to Lord Jesus my Willie's head don't smash open all over that football field, and make everybody out there as sick as I am at home."

Johnny was bewildered at the Mendelian breakdown: from

the skeletal father and the jelly-roll mother to the Herculean son.

"How come, Doctor, you send my boy Willie out with a smashed head?" She had stopped chuckling. "I don't care what his old no good man says, I see him at night holdin' his head like it was a soft-boiled egg. Can't you see he is a sick boy?"

Johnny answered her gently, expressing his happiness at meeting the fine mother of such a fine boy and assured her he was fine.

"He is not. He is sick. We is all sick."

Johnny remembered the sister, and suddenly—*the little brother*. The sickelemia.

"The specialist you sent him over to in Philadelphia, he says he is *bad* sick. He wants to see everybody, all the kids."

Not Willie, Johnny assured the mother.

"Willie ain't no superman!" She loudly rebuked Johnny, her soft, jello-like body tensing into a mass of spastic muscle fibers. "When he gets smashed, out comes the same jelly and guts as the next guy. You don't need no X ray to see. How come you make him out to be a superman? He says you tell him he is special. Nobody is special. The Lord calls us all and we all got to come."

Momma Washington sighed heavily and said quietly, "Why don't you finish your coffee, Doctor, you need the strength of a thousand cups of coffee what you have to do." She poured a fresh hot cup and he gratefully relieved his icy stomach lining and he thanked her.

She said gently, her voice pleading, "Can't you keep my boy from playing again? He has done his part. Tell him he is nobody special, tell him his body got weak cracks in it like anybody else's. Tell him, even if you have to lie."

Johnny bit into his nailbed and wished she would melt into the carpeted floor and he could just go into the men's room and hide for a while.

"Keep my Willie alive, Doctor," she whispered. "You say you are his friend—show him what is a *real* friend."

. . . .

Afternoon

12:15   **JONATHAN J. SHOEMAKER, M.D.**
                        1555 Centre St.
                  DOCTOR'S OFFICE—ONE FLIGHT UP

. . . .


```
┌─────────────────────────────────────────────┐
│   GREENVILLE POLICE SQUAD CAR #479            │
│   OFFICER ON DUTY—NICHOLAS GOLOPAS            │
└─────────────────────────────────────────────┘
```


—Hey, Moneybags, she beat us to it, she shot the husband.
Better get to her, she's up there laughing herself hysterical
crazy. . . .

. . . .

1:00

| STATE OF NEW JERSEY |
| CERTIFICATE FOR HOSPITALIZATION |
| (Under Title 30; NJSA) |

Certificate of Mental Illness

I, _Jonathan J. Shoemaker_, M.D. of _1555 Centre St._
(Print)   (Street and Number)
GREENVILLE, _NEWTOWN_, _N. J._
(City or Town)   (County)   (State)
_17858_ of _N. J._ do hereby certify that I personally
(Medical License No.)   (State)
examined _FRANCES COOPER_ on the _20ᵈ_

day of _Oct._, 19 _70_. I am not the director, chief executive officer or proprietor of any
(Month)
institution for the care and treatment of the mentally ill to which application for admission is being prepared;
nor am I a relative, either by blood or marriage of the patient. My staff appointment to the receiving hospital

_____

The following is a description of the patient: _FRANCES COOPER_;
(Name)
1610 S. WILSON RD. - EASTVILLE; date of birth: _NOV. 12, 1934_;
(Address)
Height _5'5"_; weight _144_; color _W_; sex _F_;
Marital status _SEP._; color of eyes _BR_; color of hair _BR_.

The following is a report of my medical findings:

1. History of Relevant Previous Illnesses (include mental illness and or previous hospitalizations):
No other relevant history
_____
_____
_____

2. History of onset of previous illness including predisposing factors:
No other relevant history
_____

3. Mental Status (Describe in detail the patient's behavior, appearance and manner. State what the patient said.)

Patient has over the past several months shown despondent and then exhilirating moods, change of dress, complaints against family, friend, patients in office. Patient admitted to hopelessness, and finally to stealing

4. Additional facts and circumstances (including facts communicated by others) upon which my judgment is based: *Patient's son claimed mother smoked pot (?) Patient took overdosage of prescribed and stolen (?) medication.*

5. If applicable, carefully delineate and describe any destructive, homicidal or suicidal behavior; depression, violence or excitement.

Patient's mother claims patient sat in darkened room many nights, uncommunicative. Patient revealed today she would like to kill.

6. Medications (give all known information about medically prescribed or self-administered use of medications or toxic substances.) *Patient's most recent drug (3 days) TENSIG -50-100 mgm q. i.*

7. History of Use of Alcohol *None Known*

8. Describe the patient's physical findings; physical status; vital signs; blood pressure; laboratory data; please forward abstract copies of medical reports.

None relevant

On the basis of the foregoing, I believe that the condition of this person is such as to require evaluation, care and treatment in a mental hospital.

Jonathan J. Shoemaker M.D.

1:30

> ### CENTRE PHARMACY (Formerly Shoemaker's)
> ### MARVIN SWARTZ, REG. PH.

. . . .

They ate together in the back room where once Johnny lived. Marvin still was able to throw together an egg salad sandwich, even though the lunch counter had long since been taken over by all that smelly stuff women used to keep things away from them or magnetize toward them.

"If Pop ever came in and saw his fountain—"

Marvin had taken over even while Poppa Shoemaker had been occasionally sick, while he was still in pharmacy school. It was only natural he would buy in as soon as Pop took the final turn. Obviously he and Johnny had been close, Marvin at least assumed close enough to tell him things like:

"What are you doing to yourself, you step in roses and come up smelling shit?"

Johnny told him he used too much mayonnaise in the sandwich, his cholesterol was 320 last week.

"Another nail," Marvin said impatiently. "If you're setting yourself up for hellfire and damnation, you're doing one helluva job. Willie, you already have the ax three inches over his head. Your girl upstairs, you knew she was getting ready to knock off this guy. What kind of thrill show you running?"

Marvin drank diet soda. He was five-five and weighed over two hundred last count, and after a few sandwiches and a handful of pretzels and a chocolate doughnut, he didn't take any chances with the sugar drinks. "A guy's got to look out for himself, or else who cares."

Over his second diet cola he said to Johnny (who rested with his eyes closed and his feet up on Pop's rolltop desk), "You know, I used to think a guy who looks out for himself, somebody who's got this world by the balls, Johnny Shoemaker, it's him. When I took over this store, for about a year or so, you know what, Johnny, *I* felt the same way. I figured, Johnny, he's got it made *his* way, me, I got it made *mine*. Then," Marvin sucked the soda dry and opened another, "I started filling these Rx's for all those shmucks who I went

through high school with and I see the gravy train is really on
the other side of the fence. I then said to myself, 'Mirror,
mirror, on the wall, who's the biggest shmuck of all?'
You—you it said back to me, then cracked into a thousand
pieces—which I naturally bottled and sold as ground glass for
the cure of mother-in-law fever—"

The store bell rang and a customer came in looking for her
runaway child. Marvin told her he had baked him in the oven
and was eating him. The customer oh-pshawed him and said
you're just like your father, bless him. Marvin came back to
Johnny, shook him awake, and said, "They still think I'm the
third Shoemaker."

Johnny warned him the world couldn't take another.

Marvin opened a bottle of diet orange drink. "Like I said,
I'm hot now on you doctors making all the bread and me
making all the crumbs. I used to see guys like Abe Green,
Oscar Lederman, Charlie Quintero, Pagliacci, or whatever the
hell that hairy one's name is, shmucky kids who out on the
street a few years ago you wouldn't give a shit for."

Johnny remembered these kids. Under other circumstances,
would Marvin had included the name Shoemaker on the list?

"When I see these nincompoops driving in their Lincolns
and their Jags and their Caddies" (Johnny felt relieved) "and
then calling me and bawling *me* out for charging an extra
quarter for a goddam dollar-and-a-half prescription I make
fifteen cents on, then I get my fuzz up." He downed the
orange drink and opened a diet grape.

"Then I said to myself, I'm gonna go back to school, and
I'm gonna get a diploma that says doctor on it and I'm gonna
call my corner pharmacist and tell him to shit in his hat and
mix it up and bottle it, cause it'll do about the same good all
his other crap he is selling will do."

Marvin finished the diet grape and waited for a response
from a wordless Johnny, who was only too happy to have
had someplace to come and feel invited and warm. Even
though Marvin was carrying on with average Marvin exuber-
ance, Johnny was able to find a modicum of repose in his
father's old back room, something he needed today. He
floated through Marvin's continuing biographical tirade, pick-
ing up the gist of the story between short catnaps.

"So what do I do," Marvin continued, his eyes searching for his next diet drink, "finally after ten years of saving every goddam extra cent, and figuring how I'm gonna keep the kids in school and where the wife can get a job while I'm in college, finally a few weeks ago I have it all worked out and I'm gonna make the move."

Johnny actually snorted, like a miniature snore, but Marvin continued, having found new energy in a bottle of diet punch.

"Make a move, I say to myself this week? After what I see is with Shoemaker, this is what I want? I go back to the mirror and it says, 'Shmuck, what kind of grass you think grows in Shoemaker's yard—weeds, that's what.' "

Johnny awakened and agreed with that.

"Then I say, to hell with it, who needs your headaches? What am I doing? I got the easy end of the stick. I got less cash, but boy do I have a night's sleep."

Johnny remembered Billy Brown and the cold sweats and the nightmares, and he wondered if he still would be interested in a nursing home partner. Then he remembered Poppa and decided he wouldn't be interested in Billy Brown.

"You know, the more I think of it and the more I deal with you guys," Marvin opened a box of Bendelman's pretzels, "the closer I get to the truth. None of you are human. You're all from some secret planet and you been sent down here to destroy us. You can't tell me a doctor comes out of a mother's belly."

Johnny yawned and shrugged and took a pretzel from the box and saw Bendelman's label and thought only of Mrs. Washington's wormy legs.

"Believe me, Johnny Shoemaker, I don't know what's got into you, but I am highly suspicious. Would you open up your shirt and let me look—I say you got no navel. . . ."

. . . .

2:30

GREENVILLE HIGH SCHOOL
—Est. 1917—

Health Office — Mrs. Alice McGibbon, R.N.

—We're doing girls' ice hockey today. There was a call for over a hundred girls, but I doubt whether all will show. I notice when it is a girl call, more show than boy call. I sometimes wonder whether the little darlings are happier than they look unbuttoning their blouses.

Have you heard what's going *on* here? Why, we must be infested with nests of orgies right under our noses that have been scandalizing the school. Mr. Leader has uncovered six secret societies just today. He claims that one in every three girls in the school will be pregnant by the time she is a senior. The nurse's office has been alerted to search each girl's handbag for birth control pills. The athletic department has been warned to look through the boys' wallets for contraceptives. Can you imagine, these sweet little darlings that I have coddled like my very own children, right before my very eyes fertilizing each other like pollen on the lawn.

We're getting a male nurse in for the boys. Thank goodness. Can you imagine I have been alone in a room here with some of the *actual* leaders. They are a handsome bunch, you know, and at *my* age. . . . I wonder what the male nurse will be like? . . . All right, girls—here we go, Doctor, now don't hesitate to pull out any girl that looks a bit, you know, whorish to you. . . .

. . . .

4:00

OFFICE OF THE PRINCIPAL
—DR. HENRY L. LEADER—

Johnny's brief resignation note had been filled with Leader's pencil holes.

"That's what I think of your approach to this insignificant problem. Not only full of holes, but it can't stand up to our credo, Johnny boy." The Leader worked hard at a half grin, snapping instantly back to a period of grinding his teeth.

"Dr. Shoemaker," he said distantly, "no matter what your personal ambitions are, you are hired by the township to examine and treat these football players and by God, you must do this. True," he forced a separation of his lips, "you do have cause to doubt your judgment. Willie Washington went on to win the game as I announced, and recorded statewide acclaim for our school."

The phone rang and Leader barked out an order "... Then she is fired. There will be *no* further sex education classes!"

He grinned satisfyingly and turned to Johnny.

"You can't run away from things, my boy. How would it be if I were to have left my school yesterday because my little girl has been made pregnant by one of our misfit bastards who did not hear the sound of my drums? Is that reason for me to run? Uh-uh, Johnny boy, that's the time for action. This is the seventies, a time of revolutionary change. You see the program I've already put into action here—only the beginning. Within a year I may be in Washington—however—" big, toothy, overpowering grin.

Johnny quickly ran through the list of political tickets and made indelible notes to check out who he must vote *against* next month.

"And now, Johnny boy," Leader grinned incessantly, "a show of confidence in the Henry L. Leader credo—we can do anything. *Anything!*"

He leaned over to the microphone, switched six separate buttons, and spoke with avaricious pride, the grin literally breaking apart the corners of his mouth into blood-filled cracks:

"... Attention, school, this is your principal, Henry L. Leader. All of you stop what you are doing and listen. Tomorrow there will be a special assembly in Green Hall. You are all invited to attend the wedding of my daughter, Susan, to ... "

. . . .

4:30

> **ATHLETIC FIELD**
> **STAFF PARKING ONLY**

—Dr. Shoemaker, I got this hip pointer I want you to look at ...

—Hey, Doc, the knee won't bend ...

—Doctor, can you help me, I got this headache ...

—Shoulder ...

—Leg . . .

—Back . . .

—Itchy crotch . . .

—What the hell goes, Doc? Hey, kids, g'wan back to your scrimmage. Come on, goddam you, run, never walk, *run*. Doc, Chris', you peed off or somethin'? I sent over three kids today, you send them back. I *need* them kids for Saturday, what'll I do without them? Have a heart, Doc. Between the old man trying to stop the game altogether and cutting out the cheerleading and segregating the stands and *you* cutting out on the kids—well, Chris', Doc, I got my own kids at home to feed, have a heart. You know I lose this season I could find myself in Louisiana or Kennebunkport, Maine. Six times I done this in the past twenty years. Have a heart, Doc, I got a good deal here. You nearly lost it for me last week. A coach needs a Willie every few seasons to keep up. Look at that kid out there. —Run, you goddam turtle, *run*—gotta keep right on top of them, Doc, they just would lay right down in the middle of the field. What the hell do they care for my job? They make a mistake, so, they take some broad out and break training. You make a mistake, so, you can bury yours. *I* got to move to Kennebunkport, Maine. . . .

. . . .

5:00 HC - <u>STELLA PODALSKY</u> - 8 Central Ave., Greenville—Age 64—Home (Frances' mother)—File #2128

—Doctor, I warned you. I called. I told you first she was acting crazy. I told you she had a gun. I told you he was a no good bastard, that you should do something for her. I told you she was taking too many goddam pills. Doctors give pills like they are Cracker Jacks. You ever give your wife or kids pills? You see what they did to my Frances, carried away in a strait-jacket like out of a funny paper. Nobody laughed in this house, Doctor, nobody laughed.

Her father is out drinking it away. Soon he'll come home and throw me into bed and then we'll both forget for a few hours. But how about tomorrow?

And her sons? The big one is all ready to join her. Where do they get all these pills? What kind of age are we living in?

The doctor who was our God, our Jesus Christ, the doctor now is a pusher for the poisons of big business.

What's the matter with you, Dr. Shoemaker? You must have known what was going to be the end of my Frances. Do you realize all you do for a living is make people crazy from your pills? . . . Do you know this? . . . Do you care? . . .

. . . .

5:15 —SERVICE . . . Yes, Doctor. Oh, Dr. *Shoemaker*, has *your* line been ringing. Whatever happened? You've got to call the Greenville Police right away, the state hospital needs some information, your attorney said to call him at once, Greenville Hospital called, the *Greenville Post* wants to send out a reporter. My goodness, Doctor, do you know you're a celebrity? . . . Oh, yes, there is a message from Dr. Applewhite. He would like you to call him as soon as possible about a case you sent him. . . .

. . . .

5:30 DR. ABNER APPLEWHITE
—Osteopathic Physician—

DOCTOR IS IN

NO SMOKING

—The kid's back is perfect, Johnny. Not many perfect backs around, but this kid has got one, right out of a textbook. I put him through every didactic and clinical maneuver— nothing. Twenty-four beautifully constructed well-aligned vertebrae, and not a single lesion. I'd be out of business if you sent me many more of these. Now why does Johnny Shoemaker send me this, I say, after I put this anatomical specimen through the paces, he could have found the same nothing I found. Must be Johnny Shoemaker suspects dirty work and I'm going to be his fall guy. No, some other of his not-so-genteel colleagues, but not Johnny. If anyone cares, this is the guy.

So, I figure he's busy—who isn't?—and is spreading out his cases. So, I take it upon myself to do whatever I can to dig out the boy's backache. But it's not his back. So what is it? Sure hurts him, he jumped a full foot when I punched it. So? Why didn't Johnny Shoemaker punch it? *Positive Lloyds'.* Must be his kidney.

I asked the boy about his peeing ability, he said no sweat. He feels no pain when he urinates, no burning, no dribbling, no frequency. But, he does kind of recall back there at the beginning a drop or two of blood on his underwear. Hell, he figured, everybody has a drop of blood on his underwear sometimes. And that was all.

For the hell of it, I took a hemoglobin, 10.4 grams. That's low.

Come with me, Johnny, I want to show you his X ray....

... Now, here, I used a variance on KVP's and was able to bring out something here in back of the Psoas muscle. There, look right alongside the eleventh and twelfth dorsal on the left. Now, trace this shadow around and you can just about make out a line of a kidney. Now, if you follow up along the lateral border, suddenly right here—here—you see a black out—OK—then a few centimeters above it follows a clear-cut line.

Now, make of this what you will. I'm only an old time D.O. with thirty-three years of general practice to turn to, so you can't judge by me. But if that's not a tear on this kid's kidney, I'll turn in my Spinalator....

. . . .

6:30   **JONATHAN J. SHOEMAKER, M.D.**

_____

DOCTOR IS OUT—RETURN 9:00 A.M. THURSDAY

_____

NO SMOKING

_____

NURSE ON DUTY: MISS GEORGIA JONES

—I called everyone. Most people understood. The same few sounded like they always sound—how come they can't come in tonight and eat a little of your brains, they wouldn't mind the smell. They understand your problem, but what about theirs.

Made an appointment with Dr. Kohn for Willie.

Mrs. Katz is coming in at seven. She understood the message.

Your wife called and said it would be nice if you called back.

Otherwise that's it. Typical day in a country doctor's office.

I worked once for a doctor like you down in Atlanta when I was still a junior in high school. He said I looked good just to have around the office. I did some filing and odd running jobs to the lab and the post office. He never laid a hand on me once. I saw a glint that said he'd wished he'd try, but it never got past his eyeball.

He was a nice looking man—kind, understanding, old-time storybook doc—the kind I figure you'd be if you gave yourself a chance. He sort of carried me around with him like you would a pocket secretary, brought me to the hospital, took me on rounds, showed me my first dead body. I'll never forget this, it keeps cropping up in my head, especially around here this past week. It keeps pushing itself at me and it says, spit it out, Georgia, tell him, spit it out.

I'll never be able to forget this kid, he was stone dead. A healthy, strapping farm boy, he was in the office as alive as me or you just a day before, he needed a tetanus shot, he punctured his wrist with a rusty icepick. Then all of a sudden, you blink an eye, and there he was in that hospital bed, cold and dead, and just that same smell we got in here, a dead smell.

It's still in my nose, I can't get it out all week. Then tonight it is in my mouth and in my head. I had to tell you before it busts me apart.

A bull had gored a hole in this nice kid's belly, and he just bled to death out there in the field. They thought he was still alive, so they rushed him into the hospital for Doc to see. But all Doc Cuthbert could do was pronounce him dead.

That's what I can't ever forget. That's what keeps pushing up at me and says for me to tell you, Doctor, about Doc Cuthbert pronouncing him dead.

I was there, standing right alongside him when he pronounced him dead. The words stuck right in my throat. I'll tell you it scared me so I have never forgot it.

What was I so scared about? A dead kid? Hell, no, at fifteen I was strong enough to eat live fish. It was old Doc Cuthbert who made my blood turn cold. You see, it's like it's you, and you are him, and I'm living it all through again—you don't see.

Take you. It's like what's happening around here all week, all of a sudden you're not you. Like old Doc C., was he really himself that night? How would I know when you're really what you are? You've changed. Whether you know you're changed or not I can't tell, but you have really changed.

A few weeks ago it would be nothing for me to send in a crumbly old soul praying for her last breath, and she'd come out spirit and body pasted together with some magic glue you've got hidden away behind those office doors. Today, I wouldn't feel safe sending you a canker sore. You're like a sour old pouty child. You feel sorry for yourself that you're a doctor. Your parade has marched away leaving you holding the green and white crepe paper.

You know what scared me about seeing Doc Cuthbert and the dead kid? Not the face of the dead kid, but the face on Cuthbert, smiling, yeah, *smiling* like a Halloween pumpkin, and cheering himself on. You know he actually looked happy to see that kid was laying there cold smelly dead.

I saw an unbelievable look of devilish, soulless satisfaction in his face. They had called him to pronounce this boy "dead." He'd been dead for half an hour, but without Doc the kid wasn't dead. He placed his stethoscope to that already decaying body and with all his bedside decorum and artful hesitation, he said finally—he's dead.

And it was right then, at that moment of weird silence when he said he's dead, it was right then that I saw it. It came over the face of Doc Cuthbert like a veil, and then it was gone. But for the brief seconds it was there, Doc Cuthbert had the face of Satan himself. It is the face that comes over a doctor when he has passed his final judgment, a look that he reserves only for himself—and God.

Do you understand, Dr. Shoemaker, *this* is the scare? Momma forgive me, but this is you. This is where your trouble has got to be, this is why you count yourself dead. It's not because your nurse is in a booby hatch. Plenty of nurses end up there. It can't be because somebody got shot up in your office—it doesn't happen every day, but you've seen enough of this. It can't be a dead baby, this happens too.

You are chickening out on your responsibilities for one reason, and that's got to be because you didn't get the chance to say—*he's dead.* That's one helluva pronouncement, but I was there. I get that awful sick stomach feeling that says you *wanted* Willie to get it at that game, and when you didn't get your doctor thrill, you went off and pouted like a kid who had his bag of jelly beans taken away.

I think you feel you were cheated. I think this is what it's all about.

So, I think you better get yourself to a church or whatever they got around here to wash up with, and you better ask yourself out loud—*did I really want Willie Washington to get killed?* . . . .

. . . .

:00 —MILDRED KATZ
—I'm ready when you are, J. J. . . . .

. . . .

vening
:00

> OLDE CASTLE INN—In the Pennsylvania Dutch Manner
> GOODE FOODE—PLEASANT LODGING
> YE TAVERNE ROOME
> MENU

—Greetings, guests. We urge you to relax, enjoy your meal at Ye Taverne Roome, spend time in contemplating the pleasures of this evening. Your chef will prepare for you the savory yet homelike dishes that have made the Pennsylvania Dutch known the country over. It has been said that the kitchens of the old Dutch homes were filled with the appetizers and the bedrooms filled with the dessert. Make eat now and pleasant dreams later.

. . . .

9:00

| LODGING – REGISTRATION |

Mr. & Mrs. William Jones
726 Canal St.
Williamstown, N.J.

Rm. 278

—Notice Ye Guests—

According to the regulations of the State of Pennsylvania, the fee for lodging shall be based on double occupancy whether one or more beds are occupied.

Lights must be out at midnight.

No smoking after lights out.

Guests checking out before midnight will be charged for the full day.

Please sleep quietly.

. . . .

11:35

| KATZ RESIDENCE—1210 Erie Drive |

—Whatever it was, Johnny, a doctor can't help. You should know that, you're a big boy. The food was good anyway.

And don't worry about Millie, she'll find a way. The Sealtest man gets here around five. He's no Richard Burton, but I know he makes the scene. Goodnight, J. J. Thanks for the ride in the country—and the diet pills. . . .

. . . .

THE SHOEMAKERS
692 LAKE DRIVE

———————

WELCOME

———————

—Johnny? For God's sake, where were you? I've been trying to find you for hours. Service is calling every ten minutes. Where have you been? The hospital is frantic—Marvin brought in Willie Washington about nine o'clock. He collapsed at work and they think he's about *dead*! . . .

. . . .

WEDNESDAY

1970	OCTOBER					1970
S	**M**	**T**	**W**	**T**	**F**	**S**
				1	2	3
4	5	6	7	8	9	10
11	12	13	14	15	16	17
18	19	20	21	22	23	24
25	26	27	28	29	30	31

21

OCT. 1970

12:05 A.M.

> N.J.
> MD—K885
> GARDEN STATE

ROUTE #41 N.J.

The heater in the Buick had blown out and it was cold. The radiator was hissing water, and the muffler coughed fumes, and the front end rattled. (Millie Katz had said, "That makes two of you.")

Johnny pulled the short collar of his topcoat up over his neck. His chilled head, quietly aching these past hours, now screamed *help* above the leaking sound of wind from the broken front door.

There was a hollow emptiness like in a deserted cellar.

Lem came to him, and Johnny pounced on the accelerator as if to leave his brother behind on the cold empty road. See how it feels in the dark, rats running over your feet, Pop waiting at the other end with a hose? See how it feels to be left alone just to touch a pair of black lace panties?

Lem's voice: "Where are you rushing to?"

Johnny let up on the gas pedal.

"Slow down, what's your hurry?" Lem never awaited his brother's reply. "You don't have to answer this call. You gave up on these kids, remember, Jonathan? This is your trouble, you know—inconsistent. You gave them away. Especially him, you gave Willie away, so where are you going in such a hurry?"

Johnny toyed with the gas pedal. He had raced out of the house, not waiting for any further explanation from Mary, and suddenly here he was, hell bent for the hospital. He didn't know what happened, how long ago, if it was a new accident, who brought him in, who was taking care of him, was Willie alive.

"Don't go running into that hospital," Lem said, "just to make a fool of yourself. Don't you have enough problems now? Turn around, go on home, go to sleep. You'll wake up in the morning and read about it in the paper. Don't involve yourself. I won't go with you, Jonathan. I swear, you go into that hospital and you're on your own."

The Buick clattered to a coughing, choking halt. Johnny wasn't sure whether he had intentionally choked it out so he could turn around and go back home, or whether it had developed the inevitable death rattle all by itself. He pumped gas, turned the key, and pumped again, using Lem's old advice—"*OK, now, take up on the clutch, down, slow, down with the accelerator. . . .*" The Buick pulled itself off the shoulder onto the main road and Johnny felt himself riding alone in the direction of Greenville Mercy Hospital.

He switched on his car radio. ". . . And if this doesn't bring Hanoi back to the conference table, the President stated he will go directly to Vietnam himself. . . . And now WGRN brings you Ransom B. Otwell, commenting on a local news event, a regular editorial feature of this station. Mr. Otwell."

". . . Lying in a local hospital bed suffering from a massive hemorrhage from one of his internal organs, legs paralyzed, near death, his helpless, devoted parents sobbing softly over his bedside, doctors scurrying about darkened hospital corridors preparing for emergency surgery, lies a township hero, Willie Washington. Willie, Greenville High School's star halfback, only months away from graduation, a scholarship to three major universities already assured, a life of release from darkness that has clouded our country's urban ghettos, has possibly only hours of life remaining in him. We know there are stories which can be related by all of us comparable to this catastrophic blow, but the sadness and the blasphemy of Willie's story is that it should never have happened. A football injury and a death upon the field of battle is an unfortunate and disastrous event. In spite of all the efforts of control, we have grown up to accept the freakishness of the gods when such an accident occurs. But a death days or weeks following an injury is a death laid directly upon the heads of the school authorities of Greenville High School. We are at once beginning a complete investigation of our high school's sports controlling body, and we assure you your local network will not rest until the lives of all the Willie Washingtons in our community be safeguarded and protected."

"Thank you, Mr. Otwell. Continuing now with the national news. Twenty-two dead, four hundred injured and missing is the latest count in from the Plattsville section of Minneapolis, where rioting has continued now into its third day. . . ."

At twelve-twenty Johnny pulled into the doctors' parking lot and quietly noted Alex Kohn's silver Rolls and Grawtch's black El Dorado.

In minutes he was at the Surgical West nurse's station and was advised that Willie was prepped and sedated for surgery. But the parents were waiting for Johnny before signing his surgical release. "We've been calling you for hours," McKay, the night surgical nurse, told him. "Where you been, you sly fox?" She poked a skinny elbow into his rib and winked like in the old days. "Even your wife couldn't find you."

Cassello, the night intern, told him he hadn't had a chance to go over the kid yet. "I'm up to here with work," he complained. "Would you write a few pre-op notes on him, you know, background stuff, how it all happened. I got three histories and physicals before I can hit the sack, and there's this one Italian dame with boobs like black olives. . . ."

SURGICAL W. #248

Willie lay cold in his hospital bed, his face puffy like a blowfish, little whining sounds coming from his cracked lips. Grawtch had been at work: Tubes pumped blood into one arm and antibiotics and cortisone and other life-saving medicines into the other. Alex Kohn had been at work: A rubber Foley drained red fluid from Willie's penis into a plastic bag. Johnny ran his hand over Willie's exposed face, not as a doctor but as an instinct to touch the boy like his kids who wanted to touch him last night in his house. But there was no hidden childrens' glee here. Instead, Johnny was openly repelled at its clamminess. He reached under the sheet for Willie's hand, his right throwing hand, the one that would grasp Johnny around the waist and fling him into the air. It was cold, and lifeless. *The insertion of the Palmaris Longis is—someplace in the hand?*

The room hung heavy with the smell of pungent incense, the kind they burn at old revival meetings. Willie's minister had been here and already had received some kind of final word from God.

What was happening?

Johnny paled at the insistent answer. For the first time this

---

evening he was suddenly struck with the awesome medical fact: This boy is dying, he really is. My God . . .

12:45

| OPERATING ROOMS |
| DO NOT ENTER |

| —ALEXANDER KOHN, M.D. F.A.C.S.— |

—I thought we could wait it out, Johnny, sometimes you can. With a conservative period of rest and medication these things can often wall themselves off and heal. But we have to go in, there's no other choice. . . . It looks like it busted wide open. The kid came in in shock with a hemoglobin of 8.2. He's probably been bleeding for weeks, and suddenly *kaboom*, the explosion. It was bound to happen. Lucky it didn't happen right out on the playing field. Your friend, Marvin, brought him in—nice guy, said the kid was lifting a carton of jelly beans or something and gave a yell and that was it. Get those papers signed, I don't want to wait any longer. . . . I don't know what it'll be, Johnny, until I go in. Maybe a wedge cut, maybe the whole kidney has to go, I don't know yet. Either way is usually no great risk, we do this every day. But there's a great big fly in the ointment. Wedge cut, whole kidney, or stick your head in the sand, this poor kid's chances are like zero to plus one.

I'm getting scrubbed. You want the medical story, go see Grawtch. I'm only the plumber, he's the contractor.

2:55

| HUBERT GRAWTCH, M.D. F.A.C.I. |
| —OFFICE— |

Grawtch had aged gracefully. When Johnny was his intern on medical service, he had enshrined himself with a fitful reputation designed for the devil himself. Although he had pinned Johnny against the corridor walls many a day battling for his diagnostic preeminence, he always managed to put over a medical point which somehow or other carried an intern a little bit farther up the road of professionalism. Johnny was first to recognize that Grawtch was dedicated to three principles: one, the accuracy of medical diagnosis; two, the recognition of new, young doctors; and three, the dependence of these new, young doctors on the accuracy of Grawtch's medical diagnosis.

Over the years, therefore, Johnny ran battle with Grawtch's supremacy system, and in facing the old man tonight, he suddenly was aware that here was the elemental figurehead behind the hangup he had on the G.P./specialist thing.

At this moment, however, Johnny's only concern was—how do we save this poor kid? Grawtch, I love you, you old money-hungry, medical Fagan. Tell me how we save my Willie.

"We probably don't." Grawtch blinked at Johnny, squinted up his eyes, and wiped a tear from its corner. Along with the trouble with his urinary system, he had developed cataracts and he made artifact movements to cover these encroaching elements which were and would slowly rob him of his domain.

"It's a simple case of a body outliving its time," Grawtch said, blowing his nose (tears often running into the blocked lacrimal ducts). "Any second-year student could have picked it up the first day this lad walked into his office. He followed a most classic textbook pattern."

Grawtch twitched one eye and for a moment hesitated as if in deep thought. However, he was fighting back both eyes from snapping shut on him.

"This boy, Dr. Shoemaker, is a black boy. Naturally this should at once relate to you the predominant disease patterns of the race. The head injury was a white elephant, and while all of you were amusing yourselves with concussion phobia, this insidious flank pain continued its insistent prodding, but nobody answered. The blood continued to seep away, and because of the boy's inherent disease pattern, his chemistry failed to answer the call for help. A simple blood smear would have given you the immediate clue: sickle cell anemia. You may fill in the rest, doctor."

Grawtch, like a spent old county judge who had just charged his jury with their duties regarding the sentence to death, placed his elbows upon his desk and covered his eyes with his palms in momentary silence, allowing the court to adjust its defenses.

But Johnny had none. Willie Washington had sickle cell anemia. The whole family had it. But he is seventeen years old, Johnny consoled himself, and he's made it until now. He'll be fine. He's a ramrod. He's as strong as an Atlas. You don't destroy a body like Willie's so easily. Willie Washington is not like everyone else, he's Professor Arturo's *Ultima.*

"I would hate to be the family doctor on a job like this one," Grawtch said with honest compassion. "Johnny, we have had some differences over the years, but never a loss of respect. You're a good G.P., and glory knows we need you all, but dammit, boy, don't you know you've got to start sharing some of this awful medical blame? I swear, Johnny, you G.P.s are the death of yourselves, you want to be heroes right to the grave.

"Ordinarily," Grawtch removed his hands from his eyes and rubbed away the discharge, "I would never interfere in such a case, but I have always had a special place for you, Johnny, and I want you to know that this boy has been given whatever there is known about his case to help pull him through. But a surgical crisis to a sickelemia—this is even beyond me."

Hubert Grawtch said that.

.   .   .   .

At 1:15 A.M. Dr. Shoemaker convinced Willie's mother and father of the urgency of signing the surgical release, and in minutes Willie Washington was wheeled into the operating room. Alex Kohn sent Johnny out and said he would call him when it was over.

"Go to sleep," he told him. "You G.P.s all look like you could use just one more hour in the sack."

.   .   .   .

1:30

> ## DOCTORS' LOUNGE AND LIBRARY

Wagner's Text on Clinical Hematology—Sickle Cell Anemia
AMA JOURNAL—The G.P.'s Waning Role In Hospital Procedure
CLINICAL MEDICINE—Impotence After Forty
Medical Review and Opinion—Marriage, Divorce, and Mental Breakdown
in the Medical Family

. . . .

2:30

> ## DINING ROOM—For Hospital Personnel Only

To Johnny, Jonesy appeared ageless. Over the years, through maneuvering the nurses credo of tender loving care upon herself even more lavishly than upon her patients, she had somehow managed to retain a firm hold on youth, and even in her hospital scrubs she continued to give off more understated sex than Johnny felt prepared to handle at this hour.

"I heard you were in," she smiled, "and I worked my break for now. You usually got hungry around two-thirty. I hoped I'd see you. It seems like years. How are you, J. J., you look tired."

Johnny told her why he was in the hospital.

"Not much night work for the old G.P. anymore," she said. "I remember when the halls were full of them. Now it's interns and residents and covering ambulance chasers. Glad to see ol' Doc Shoemaker still believes in making a few miracles on his own. Remember we saved one a night, anyway?"

She smiled and showed newly made teeth. Jonesy used to have a thing about her graying front teeth. She had been in a car accident, and the nerves had been destroyed, and the teeth discolored, and Jonesy seldom smiled in bright lights. He figured this is why she worked nights, and he looked at her now and wondered what there was about her then that was so appealing. But now he liked Jonesy's teeth. He smiled at them as she talked, and she knew he had come back to her. Jonesy had always known J. J., and she knew which night would be theirs within minutes of his start of duty.

"God, J. J.," she smiled, "it's good for me to see you. I

hate like hell telling you that, but it feels so good. When the word went out that you were here, my heart just took an old-fashioned flip-over and I worried that my hair was too light blonde. You never liked it that way."

Johnny assured her her hair was likable. He told her he liked her teeth.

She smiled and said, "You're going to stay all night, I know that. It'll be daylight before you get the word on your patient. You are going to stay, J. J., it's been so long. I can't believe so much time has gone by. How's Mary? Now why did I ask that? Damn lucky woman, I hated her. Big-time liar, me. Oh, no, J. J., I said, I don't want to hurt Mary, she's your wife, I would only think less of you if you would leave her. She never did anything to me, just lived with you, and slept with you, and held you every night, that's all she did."

Jonesy didn't feel like smiling. It had been a lousy deal, and she had never gotten over it, and why the hell should she smile.

"It's been rotten, J. J., let me tell you. There's not a night I don't walk these halls that I don't see you in every white coat that passes me by. I want to grab onto one and say to it, "J. J., it's me—look at me, it's me." I don't want much out of life, just come by once or twice a week, say hello, touch my face, run your hand through my hair. . . ."

Johnny studied her and thought of Mary. Wonder if she's asleep? He tried to remember Mary's smile and could not make out the shape of her mouth, the condition of her teeth. She has a nice mouth, he thought, good strong straight teeth, nice clean-cut lines to her face, doesn't wear too much junk. Fact is, Mary is a damn good-looking woman. Can't think of anything wrong with her other than what she can't help.

Johnny stared at Jonesy and wondered what it would be like taking off with her, chucking the whole mess, maybe running off to one of those small towns in Nebraska or New Mexico where they don't even have one doctor and they give you the whole town. Jonesy had a surgical menopause twelve years ago. It could work out.

Jonesy got up from the table and said simply, "I'll be on the third floor at three-thirty. The linen room keys are on the same rack above the door."

·   ·

3:30

DOCTORS' LOUNGE AND LIBRARY

"Dr. Shoemaker, call extension 295. Dr. Kohn is waiting to talk with you."

—It's all over, J. J., the kid looks fair. We had to take the whole kidney, it was spurting like a stabbed pig. Whether that does it or not, I don't take bets, but he's alive and he's young—so what else can a big doctor offer you? Go to sleep. He's good for maybe twelve hours before we know. . . . You sound tired, J. J. Hell, *I* did all the work.

. . . .

At three thirty-three Johnny dialed his home and found Mary awake.

"I'm glad he's alive, John. How are you?"

He told her he was tired but relieved, and would she mind if they talked for a while.

"It's like turning back the clock," Mary said to him. "Three-thirty was always a good time to talk, until the operator got tired of holding open the switch."

John told her he would stay on for the night, would she mind.

"I knew you'd stay," she told him. "You didn't have to call, but I'm grateful. I haven't really slept. I've been walking the halls with you. It's something I always felt I'd like to do, but somehow never got around to it. I'll come down now, John, if you want me. It must be endless, the night in a hospital, just hanging around waiting for that one good breath. Where will you sleep?"

He told her he'd just spread out on the couch so he'd be near the phone.

She told him she would think of him.

He said thanks.

And of Willie.

He said he'll need more than thoughts. She said, "I did a miserable thing, John. When you left the house, tonight, I called Willie a name and wished him dead."

John said nothing.

"I wished *all* of your Willies dead. How's that, Johnny, the whole last Willie that walks into your office and eats from your heart so that there is nothing left for me. And when the telephone rang, I knew you were calling to tell me Willie had died, and I knew *I* had just as well smashed his head. He's going to live, John, we don't want him to die. We don't want all your Willies to die, Johnny—do we? . . ."

Johnny slept restlessly until seven and awakened with a driving need to talk to somebody. First he checked with recovery room, and Willie was still under. Then avoiding the main halls and lobby where a small army of family and friends had gathered, he slipped off into the early morning drizzle.

.   .   .   .

7:30 A.M.

> ## FIRST CHURCH OF CHRIST
> ## —OFFICE—
> ---
> ## REV. CHARLES W. ABLEMAN

The man had been as tolerant a person as Johnny could imagine was available. And tolerance and understanding was what Johnny was seeking, perhaps even revelation. He could only remember the boy Reverend had hit with the Bible, only days later being welcomed back into his loving and praying arms. But the stern greeting and the stiff posture belied Reverend Ableman's clerical position. He looked only out into the chapel when he spoke to Johnny.

"Jonathan, could I tell my brother's wife that his doctor, in failing to respond to her call, killed her husband as directly as if he had injected the devilish bacteria into his vein?"

Johnny had no answer. He had come himself with the same question.

"God has told me," Reverend Ableman went on, his eyes fixed into the dimly lit chapel, "that man is a sinner and that I am to help Him cleanse these sins through the grace of His son, Jesus Christ. If you have come to me as a minister to tell that your sin of omission has been the cause of the pending death of a young boy, I will accept you into my prayers and ask for deliverance of your soul from the devil. But if you have come to me as an old friend whom I, at one time, proudly counted as one of my associates, and are seeking an answer to whether you are guilty or not, you have come at a poor time in my life."

Both men sat silently avoiding the other's deepening confusion. Then, after what seemed like hours, Reverend Ableman turned his crimped face from the chapel and with eyes resembling ground glass, stared grimly at Johnny and said, "Of course you are guilty, all doctors are. There is no hope for any of you. Your days are filled with the terrors of other lives which you poison with chemicals, maim with knives, desecrate with words, destroy with desertion. You are licensed to kill and you blindly, faithlessly revere this license as a hunter would his gun."

The reverend stood up from his desk, and looming against the early morning light shining through his window, he was a massive shadow of doom to Johnny as he waved him away.

"I have no sympathy with your problem this morning. My heart is so full of hate that even God cannot reach me. I have no words from Him for you. Go elsewhere, find Him for yourself, Doctor, but hurry, because you are wrapped in the ways of the devil, and God will soon be helpless, too. . . ."

. . . .

8:15

SACKS' DELI-LAND

BREAKFAST 7 to 9

"It's just like doctors' hours," Sam said, sliding Johnny's plate of eggs under his nose. "One to three, seven to nine, six to eight. It's like a doctor's life, work two hours a day. Up all night, *boychick?*"

Johnny briefly mentioned Willie.

"If they don't cause you trouble while they're alive, they got to be trouble trying to die. Tragedy, the world is one big tragedy. My poor Myra, three days in the hospital, they already cut her open in two places, took out a dozen parts and put six back in. It's like when you're a child and you take apart your Poppa's watch and when you put it back together you got six pieces don't fit. How do they know she can work without the pieces they didn't put back?"

Johnny assured him they knew. "They're specialists, aren't they?"

"That you didn't have to say," Sam took away the half-eaten eggs. "Big eater. No matter what you say, Doctor, to me you're still a *pisher* and I'm the *alter.* All you would need in your mind now would be my Myra. Thank me for sending her away, learn to thank people for relieving you of burdens and making decisions you don't like."

Johnny said an unsmiling "Thank you," downed his coffee, and got up to leave.

Sam took hold of Johnny's jacket collar, and waved his shaking finger under his nose.

"Dr. Johnny, you think yours is the only hard road. Don't feel so sorry for yourself. It's not so easy, let me tell you, coming down here and she's not here. You think it's easy running across the river every day and waiting to see if she's still alive in some stranger's arms. I closed down Monday, and I closed down Tuesday, and I said to hell with it all and I stayed next to her bed day and night. Such a big help I was to her. And the doctors and the nurses needed me, oh, yes, they really needed me. I'm great with watching transfusion blood dripping. I fell asleep three times counting drops. So this morning I marched out of there and opened the store. I felt like Myra said it was OK. What else we got to go by? The voice says OK, and I opened up the store and started slicing lox again."

Johnny said to Sam he understood, there comes a time when you've got to start slicing again.

"So?" Sam said to Johnny. "Slice."

And at the door, Johnny said to Sam uneasily, but effectually, "It's not the same, Sam. If you should shred a piece of lox or come to a fat end, you dump it in the garbage. The fat man comes and takes it away, and it all comes out as sweet-smelling soap. Where do I drop my shredded pieces or my fat ends? Is there a doctors' garbage can? . . ."

. . . .

8:45   JONATHAN J. SHOEMAKER, M.D.

DOCTOR IS OUT

NO SMOKING

Nick Golopas was waiting for his daily shot. Johnny didn't
bother checking his chart. It was either number three of the
fifth series or number five of the third series. It really didn't
matter, Golopas was hooked. Like we're all hooked on our
own garbage, Johnny said.

"What are you talking about garbage?" Golopas said to
Johnny.

You're too stupid to understand, Johnny said to himself,
shoving the needle deep into the fat buttock. Golopas jumped
and said "Ouch" and said "Is this number three or five and
what if I get another dose tonight, do we start all over
again?" We're both stupid, Johnny said to himself, but he's
enjoying it.

. . . .

9:00 Mail   **GREENVILLE MERCY HOSPITAL**
                        GREENVILLE, N. J.

SPECIAL MEMORANDUM:
ALL DOCTORS ATTENDING THE REGULAR MONDAY
EVENING STAFF MEETING, PLEASE DISREGARD
IRREGULARITIES.

. . . .

GREENVILLE MERCY HOSPITAL
GREENVILLE, N.J.

Annual Dues (payable before Nov. 1)
General Staff . . . $100
Obstetric Service . .   50
Due $150

. . . .

GREENVILLE MERCY HOSPITAL
GREENVILLE, N. J.

Office of Frank Lenihan, M. D.
Chief of Staff Obstetrics

October 16, 1970

Dear Dr. Shoemaker:
　　　　　This is to officially notify you that as of the above
date, you have been removed from official staff of Obstetrics and
all privileges have been suspended. The Greenville Mercy Hospital
will accept no responsibilities for any of your patients entered
after the above date.

Yours fraternally,

Frank Lenihan, M.D.

Note: Johnny, any pending OB cases you can slip in under my
service. Drop by and I'll work out the deal.

F. L.

.　.

October 18, 1970

Dear Doctor,
　　　　　I am enclosing a form for the insurance to my son's injury
which you kindly took care of. His school insurance paid you
twelve dollars and there is a bill from you for ten dollars extra I
don't understand, although if you still need the other ten dollars,
just fill out those papers and I will take them to my Blue Cross
and see if they got the money for you—I don't.

Yours very sincerely,

(Mrs.) Jane Gordowski

.　.

KONA KAI INN
Osabe, Hawaii, U. S. A.

Monday

Aloha, you stupid artist—
     And you make believe, Doctor. Here I am—so where are
you? Loosen your damned tight tie, you worthless creature of
habit. Breathe in. Breathe out. Open your belt. Take off your
pants. Wiggle your bare ass at your packed waiting room. Here
I am, I made it. One night I have already run naked in the ocean
and painted twenty titties on a foam rubber canvas. It's warm
and it's mellow and it's freeee man, it's like freeee. I'll give you
just twenty-four hours to make it man—or you are lost—L-O-S-T—
forever and ever.
     . . .Please Baby, come and get me—I can't stop runnnning.

Your boy,

Pauly Baby

.   .   .   .

GREENVILLE MERCY HOSPITAL
GREENVILLE, N. J.

PATHOLOGY DEPARTMENT
CLINTON ALTSHURER, M.D., F.A.C.P.

Oct. 19, 1970

Jonathan J. Shoemaker, M.D.
1555 Centre Street
Greenville, N. J.

Dear Dr. Shoemaker:

     Preliminary reports on the gross findings of the Dusharme
newborn indicate anomalies of many of the major organs. There
was a dextroposition of the heart, deficient ventricle development
in the brain, all these possible biologically inherited deficiencies.

However, most important to you, there was a complete atelecto-
sis of the right lung, totally collapsed; fact is, never developed.
The kind of thing you see in a perforation wound. Probably
they tried a knitting-needle abortion the second or third month.
Regardless, the infant was pre-doomed, possibly dead before delivery.

I am sending a copy to Drs. Lenihan and Kohn, and
Mr. Kleinert and attorney Paltzinger as you requested. This is
not general procedure, but I understand.

An official pathological report with micro findings
should be available in three or four days.

Sincerely yours,

Clinton Altshurer, M.D.
Chief Pathologist

. .   . .

SOUTHERN ILLINOIS MEDICAL COLLEGE
BROWNSVILLE HOUSE
CHICAGO, ILLINOIS

Oct. 19, 1970

Dear Dad,

Glad to have you aboard.

I read your letter with respectful relish. You nailed
yourself to the wall, but you wisely packed a suture kit.

You masterfully destroyed the old threadbare G.P. legend and made me proud you are my dad. How many of the
establishment would take the stand you've taken? It's too mon-
strous a task, this practice of medicine, to allow it to remain in
the hands of mystics and "feelers." I'd like to put you up before the licensing boards of every state in the union and say,
listen to this man before you stamp out any more G.P.s into the
old mold—listen to him—he knows what goes on behind that
door that says Private, Consultation Room. He knows that
every poor soul who walks in is lucky to walk out. Hear him
tell it, the practice of medicine is for the quick and the tough
and the hard cold fact.

Good for you, Pop. Although you told me never to

hedge on you, I couldn't just run you over without smoothing out the wrinkles. But now that you see the light and you're leaving General Practice—even though you're using some kind of subterfuge called Willie Washington—now I can tell you what was really behind my decision to move out of your world.

I've joined SHO, the Student Health Organization. Don't worry, I'm not growing a beard—yet—but I do have an extra inch of hair over my ears and I just bought my first pair of bellbottoms and maybe I'll throw on a pair of granny glasses, but that's not the issue. The point is we are not interested in modifying the medical scene, we're going to overthrow it. Recently I wrote an article for one of the SHO bulletins that I'll send on to you, but it reemphasizes only what I already told you—today's doctor is up for grabs. The practice of medicine today is an abomination. My God, I look back at my days with you in the office and I say, how did you ever sleep nights? The whole system is antihuman. It's the ever-loving buck and who's next. Sorry, Pop, but comes the revolution and white coats will roll. I'm sure glad you're folding yours away before the ax falls.

Why don't you come out here, Pop? I'll show you around. See what we're doing—come to one of our meetings and maybe give the boys a talk on the follies of general practice. Who knows, maybe we'll grow beards together.

Gotta run, Pop, there's a student rally to bring the medics home from Vietnam. Keep me posted. And above all, no matter what you do—send money.

Love,

Tom

. . . .

10:45

**GREENVILLE MERCY HOSPITAL
DOCTORS' PARKING ONLY**

—It's Wednesday, Dr. Shoemaker, go on home. Only ones here today are interns, residents, and ambulance chasers. . . . Now, look, Doc, about my shoulder . . .

DOCTORS' LOUNGE

—So what the hell, Shoemaker, if I don't answer the phone, I'm not responsible. Come Wednesday, I am unavailable—but absolutely. Don't I have the same right as the goddam unions fighting for a three-day week. . . .

—The whole country is standing at relief windows, where do we stand? I take a lousy day off and get slapped on the wrist. I gave up my answering service, who needs them tailing me all over town? . . .

—Life is short, Shoemaker. I'm going out and whack that goddam little pill and hope it drops into a hole before I do. . . .

—Go on home, Johnny, sign off. How many lives do you think you're going to save today? . . .

11:00

SURGICAL FLOOR	EAST↑	WEST↓
SURGICAL WEST	RMS 200-240 ←	RMS 240-260 →

NURSES STATION

—Nothing, not a peep. He keeps breathing, but not a move, poor kid. He just lays there, almost looks white. The whole colored population of Greenville has been in and out. I never said a word, who needs trouble? There's another guy, he's been in and out every ten minutes. They told me he was the school principal and to leave him alone. I swear he wants to pull the kid out of bed to do thirty pushups. . . .

. . . .

Henry Leader was a desperate man. Just at a time when he had finally found in his daughter's pregnancy an excuse to reorganize the school system in the image of his unpublished papers and possibly catapult himself into an executive suite in Washington, *this* had to happen.

The uncontrolled sardonic grin was gone.

"Johnny, my boy, I am glad to see you. What's it going to be? I've been talking to Willie every few minutes—come on, breathe boy, I tell him, get up and at it for Greenville High. It's your duty boy, up, up, up."

Johnny looked in on Willie. He lay as silently as he had left him, tubes still pumping blood, skin still cold. The only difference was that he was now minus one kidney.

Isn't that awful, Johnny thought wearily, my beautiful baby, damn—*he's no longer perfect.*

"Is he going to make it, Johnny?" Leader insisted on positive accord. "Now, say it, *he is going to make it.*"

Johnny merely shrugged his shoulders. He wasn't listening.

"Do you know," Leader said threateningly, "this will be the first time anything like this has happened while I have been principal. You should have acted on this sooner, Shoemaker."

Johnny eyed Leader disbelievingly.

"This didn't have to happen, you know," Leader pushed the point. "Why didn't you warn us more forcefully, boy, *forcefully*. You know you sat back and let us go on destroying this poor innocent boy, and now you can't save him?"

Johnny assured him he was in good hands, but nothing more could be done at the moment.

"*Anything* can be done, now you know that."

"Everything *is* being done."

"You don't know what this means to me."

Johnny nodded.

"No, you don't understand. Who understands?"

"We will know later," Johnny said.

"Can't you do any more *now*?"

"No."

"That's ridiculous. I demand you do something now."

"It's all been done."

"But you haven't *saved* him!"

"We're trying."

"That's not enough. Doesn't anyone understand, I want that nigger pulled through."

Johnny shuddered, and placed his thumbs up under his skull to release the pressure. He turned shamefully to walk away. But Leader, now overwhelmed with the helplessness of his plight, wildly grasped for Johnny's uplifted hands.

"*Save him,* my boy," he cried out plaintively, and like they were the last floating logs in an ocean of strangling weeds, he desperately tore at Johnny's fingers, at once ripping blood from the old chronic sores.

"For God's sake, Leader," Johnny sucked at his cut fingers, "keep your goddam hands off me." He pushed Leader forcefully to one side. Leader whimpered, "My boy," and Johnny said bitingly, "I am not your boy, I'm nobody's boy. Whatever you were cooking up, Leader, you're going to have to stew in it alone. I know where my guilt is—God, do I know—and I'm going to have to pay for it, but it sure as hell isn't going to be your way."

"Johnny," Leader's voice rattled with uncertainty, like the old cold Buick readying to stall out. "You know the credo—anything can be done. . . ."

Johnny turned full face to Leader and stuck two bloody fingers under his quivering nose.

"Don't you ever believe it, Leader. Some damn things can *never* be done—go ask Willie."

Johnny's fingers continued to bleed, and he let them run wild, red sticky warm blood trailing down his wrists and over his watch and under his shirt and into his sleeve.

"It hurts," he said quietly to himself as he raced to his car. He pumped gas, pulled the choke, and felt the hurt all the way up into his shoulder. He cried out in joyous pain, "It hurts—I feel it—*it hurts like hell!*" And he sucked away at the raw edges and pulled new flesh away from the nail and blood spurted onto the wheel and he rubbed it and wiped it over his mouth and the hurt was sharp and deep. The attendant waved him on and pointed painfully to his shoulder. The Buick lurched out of the parking lot, and Johnny called back to the man, "Be happy, you damn fool, let it hurt . . ."

. . . .

Riverview Park/Buick
2:00 p.m.—Wednesday

Dear Tom,
I've been in the park for the past hour, just hanging
around, making it with the ducks, flipping stones into the river,
watching them dance over the edge like a bouncing sing-a-long
ball. It turned out to be a cloudless, magic, balmy kind of day,
the temperature somewhere around fifty-five to sixty, the air
smelling crisply of falling leaves shaken gently from the trees in
bright sunlight—in short, an almost unbelievably beautiful October day.
I'm sitting back in the Buick now. Over on the other
side of the river a gang of kids are tackling each other in a hop-
ped-up game of touch football. I was there a while ago and
Band-Aided a cut chin on a little nine-year-old who will from
this day forward never be long without Band-Aid or some other
medical paraphernalia. He could not for one second stop jumping, screaming, running, tackling, arguing, twisting his ankle,
butting his head, cutting his chin. Oh, that chin, he will lead
with it forever.
A few minutes before I settled into the car to write to
you, I called my Service. It is, you know, the official sign-off
day, and I told them I am not signing off. I told them to take
calls and refer them to me as soon as they come in. I'm going
to see how many lives I can save today.
I figure if I am not a real doctor as you say, I might as
well stop acting like one. The first thing you do, then, is answer
your own telephone, and work on Wednesday. One thing leads
to another, and pretty soon you're even rushing off on a house
call.
I hate to destroy your newly found versions of medical
practice, and I must refuse your invitation to the young radicals'
necktie party, but all of a sudden I like my version of medical
practice, and I like my neck, and let me tell you, I'm going to
save both of them.
Because after thirty years in limbo, I think I know what
is going on inside me, and who can say more sometimes after a
hundred?
Early this morning I pounded a footpath up and down

the corridors of old Greenville Mercy. Lying just about dead in
Room 248 Surgical West is poor Willie. Yes, Willie finally gave
out, just as I predicted. Thrills and overjoy, right?

Shame and stupidity.

If I had been man enough to assume my birthright as a
physician and not as a stand-in doctor, Willie wouldn't be the
center of the universe, but at the same time your daddy wouldn't
ever have found out what it is all about.

When your Uncle Len. got burned to death, I had no
more inclination to be a doctor than the little kid running the
football across the river. He's too busy living it now. Who cares
about later, he says, throw me the ball, run, run, run. When I
was old enough to realize that in our house it was Lem who was
In and I was Out, I was too busy. Throw me the ball.

Crazy how the fire started down in the cellar. Probably
some old sulfur bottles exploded and the cotton balls and bandages went up like confetti. Pop fought with Lem to salvage
the old trash, and Lem got trapped shoving Pop out of the
debris.

That's the thrilling autobiography of how your old man
became a successful physician. Think Mrs. Carbone would like
to hear it? She told me yesterday, if anyone was born to be a
doctor, it certainly is me.

Now what do we do for the second laugh? . . .

But somehow I have gone about my business of being a
doctor. The years of *Gray's Anatomy* and *Boyd's Pathology*
and *Clinics of North America* and Medical Tape Digest have
managed to involve me deeply enough into the meat of medical
information so that I have assumed with some success the role
of doctor. Honored, cultured, esteemable, community-spirited,
and clandestinely admired by one and all. And in spite of the
barbs of despair stuck into my profession by those who stick
barbs, I go on—there he is, see him, Jane, that is *our* doctor, he
saved Grandma's life.

God only knows, but in some damnable way I saved
Grandma's life. Now, you see, here is the rub. How in hell does
a doctor like me save Grandma's life?

Now a guy has got to know how he does these little
miracles or soon he doesn't even believe he is doing them.
Especially if a guy never believed he was who people pointed

him out to be, anyway. Then who got Grandma well? Must
be Lemuel, he gets all my patients well. Lem is totally responsible for all my results, and naturally they are damned good
results, because Lem is the best doctor.

However, there comes an uprising in the practice. Grandma doesn't get well. Lem, what happened? And a baby dies—
Lem?—and Myra Sacks busts wide open and Fran Cooper puts a
hole in husband Sal, and Willie Washington's body falls apart.
Lem?

How come the walls are tumbling down? How come
magic has gone out of the doctor's wand?

Very simply answered: Because I fumbled the ball.
That's right, not Lem, but *I* lost it. It's great to be able to
hide for thirty years, but come this morning the old Buick
pulled out of a near-death stall, and Lem was no more.

The only one here, Tom, the only one ever here was me.
I am the doctor. *I* put Willie where he is, totally responsible me.
Lem is dead, thank God, and I am *ME, ME, ME*. It was like
being buried alive and unable to move even an eyelash. And inside I was screaming, I am here, I am alive, and nobody heard.

I knew I had to get out, Tom, but I had to paw and
scratch and rip away at myself until I bled, and hoped just to
feel. To be there. . . .

And suddenly, Tom, that was my answer.

Willie getting clobbered two Saturdays ago made me, for
a brief moment, *be there*. And the haunting thought kept coming
back to me: Through Willie, I could be *there*.

What other chance does a G.P. get to hear the applause?
So I wished that colored Willie (I don't *think* I thought "nigger")
would just get hurt, and I would run out and help him hobble off
the field. *Or* he could be knocked out cold, and I would call for
the ambulance and the stretcher team would rush him and me to
the hospital with a police escort. Or—now there is a thought—he
could even be dead, and I would shake my head and say, he's
dead. Now, tell me, son, do you know of a better way to be
there.

All right, so Willie got up and in a week's time got ready
for the next battle. I knew he was in no condition to play, but
hell's bells, I said—desperately seeking escape from the shadows
of the grave—hell, said I, if this crazy nigger (I guess I did say it

this time) wants to go off and kill himself, I'll just stand by until
he does and then I'll say—he's dead. The crowd won't cheer, but
they'll know that I had said quietly don't play, and now I'm
standing over him in all humility and must pronounce him dead
—God bless me.

You know, Tom—*now, Tom, you hear this:* Maybe we
want our patients to be sick, and we *want* our patients to suffer,
and we *want* our patients to die.

Do you remember Old Dr. Mueller, Poppa's checker-
player friend? One day he came into the store and Poppa
says, "How's business?" and Mueller smiled and said, "Thanks
God, business is good."

I shriveled out of the store and for years couldn't look
at a doctor without thinking he wished me sick or maimed so he
could, "Thanks God——" But that's the truth, this is what we
really are. We, too, must live. Can we help it we must live on
life's imperfections?

You think the computer might possibly fix this up for
the next wave of young doctors? You work on it, son, although
I don't really give a damn what you and your computer think, I
know who ME is, and it sure is not Lem. Poor kid, what he
missed. And what nearly was me! Hell, Tom, I'll be on Lesson
Number Five for a dozen years, so what? I'll get to charcoal in
Lesson Seven, and in Ten I get to draw a real live breast. (Maybe
they send it through the mail; or Pauly Baby delivers it in person.)

What the hell do I care now. Me is ME. I am a G.P., I
always was, and always will be the best damned G.P. in Greenville or maybe even all of New Jersey. And I don't want any of
my patients to die or get sick or even hurt a little bit. I *need*
these people. I need them probably more desperately than they
need me. I want Mrs. Reilly to come in and cry over my desk,
it might wash away some of her fat cells. I want Mr. Pugliese to
smoke his goddam cigar in my office so I can tell him how it's
destroying his health. Who else is there to tell him, the American
Tobacco Institute? I want to be there to see the kids suck on
their lollipops and kiss my cheeks with their sticky lips. I want
to hold Mrs. Carpenter's hand and tell her not to worry, her
husband will live. I want Essie Howard to know she has someplace to come to replace her "lost" narcotics. Where should

she go, to a policeman? I *want* Clara to call me and tell me Lisa
only eats two and a half ounces of baby peas when she should
be eating two and three quarters. Who else can she talk to,
Dr. Spock? I want Ruben Myerberg to be able to come in once
in a while and look at me and feel better. He feels better, he
feels, he *feels!*

And oh, how I want Willie to live. I want him to live as
bad as I want Lem to stay dead. If this boy dies now, well—it'll
be like starting all over again. But what the hell, son, that's what
the G.P. is, the fall guy, the guy who has to pick himself up,
laugh, and start all over again.

You boys are on the right road. I'm certainly not against
a revolution in medicine—can't say it's not needed. But in the
meantime, somebody has to mind the store, a damn big busi-
ness-as-usual-kind of store. And I am glad it is me. I'm going to
go on, Tom, and make it on my own, not because I'm stepping
into someone else's dream, not because I hear the crowd cheer,
but because I've got to be what I was meant to be, and I've got
to do it my way, or I'm as dead as my brother Lem.

. . . So put that in your computer and watch it smoke.
You push your buttons and I'll push mine. And you know,
come reckoning time, I bet I get as good a score as you—maybe
a few better. Sure as hell, kid, there are a lot of lives to be saved,
and sure as God made vinegar and honey, you'll save as many
with either spoon—just so long, son, as the spooner is real.

Signed: The Real *ME.*

P.S. I love you, boy . . .

. . . .

3:30

GREENVILLE MERCY HOSPITAL DOCTORS' PARKING		
SURGICAL FLOOR	EAST↑	WEST↓
SURGICAL WEST	RMS 200-240←	RMS 240-260→

NURSES STATION

—He got up just for a second, Dr. Shoemaker. Mrs. Ames saw him sit up straight in bed, and when she tried to put him down, he just stared at her and said, "Doc, you know I got to get back into the game, I just gotta," and he dropped off. Dr. Grawtch came right over, but it was useless—he was gone. Ames couldn't get over it how real he made it sound, "Doc, I just gotta get back. . . ."

NEW JERSEY STATE DEPARTMENT OF HEALTH

1. PLACE OF DEATH
a. COUNTY — *Newtown*
b. CITY ☐ (Check box and give name) BOROUGH ☐ TOWNSHIP ☑ — *Greenville*
c. LENGTH OF STAY (in this place) — *1 Day*
d. FULL NAME OF (If not in hospital or institution, give street address or location) HOSPITAL OR INSTITUTION — *Greenville Mercy Hosa*

2. USUAL RESIDENCE (Where deceased lived. If institution; residence before admission)
a. STATE — *N.J.*
b. COUNTY — *Newtown*
c. CITY ☐ (Check box and give name) BOROUGH ☐ TOWNSHIP ☑ — *Greenville*
d. LENGTH OF STAY (in this place) — *8 Years*
e. STREET ADDRESS If rural, P. O. Address — *12 Lark St. Greenville, NJ*

3. NAME OF DECEASED (Type or Print) — *William George Washington*
4. DATE OF DEATH — *Oct. 21, 1970*

5. SEX — *M*
6. COLOR OR RACE — *Negro*
7. MARRIED ☐ NEVER MARRIED ☑ WIDOWED ☐ DIVORCED ☐
8. DATE OF BIRTH — *Oct 24, 1952*
9. AGE (In years last birthday) — *17* — If Under 1 Year If Under 24 Hrs. | Months | Days | Hours | Min.

10a. USUAL OCCUPATION (Give kind of work done during most of working life, even if retired) — *Student*
10b. KIND OF BUSINESS OR INDUSTRY
11. BIRTHPLACE (State or foreign country) — *Georgia, U.S.A.*
12. CITIZEN OF WHAT COUNTRY? — *U.S.A.*

13. FATHER'S NAME — *Sam Washington*
14. MOTHER'S MAIDEN NAME — *Mildred Parker*

15. WAS DECEASED EVER IN U.S. ARMED FORCES? (Yes, no, or unknown) (If yes, give war or dates of service) — *No*
16. Social Security No. — *025-38-69??*
17. INFORMANT — *Mother* — Address

18. CAUSE OF DEATH [Enter only one cause per line for (a), (b), and (c).]
PART I. DEATH WAS CAUSED BY:
IMMEDIATE CAUSE (a) — *Cardiac Arrest*
Conditions, if any, which gave rise to above cause (a), stating the exciting cause last. DUE TO (b) — *Internal Hemorrhage*
DUE TO (c) — *Post-Surgical Nephrectomy (Sicklenia)*
INTERVAL BETWEEN ONSET AND DEATH — *Minutes* / *12 Hours*

PART II. OTHER SIGNIFICANT CONDITIONS CONTRIBUTING TO DEATH BUT NOT RELATED TO THE TERMINAL DISEASE CONDITION GIVEN IN PART I(a) — *Sickle Cell Anemia*
19. WAS AUTOPSY PERFORMED? Yes ☐ No ☐

20a. ACCIDENT ☐ SUICIDE ☐ HOMICIDE ☐ to the best of my knowledge.
20b. DESCRIBE HOW INJURY OCCURRED. (Enter nature of injury in Part I or Part II of item 18.) — *Football Game*
20c. TIME OF INJURY Hour — a.m. p.m. — *Oct 10, 1970* — Month, Day, Year
20d. INJURY OCCURRED WHILE AT ☐ NOT WHILE ☑ WORK AT WORK
20e. PLACE OF INJURY (e. g., in or about home, farm, factory, street, office bldg., etc.) — *Football Stadium*
20f. CITY, TOWN, OR LOCATION — *Greenville* — COUNTY — *Newtown* — STATE — *N.J.*

21. I attended the deceased from *Oct. 4, 1966*, to *Oct 21, 1970* and last saw ~~him~~ her alive on *Oct 21, 1970*. Death occurred at *3:15* P m. on the date stated above; and to the best of my knowledge, from the causes stated.
22a. SIGNATURE — *J.J. Shoemaker M.D.* (Degree or title)
22b. ADDRESS — *1555 Centre St. Greenville*
22c. DATE SIGNED — *10-21-70*

23a. BURIAL, CREMATION, REMOVAL (Specify)
23b. DATE
23c. NAME OF CEMETERY OR CREMATORY
23d. LOCATION (City, town or county) (State)

24. FUNERAL DIRECTOR'S SIGNATURE — N.J. LICENSE NO. — ADDRESS
25. DATE RECD. BY LOCAL REG
26. REGISTRAR'S SIGNATURE

4:15

┌─────────────────────┐
│   HOSPITAL LOBBY   │
└─────────────────────┘

Most everyone had gotten the word and had either gone off to their private mourning areas or had remained numbly behind huddled in mumbling, disbelieving groups around the stuffy, outdated hospital lobby.

Coach Bocca had remained on vigil since early morning, being joined slowly by other coaches, then the team. He stood alone now, his squat paunchy hulk sagging in unacceptable defeat.

"Jesus, Doc, he didn't *die*, really die?"

Johnny nodded his head wearily: yes.

"Never in eighteen years coaching did a kid die. Hell, we got broken legs and busted up knees and fingers, a couple of concussions, once had a broken back, but Jesus, Doc, that's the name of the game. But to die on us——"

Bocca pulled up his drooping belly, and standing on his toes reached Johnny's ear and whispered nervously, "It *was* an accident, wasn't it, Doc? Nothin' we did?"

Johnny assured him it was nothing he did.

Bocca breathed cautiously. Still and all it was one of his kids.

"I mean things like this can happen—I tell the kid's folks it's like crossing the street. Jesus, Doc, but to *die*. Did it hurt? Poor kid, he sure could carry that ball. Now what the hell is going to happen to the rest of the season? . . . —Hey, Doc . . ."

One by one the boys shook Doctor's hand, or touched his coat, or waved hopefully, awaiting Doc's word that this was like it had always been, the kid always got up, and tomorrow it was always better. Out of uniform they were all clean, quiet-appearing in their school clothes, unlike the killers they would be forty-eight minutes a week. They were, in the last analysis, children.

—Hey, Doc . . .

—Hello, Doc . . .

—Yeah, Doc . . .

—Hi, Doc . . . you gonna be out there Saturday? . . .

—You gotta be, Doc . . .
—Willie told us . . .
—Yeah, Doc . . .
—I got a little headache, Doc . . .
—My back . . .
—My arm . . .
—My leg . . .
—Hi, Doc . . .
—Hello, Doc . . .
—Willie told us, you're our boy, Doc . . .
—Yeah, Doc . . .
—Stay with us, Doc . . .
—Yeah, Doc . . .
—Hey . . .
—Please, sir . . .
—My head . . .
—My foot . . .
—Jesus, Doc, Willie is really *dead*? . . .

. . . .

"The letting go will be more difficult than the finding." Dr.
Arturo's words pulsed rhythmically in Johnny's head. He
stood in the damp cold basement alongside Willie's covered
dead body and he made himself as motionless as he could,
reducing his own heartbeat, his own body sounds, to the
faintest murmur. He must be sure Willie was dead.

When he was an intern and his first patient on his service
had died and he had to pronounce him dead, he spent well
over half an hour testing and retesting all the known signs of
death, adding even a few he made up on the spot. He stepped
far aside, held his own breath, and swore the dead patient's
chest was moving and under the sheet the heart was
fluttering. When finally he had said, yes, he's dead, he
shivered inside, felt a wave of uncontrolled nausea, then
followed the cart into the morgue. And after everyone had
left, he went through all the signs again.

Just as he was doing now with Willie.

*"He will have six hundred and forty-seven muscles in
exacting origin, with exacting insertions, and exacting actions."*
They all were at rest.

"And he will be your gift, your only chance at being a real doctor . . . and he will die only if you allow him to die, for his death will be a tragic blunder."

"But Arturo," Johnny screamed into the echoing hollow of the hospital morgue, "he wasn't the one, he wasn't perfect. You old fool, *nobody* is. You want me to write the origin, insertion, and action of Willie Washington five hundred times?"

A passerby observing the next moments would say he saw Dr. Shoemaker shake the hand of the massive form on the cart, and if he would blink his eyes once, he would see this powerful hand lift the doctor to the ceiling, and if he would listen carefully, he would hear the band play "Hail Greenville High" and a roaring whisper of "Olé!" coming from somewhere above. And then if he would blink again, he would see Dr. Shoemaker pull aside the cover sheets and *behold!*—a giant, pulsating specimen, free of wounds and scars, clean and flawless: the Absolute.

Johnny replaced the sheet gently, pulled the folds up over Willie's head, and said softly to the boy, "You're beautiful . . ."

And as if in final misgiving on leaving him alone, Johnny turned back to him from the door and said, "If you get hurt again, you crazy bastard, you call me immediately, you hear?"

.   .   .   .

6:30   **THE SHOEMAKERS**
                                    ———————————
                                    692 LAKE DRIVE
                                    ———————————
                                    WELCOME
                                    ———————————

The lawn had been cut and trimmed and swept, the bushes clipped and mulched with peat. The mimosa hung limp but vigilantly alive, one of the standard-bearers of life after most of the other leaves had gone to rest. Johnny was happy to see his home as he drove the big car into the driveway. It was a good-looking home and he felt good things about what was good inside. For a moment he remained in the car, brushing a speck of lint from the seat, testing the thermostatic heater, pushing the chromed locks, running the windows up and down with the chrome-edged button. Before finally stepping to the driveway, he turned the key once again and listened to the automatic choke take over and heard the motor purr. Then he turned the key to *off*, blew on his horn several loud but muted notes, and walked briskly to his home door.

—Hey, it's Pops. Pop's home, everybody--oh, no! Holy cats, hey, Mom. Hey!

—No . . .

—Yeah . . . Pops got a new—*car*?

—It really is . . .

—What is it?

—It's a new—I don't know, Hey, Pimples—What is it?

—Stupid girls—its a *Gremlin* . . .

—A new *blue* Gremlin . . .

—Gimme the keys, Pop—

—I'm sitting in front . . .

—Shut up, Skin . . .

Mary smiled tolerantly, then scowled and said, "We don't have the playroom furnished yet."

And Johnny began the count . . .

"Five, ten . . ."

"John . . ."

"fifteen, twenty . . ."

"Service called, they have several messages."

"Twenty-five, thirty . . ."

"There's one from Clara, she says Lisa swallowed some air, and she read about this pollution—"

"Thirty-five, forty . . ."

"Laurie Lee's husband called and said *he's* sick."

"Forty-five, fifty . . ."

"Nick Golopas says he wants you to know as soon as you come home from your golf game, tomorrow morning has to be number one again . . ."

"Fifty-five, sixty . . ."

"John, the kids—"

"Sixty-five, seventy . . ."

"It's warm in here . . ."

"Seventy-five, eighty . . ."

'John, I could become pregnant—"

"Eighty-five . . ."

"John—could I?"

"Ninety . . ."

"Don't—push—me . . ."

"Ninety-five . . ."

"*Push* me—"

Mary clicked the lock on the bedroom door.

"Push me. I signed out anyway. Ha! on you, Johnny Shoemaker."

She undid the silk scarf and let her hair fall softly to her shoulders.

"One hundred, one hundred, *one hundred!*—And I told them the doctor was spending the rest of his night saving a life. . . ."

. . .   .

THE ~~END~~ BEGINNING